STANDARD DEVIATION

DAVID HARRY

STANDARD DEVIATION
The standard deviation can be thought of as a boundary defining the limits of normal with respect to any measured set of data, such as behavioral data. Individuals whose behavior falls within the standard deviation boundary are considered "normal". Persons who exhibit behavior beyond the boundary are considered outside the range of normal.
Readers should decide for themselves as to whether a particular character depicted in this novel falls within or outside the standard deviation of human behavior.

DISCLAIMER
This novel is a work of fiction. And while there is speculation that many creative scientists, including Isaac Newton, Alexander Graham Bell and Albert Einstein, were on the Asperger's Syndrome spectrum, it should be understood that all of the characters in this novel are imaginary and not based on any person living or deceased. Any similarity to any person is purely coincidental.

Copyright 2013 by Union Beach, LP

All Rights Reserved

Printed in the United States and published by Hotray LLC

ISBN – 10: 098467845X

ISBN – 13: 978-0-9846784-5-7

Author's Note

I am not an expert on Asperger's Syndrome. However, there are numerous people around us who either have the disorder, or who care for someone who does. Autistic spectrum disorders manifest themselves in a myriad of ways, ranging from imperceptible to immediately obvious. Some people on the autistic spectrum are highly functional, while others require constant care and supervision.

Our society has a tendency to push autistic folks to the background. Our educational, healthcare, and transportation systems, to name a few, are ill equipped to handle the special needs of people who through no fault of their own live their lives close to the standard deviation boundaries of human behavior.

Inspiration for this book came from the vast army of caregivers who everyday dedicate their lives to helping their loved ones cope with what most people take for granted. May God bless each and every one of you for the wonderful work that you do. Your caring makes all the difference in the world.

ಸಂ

OTHER BOOKS BY DAVID HARRY

The Padre Puzzle

The Padre Predator

The Padre Paranoia

The Padre Pandemic

Book One

ONE

Cecil Harris was socially challenged from his first breath. The boy should have been heralded at birth for being the first baby born in the south Texas town of Cosper in the year 1979. In point of actual fact, the child arrived at precisely ten seconds past the stroke of midnight on the first day of that year. His frenzied non-stop crying lasted twelve hours and twenty-two minutes, setting a new hospital record not since matched.

During that time, several nurses exhausted their many tricks trying to comfort the boy. Nothing worked. At one point the attending pediatrician, acting at the request of the nursery staff, considered medicating him. The doctor instead moved Cecil to a private room at the end of the corridor. The noise continued, but proved less disruptive. And while the medical team could not possibly have known this at the time, their accommodation of Cecil was a prelude to how people throughout Cecil's life would cope with his unorthodox behavior.

While Cecil was busy screaming his lungs out, the award and the prize money that went with it, was given to the family of Alice Spencer who was born a half-hour after Cecil. The Spencers, as it just happened to turn out, owned the local paper and were major contributors to the hospital. The celebration of Cecil's life would have to wait.

Cecil's first quiet breath finally occurred twenty-two minutes past noon on New Year's Day, much to the relief of the exasperated nursing staff. His screaming and wild gesturing had been so violent that the anxious parents, Maggie and Joseph Harris, were not even allowed to hold him until he quieted down.

Despite his noisy beginnings, Cecil was mostly a quiet child, sitting on the floor in the kitchen and staring through the glass panes into the backyard. Later, when he learned to move on his own, and when he was not staring off into space, Cecil's favorite pastime was jumping off the bottom step leading up to the family bedrooms. Over and over he would jump, usually landing on his feet, but sometimes on his back. Sometimes even nose first. But, regardless of how he landed, feet first, butt first or head first; he would pick himself up and compulsively repeat the ritual.

His parents, Maggie and Joe were faced with the lose-lose choice of either standing by and catching him or listening to his screeching if they prevented him from jumping.

In due time, Cecil graduated to the second step, encouraged by his sister Caroline who was three years his senior. Other than Caroline's occasional interferences in Cecil's play routine, she was in every aspect a model child. She was an excellent student—bright and lively. Her biggest failing, and a source of agitation to the family, was her low tolerance for Cecil's manic-compulsive behavior. Caroline spent long hours in her room separating herself from her baby brother, seemingly only interacting with him in a manner calculated to get him in trouble with their parents. At first, it had been fun to stir him into a frenzy, causing him to go into a mantra of repetitive outbursts. But soon the fun faded, and Caroline would flee at the first signs of his loop mode as she called his outbursts.

For the first three years of her life, Caroline had thrived at being the center of her parents' universe. They had taken her with them everywhere they went, their eyes filled with joy, their mouths full of praise. But that all changed when Cecil was born. And Caroline despised her brother for it.

The hatred came, not so much for what he actually did, but because he emotionally drained her parents to the point where there was literally nothing remaining for them to give Caroline.

The few times the Harrises went out in public with Cecil he managed to work himself into a tizzy for one reason or another, causing the excursion to end painfully for all involved.

When Cecil began jumping from the fourth step, the distraught parents sought the help of Dr. Regina Goldschmidt, a psychologist with extensive experience in early childhood behavior. Her conclusion after several weeks of testing and observation was that Cecil needed distraction. "We must find something the boy likes to play with," the psychologist advised. "That'll get his mind off the jumping and should eliminate, or at least reduce, the aimless staring."

Joe Harris was not convinced. "What about his inattention to everything else around him, including TV? He doesn't seem to be aware of anything except what he's focusing on at the moment. I've never been around anyone so...so...what should I say?...self-absorbed."

"It's apparent that the behavior Cecil exhibits is out of the normal range," Dr. Goldschmidt confirmed. "The good news is your son shows no cognitive developmental impairment. However, his fixation on repetitive activities certainly bears watching."

"It's really hard to know what to do," Maggie said, keeping her eyes on her lap. "I try to read to him and he sits for maybe a minute and then runs to do something else, usually jumping off the stairs. It doesn't make a difference what story I try, he won't sit still."

"As I said," Dr. Goldschmidt responded, "his tests confirm there's nothing wrong cognitively. In fact, I'd venture to guess he's actually at the high end. His attention span, however, is below his age level. Consequently, he'll be a late reader, but I'm confident he will learn to read in due course. Focus is what is important here. Focus. It is important to find something constructive so he can channel his interest."

"You mean other than jumping from the fifth step!" Maggie responded, clearly upset and struggling to hold back tears. "Cecil's so different from Caroline, his older sister. She'll read or play by herself for hours on end. When I gave her picture books before she could read, she'd sit for hours making up stories to go with the pictures. Cecil just throws the books on the floor."

"Boys will be boys," Joe offered lamely, trying to console his wife and failing miserably.

"What does he like to do?" Dr. Goldschmidt asked. "I mean, other than jumping from the stairs. Is there anything that captures his attention?"

"Nothing that I've seen," Joe responded. "He's not interested in balls or other typical boy stuff. For that matter, he's not interested in Caroline's old toys either."

"Nothing?" Goldschmidt pressed. "Children like Cecil usually have multiple activities they get involved in."

"Well," Maggie began, "he does seem to have a fascination with things that move, that go around."

"Please give me an example."

"The washing machine. Well, actually, the dryer. He sits in front and watches the clothes tumble. He won't move away while it's running. I hate to say this, but when I can't take any more jumping, I put rags in just to keep him quiet. He can sit there for hours, his arms going in circles, all the time concentrating on what's inside the machine."

"Tell her about the park," Joe coaxed his wife, leaning forward in his chair. "Maggie's been telling me about his attraction to moving things in the park."

"Yea, I forgot about that," Maggie said, finally looking at the counselor. "The first time I became aware of him liking circular things was on the playground. I don't know what you call it, that circular thing where kids push the outside edge and other kids can jump on."

"You mean a carousel?" Goldschmidt volunteered.

"Right," Maggie answered. "There's no music or anything, just a big platform the kids push around in a circle. But..." Maggie paused, not sure how to explain Cecil's behavior.

"Go on," the doctor coaxed. "But..."

"But...but it's not the carousel he's interested in. The other kids push or ride it. Cecil crawls to the center and is fascinated with whatever's there. The children tease him. They call him stupid for looking the wrong way on the platform. All he cares about is watching the gears, or whatever's in there."

"Is there anything else?"

"I can't think of anything else he cares about," Joe answered, clearly resigned that this was going nowhere. Goldschmidt was expensive and seemed to be going in circles herself.

"Okay," the counselor said. "Let us focus on toys that go around. If you could buy him a toy carousel or perhaps a toy motor, that would be good. We must determine where his interests lie."

Two

For Cecil's eighth birthday Joe Harris turned to his friend, Bart Holbrook, who owned an engine repair business. After hearing about Cecil's fascination with rotating machinery, Bart suggested giving Cecil a worn-out lawn mower engine. "I can have one of my guys soak it clean and rebuild it. That way, the boy can take it apart," Bart offered. "He might get a bit frustrated putting it back together, but I'll come over and help if that happens."

When Joe protested, Bart replied, "It doesn't work, so I'm about to toss it out. He can't get hurt because it won't run."

"What's wrong with it?" Joe inquired, as if the answer, *whatever* it was, would make any sense to him.

"Since when have you become an engine guy?" his friend teased. "Actually, my guy ripped it down and says it's well beyond repair. Something must have worn out—or broke. Not worth my time trying to figure it out."

"I'm asking 'cause Cecil will ask," Joe said.

"He'll never know there's anything wrong," Bart said. "If my guys couldn't find it, the kid certainly won't. In fact, clever as he might be, without a manual he'll struggle to get it back together."

"You're right. He'll get upset and go into his repetition thing. I'll have hell to pay at home."

"I've heard that the boy gets locked on a word and repeats it until the other kids can't bear it. Better get it checked out. That's not normal. Know what I mean?" Bart cautioned.

"We've spent a ton already on shrinks. They have a fancy name for it; *perseverative thought*. In some children that's a big problem, but apparently not so much with Cecil. The doctor's exact words were, 'It's clinically significant only if it interferes with his functioning.' Seems it happens when his stress level goes up and he locks onto a thought. Like when everyone's laughing at a joke and he can't figure out why they're laughing," Joe explained. "That's when he locks onto a repetitive mantra."

"Didn't know there was such a thing." Bart looked away before continuing. "Junior says the kids rag on him constantly. When he reads in class Junior says he sounds funny and they tease him. Have you thought of private school?"

"The doctor says it's important to keep him mainstreamed, whatever the hell that means. I'm not sure we can afford some fancy-pants school anyway. Maggie can't work at anything like a full-time job 'cause the boy needs constant supervision from the moment he gets home from school."

"Hope the engine helps," Bart said. "He'll get it apart easy enough, but the little sucker'll keep him out of mischief a long while trying to get it back together. Be sure to tell him I'll come help when you give it to him. This just might keep him from going crazy. I allow my guys a full day to rebuild an engine like that. That's assuming they already know how it goes together. Good luck."

Two hours after Cecil received his present, he had the engine fully torn down with all the parts carefully laid out on the kitchen floor.

"My God!" Maggie exclaimed upon discovering that there was nowhere to walk without stepping on a pulley or a spring or a piston. "It'll be weeks before I can get back in here to cook! I suppose it'll be take-out until then." She turned to see Joe's reaction, but her husband had slipped outside and was busy with the weed-whacker. He had been trimming the bushes and working on the yard a lot lately. Cecil didn't like the sound of the cutters, so he kept his distance, which, truth be told, suited Joe more than he was willing to admit.

Maggie picked her way to the sink to clean the lunch plates. Cecil looked up from the floor where he was sitting, the parts surrounding him. "Don't step on parts. Don't step on parts," he said, his face revealing nothing other than his ordinary bland expression.

"You can't just spread things on my floor like this, young man," Maggie scolded, being careful to keep her tone pleasant for fear of setting him off on one of his endless mantras.

"It's my floor too," the boy replied, not understanding why she was complaining. "My floor too."

"Daddy says it will take you a long time to put this back together. I can't cook with this mess under my feet."

"A real long time," Cecil replied. "You can watch."

"I won't be able to cook."

"Done by time to eat." With that, the boy began reassembling the engine. He had laid out the parts in a big spiral during the disassembly, putting the first mechanisms as far away from him as he could. Then he had placed each removed part on the floor in a circle around the engine, working from the outside toward the middle.

Now, during the reassembly, Cecil was circling the engine block, working from the inside of the circle to the outside, picking up the parts one by one and installing them accurately in their proper places. The engine grew larger by the minute. Moving quickly, but deliberately, round and round, the parts disappeared from the floor in a steady progression.

By three in the afternoon only the outer ring of parts remained on the floor.

Suddenly, Cecil let out a scream and ran to the stairs. He clambered to the fifth step and jumped off, landing on all fours, his knees scrapping the hardwood hall floor. He picked himself up, climbed again to the fifth step and again jumped off.

Joe came in from the yard just in time to see his son leap into the air. This time Cecil's right arm buckled when he landed and his chin thudded against the floor.

Joe expected a bellow of pain, but Cecil only shook his head as if to clear his vision and raced up the stairs to jump again. Blood from the gash along the side of the child's chin trailed across the wood floor and up the steps.

This time Joe caught the boy in mid-air and carried him to the kitchen. Seeing only a few parts not in place on the engine, Joe exclaimed, "I thought you had it apart already! What was your mother complaining about?"

The boy squirmed in agitation. "Hold still, son! We need to stop the bleeding and get a bandage on your chin. This may need stitches."

The boy wildly gestured toward the engine, yelling something like, "Wrong peen. Wrong peen." Cecil repeated the words like a mantra, over and over and over again, making it difficult for Joe to stem the bleeding.

Maggie, coming back to the kitchen to retrieve something she had forgotten, noticed the floor before she saw Cecil. Not realizing her son had split open his chin, she exclaimed, "Where did all the parts go? That's why he's screaming! Someone moved his parts."

Before her husband could respond, she yelled, "Caroline! Caroline! Where are you? Get down here this instant!"

"Hold it," her husband said. "Caroline's not the reason he's upset. He cut his chin. Help me get the bleeding stopped. He may need stitches."

"Oh, my God! I didn't see that! What happened?"

"Steps again. Cracked his chin this time, on the hall floor."

"I don't understand why he was on the steps. He was working on that motor. Parts were all over the floor last I saw."

"We'll deal with that later," Joe responded. "Let's see to the damage to his chin."

Joe carried the boy over to the sink and Maggie dampened a paper towel and wiped at the blood. Cecil didn't protest or even seem to pay attention to what they were doing. He continued his pointing and chanting, "Wrong peen. Wrong peen."

"What do you want?" demanded the just-arrived Caroline. "I'm in the middle of a game. I've managed to trap the dragon and he'll get away if I don't get back!"

"Never mind," Maggie said. "False alarm. Go back to your game!"

"What happened to him now? Why's he screaming about a pin?"

"Like your mother said," Joe replied, "never mind. Go back to your dragon or whatever's so important."

"Hey, that's my life! I didn't do anything here! All you ever care about is him, him, him! You spend all your time catering to his nonsense with those motors, and never care what I'm doing! The only time you care about me is when you think I've done something to that jerk! That's what he is, a class act jerk! The kids in school make fun of him. They tease me because of him. I hate him. He's messed up my life! I hate him!" Caroline turned and stomped back to her room, mumbling about being tired of being blamed for her stupid brother's antics.

"What's got into her?" Joe asked. "We haven't seen that for a while."

"Her friends have been getting on her. Janet Spencer is in Caroline's class and her sister Alice goes to school with Cecil. Kids talk." Maggie studied Cecil's chin. "This cut isn't as bad as it looks. The blood is coming from his lip. He must have bit it when he fell. I think it's stopped."

Joe inspected his son's face and realized that the boy's features were beginning to mature ever so slightly. Cecil was going to be a handsome young man, if only he would learn to look directly at people instead of down to the floor or off to the side. "Hold still a minute, Son. You'll be fine. Now what's bothering you? Something about a pin? What pin?"

Cecil ran across the room to the engine and pulled out a pin that had been holding what Joe took to be a piston to a shaft. "Wrong," the boy said. "Wrong."

"Then put in the right one," Joe replied, looking around to see if he could find the right pin. Not finding another pin, he turned to his wife. "Maggie, did anyone touch anything? A pin seems to be missing."

"Not unless Caroline did. But I don't know how she would have taken a pin and been able to replace it with another one. Where in the world would she get it?" "Wrong pin! Wrong pin!" the boy resumed his chant, agitation clearly rising. Now that his mouth was not full of blood it was clear what he was saying. "Wrong pin! Wrong pin!"

Neither of them could do anything to calm him. Maggie offered him a sandwich and he refused. As soon as Joe let go of him he ran toward the steps. Again Joe caught him in midair. "Enough is enough!" Joe shouted, his patience long gone. "Calm yourself down!"

Maggie, playing the conciliatory role, replied as calmly as she could, "Remember what Dr. Goldschmidt told us. Stay calm."

"Then let the frigg'n doctor deal with him! I've had it! The child's impossible!"

"Didn't Bart say to call if Cecil had a problem? Maybe he can figure out what this *wrong pin* thing is all about."

Joe sucked in a deep breath, blew it out and said nothing.

"Just call him!" Maggie insisted, and then, frustrated and exhausted, she dragged herself upstairs. At the top of the steps, realizing Joe was tuning out, Maggie resolved to call Bart herself.

Joe, meanwhile, plopped himself down on the bottom stair step blocking Cecil from jumping. Instead, Cecil threw himself on the sofa and curled into a fetal ball, all the while chanting, "Wrong pin! Wrong pin! Wrong pin! Wrong pin!"

Three

"He did what?" Bart exclaimed, when Maggie explained about the parts being spread out on the floor. "That's not possible! You say it took him about two hours to tear it down. But it's not torn down."

"I know," Joe said. "Seems he put it back together."

"Not possible. I've rebuilt hundreds of these and I'd be hard-pressed to do it that fast."

"All I can say," Maggie continued, "is parts were everywhere. I couldn't walk in my own kitchen!"

Joe, on the sofa still restraining Cecil, pointed in the direction of the engine. "Maybe it's not put together proper, but judge for yourself."

It was hard for conversation to take place over the boy's incessant mantra, *"Wrong pin, wrong pin!"* But Joe pressed on. "He seems to be saying there's a wrong pin or something. I don't know what he's screaming about."

Bart bent over the engine, examining it closely. He straightened up, rubbed his balding head, and then turning to the strung-out parents, said, "The boy's right on, by God! The pin's indeed wrong. That's a *Lawn-Boy* pin, but it's a *Stratton* engine. There's a locking ridge missing. That piston won't lock to the rod and the engine can't work. It's beyond me how he'd know that." Staring over at the almost re-assembled engine, he asked, "How long did you say it took him to get this far in the rebuild?"

"No more than four hours," Maggie replied. "Most likely three. Why?"

"You certain?"

"Positive. He had parts all over the kitchen. I didn't think I'd be able to cook dinner. He said he'd be finished by cooking time."

"I've never seen anything like this! Most of my men wouldn't ever have known the pin was wrong. Actually, I may have the right one out in the truck. Give me a minute." Bart turned to Cecil, who was now much calmer, but still chanting, almost to himself, *wrong pin, wrong pin, wrong pin,* and said, "Young man, you're right. There *is* a wrong pin in there. Rod won't hold. I'm going to my truck to see if I have the right one. Would you like that?"

To the astonishment of both parents, the boy stopped the mantra, and nodded his head. "It will work. I know it will work."

"You're right, son. I'll be right back."

Cecil calmed down and climbed off his father's lap where he had been held captive. Instead of racing for the stairs, he nestled his head in Joe's lap and lay there rocking softly.

"Cecil, can I get you something to eat?" Maggie asked tentatively. "I mean, while we're waiting."

"Sandwich and milk," the boy replied, as if nothing at all unusual had happened.

Maggie quickly busied herself getting the boy what he wanted. By the time Bart walked back into the house triumphantly holding a pin the size of a small rod, Cecil was well into a ham sandwich, plain, with no condiments, just as he liked it.

Bart started toward the engine. The boy yelped, slid off the sofa, and ran to intercept him.

"I suppose he wants to change the pin himself," Bart said. "It's not all that easy 'cause you need to keep the piston in the exact right position to lock the pin."

"Let him do it," Joe urged, "I can't take another round of stair-jumping and chin bashing just right now."

Bart handed Cecil the pin and stepped back.

The boy laid the new pin carefully on the floor, sat down beside the engine, placed his left hand on the far side of the block, his index finger slightly inside, wedging the piston against the shaft. He then slowly pushed on the existing pin until it was partially out of the slot. Before it fell all the way out, he retrieved the new pin and fitted it into the vacant portion of the slot. Then, using the new pin, he pushed the old one all the way out until it fell onto the floor with a dull clank.

"Now I've seen everything!" exclaimed Bart. "My most experienced mechanics are not that smooth. Beats me how he knew to do it that way. Also beats me how he knew it was wrong. The only difference is that small detent at the leading end. That sucker was tore down twice and no one spotted the wrong pin. One of the guys must have misassembled it the first time."

While they were talking, Cecil resumed his circular attack on the remainder of the parts. Within five minutes he had finished the rebuilding. But before anyone had a chance to say "good job" or anything else, the boy immediately began taking the engine apart again. When Maggie realized what he was doing, she exclaimed, "Move him into the dining room! I need my kitchen back. We can eat in the kitchen."

Joe carried the engine to a corner of the dining room, only to have Cecil take up a new chant: "Middle, middle, middle."

The men looked at each other, confounded as to what was *now* troubling the boy.

But Maggie, having already been exposed to Cecil's modus operandi, knew *exactly* what the problem was. "He wants the motor in the middle of the floor so that he can spread the parts out in a circle. Go ahead, move the table. We'll cope."

With the table moved, Cecil set the parts that he had already removed in a circle just as Maggie had described. Then he continued tearing down the engine while Bart stood in the doorway transfixed. "Never seen anything like this in my life," he exclaimed at one point. Look at his fingers work. He seems pretty awkward in most things, if you'll forgive me for saying, but this...this is like watching the fingers of a virtuoso musician. Never seen anything like it, I tell you."

Joe wasn't watching the boy's fingers. He was studying his son's pleasant face. Cecil's mouth was slightly open, his grey eyes intent on his work, the intensity of his focus sending shivers down Joe's spine. His son appeared to have floated off to a place Joe could not imagine. His fingers seemed to move by themselves, as if by muscle memory, without any guiding thought process. Cecil moved around the engine in a clockwise circle, and as he went, parts disappeared from the engine and appeared on the floor in a spiral, working inward from an outer ring.

Bart checked his watch. "Unbelievable! Thirty-five minutes and the whole thing is apart!"

But not for long.

No sooner had Cecil placed the last part on the floor in the middle of the room than he began to reassemble the engine.

"Mind if I stay a while?" Bart asked. "I want to see how long it takes him. No one will believe any of this!"

"Want something to eat, drink?"

"Beer will work nicely. From the speed he's moving, I probably won't finish even one."

Bart didn't have long to wait. "Holy crap. Thirty-five minutes to tear it down, fifty-five minutes to reassemble! That has to be a world record, if there is such a thing. If I hadn't seen it, I wouldn't have believed it! And I still can't figure how he knew about that pin." Bart thought for a moment, then said, "Hey, how about bringing him over to the shop on Saturdays? I can always find something he can work on."

"If you're sure you want him underfoot. He can be trying."

"All we can do is try. One of my men can keep an eye on him. There's always an engine that needs rebuilding. Cecil will be in his element."

Cecil, meanwhile, had once more begun to strip the engine.

"Will he just keep doing this?" Bart asked, struggling to understand a behavior that could only be described as bizarre. "I've never seen or heard of anything like it. He sure is different."

"He's different," Joe acknowledged, "that much I can attest to. He's a good child, but when it comes to something he's focused on, he can't stop obsessing over it. Child psych called it 'circumscribed interests', which is a form of perseverative thought."

"Like what else is he into?" Bart inquired, confused over the fancy words.

"Seems it's anything that goes around. Rotary stuff," Joe replied, fascinated by the speed at which his son's fingers moved.

"So why don't you give him one of those old windup clocks to play around with?" Bart suggested. "From what I've seen, he'd probably make it keep better time than when it was new. The kid is a regular mechanical genius."

"Genius?" Joe thought to himself, reflecting on the day's events. "More like savant." He was about to say it out loud— *mechanical savant*—but changed his mind. Truth be told, he was afraid of what it all might mean.

Four

Cecil was given the workings of a pendulum clock Joe had picked up at a yard sale for three dollars. The hands were intact, and so was the mechanism, but precious little else had survived. The seller had no idea if the clock could be made to work.

In anticipation of problems, Joe had stopped at a watchmaker's shop for guidance. After speaking at length with the owner, Joe bought several small tools, among them a gear puller. The proprietor took time to show Joe how the various tools worked. But the gear puller eluded him. Exasperated with Joe's lack of intuitive understanding, the owner said, "If need be, bring the boy in here and I'll be happy to show him how to use it."

Cecil was delighted with the clock. But when Joe handed him the gear puller, the boy's eyes immediately came alive. "I'm not sure I can help you with this," Joe said, "but I can try."

Cecil refused to part with the tool, chanting, "I know," several times.

Joe, having learned to back off when Cecil went into loop mode, didn't press the issue. Instead, he asked, "What do you know?"

"I know it pulls gears from pins." The boy then proceeded to remove two gears, one after the other. "See?"

Joe shook his head while he recalled how he had struggled at the watchmaker's with the tool. Meanwhile, gears, pulleys and all kinds of little parts began to appear on the dining room table, as always in a circle around the main clock housing.

The housing was soon empty.

Joe knew they were at a crossroad because now the boy would have to put it all back together. Again, Joe knew he was unprepared to help, other than to spread a plastic sheet on the floor where Cecil was stationed. He handed Cecil a small bottle of solvent, a lint-free cloth, and some lubricant.

Cecil carefully put solvent on one cloth, wiped a small gear clean and then dried it with a second cloth. He slipped the gear onto a shaft. Cecil repeated the process and cleaned a tiny pin so small Joe had trouble seeing it. When the pin was dry, Cecil carefully inserted it into a small hole in the gear, locking the gear to the shaft.

In places where parts were supposed to rub together Cecil applied the faintest trace of lubricant. This process was repeated for several minutes, when suddenly the boy became agitated and his head began to move wildly from side to side. "Wrong! Wrong! Wrong!"

Joe rushed to his side, remembering all too vividly the scene that had played out with the engine six months earlier. "What's wrong?" Joe asked, trying to sound positive despite the deteriorating situation. He was fearful that the relative calm of the past six months was about to end, but he knew it was not good for Cecil to endlessly focus on one thing alone. Tearing down and rebuilding the engine had become Cecil's new mantra.

The boy stopped his chant and said. "Gear and pin are bent," he said, holding them up for his father's inspection.

"We can straighten the pin," Joe replied. "I don't know about the gear. Come out to the garage and we'll use the vise."

Obediently, the boy climbed down from his chair and followed Joe out to the garage, clutching the bent parts in his hand. Joe took the pin, which was the diameter of a mechanical pencil lead, and grasped it with the jewelry pliers the watchmaker had sold him. He then carefully positioned the pin between the jaws of the vise. "Turn this handle," he instructed Cecil.

The boy followed Joe's instructions and slowly the pin straightened. When the vise was opened the pin fell into Cecil's hand and the boy was ecstatic. "Good, good, good," he repeated. "Will work." Cecil placed the pin in his pant's pocket.

The gear proved more difficult. A few teeth were missing, and several others were bent. The boy meticulously positioned one of the bent gear teeth in the vise and turned the handle. He then removed the part and examined the teeth by rotating the gear several times.

Joe stood off to the side observing his son. He took particular notice of how totally focused the boy was, and how his face remained emotionless, serene.

Cecil then placed another gear in the vice, turned the handle, and repeated the process, again rotating the gear in his hands.

Joe said, "I'm sorry we can't fix the missing teeth. Maybe we can buy a new gear from the clock maker."

Cecil didn't seem to hear his father's comment, as he continued to study the broken gear.

A few minutes later Cecil again held the gear up to the light, rotated it in his hands several times and slipped it in his pocket. He said, "Work now." He then ran back into the house, heading straight for the clock.

By the time Joe arrived in the dining room, the pin had been inserted and the gear was in place. Joe wondered how in the world the boy could work so fast, particularly since he had never before seen an escapement mechanism in operation.

Fascinated with the boy's manual dexterity, Joe watched from the doorway as Cecil added a few more parts, and then turned the mechanism over to study the pendulum. Joe mentally braced himself knowing that when the gear jammed he'd have to deal with what he was sure would be the inevitable meltdown.

Then suddenly the boy was shouting, "Works now! Works now! Works now!"

Joe hurried across the room to where his son was standing and was surprised to see the clock set to the proper time, even though Cecil could not yet tell time.

Cecil was holding the clock above the table allowing the pendulum, which looked like a hockey puck fashioned to the end of a tail, to swing from side to side. This model had been designed for wall mounting and without a base the pendulum would hit the table and stop working.

"How in the world did you get it running? I was told the windup key was missing."

Cecil simply said, "Pulled chain up."

"I'm not sure I know what you're telling me, but it works. Here, give it to me and I'll hang it on the wall for you."

The boy pulled the clock tight against his chest. Panic filled his eyes and he ran to the far side of the room.

Joe quickly realized what was wrong, "I guess you want to tear it down again and rebuild it. That's okay too."

The boy immediately calmed down and set the clock on its side on the table. He unhooked the pendulum and began to disassemble the mechanism once again.

The engine was all but forgotten—at least for now.

☙❧

Several weeks later, Miss Palmrose, Cecil's second grade teacher, phoned and asked if she could stop by to speak with Cecil's parents.

Palmrose appeared ill at ease when she arrived. Cecil was busy in the dining room rebuilding his engine yet again. She stood in the doorway watching Cecil. Her discomfort level rose when she saw that the floor was covered with engine parts, including endless bolts, nuts and washers. The teacher continued to study the boy as he meticulously laid one part after another on the floor, spiraling inward toward the mechanical carcass. She had never observed anyone working in this fashion.

Palmrose turned to face Joe. "Can we please talk out of hearing of the child," the teacher began.

Moving into the living room, she said, "I need to discuss some disturbing behavior, and it would be best if he was not privy to the conversation."

"He's concentrating on his engine now, and when he works this way everything else seems to be blocked. Maggie will join us in a moment. She's out in the kitchen brewing tea. Is there anything else I can get for you?"

"No thanks. The tea will be fine."

They sat in silence a few moments until Maggie joined them. The teacher, a tiny, severe-faced woman, sipped her tea and then began, "Well, it seems that Cecil's social development is very much out of kilter. His first grade teacher noted the situation, but thought he would grow out of it. Unfortunately for all of us, I don't see much progress. He's oblivious to what anyone else is doing or saying. He never makes eye contact and often has his head down. He seems to be in his own world. Much like he is now over there."

"But he's not disruptive, is he?" Joe asked, defensively.

"I'm afraid he is. He has no friends, except possibly for little Sally, who...shall we say...also has...'issues.' I must say, wherever Cecil is, Sally's not far away."

"Where is this leading?" Joe pressed. "Is he bothering the girl?"

"Oh, heavens no. Not Cecil. He's too busy trying to see how things work to bother with the other students. Sally seems to want to talk with him, but like I said, he's in his own world." Palmrose paused, sucked in her breath and then continued. "In fact, that's why I'm here. Like I said, to be blunt, Cecil has major social issues."

When neither Maggie nor Joe responded, the teacher went on. "The boy has not developed age appropriate relationships and to make matters worse, he does not have a sense of humor appropriate for his age. We might be discussing one topic when all of a sudden, out of nowhere, he blurts out something that is not appropriate for the topic being discussed." The teacher sipped some tea before continuing. "And that thing he does with his arms. I mean holding them out like an airplane and waving them around. The other kids mimic him. On the playground they run around with their arms waving and flapping."

"I don't get where you're going with this," Maggie replied. She was mortified to be the subject of a home visit, but hid her discomfort as best she could. "What are you talking about?"

"I'll give you an example. We have a joke telling session each week. The idea is to make the children comfortable in public speaking. This week it was Billy Edwards who told the joke. Cecil didn't find it funny. He never does. But this time he told Billy it was a stupid joke. The class then started teasing Cecil about not getting the joke. I'm afraid they are still teasing him."

"What's the joke?" Joe asked. "Maybe Cecil's right, it wasn't funny."

"The joke's not the issue, Mr. Harris. He just doesn't seem to fit in with the class."

"Please. What was the joke?"

"If you insist," she relented, checking her notes. "One student says to the other, 'Why are you always scratching yourself?' The other student answers, 'Because no one else knows where it itches.'"

Joe looked at her, not sure how to say what he wanted to say. Finally, he asked, "So what happened? It's certainly not the funniest joke I've ever heard."

"Your son yells, 'You're stupid! Of course you scratch it yourself! Nobody knows where to scratch your own itch!' That's inappropriate for his age."

"That's why you came to see us? Because he didn't get a joke? Because he called another kid stupid?"

"That, and then your son added, 'Except my daddy always scratches my mommy's itches because they are always on her butt.' For Cecil, nothing is ever in proper context."

Joe's neck felt suddenly warm, and he was certain his face had turned bright red. "Well, I...I don't know what to say. Cecil does tend to speak his mind, I'm afraid."

"I'm here as his teacher, but more importantly because I care about the boy. I suggest you seek professional help."

"We're already going to counseling. We're getting all the help we can afford right now," Joe answered, anger creeping into his voice.

"Are you certain he's in the right school? Perhaps a school more...more shall we say...appropriate for his situation."

"His therapist wants him in the public school. She says it's important to keep him mainstreamed. And we happen to agree with that."

"This is only the beginning of his problems I'm afraid," Palmrose pressed. "The class is picking on him. When they do, he starts mumbling, says things over and over like a broken record. We can't do our work when he gets like that. It's disruptive and getting worse. The other kids are imitating him, repeating words and rolling their eyes. Cecil doesn't know exactly what they are doing, but he knows they're making fun of him. He puts his head down and he becomes unapproachable."

"We *are* working on it, Miss Palmrose," Maggie responded, breaking her silence. "The official term for it, in case you're interested, is perseverative thought. He has a mild neurological impairment, but it's not expected to get any worse. He's really a very bright boy and he wants very much to be accepted."

"I have to agree that when he's not in broken-record mode he's really very sweet. He always wants to please, but doesn't know what to do."

"So why are you here?"

"In short, he's disruptive to the learning process for the other children. I really think—"

"The school will just have to figure out a way to cope!" Joe broke in, his patience having evaporated. "We're doing our best."

"I'm trying to do what's best for Cecil," Palmrose responded. "You do understand that, don't you?"

"I understand you're trying to get him out of your classroom. I'm sorry he doesn't fit your tidy little mold, but he won't be going to a private school."

"I'm sorry you feel that way. I have nothing further to discuss." Palmrose stood. "One other thing," she said. "I suppose you know the boy has an obsession with clocks. He took ours off the wall, then proceeded to take it apart."

"He's good with mechanical things," Joe commented. "Didn't he put it back together?"

"I took it from him when I realized what he was doing. It's broken and in the closet now."

"Just give it to him and he'll fix it good as new."

"I'm afraid I can't do that."

"Why not?"

"The other children grabbed the springs and things and now they're gone. When Cecil found out the parts were missing he went into one of his mantras. It took hours to calm him."

"I'll pay for a new clock," Joe said, reaching for his wallet.

"That won't be necessary, Mr. Harris. I just brought it up to point out some of the issues."

"Next time he takes something apart, keep the parts safe. He'll rebuild it good as new."

"That's not the point, I'm afraid. Please instruct Cecil to keep his hands off school property. I can't have him pulling things apart. He's disruptive as it is. Anything you can do to help would be greatly appreciated."

"We'll do our best, Miss Palmrose," Joe replied, anxious to see the teacher on her way, "but I can't promise he'll listen. The boy has a mind of his own."

"That's the least of it," Palmrose commented, glancing at Cecil in the next room and noting his concentration as he placed the last few parts on the engine. "I don't know how we're expected to cope with him, but I'll do my best."

FIVE

After Palmrose's visit, the school administration assigned a specially trained helper to Cecil. The woman spent her days in the classroom keeping the disruptions to a minimum. This arrangement continued for several more years as Cecil progressed from the second grade to the eighth grade. His grades were average, except for reading where he lagged behind the class. He had little patience for the science experiments, but he excelled in math. He sat for hours working the problems over and over, very carefully writing down his work. His homework papers were always perfect. But test taking was difficult because he did not have time to do each problem several times as he did with his homework. At times, the frustration pushed him into a mantra which proved disruptive to his classmates. The solution was that in sixth grade the school assigned him a monitor and allowed him to take his tests in a private room. From that point on his math and science grades were never less than an A.

Richard Henderson, one of his eighth grade teachers, quickly realized that while Cecil hadn't mastered all that had been expected, especially in reading, he did have a fabulous memory. It seemed that if he heard something even one time he would remember it with near perfect recall.

Henderson approached Cecil's mother one afternoon when she was in the building helping in the library. "Would you mind," he began, "if Cecil was given a part in the class play?"

The question caught Maggie Harris unprepared. Never had she even dreamed Cecil would have any part of being in a play — with other children. "I'll have to discuss it with my husband," Maggie answered, flabbergasted at the thought of Cecil being on stage. "I'm not sure he can read his lines. He has such trouble with written words."

"That won't be a problem," Henderson replied, having anticipated the concern. "Actually, I plan to read him the lines. When he hears something he never forgets it. With his memory he should have no trouble remembering his lines."

"If we agree," Maggie responded, uncomfortable at the thought, "please don't give him a big part. I don't want pressure on him he can't handle. He's a sensitive child."

"I understand," Henderson replied. "It will be good for him. Cecil's a good boy, but he gets wound up over trivial stuff and misses what's really important. I'm hoping this will get him to interact with his classmates. As far as I can tell, the only person he ever talks with is Sally Mascar."

Maggie knew Sally only as the slow learning child in Cecil's class. She was a pretty girl in a homespun way; always friendly, always smiling.

Sally's mother never came to PTA meetings and Maggie knew nothing of her. Maggie also didn't know if Sally's father lived at home, or whether he was even alive. "Will Sally be in the play with him?" Maggie asked.

"I hope so. But I'm not sure she'll make it. The girl has trouble remembering things. I'll try to work with her, but I don't hold out much hope. She doesn't have the...capacity...that Cecil has."

Joe Harris was skeptical, but relented when Cecil said, "Mr. Henderson says I can do it. I'll work hard. I can do it. I want to be like the other kids."

"Okay, son, you can do it. I'll help you with your lines, if you want."

Cecil ran off to play with the latest engine Bart had dropped off. Joe turned to Maggie and shook his head. "This is not going to end well. Try to stay close and let me know at the first sign of trouble. I can't imagine Cecil in front of an audience."

"By the time I see anything wrong," Maggie exclaimed, "it might just be too late."

༺༻

The weeks leading up to the play were hectic for everyone but Cecil. He had been the first to know his lines, and in each rehearsal had recited them flawlessly. The only problem was that, despite repeated coaching, his lines were still being delivered with no inflection and with a facially flat affect.

Joe Harris sat in on the final dress rehearsal and commented to the teacher, "Everyone is so good and Cecil seems to be odd man out. Flat. I'm sorry he's a problem."

Henderson shrugged and replied, "I'm thrilled he's participating. Look, this is only eighth grade. It's no big deal if he's not perfect. At least he knows his lines. That's more than I can say for some of them."

"I'm glad you feel that way. His mother's a wreck."

"Tell her to relax. He'll be just fine."

༺༻

On the morning of the play, Maggie asked Cecil if he was all set.

"I know my lines. I'm ready."

"Good luck. I guess I should say break a leg."

His eyes fell and his head went down. Maggie should have expected that reaction after all these years, but she was so nervous about the play that Cecil's likely reaction to what she said completely escaped her.

"What's wrong now?" she pressed.

"You want me to break my leg. That's a mean thing to say. Sally said the same thing yesterday. It's mean. I don't want to break my leg. I can't do my lines if I break my leg."

"It's an old show business saying, dear. Break your leg is a way of saying good luck. In the theater wishing someone good luck causes them to mess up. A superstition. Like throwing salt over your shoulder."

"Why would I throw salt—"

"Never mind, Cecil. Everyone means you well."

"I still don't understand why you told me to break my leg."

His mother sighed. "I'm just wishing you good luck tonight."

"I don't need luck. I know my lines."

"Okay. Just go to school and I'll see you after the play."

Caroline, already late for school, rushed through the kitchen. Seeing Cecil and being uncharacteristically friendly, she called over her shoulder, "Break a leg!"

"Stop saying that. Stop saying that. I don't want to break my leg. You are mean."

"What's the matter with him now? God, will he ever join society? Jerk!" Caroline slammed the door behind her.

Cecil again hung his head and turned away.

"Cecil," Maggie said, "I told you, she was just wishing you luck tonight."

"Party after the play," the boy said, already forgetting the mean statements. "Want to go."

Cecil had never before asked to go to a party, or for that matter to go out with anybody for anything. Maggie was caught off guard. "Sure you can go. I'll find out more about it, and you can go."

"Alice will be there."

"Who's Alice?"

"A girl in the play."

"What part does she play?"
Cecil looked blank, confused. He remained silent.
"Never mind. I'll figure it out later. Is Alice special?"
"Pretty." Cecil's face turned red and his head bent forward again.
"Does she have a last name?"
"Alice Spense... or something."
"Oh, that's the Spencer girl. I forgot she was born the same time as you. Jennie Spencer's daughter. I didn't know you talked to her. She's always been mea—"
"Makes fun of me. Don't want to talk anymore."
Maggie had long ago learned that when Cecil didn't want to talk, it was best to leave him be. "Okay, have a good day."

༺༻

Later, on the way to the performance, Maggie mentioned the morning's conversation to her husband. Then added, "What do you make of him and Alice Spencer? Alice has always been mean to him. I've mentioned it to Jennie Spencer, but she doesn't seem too concerned with what her daughter says or does."

"Alice Spencer," Joe immediately responded, "plays the second female lead. Cute kid, but too much of a little vixen, if you ask me. They have a scene together. Maybe that's what got into him."

"Cecil seems to have his eye on her. Should we be worried?"

"They're only fourteen, for goodness sake! He's fine."

"Who knows nowadays."

"You're worrying for no good reason—as usual. From the look Alice gave him on stage at the dress rehearsal you've nothing to worry about."

Maggie, Joe and Caroline sat in the second row. Caroline leaned close to her mother. "He's not going to embarrass me, is he?" the seventeen-year-old asked. "I have friends here."

"You're in high school. This is middle school. Your friends won't even know."

"Wrong, Mom! My friends have little brothers and sisters. Many of them are here tonight. God, I hope he doesn't screw up like he usually does. He's a jerk."

"That's not nice, Caroline. He's still your brother and hasn't been a bother to you for years. Behave yourself."

"I'm sorry I came! What the hell's he doing in a play anyway? He'd be happier building a car or something. I get all creepy being around him."

"Caroline!"

"That kid is still obsessed with his motors and clocks, and God knows what else. How many does he have now? Five, six?"

"Ten, if you're really counting."

"Why do you put up with his mess? I get the littlest thing out of order and you come down on me! The dining room is unusable and you do nothing. I can't dare have friends over. Shit!"

"Caroline! That's about enough from you!"

"He doesn't care about anyone. Machines are all he knows or cares about."

"It's a small price to pay to have him act mostly normal. And besides that, he's doing okay in school now."

"With a full-time sitter! Just keep him away from me and my friends, that's all I ask."

While they were talking, the curtain had gone halfway up and stopped. Then it came down and stayed down. The outlines of several people could be seen with their hands on the curtain jiggling it.

A few minutes later, the lights again dimmed and the curtain started up for the second time. Again it stopped in the same place, about a third of the way up. The house lights came back on full.

Nothing happened for several minutes and then the legs and parts of the torsos of two adults could be seen working on something behind the curtain.

From the background Joe began to hear an all too familiar sound. His senses locked onto it.

Maggie, noticing the pained look on her husband's face, asked, "What's wrong, honey? You feeling okay?" His face tightened even further.

She was thinking heart attack.

Then Maggie heard it herself. Her stomach instantly knotted. She grabbed her husband's hand. Even by squeezing with all her strength she couldn't get the tightness in her chest to ease.

The sound was louder now and at least one woman sitting several rows behind them said, "Who's moaning? Someone's been hurt. Someone's moaning back there."

Maggie knew it wasn't anyone moaning. It was Cecil in deep agitation, repeating over and over, "Wheel off! Wheel off! Wheel off! Wheel off!"

Henderson walked out onto the stage in front of the partially opened curtain and announced, "As you can see, we are having what they call *technical difficulties*. In truth, we simply can't get the curtain to go up. It appears to be jammed. Hopefully, this won't take much longer to resolve and we'll get on with the play. We hope to restart in fifteen minutes. You can go to the lobby if you wish. We'll flash the lights when we're ready."

Henderson started back toward stage right. As he did so, the noise from Cecil increased in volume. Suddenly, he burst from the left corner and ran to the center of the stage. The mantra, "Wheel off! Wheel off! Wheel off!", continued as he pointed straight up over his head.

Henderson ran back to where Cecil was standing. "Son, please stop yelling. Why are you so agitated?"

Cecil, his voice a little softer, continued with, "Wheel off! Wheel off!"

Joe Harris jumped from his seat, excused himself getting to the aisle, ran to the front and climbed onto the stage. Reaching the teacher, he said, "Cecil is trying to tell you what's wrong. Is there a wheel up there?"

"I wouldn't know a thing about what's up there," Henderson snapped. "But I'm told the problem's down here, not up there."

Joe tried to see what his son was looking at but could only make out a mass of cables extending far upward. "Cecil, is the problem a broken wheel up there?"

The boy nodded, but did not look down.

"Are you certain?"

Again he nodded. The mantra had stopped.

Joe ducked under the curtain and found the school custodian. "My son says the problem is with a wheel up there. Could that be the problem?"

"Anything could be the problem, mister. This is an old building. But that's never what it's been in the past. Usually it clears if we straighten the wires down here."

"Could the boy be right?"

"How the hell would he know what's broken? Boy can't possibly see up there from here."

"He knows what he's saying. He always knows. Could you please check?"

"I wouldn't know where to begin. So what's the use?"

"Maybe he could fix it?"

"Buddy, you kidding me? That's not something a kid could do! You nuts or something?"

"Just let him try. He has a way with machinery. Can we go up there safely?"

"There's a catwalk over that part of the stage. We can get there from the fourth floor, but I can't allow a kid up there."

"I'll give permission," Joe quickly replied, not so much because he wanted to fix the curtain, but in self-defense. He didn't want his son to restart his mantra. "I'll go up with you."

"If Henderson okays it, I'll humor you. But I'm telling you right now, it's a waste of time."

"You're not making much progress down here. If it's not fixed I suppose the play will be cancelled."

"You got a point."

Henderson bucked the request to the principal, who had come onstage to see for herself what was going on. After a brief discussion, she nodded her consent.

A few minutes later, the school custodian, Joe, Cecil, and Henderson left the stage, climbed the steps toward the fourth floor and made their way out onto the catwalk. Halfway across the catwalk, Cecil, still dressed in the costume of an old professor, went down on his stomach. At first Joe thought he had fallen, and both he and the custodian quickly reached to snag him. But the boy was positioning himself to better see the curtain-lifting mechanism.

Cecil leaned over the side, studied the pulley and cables and began pointing. The maintenance man looked at Joe puzzled.

"He wants you to lie down and look at what he's pointing to."

The man positioned himself head-to-head with Cecil, leaning cautiously over the side. "Hell, the boy's right!" he exclaimed. "The wheel's broke. The cable's hopelessly wrapped around the shaft and jammed tight. We can't fix it tonight. It'll take a repair crew."

"Curtain down! Curtain down! Curtain down!" Cecil began.

"Okay, son," Henderson called from the end of the catwalk. We heard you. Don't start that now."

Joe turned to the custodian. "He wants you to lower the curtain. Can you lower it?"

"Went down before, so I suppose it will again." He gingerly climbed to his feet and made his way to a small control panel off to the side. He produced a large key ring and began moving them aside one by one, searching for the key he wanted.

A moment later, key in hand, he reached for the switch. "Here goes nothing," he announced. "Be careful, the entire curtain mechanism is supported by this catwalk. Get your hands inside the rail."

Cecil did as he was told. The catwalk suddenly jerked and began to shake as the massive control rod started to turn. Slowly, the cables holding the curtain moved downward. When they came to rest, Cecil lay back down on his stomach, pressed his shoulder through the guard bars and hung his arms far over the side. His face was turned sideways and was pressed hard against the grated surface.

Joe grabbed his legs to be sure he didn't fall through. "Be careful where you put your fingers," Joe admonished. "Keep your hands away from the gears."

"Okay," the boy replied, and kept working, his body sliding even further through the bars.

The custodian, curious as to what the boy was doing, got out a flashlight and again positioned himself head-to-head with Cecil, both of them flat on the walkway. The burly man had to force his shoulders through the bars to see what was being done. He remained silent observing what the boy was doing.

After a few minutes, he called back to Joe, "By golly, I'd never have thought of this. The kid's a genius or something. The pin holding the wheel to the rod snapped off and the cable was tangled around the rod. He's removed the cable from the wheel and wound it directly around the shaft using the protruding pin as a lever. Hey, this just might work. How he could do this one-handed is beyond me."

Minutes later the custodian pulled himself fully back onto the platform and stood. He then helped Cecil to his feet. When the boy was standing, the man reached out to shake his hand. "Nice piece of work, young man. Nice piece of work."

When he took his hand away from Cecil's it was black from a half century of dirt and grime, all imbedded in a thick layer of grease. Seeing the custodian's hand, Cecil looked down at his own hand and before Joe could say anything, Cecil wiped his hand across his shirt and onto his pants. His costume now looked the part of a car mechanic, or coal miner, instead of the college professor he was playing.

The maintenance man walked to the control panel, exclaiming, "Let's give it a try. I'm sure it'll work. Actually, the way he fixed it, we won't need to repair it. Those wheels aren't necessary." With that, he flipped the switch up and the curtain rose just as smoothly as it ever did.

When the curtain was fully up, the folks who remained in the auditorium gave a hardy round of applause. Joe smiled proudly in spite of himself.

Cecil, on the other hand, had his head down and had begun a new mantra: "Ruined costume! Ruined costume! Ruined costume! Ruined costume!"

Six

While Cecil was fixing the curtain problem on the fourth floor, Sally Mascar was experiencing her first sexual encounter one floor away. However, that is not how Sally viewed it. To her, she was just having some fun with Wade Spenser, a classmate's older brother, whom she had met back at Christmas at Alice Spencer's house. She and Alice were not best friends, but they shared a love of music. Often Sally would sleep over so the two could spend the night jamming.

Wade had come home for the holidays after finishing his first semester at Holbrook College. Sally and Wade played Atari games late into the night while Alice watched movies on TV.

Just before the Christmas break, Sally had been told she would not have a part in the play. She had a better-than-average voice and had hoped that this year's play would be a musical. Unfortunately for her, it was not.

"Don't take it so hard," Alice had counseled. "This way you'll have more time to work on passing math."

"I really don't care anymore," Sally replied defiantly. "I just can't do it."

"You'll care when you have to repeat this stinking year again. It's no fun to flunk eighth grade."

"I'm going to drop out anyway. I'll get a job at the new mall. I don't see any use for this stupid school stuff."

Then, six weeks ago at Easter break, Sally, Alice, and Wade had taken a ride in the country, Wade was at the wheel. They ate a picnic lunch overlooking a pasture. Cows were meandering about, slowly chewing the grass as they went. Sally was fascinated with the white birds that seemed to be part of the herd.

"Cattle Egrets," Wade announced. "They eat the ticks and flies from the cows. Works out well for all concerned."

A sudden downpour interrupted the outing. All three were soaked when they finally managed to get back to Wade's car. Alice rode in back and Sally sat next to Wade as they drove back to the city. Wade pulled Sally close to him to stop her shivering. His right arm was draped over her shoulder.

Sally shuddered with excitement at his touch. It felt good, different from anything she had ever before experienced. While his arm was around her the ever-present cloud of defeat lifted. She felt warmly content and it seemed to her from the look on Wade's face that he was content as well.

"What the hell were *you* doing?" Alice demanded of her brother when she climbed into the front seat after Wade dropped Sally off in front of her house. "She's not all there, you know."

"Yeah, she's a little slow on the uptake, but she's fun anyway. And tell me, just why do you hang around with her? She's not your type."

"Her mother works at the bank and father doesn't want to explain why I won't include her. *It's a small town, have to get along.* How many times have you heard that lecture?"

"Enough to last a lifetime. She's always smiling and friendly. I'm glad she's your friend."

"She's not really my friend, but leave her alone. You're four years older than her! Find yourself a girl your own age!"

"Hey, Sis, cool it! I got plenty of girls at school. She's just fun, that's all."

"I saw you ogling her chest, you idiot, so don't give me *she's just fun*. Keep away from her!"

"Wet T-shirt day! What can I say? She's got a great set. You show 'em, I look at 'em. Can't blame a guy for doin' what comes naturally."

She slugged his shoulder. "I'll tell Mother on you. You'll find out what comes naturally! Stay away from Sally. She's way too young for you. Go play with girls your own age. If father finds out, you're in big trouble. Real big trouble."

"Mind your own business, Little Miss Know-It-All. I'll do what I want."

ஐஒ

That was Easter. It was now late May. Wade's school was out and he came to see his sister, Alice, in the class play. But instead of sitting with the family, he asked Sally to meet him in the hall beside the auditorium. Sally, as his sister continued to point out, was four years his junior, but girls his age seemed threatening in a way Sally didn't. She looked up to him, was impressed by him and, he believed, wanted him.

Sally, for her part, was indeed excited. The thrill of the upcoming meeting had been building all day. For over a week she had been planning what she was going to wear on her first real date. She had thought about going to the mall and buying something special, but at the last minute thought better of it. She had never before asked her mother to take her shopping, and she didn't want the questions that would come with such a request.

It had been bad enough in the morning, when her mother yelled through the bathroom door for her to hurry up and finish her shower. "And for God sakes, pipe down," she added. "You're singing at the top of your lungs. The neighbors will think someone's being slaughtered over here."

Finally, the time to meet Wade had arrived. Sally didn't hear him approach, and before she knew it, he had grabbed her arm from behind, spun her around and held her tightly against him. When she didn't pull away, he kissed her on the lips. She collapsed against him, desperate for more.

"Come," he suggested, making it sound spontaneous, "let's find a place to ourselves." Wade had remembered an out of the way janitor's closet from his days at the grade school. He guided a willing Sally up two flights to the third floor and started down the hall toward his destination.

"I hear a voice," Sally whispered, a bit too loud. "Someone is coming up the steps."

Without a word, Wade grabbed Sally and moved as far from the stairs as he could. The footsteps came closer and now the voice came from exactly where the two of them had stood not ten seconds before. Sally's heart pounded as Wade pulled her close to him, the two of them pressed hard against the wall.

The voice belonged to Mr. Henderson, but it was a custodian who first came into view, accompanied by another man whom Sally knew vaguely, but couldn't immediately place. The two men continued up the steps toward the fourth floor, followed moments later by Mr. Henderson.

Sally gasped when Cecil turned the corner behind Henderson. He was dressed as an old professor with his hair grayed, but the costume did little to hide the characteristic awkwardness of Cecil's movements. Cecil stopped at the base of the steps leading up to the fourth floor and squinted down the hall in Sally's direction.

Sally pulled back even tighter against the wall, certain that Cecil had seen her.

Henderson, realizing something had captured Cecil's attention, retraced his steps to the third floor landing to see what it was. Seeing what he thought was a human shadow, he yelled, "Who's there? Who is that?"

Sally felt Wade's body tense, as if he was about to run. But he held fast.

"Who's down there?" Henderson repeated, anger now in his voice. "No one is supposed to be on this floor!"

From above him the custodian called, "Is there a problem down there? Need help?"

"Someone's here. I'll be up in a moment."

Henderson took a step in the direction of the shadow. Cecil ducked in front of him and started up to the fourth floor, a mantra beginning to form. "Need to hurry. Need to hurry."

Two steps up, the mantra, amplified by the stairwell, distracted Henderson. "Be quiet, Cecil!" They can hear you downstairs."

The mantra continued. "Need to hurry. Need to hurry. Need to hurry. Need to hurry."

Henderson returned his attention to the movement he had seen, and started in that direction. "You there," he shouted, "go down to the first floor immediately! You're not allowed on this floor! Go downstairs!"

"Need to hurry. Need to hurry. Need to hurry. Need to hurry," Cecil continued.

Henderson, caught between doing his duty as a teacher and clearing the floor and silencing Cecil, turned back toward the steps and took them two at a time, following Cecil up to the fourth floor.

Wade held Sally against the wall until the footsteps could no longer be heard. Then he whispered, "Follow me and stay quiet." With that he led the way to the janitor's closet, and they both slipped inside.

Not bothering with the light, his lips found Sally's. Again she melted against him. She gasped with excitement — and then fear — when his hand locked around her breast.

Then the other hand was on her other breast. It felt wonderful to be wanted and she grabbed his hands to press them against her breasts all the harder.

Then his hands were under her blouse behind her, and she felt her bra come loose.

Something deep within her rebelled. She pulled backward, bumping against a shelf and causing a bucket to fall to the floor with a deafening boom.

"He'll come back!" she said, now in a full-scale panic. "He'll be back and he'll catch us! I'm in trouble already for flunking math. I'll be expelled! My mother'll kill me! Let's get out of here!"

"Don't be so scared, Silly Billy," Wade coaxed. Nothing will happen. They'll never find us in here. This will be fun," he cooed, bringing his hands around underneath the unclasped bra and reaching for her bare breasts.

"This is wrong! I can't be here. It's wrong!" Pushing his hands away, she quickly reached under her blouse and re-clasped the bra. Sally then found the door handle and eased the door open, fully expecting to see Henderson standing on the other side.

The hall was empty. She crept toward the steps, listening intently for footsteps. Wade was following several yards behind, but made no attempt to stop her.

They were down to the second floor when Sally heard Henderson's voice directly above them. Footsteps echoed off the walls and were growing louder as several people came swiftly down toward where she stood frozen.

Sally didn't know if there was enough time for her and Wade to make it all the way to the ground floor before being spotted. Sally's stomach tensed, certain she was about to be busted. A hand landed heavily and tugged at her right shoulder. She glanced back in time to see Wade turn and start back up the steps toward Henderson. Instinctively, she did the same.

Henderson, followed closely by Cecil and the man whom she now recognized as Cecil's father, turned the corner of the mid-flight landing. Cecil was mumbling something about being "ruined," but the clatter in her head prevented her from understanding what he was saying.

Henderson spotted the two people coming toward him and immediately snapped, "Where the dickens are you two going? Sally Mascar, you know the upper floors are off limits after school hours. Get back downstairs pronto! Both of you."

"Sorry, sir," Wade intoned smoothly. "Just looking for the bathroom."

Henderson shot him a puzzled look, glanced at Sally and was about to say something when Cecil's, *ruined costume* chant broke through.

"Bathroom? It's downstairs next to the auditorium. Now turn around both of you and get moving! And hurry, you're blocking the way."

SEVEN

The first act had come off without a hitch. The audience regathered after the intermission, the pre-play curtain drama having been all but forgotten by everyone except Cecil. The longer Henderson worked to remove the grease from his costume, the worse his agitation became.

During the intermission, Henderson had said to Cecil, "You are going to do fine. Just fine. Now I want you to concentrate on your lines and forget about the costume. The dirt is mostly gone. No one will see it anyway. Can you do that?"

The boy had not replied, but continued to mumble, "Ruined costume! Ruined costume! Ruined costume!"

"Cecil! You're going on stage in less than five minutes. I need you to be ready. Will you be ready?"

"Ruined costume! Ruined costume! Ruined costume!"

"Dear God!" Henderson intoned to no one in particular.

"Ruined costume! Ruined costume! Ruined costume! Ruined costume! Ruined costume!" The boy's head was down, his shoulders slumped forward as if he wanted to fold in on himself.

Then an idea came to Henderson. He took Cecil by the arm and walked briskly to the back of the stage. "Hold the curtain," he barked to the stage manager, "we'll be right back."

With that, he marched Cecil down a flight of steps to the dressing room. He had the boy change into his street clothes and then the two of them raced back up the stairs.

Henderson nodded to the stage manager and the lights in the auditorium slowly dimmed. A moment later the curtain went up, and Act Two was underway.

Henderson turned to Cecil. "Do it like we did in rehearsal. Say your lines just like we practiced. Can you do that, Cecil?"

The boy looked up at the teacher, his face now calm, his posture having returned to normal. He replied, "I can do my lines. I can do them."

"Okay, now listen to what is being said on stage because you are almost on."

"I know. I hear them." The boy's mouth began to move in unison with what he was hearing. When he mouthed the words he was waiting for, he said, "It is my turn now. Here I go."

With that, Cecil came onto the stage as he had been coached and immediately shielded his eyes from the bright lights in order to locate the small X that marked his spot. He found the spot and ran to stand on top of the tape. Once there, he turned to face Alice Spencer who was wearing a black hat, cape and exaggerated witch makeup.

Cecil, using the deep tones he had rehearsed, said, "What am I to make of this? I was told you and your friends had ceased dressing up and pretending you are witches. That most certainly is not the case, as I now see. I must deal with this behavior of yours."

"You are mistaken, dear Professor," the witch replied, "I'm not *pretending* to be a witch. I *am* one!" With that, the witch spread her arms over Cecil, her cape engulfing him. When the cape had settled over him, she said, "'Tis a spell I will cast, spread about and let it last. For he who thinks himself so clever, let him be a tree forever!"

With a flourish Alice flipped the cape off of Cecil, who dutifully pretended to be frozen, his arms extended straight out in front of him, his hands hanging limp.

What the audience hadn't heard was what Alice had said to Cecil just before the cape was removed. "You're a fool without your costume," she had hissed. "You look stupid."

Alice exited left just as the hero came on from the right to find the professor, played by Cecil, frozen into a tree. The hero began delivering his lines to the tree. As he did so Cecil's head slowly bent forward and his arms came down.

The hero, not knowing what to do, continued with his lines as if nothing were wrong. "Oh, professor. What has happened to you? You are a tree, forever standing here, branches outstretched. I beg of you, speak to me."

Of course, Cecil should have remained frozen in place as a tree, unable to speak. This called for the hero to recite, "Oh, a spell has been cast on you. It must have been by a witch."

Except, when the hero begged Cecil to speak, Cecil, his head still down, shouted, "I'm not stupid! I'm not stupid!" Soon, Cecil was repeating the mantra, *I'm not stupid! I'm not stupid! I'm not stupid! I'm not stupid!* loud enough so that even those in the back of the auditorium could clearly hear the forlorn cry of a boy in distress.

At first the hero stood waiting to deliver his next lines. He eventually turned to the wings and shrugged his shoulders as if to beg, *What am I supposed to do now?*

Henderson, frantically trying to save the situation, motioned for the hero to come off stage. When the boy tried to follow his teacher's instructions, Cecil gave him a shove that sent him sprawling.

Cecil sat down and continued to chant, "I'm not stupid! I'm not stupid! I'm not stupid!"

In an act of desperation, Henderson came onto the stage, and escorted Cecil off.

"Pretend he's still out there," the teacher said to the actors around him. "He has no lines until near the end, so play it as though he's still there, an invisible tree."

The actors, all eighth graders, continued on with the play the best they could. Many of them were unable to suppress their giggles as they delivered lines to an invisible tree. Several boys rolled their eyes.

Downstairs in the dressing room, Henderson worked with Cecil, trying to calm him. "Cecil, I don't know what happened, but you're not stupid. Do you hear me, you're not stupid."

The boy just kept his head down, repeating the words, "I'm not stupid! I'm not stupid! I'm not stupid!" over and over.

"Did someone say something to you out there? Is that what happened?"

The boy nodded, but continued chanting.

"Let me tell you, you're not stupid. Look how you fixed the curtain. That was good work. You are a genius."

Cecil's chant became less intense, finally stopping altogether. His head came up. Seeing this, Henderson, continued, "Cecil, we're all very proud of you tonight. You saved the play."

A small smile appeared at the corners of the boy's mouth.

Henderson closed his eyes, straining to hear the dialog proceeding on stage above them. He then turned to Cecil. "If we hurry, we can make it in time," he said. "You can wake up from the spell and deliver your last lines. Do you want to do that?"

"Yes."

"Then hurry, we have just enough time."

The boy raced up the steps and across the back of the stage to where he would enter. It was almost time for his lines and he was already supposed to be on stage. He froze, not knowing what to do.

Henderson, flushed and breathing heavily, caught up to him and instructed, "Run out there and take your position directly in front of Alice. Freeze like a tree. She is about to remove the spell."

Cecil ran out, pushed a boy off the taped X and positioned himself exactly where he was supposed to be. Only then did he resume his stance as a frozen tree.

Several in the audience had more or less figured out what had happened, and they began to clap. This further distracted the actors, who stopped delivering their lines.

Henderson frantically waved for the actors to resume the play. The children obeyed, as best they could. Cecil waited for his cue, and when it came, he delivered his lines perfectly.

Henderson mentally noted a real inflection in Cecil's voice this time and not the flat monotone that Cecil had always used in practice and earlier in the play.

EIGHT

Joe Harris had seen enough. Not known for having a long fuse, he was red in the face when the curtain finally came down. Turning to Maggie, he said, his voice barely under control, "This is an unmitigated disaster! That girl said something to him on stage. That's bullshit and I'm going to get to the bottom of it!"

Maggie quickly stood and faced him, trying in vain to block the sound of Joe's voice from escaping past her. "Keep your voice down," she scolded in a stage whisper. "The Spencers are right next to me."

"I don't care if the President of the United States is next to you! That girl had no right saying anything to him!"

"Lower your voice. Remember who Spencer is! Alice is a kid. This is eighth grade. Maybe Cecil said something, who ever knows with that boy. He wasn't in costume, maybe that caused the problem."

Maggie's reference had been about Jackson Spencer, Alice's father, and publisher of the Cosper County *Sentinel*, the region's main daily newspaper.

"He got grease all over his costume," Joe responded. "The boy rebuilt the curtain control up there leaning over the catwalk like a monkey hanging from a tree. Then he gets dumped on? That's not right. He saved the play for God's sake!"

"This is not the time," Maggie scolded. "Talk to Mr. Henderson privately. Don't make a scene."

"I know one thing," Joe went on, his voice lower than before. "He's not going to any party tonight. He's had enough of these kids for one day!"

"Don't be so quick. I think the Spencers are taking a group of them for burgers. Let's see what he wants to do."

"It's best if he comes home with us," Joe insisted. "Those kids can be merciless."

"We'll see," Maggie responded, turning to greet Alice's parents. She began to congratulate them on their daughter's performance. Her words fell on deaf ears because Jennie Spencer abruptly turned her back and followed her husband down the aisle without acknowledging Maggie's attempt at being sociable.

"I see what you mean," Maggie said over her shoulder to Joe as they followed the Spencers out of the auditorium. "Let's find Cecil and take him for ice cream. He'll like that better anyway."

Caroline, who had been mortified by Cecil's behavior, caught up with them in the lobby. "Mother," the seventeen-year old exclaimed, "He did it! I knew that jerk would do it! He embarrassed me in front of my friends."

"It's not his fault, he's—"

"It's never his fault! There's always some reason. He's just plain weird! He has no idea what anybody thinks—no clue what's going on!"

"Stop that talk this instant," Maggie hissed. Then added, "We're going for ice cream. Want to come?"

"Not on your life! I've had all I can take of his foolishness. I wouldn't be caught dead with him!"

"Caroline!"

"And besides, I'm going out with friends. Be home by midnight."

"Where are you going?"

"To *The Pit* for burgers. Then over to Liz's house to listen to music."

"Liz?" Maggie asked, her face wrinkled in puzzlement.

"Liz Classico. We talked ab—"

"Oh, yes," Maggie replied, recalling their earlier conversation. "Now I remember. Be careful."

"I will," Caroline called over her shoulder, racing to catch up with a group of teens quickly disappearing out of the school into the parking lot.

A few minutes later the eighth-grade actors began arriving in the lobby. The decibel level rose dramatically as parents hugged and congratulated their children.

Cecil was not among them.

Slowly the lobby emptied. Soon only a few maintenance people remained, standing by the school doors waiting to slip chains around the grab bars.

Eventually, Henderson appeared, his body telegraphing fatigue laced with a large dose of distress. "Just the folks I was looking for," he began. "Your son is refusing to leave the dressing room. He says the other kids are blaming him for ruining the show."

"He *saved* the show!" Joe exclaimed. "You kidding me?"

"They don't care about the curtain. That's our problem, not theirs. They don't even know—or care—that Cecil fixed it. They only know that they felt foolish talking to a nonexistent tree. Simon, that's the boy Cecil knocked down, is unhappy. I had a little talk with him, but I never can tell how that goes."

"How bad is Cecil?" Joe asked.

"At least he hasn't gone into a mantra. That's the good news. The bad news is he won't leave the dressing room. He locked himself in a closet while everyone was there. He's out of the closet now, but won't leave the room."

"I'll go back and get him. What's the school going to do about the Spencer girl taunting him on stage? I assume that's what triggered Cecil."

"I'll speak to her on Monday, but we'll never know exactly what happened. And by the way, I don't for a moment think the play was ruined. Your son should be praised."

"We can calm him down for now. But what about Monday?" Maggie asked, ever the practical one. "The kids will be making fun of him."

"I've actually been thinking about that. There's only one more week of school and mostly nothing happens. Book turn-in, that sort of stuff. The principal agrees that Cecil should be rewarded for fixing the curtain. His reward will be that he doesn't have to come to school next week. Just come to graduation Friday afternoon."

"That will work nicely," Maggie replied. "Next semester he'll be at the high school. Maybe some new faces will do him well."

"We can only hope," Joe said, with a big exhale. "We can only hope."

NINE

Twenty minutes later the Harris family was seated in the ice cream parlor with Cecil devouring a triple scoop of vanilla ice cream stuffed into a massive waffle cone.

While the family was enjoying their ice cream, less than five miles away, Cecil's sister, Caroline, and three of her friends finished their hamburgers at *The Pit* and piled into a convertible. The driver, impatient to make a left out of the parking lot, spotted a slow moving bus and mashed the accelerator to the floor.

At that very instant, the driver of a fully loaded new-car carrier pulled out to pass the bus on the far side. The truck hit the convertible broadside, sending car and body parts flying. The convertible landed upside down twenty feet down the road and barrel-rolled several hundred feet further before finally coming to rest. The truck driver watched in horror as the driver's head was severed and the girl in the seat directly behind her was tossed high in the air, landing directly in front of him. Braking desperately, he maneuvered his vehicle so that the tires would not run over her already lifeless body. He also avoided hitting the convertible a second time as it lay upside down directly in front of him, its wheels still spinning.

That act spared the lives of the two girls who were still alive and trapped inside the mangled car.

Ten

"So young man," Joe Harris began when Cecil had almost finished his ice cream, bits of waffle cone sticking to his lips, "you did a nice job of getting the curtain working. You saved the play."

"It was real easy. The wheel didn't work. I moved the cable to the drive rod. Don't need the wheels."

"Was it a bad design?"

"Most things are bad designs."

"How do you know that?"

"I can see it."

"You have a gift. Let's hope you do something with it."

"When I grow up, I want to fix things. I can make things better."

"You will, my son. You will," Joe replied, working to bolster Cecil's confidence. "So, tell me. What happened on stage tonight?"

Maggie jabbed Joe's ribs with her elbow. When Joe looked her way, she gave him a quick grimace, her face setting hard.

Maggie had no cause to worry about her son seeing her communicate her displeasure. Cecil couldn't read the signals.

"I won't be mad at you," Joe pressed, observing his son's shoulder drop. "I would like to know what happened. I know it was not your fault."

Cecil fixed his eyes on the floor and refused to look up.

Maggie leaned in close to her husband. "Leave him alone. You'll just get him all worked up again. That's all we need. Enough's enough already. I can't take much more."

"I'm tired of everyone picking on him," Joe snapped back. He was determined not to be deterred. "I'm going to get to the bottom of this one."

"Maybe it'll be better for him next year in high school. Let it go for now."

"I hope so," Joe replied, returning his attention to his son.

"So, Cecil, please tell me what happened?"

To his surprise the boy stood up, pulled himself tall and replied, "She called me stupid for not wearing a costume. Teacher said it was okay. Teacher said it was a rehearsal. Grease on the costume."

"You did fine tonight," Maggie said, studying her son for signs of agitation. Seeing nothing, she continued, "We're all proud of you."

Before Joe could say more, the door to the parlor swung open and a gang of kids, Alice Spencer among them, flooded in. Behind them came Jennie Spencer, Alice's mother.

"Oh, it's you!" Alice called over to Cecil. "You ruined our play! Now you're ruining our treat. You're such a jerk!"

"That's enough, young lady," Jennie snapped. "Not another word!" Jennie looked around to see who had heard her daughter's outburst. "Everyone, get ice cream and go out to the porch. No more talk about the play. You hear me?" She then turned to Maggie and forced a smile, pretending nothing had happened tonight to dampen their friendship. "We tried to get burgers at *The Pit*, but couldn't get near the place. There were sirens everywhere and traffic was stalled. Jackson jumped out of the car to see what's going on. You'd think he was still a cub reporter and not the publisher. I gave up and came down here. "Anyway, I'd rather have a waffle cone than a burger."

"So would I, actually." Maggie replied, matching Jennie's smile tooth for tooth. "I can stick to the ices and control my waistline." Delivered with a polite South Texas smile, the words were designed to cut deep. Jennie Spencer carried an extra fifty pounds; Maggie's figure was trim and well-maintained.

"You've got nothing to worry over," Jennie was forced to respond, acknowledging Maggie's waistline, her smile wilting. "Please excuse me. I have to check on those kids." She hurried over to the counter where the group was sampling small tastes of various flavors.

Several minutes later Maggie smiled to herself when she heard Jennie order a small lemon sugar-free sherbet.

Cecil, seeing a bicycle propped against the railing outside, went to investigate.

Joe nodded to Maggie and the two of them followed Cecil out to the patio. Coming through the door, Joe heard Alice exclaim to her friends, "Pay no attention to Cecil. He's the class retard!"

It took Cecil less than two seconds to cover the distance from the railing to the table where Alice had sat down. With a sweeping motion of his hand, he slammed Alice's double-dipped chocolate cone up into her face.

Joe ran over to pull Cecil away, even while silently applauding his actions. The others at the table were frozen into silence. Alice wasn't screaming because her nostrils were packed with ice cream and she was having trouble breathing.

"I am not a retard!" Cecil screamed. "And I am not stupid! You're the stupid one! I hope you suffocate!"

Jennie Spencer rushed over, "Get that little beast away from my daughter!" she screamed. "There's something wrong with him! He should be locked away! You should be ashamed of yourselves for allowing him to be with normal children!"

Joe started toward the woman. Maggie grabbed his arm to pull him back. "Joe!"

Joe shook his arm free. "If you weren't a woman," he screamed, his mouth inches from her face, "I'd deck you sure as hell! Your daughter is the beast! You should teach her manners. But considering the source—"

"Joe!" Maggie's tone instantly told Joe he had gone over the line. He'd have hell to pay at home if he continued. "Let's leave," she said.

Truth be told, Maggie also thought Alice Spencer had received what was coming to her. But she thought it prudent to mollify Jennie Spencer and to try to defuse the situation. "Cecil had no right doing what he did," she announced, loud enough for all to hear. "I appol—"

Joe interrupted. "That little brat has no right calling Cecil... what she called him." Joe couldn't bring himself to say the word "retard." "She's the one who started this. Serves her right."

Maggie had Joe by the arm. "We need to go! Cecil, come. Right now!"

"I'm not a retard," the boy replied. "I'm not a retard! I'm not a retard!"

"No, Cecil, you're not. This young lady owes you an apology."

"I do not!" Alice yelled. "He ruined my new dress!"

Joe turned back to say something, but Maggie pulled him toward the car.

Cecil continued to repeat, "I'm not a retard! I'm not a retard! I'm not a retard!"

Once inside the car, Cecil immediately calmed down.

Joe glanced in the rear view mirror and saw that the boy was already engrossed in a new activity—taking apart a toy bicycle that had been left on the car floor months ago. His face was placid, the incident with Alice Spencer seemingly forgotten.

Eleven

Sally and Wade left the school during intermission, on their way to *The Pit* for burgers and fries. Afterward, Wade suggested they go for a ride. Sally reluctantly agreed and positioned herself against the passenger door keeping as far from Wade as possible. Wade reached over to pull her closer and she batted his hand away. "Don't touch me," she said, frightened and excited at the same time and struggling to know what to do. "You scared me when you put your hands...um...you know where."

"I thought that's what you wanted," Wade replied, playing the role of an innocent, wounded suitor.

"I've never been with a boy. I mean in that way. I've never even...kissed a boy! I should go home."

"Did it feel good?"

"Until I got scared," Sally reluctantly agreed. "You scared me, you know."

"It's really fun. Now come over here and stop being a silly girl."

"I'm not a silly girl. I want to go home. Please take me home."

Ignoring Sally's pleas, Wade said, "Now come here and show me you're not a silly girl."

"Promise you won't...won't touch me...there."

"Promise. Boy Scout honor." He held his right hand up in a mock pledge.

"You're not a Boy Scout."

"I was. That counts. All them stink'n badges count for something."

Sally giggled.

"Now move over here," Wade said, sensing a victory.

Sally slid partway across the seat. "Now watch where your hand goes. I don't want...your hand...there."

Wade kept his hands on the steering wheel, his mood lightened and he told her stories and jokes.

At first, Sally sat with her back to the seat, rigidly looking out the window. As they drove, her resolve softened and she laughed at a joke, then another. A few minutes later she leaned her head on Wade's shoulder and closed her eyes. Wade's warmth made her feel good and her concerns faded.

When she opened her eyes, she blinked, sat upright and said, "Where are we? It's dark out here."

"You afraid of the boogey man? Come, put your head back where it was. That felt nice. I love the smell of your hair."

Sally did as Wade asked, saying, "Not many cars or houses. Where are we?"

"Taking a drive is all. Relax. Put some music on the radio if you wish."

Sally found a station she liked and began singing along to the music."

"That's the way," Wade said. "You have a nice voice. You should be a singer some day. You're that good."

"You think so?" Coming from the son of the newspaper owner and the richest boy in town, Sally felt an elation she had never experienced before.

"Now move the rest of you a little closer," Wade said, "and sing to me. It's nice when you're against me."

She pushed her hips against his. "Now keep your hands where they're supposed to be, like you promised."

"I am. See, my hands never leave my wrists."

"Keep it that way," she giggled, content to be snuggled against him. The movement of the car, coupled with the warmth of his body, intensified by the catalyst of his scent, erased the bad memories.

Sally, lost in the excitement she had felt earlier in the school as they had snuck up the steps, didn't notice that Wade had pulled off the main road. They were now on a gravel lane leading into a heavily wooded area. The car came to a stop and Sally continued singing gently, while Wade listened, his eyes closed.

Wade suggested they take a walk. The euphoria Sally felt by being wanted by someone like Wade overcame any reluctance she might have had. They walked to the top of a small rise and stood looking out over the farmland faintly illuminated by the moon. Sally now felt safe with Wade, his arm wrapped around her waist.

Wade pointed off to the left. "You can smell the fresh plowed land. Spring planting is mostly over, but it still has a distinctive smell of earth."

"Smells like chemicals to me." Sally replied, sniffing the air. "I don't get around farms much so I don't know what they smell like."

"Smells fresh to me. Something new. I like this time of year. Better than the fall, when things smell dead." Wade sat down under a small tree and Sally, after a short hesitation, followed him. A few minutes later she threw her arms around his waist and pulled him close.

This time when his hand found her breast, she squealed with delight, her fears suppressed by the ecstasy of the moment. She welcomed the feel of his strong hands on her.

Wade opened her top shirt button and she anxiously helped. The shirt fell away and a moment later her bra followed. She pressed her mouth against his even harder. Wade cupped both breasts in his hands and Sally trembled when he softly licked her nipples.

Sally enjoyed the obvious pleasure she was giving Wade Spencer, a guy who could have any girl he wanted, but who had chosen her. Suddenly, she realized her jeans were down. She opened her eyes in time to see him unzip his pants and reach inside.

She tried to stand, but tripped. "No! I don't want—" she began to cry. But her words were choked off when he clamped his hand across her mouth. She tried to roll free but she was pinned to the ground by his weight.

She ripped his hand from her mouth and again screamed, "Stop it! Let me go! I don't—"

"It's too late for that now!" he growled. "You're nothing more than a little tease! I'll show you what happens to a tease like you!"

Wade was on her then, even as she screamed and begged him to stop. He ripped her panties free, all pretext of lovemaking, of civility, of humanness, evaporated.

Sally forced her eyes open in time to see that Wade's soft, kind eyes had taken on the fervor of power and control. They were now the eyes of a beast. His body moved with animal frenzy—an animal conquering its prey.

Her heart raced with a mixture of fear and disgust. Her body shook with rage and utter helplessness. She let out an ear-piercing scream, and continued screaming until her vocal cords were raw. She punched his chest and face. She scratched his neck and dug her nails into his cheek just below his right eye, tearing a chuck of skin from his face. Her fighting seemed to fuel his rage and his body pounded into her even harder.

Wade finished and rolled onto his back, breathing heavily.

Sally was numb from screaming, numb from fighting, but mostly numb with rage and fear. She was still screaming, but was producing little sound. She sat up, grabbed her pants and blouse and hurriedly put them on, not bothering with the rest.

Wade turned onto his side, watching her. He started to say something and as he did, she kicked out at him, unleashing her fury with all the might she could muster. Her shoe impacted his rib cage, producing a sharp crack.

Deep within her, buried with the agony and shame of what had just happened to her, a twinge of satisfaction registered when he gasped in pain. "You little bitch," he yelled, "you broke my ribs!" He reached out to grab her foot, but screamed in agony when he moved his arm.

Sally ran to the car, retrieved her bag, and raced into the night, not knowing where she was going, but knowing she had to just keep moving.

She was ashamed. She had allowed Wade to touch her, to see and touch her breasts. It had felt good at first, and she shivered remembering how she had wanted more of that. She felt dirty and ashamed. *Was this her punishment?* This was all her fault. *Is this what boys do? Is this what sex is? I caused this! Oh, my God! I caused this! What did I do wrong? Mother's going to kill me! Oh, God, I really messed up this time! I'm sorry. I'm so sorry!*

She tried to visualize what had happened, but it was mostly just a blur—a nightmarish blur. She saw herself lying on the ground, her breasts glowing like beacons in the moonlight, guiding him to her. She hated her body. She hated herself.

She stopped to put on her panties and bra. Her fingers came away sticky. With what little light there was left she realized her legs were streaked with blood. She cleaned herself using grass clumps and what few leaves were scattered around.

The further she went the more confused she became. At one point she stopped and looked down at herself. What she saw was the same body parts as before. What she felt, however, was totally different, ripped apart, violated, emotionally dead. She hated Wade Spencer with a deep passion, but she hated herself even more. She lifted her head to the sky and screamed into the empty night.

What she couldn't see was her own eyes. Before, they were alive with excitement and anticipation. Now they were dull with hatred—and self-loathing.

The few times she saw approaching car headlights she ran off the road and hid. She didn't want to see, or be seen, by anybody. Her shame was overwhelming, and it was hers alone to bear. This was a secret not to be shared with anyone. *What will I tell my mother?* The question haunted her as she walked, struggling to think about what she was going to do. Her stomach knotted up and she vomited into the weeds several times.

Sally continued to focus on her mother and what she was going to say. Lydia Mascar was a woman besieged by life. For the past seven years she had worked in a local bank, working her way up to head teller and also served as assistant to the Manager. This was the longest stint she had ever managed. Sally's mother had told her on numerous occasions that she was determined to keep her bank job at all costs. Lydia worked every Saturday morning starting at eight, so Sally knew her mother would be out of the house by seven. She also knew her mother would be sound asleep early, as she always was on Friday night and wouldn't have stayed up waiting for her.

Lydia had married Nelson Mascar the summer after high school graduation. Nelson, who went by Nellie, had been Lydia's senior-year boy friend and was a year older than her. He was a good mechanic and had not yet begun drinking. The alcohol had come after Sally turned two when Nellie realized he was not cut out to be a father.

Technically, the Mascars were still married, but he only came around every now and again, usually when he needed a meal and a warm place to sleep. From what little Sally knew about her father, he worked part-time for a man in Dallas. She never once received a present from him or even so much as a phone call. He never brought her anything when he came by. They had spoken only a few times and he had seemed shy. She had always dreamed about getting to know him, even of spending time with him when she was older.

Sally's thoughts drifted now to Nellie and she again wished she knew him better. She knew she couldn't tell her mother what happened; she'd fly into a rage. She wished she had a father to talk with, a father who would help her. After all, she couldn't talk about this with her best friend. Alice Spencer was Wade's sister.

She found a clump of bushes and sat waiting for daylight. She focused on taking a long hot shower and washing Wade's smell down the drain along with the shame and guilt.

Sitting in the bushes, completely exhausted, but afraid to sleep, the conversation she had had with her mother before the play popped into her mind. It now seemed like an ancient conversation.

Lydia had learned that Sally had failed math and had done poorly in English and history as well. "I'm told they're thinking of holding you back a year," Lydia had said over dinner, which consisted of a reheated pizza. "What am I going to do with you?"

"It's my problem, I'll deal with it."

"Why didn't you tell me you were flunking?"

"Nothing you could do. I can't learn that useless stuff! I don't even *want* to learn it."

"Teachers are willing to help. I could have made arrangements."

"Those teachers don't care!" Sally cried, tossing a half-eaten pizza slice onto the table hard enough to cause the sauce to fly off. "They can't teach!"

"You have to change your attitude, young lady," Lydia replied, anger creeping into her voice. "You need to get ready for high school."

"Maybe I'm not for school. Everyone can't be good in school."

"You have to at least graduate high school. Without that you—"

"What did high school ever do for you—or Nellie?" Sally demanded.

"That's enough of that! I work hard to keep this house. You've got shoes on your feet and clothes on your back. Without my having stuck it out through high school we'd be out on the street."

"I can make money working at *The Pit*. I don't need high school for that."

The conversation had gone downhill from there, ending when Sally stormed out of the house. She had no idea how she would ever learn the math and everything else she needed to graduate high school, even assuming she could ever get there.

But that was next year's problems. Summer was coming and she would get a job and save her money. Then she could buy a tape, or maybe even some CDs, and listen to music like the other kids did.

The thought of music triggered the thought of her singing on Wade's shoulder. With that image came the horror of what had happened and her mouth went dry. A wrenching pain shot through her body as her stomach seized into a tight knot.

She bent her head forward in an effort to control the nausea sweeping over her in torrents. With her head between her knees, Sally again vomited into the weeds. This time nothing came out.

Twelve

Maggie Harris was propped up in bed reading. It was now twelve-thirty and she was nervously checking the clock every few minutes. It was most unusual for Caroline to stay out beyond midnight without calling. One ear listened for the sound of a car stopping out front, and the other listening to Joe, who couldn't let go of the earlier incidents with Cecil.

Joe was now saying, "It's good he's out of that school. Eighth grade's not been good for him. Just when I thought we had turned the corner, that Spencer girl messes it all up."

"Leave it alone already, Joe!" Maggie snapped her book closed and turned to face him. "Let's face it. Cecil is not a normal child. It's natural for the other kids to pick on him. I wish it weren't that way, but it is. Remember, that's what the doctor told us was likely to happen. Alice was expecting Cecil to be in costume and out he comes in his street clothes. She's a child, what do you expect?"

"Fourteen's old enough to know better."

"My point is she got caught off guard."

"No need to call him stupid."

"They all call each other stupid—and a lot worse—so leave it be. Enough already!"

"The boy saved the play. So he came out without a costume. Big frickin' deal."

"They had to do the entire second act pretending he was there, when he wasn't. You think that's easy for a fourteen-year-old?" She paused to focus on a sound she thought she heard. Satisfied it was nothing, she continued. "Now we're at odds with the Spencers. I'm afraid I was nasty to Jennie at the *Parlor*. I'll call her in the morning and apologize."

"Serves her right."

"I feel bad. That's all I'm saying. Two wrongs—"

The phone rang.

Joe and Maggie each instinctively glanced at the clock before Maggie picked up the receiver. Thinking it was Caroline calling with some flimsy excuse, Maggie began, "You better have a good explanation—"

Joe saw his wife's face fall as her eyes went wide with terror. The silence was broken only with a series of yes's, followed by, "Oh, my God! Oh, my God! Is she—? Where? When? How bad? Oh, God no! No! Oh, my God!"

Maggie went white, her mouth working, but no sounds emerging. Joe raced downstairs to the kitchen phone. He picked it up in time to hear a man's voice say, "Like I said, she's in Memorial General, and you better hurry."

He took the steps two-at-a-time back upstairs to get the rest of the story from Maggie. Joe found his wife slumped on the bathroom floor. He couldn't determine if she had tripped or had fainted.

Her head was hot with beads of sweat on her forehead. Joe ran for a cloth, soaked it with cold water, and mopped her forehead.

A few minutes later he had Maggie sitting up on her own, her back resting against the tub. Joe asked her what had happened.

All Maggie could say was, "Caroline! Oh, my God, it's Caroline!"

"What happened? What did he say?"
"It's Caroline."
"What? What is it?"
"Hurt. My baby's been hurt."
"How bad? Did they say how bad?"
"They said to hurry."
"Did they tell you what's wrong with her?" Without waiting for an answer, he said, "We'd better get over there. Come, can you stand?"
"I feel wobbly. I must have fainted. I don't remember falling."
"What about Cecil?" Maggie asked, as they hurriedly pulled on clothes.
"He'll sleep 'til nine, as always. You can set your watch by that kid. Think we can leave him?"
"It's better than taking him to the hospital. There's no place to drop him off at this hour. We'll be back in the morning. He'll be fine. Let's go."
"Did he say anything about how she is?"
"Something about an accident. A truck, I think I heard. I can't remember."
"You can't remember?"
"I wasn't understanding. I don't know. God, I hope she's okay."
Driving out of the driveway they caught the end of a news broadcast. The reporter indicated that two girls had survived a car/truck accident earlier in the evening, with one of the survivors being in critical condition. The reporter had said that two teenagers were known to have died at the scene. Names were being withheld pending notification of next of kin.
They drove the six miles in silence, Joe's arms shaking with fright. He didn't know for sure if his daughter was still alive, but took slight comfort in the realization he was driving to the hospital and not the morgue.
Joe steered the car into the visitor's garage opposite the emergency entrance. Memorial General was the big new regional trauma center serving several counties. At this time of night the

lack of traffic in the hospital roadways belied the activity going on inside.

Joe shook his wife out of the trance she had fallen into. Maggie had never before behaved this way and Joe was worried about her. Then the fear lurking in his stomach expanded to his chest with a sudden constricting pain. He leaned against the side of the car waiting for his breath to return. When it finally did, he opened the door for Maggie and she cautiously climbed out. Her movements telegraphed her fear of learning the horrifying news waiting for them on the other side of the hospital's gray brick walls.

Joe and Maggie crossed the roadway, deserted this time of night except for a lone ambulance sitting with its back doors open, its blue and red flashing lights playing off the walls, no one in attendance.

Several people in various states of distress were sitting in the waiting room. One man sat with his head bent far over, holding a handkerchief against his left eye. Another man pressed a dirty towel against his leg. His pants were ripped and bloody.

A tired-looking woman in her early sixties sat at a desk separated from the waiting room by a sliding glass window. The window was closed and the woman was staring with a blank expression at a screen in front of her. Joe helped Maggie to a chair and then proceeded to the window. He again looked over the people in the waiting area, looking to see if any of them were the parents of any of Caroline's friends.

Joe tapped lightly on the glass. The woman glanced in his direction and then returned her eyes to the screen. Another minute went by, an eternity in which he visualized his daughter screaming for help, but no sound reached his ears.

He rapped on the glass again, this time with more force.

The woman's expression went from boredom to anger. Her hand reached for the glass and slid it open. "And just what is your problem? You injured or sick?"

"I came for my daughter."

"What's her name?"

"Caroline. Caroline Harris."

"How old is she?"
"Seventeen."
"What's her date of birth?"
"Is all this necessary? I just want to see my daughter. We were told to hurry."
"Date of birth please," the woman continued, her eyes not leaving her paper.
"November, nineteen seventy six."
"November what?"
"Maggie, what's Caroline's birthday? November what?"
"Sixteen," came the faint reply.
"Sixteen," Joe repeated through the partition.
"Okay. Take a seat and I'll call you." The glass slid closed.

Maggie didn't raise her head when Joe sat down beside her. She appeared to be on the verge of fainting again. He wanted to kick something, pound the wall with his fist. Every few minutes he looked over to the desk, but the woman always seemed preoccupied by the computer screen. Not once did she look his way.

Now and then the big double door opened. Each time Joe looked up in expectation. But each time the gray-clad woman called a name that was not his.

Thirty minutes elapsed; the waiting room emptied. Joe and Maggie were now alone. He got up, stretched his legs and back, then walked across the waiting room and again tapped on the window.

The window slid back and the bored voice said, "They'll be with you soon. Nothing more I can do 'til they come down."

"How long will that be? I must see my daughter!"

"They're working on her. Just take a seat. They'll come see you when they can."

Again the window slid closed.

Again Joe retreated to his seat. Maggie appeared to be sleeping. A few minutes later, agitation, followed by anguish, forced him to stand. He tried to sit several times but found the chair too confining. Joe paced the room for at least an hour and then slumped into a chair, exhausted.

A hand on his shoulder brought him awake with a start. Standing over him was a tall, slender man with deep lines under his eyes.

Joe shook his head clear and glanced in the direction of his wife. Maggie was awake, her panic stricken eyes focused on the man standing in front of them.

"Mr. Harris?" the tall man inquired.

"Yes. This is my wife Maggie."

"I'm Doctor Cantor, a neurologist. Your daughter is stable—at least for now."

"What do you mean, at least for now?"

"In her condition, we never really know for an absolute certainty. Conditions can change in the next forty-eight hours, but I don't expect that to happen."

"What condition is that?"

"I'm sorry, I thought they told you."

"That old biddy over there wouldn't give me the time of day!" Harris replied, nodding in the direction of the receptionist.

"She's a temporary fill in. The regular receptionist is out tonight." He glanced around. "I don't see the triage nurse. I apologize. Your daughter was in a serious car accident earlier this evening. The car she was riding in was broadsided by a truck."

"I heard about it on the radio. Two girls died."

"Oh, my God!" Maggie exclaimed. "How is she? Will she—"

"As I said, critical condition, but stable for now."

Joe studied the doctor, trying to read beyond the words. "That means we won't be taking her home tonight?"

"I'm sorry, she won't be leaving the hospital for a long time."

"How long? And why?" Joe asked, realizing there was something he wasn't being told. "Can we see her?"

"I'm afraid that won't be possible for some time yet."

"Why not?" Joe demanded, trying to piece together the possibilities. "She's our daughter, and we have a right to see her."

"She's sustained multiple trauma. Head, neck, back. Internal bleeding. As I said, she's stable now. But we must keep her calm."

"Will she—" Maggie couldn't force the end of the sentence.

"We don't know for certain yet, Mrs. Harris. She's on the critical list. Many things must go right for her. Like I said, I'm very optimistic. Give the receptionist your phone number and I'll call you if anything changes. I'll be with her until we're certain she's completely stabilized. Go home and get some sleep. It will be at least noon before you'll be permitted in the room. And maybe not even then."

Joe glared at the doctor. "You can't stop us from—"

"Don't make this harder than it is, Mr. Harris. You simply cannot go up there now." The doctor's tone softened. "I'm sorry. I understand you want to see your daughter. But it's not in her best interest. Any movement could...could...could cause even more trauma. I must insist. Someone will call you when it is safe for you to see her."

Joe started to respond, but Maggie took her husband by the arm. "Dr. Cantor is taking good care of Caroline. Let's go home. We're doing no good here, I'm afraid."

"Are you okay to drive?" Cantor asked. "If not, we'll call a cab. I don't need to be treating you as well."

"I'll be okay," Joe responded, not sure he really would be. He wanted to lash out, kick something. Instead, he just stood there, waiting. Waiting for what he didn't know.

Cantor shook both their hands, and said, "Please be assured we are doing everything we can. As I said, I don't expect any changes tonight."

On the way out to the car they passed a young man Maggie knew well, but in her mental state could not immediately recall his name. He was walking slowly from the parking garage holding his side, a long nasty gash extending downward from his right eye.

৪০০৪

An hour later, Joe and Maggie were in bed. Maggie snapped the lights out and in the dark, said, "Pray for her, Joseph. Pray like you've never prayed before in your life."

"I've been praying for the past three hours. You know something I don't?"

"I know what I saw in the doctor's eyes. And it's not good."

"He said he thought she'd live. That's good news, at least."

"It's the way he said it. His eyes said something more. Something's wrong. Pray hard for her. She needs our prayers really bad."

Thirteen

At noon on Saturday, Joe and Maggie Harris walked back into the hospital, this time through the main door. Dr. Cantor's office had called to suggest they meet him in his office. All they would tell him was, "She's critical, but stable. The doctor will discuss everything when you get here," the faceless voice on the phone had said.

Maggie's mother had agreed to stay with Cecil. Grandma had little patience for the boy's non-stop building and rebuilding and would only agree to sit with him for limited periods. Caroline being in the hospital made this an exception.

They were now running a few minutes late because grandma insisted they stop to rent video tapes to keep her occupied. Grandma fired a million questions at Maggie who simply shrugged, being much too numb to focus on anything her mother was asking.

Maggie and Joe were ushered directly into the doctor's private office as soon as they arrived. Cantor had changed out of his scrubs and was now wearing a suit.

"First, let me tell you Caroline is stable and we are expecting her to remain that way for some time. We've contained the brain swelling and don't expect any negative change from this point on."

"Doctor, pardon us," Joe said, "but all we know is what's been reported in the Sentinel. Two girls dead, two in the hospital, one paralyzed. Which one is—"

"I'm afraid your daughter has a C-4 lesion."

"Meaning?" Joe asked, dreading the answer.

"Meaning the spinal cord at the C-4, that's cervical four, has been badly traumatized."

"Will she—"

"I'm afraid she'll not have the use of her arms or her legs."

"Oh, my God!" Maggie cried. "Oh, my God!" Tears flowed freely down her cheeks. She made no attempt to wipe her face.

Joe sat in his chair stone solid, saying nothing, struggling to comprehend what this all meant. After a few minutes he reached out to touch his wife. Turning to the doctor, he asked, "Is it permanent? Or will she recover some use?"

"Unfortunately, I've seen too many of these types of injuries to give you much hope for movement. Miracles happen, but it's not very likely. If there's going to be a change, it will occur within the next few days. However, my expectation is that she'll have only marginal improvement at best. I'm terribly sorry. I—"

"You said brain swelling," Maggie interrupted. "Is she—"

"Mentally, I expect she'll recover. I don't anticipate lasting diminishment of her mental capacity. All tests have been promising. She also has several broken bones and a punctured lung. These will all be surgically repaired, and should, in time, heal properly."

"Can we see her?"

"I have arranged a visit, but I must warn you that because of the spinal injury we have not yet undertaken surgical repairs. Her face is pretty badly lacerated, but not as bad as it looks. She's sedated, so pain's not an issue. Please don't touch her. We can't take a chance on anything shifting. You can talk to her, if you want. There's always the possibility she can hear you. But don't expect a response."

"Oh, my God!" Maggie cried again. "My poor baby. My poor baby."

Joe stood behind his wife, his hands on her arms. His intent had been to comfort her, but the feel of her skin actually steadied him. Myriad questions bombarded him, but he couldn't find the words. He also knew that if he tried to speak he would burst out crying.

"Are you ready to see her?" Cantor gently asked, "Or do you need more time?"

"Time for what?" Maggie asked. "Time won't make it better." She stood. "Come Joe, let's go see our baby."

ಲಿಂಕ್

Dr. Cantor led them down a long corridor with patient rooms lining each side. He turned the corner at the end of the hall and entered an area marked BSCIP. Cantor explained that this was one of the state's Brain and Spinal Cord Injury Program facilities. "This is one of the best in the country, if I say so myself. Your daughter is lucky to have this here."

In Joe's mind, there was nothing lucky about anything that had happened to his daughter. He began to say something to the doctor, but Cantor had already disappeared into the room.

Caroline was in the center of what was called an isolation observation room, surrounded by machinery and equipment, all unfathomable to anyone not trained in acute care of spinal cord injuries. Wires and tubes ran in a chaotic jumble in every direction. A metal ring looked to be screwed to her forehead with wires attached to a frame over the bed.

Cantor said, "We've taken her off the respirator and she's doing nicely. Also, we have her in spinal traction, that's what the halo is for. We're administering steroids to reduce the swelling. That's what I mean about being advanced here. Not many other places use steroids. I've had good results since I started."

Caroline was lying on her back, her arms folded over her stomach. She looked to be at peace, except for the facial wounds that would have looked horrendous in any other setting.

"Later today a plastic surgeon will close the facial trauma, and in the morning we plan to set her broken arm and leg. Monday, if everything progresses as expected, we'll begin to gradually bring her out of the coma."

"Coma?" Joe repeated. "You didn't say she was in a coma."

"That's a precautionary measure. We don't want her moving at this point. It's an induced coma that effectively slows her brain functioning and makes her more comfortable. By Wednesday she'll be fully back out of it and you'll be able to speak with her."

Maggie asked, "How long will she be like this? I mean in the hospital?"

"We'll keep her in acute care until we're certain all danger is past. About two weeks typically, maybe a little longer because of the other trauma. Then she begins rehabilitation."

"Does that mean walking?" Maggie asked, hope evident in her voice.

"Mrs. Harris, I'll be frank with you. The possibility of Caroline having any meaningful use of her arms and legs is extremely remote. We will do what we can to preserve the maximum possible function, but the prognosis is not promising."

"How will she live? Oh, my God, what will we do?"

"I suggest taking this one day at a time," Dr. Cantor gently replied. "We measure progress in small steps. Her life will be different, but with time, she'll be able to do most everything."

"Most everything, except use her arms and legs!" Joe snapped. "You call that everything?"

"I'm sorry this happened, Mr. Harris. I truly am. We neurologists devote our lives to helping people in this situation and we do our best to get them to a point where they can lead reasonably normal lives. Most do just that. It'll be up to her entirely. Mental attitude is crucial. Yours, as well as hers. You'd be surprised at what wonderful things people can achieve without the use of their arms or legs. Please try to be positive and take this one day at a time. She'll have first-class therapy here. It's our job, yours as well as mine, to give your daughter the tools and the attitude to do well. It will take a while, but she *will* make progress."

Maggie asked, "What are we to do? I feel helpless. I don't know what to do to help."

"We have a training program for home care-givers for patients like Caroline. She'll require your full support."

"Who pays for all this?" Maggie asked. "We don't have that kind of money."

Before Dr. Cantor could respond, Joe pulled Maggie against his chest. "We'll find a way. If I have to take a second job, we'll find a way to get through this. Don't worry, we'll take care of our baby."

"And what about Cecil?" Maggie asked. "What about him?"

"What about him?" Joe replied. "He'll just have to grow up. That's all there is to it."

"He drains my energy as it is. What will I do with two on my hands? Oh, my God, I can't do this."

"Cecil will just have to find a way to stay out of trouble won't he? The boy's not stupid."

"He can't help what he is, Joe. He's a good boy. I know you think he should be like the others, but he can't be. He's just not that way." Then, changing the subject, Maggie asked Dr. Cantor, "Did the other girl come here?"

Cantor studied Joe and Maggie Harris before he replied. "I'm sure you know the driver of the car and one of the passengers were killed instantly. The young woman who survived, her name's Elizabeth Classico, is down the hall. She has a concussion and both arms and one leg are fractured."

"I want to visit her. Joe, you remember her, don't you? Nice kid. She's the girl who slept over two weeks ago. Her family's new to Texas. I've never met them, but I spoke with the mother on the phone before the sleep over. Nancy, I think."

"Come," Dr. Cantor said, "A visit with her would be appropriate."

☙03

The scene in Liz's room was in stark contrast to the isolation room where Caroline Harris lay in a coma. Flowers covered every surface, and several children, Maggie assumed them to be siblings, were huddled around a computer, laughing at something on the screen.

"Maggie, how's your daughter?" Nancy Classico inquired as soon as the doctor made his exit. "I tried to go see her, but they wouldn't let me. She's in good hands. Dr. Cantor is the best there is. That man really cares."

"Too early to tell," Maggie replied, remaining surprisingly calm. "It'll be a long road back no matter what." She looked away as tears again formed. Forcing herself to continue, she added, "They say she'll be paralyzed. She won't..." Maggie paused to wipe her eyes. "...have much use of her arms or legs."

Nancy started to say something and changed her mind. Instead, she said, "The paper says only two survived. I feel sorry for the parents of the other two girls. They were all nice kids."

"Why'd this have to happen?" Maggie cried. When everyone in the room turned toward her, she realized she had cried out more strongly than she had intended. She looked around, then asked, "How's Liz?"

"They expect her to recover fully. It will take a while for her leg to mend. It's broken in several places. Her arms have been set and should be fine. They had to rebuild her leg with plates and screws and who knows what else. But we're told she'll be able to walk." Nancy caught herself, then said, "Sorry, I know it'll be a long while for Caroline. I don't mean to be...insensitive. Please, if there is anything we can do, please let us know."

"I'm happy for you and your family," Maggie managed. "Liz is a nice girl." Then the tears came, quietly at first, then extending to gasps and finally to uncontrolled heaving.

Joe put his arm around his wife and led her out of the room and down the hall. Spotting a small chapel, Joe steered Maggie through the door.

Once inside, Maggie's anguished cries filled the room. Joe tried in vain to comfort her, finally giving up. The more words of comfort he spoke, the deeper her emotion became. He wrapped his arms around her. Then his own tears came.

After a long while, Maggie, squinting through the mist, spotted the small altar. "So this is what we get for being good!" she cried. "This is how you answer our prayers! How could you do this to my baby girl? What kind of God are you? What kind of God does this to a nice girl?"

Maggie paused, as though she was waiting for an answer, and then continued with renewed energy. "Answer me!" she begged. "Please answer me! I need to know why you did such a thing to a nice girl like Caroline! Why did this happen? What did I do to deserve such punishment? My poor baby! My poor little girl! What will she do? Oh, God, what will become of her?"

Joe made the mistake of saying, "At least she's alive. We should thank God for keeping her alive."

"You call never able to use your arms or legs being alive! She won't be able to do anything! She can't feed herself or even go to the bathroom! Oh my God!"

"We'll get through this, Maggie, and so will she. She's a good kid and tough." Even while he was speaking he knew what Maggie was saying was true. Living with useless arms and legs was just not imaginable. In fact, Joe began to wonder if he himself was up to the challenges that lay ahead.

Fourteen

Sally arrived home an hour after her mother left for work. She raced directly to the bathroom, stripped off her clothes, and climbed into the shower. The hot water turning cold drove her out. The blood was gone from her legs, but no amount of scrubbing removed the soil pervading her soul. The towel brushing across her breasts reminded her of his hands and rekindled her anger.

She had never before experienced such an intense cycle of emotions; anger, despair, sadness and back to anger again. Her body was exhausted, but every time she dozed off she would come awake kicking and screaming and fighting to remove Wade from on top of her. Nothing she could do lessened the hammering feeling of violation and despair that had taken over her body. It was not until well into the afternoon on Saturday that she actually fell into any semblance of a sound sleep.

Lydia Mascar didn't bother knocking on her daughter's door at four in the afternoon when she arrived home from the bank because Sally was always out of the house on weekends. She opened the door to collect the clothes from Sally's laundry hamper and was surprised to see Sally sprawled on the bed. Her daughter had always been a composed sleeper, arms and legs tucked in against her body. Lydia was puzzled to see Sally's limbs flung out and twitching, almost as though she was trying to ward off a predator.

"Sally," she called. When the girl didn't respond, Lydia became frightened and shook Sally's shoulder.

Sally's feet shot into the air. "Get away from me, you pig!" she screamed." Get away. Get away. Get away."

"Sally!" Lydia screamed back. "Wake up! You're having a bad dream. Wake up. Wake up. Are you okay?"

"Get away from me!" the girl repeated. "Get away!"

"Sally, wake up. What's wrong?" Lydia put her hand on Sally's forehead to check for fever, only to have her hand ripped violently away. "Why are you sleeping in your clothes? Is something wrong?"

"Get away from me!"

"I'm not leaving this room until I can see you're alright. Please, get up!" Lydia again shook her daughter, resulting in more violent leg kicks. Only this time the teen reached out a clawed left hand in an attempt to scratch. "Stop that!" Lydia shouted, grabbing the girl's wrist and pinning it against the bed.

Sally's eyes opened briefly and then closed.

A moment later they opened again. "I'm sleeping," she intoned in a half-dead voice. "Leave me alone."

"It's after four in the afternoon! What's going on?" Lydia released her daughter's wrist, ready to grab it again if she continued fighting. But the girl calmed down and slowly pulled herself to a sitting position.

"Now, tell me. What's going on?"

"Had a bad night."

"What kind of bad night?"

"Couldn't sleep. I must have eaten something bad."

"You went to the play. What did you eat?"

"Some of us went to *The Pit* after. Had a burger. Maybe something was wrong with it."

"After the play?" Lydia quizzed. Her mother's intuition was now firmly in control of the direction of the interrogation. "How did you get there?"

Sally was ready. She had worked it out on the way home the previous night. "The Spencers took a bunch of us."

"Were you there when that terrible accident occurred? The radio said two girls were killed. I think another was paralyzed. No names have been released."

"What accident?"

"Right after the play. A bunch of girls, high school seniors the radio said, pulled out of *The Pit* and got hit by a tractor-trailer."

"I didn't see anything."

"Are you sure you were there?"

"Where else would I be? I told you, I ate something and got sick."

"Throwing up?"

"The runs."

"Are you telling me everything?" Lydia asked, certain something was going on, but clueless as to what it could be. "It happened after the play. That's where the girls were coming from, your class play. You couldn't have missed the accident if you were there."

"I was there and I got sick. What more do you want from me?"

"Just the truth is all. You look...well, horrible is the only way to say it. I've never seen—"

"I told you the truth! I need to sleep. I was up all night."

Lydia gave up, determined to get to the bottom of this later when her daughter felt better. "I hope you feel better," she said. "But please do get this room cleaned up before you go anywhere."

Sally tried to go back to sleep. She lay in bed numb, her eyes open, staring blankly at the ceiling. It was as if she could hear and see, but not feel any emotion. It was as if she was watching someone else, someone disconnected from her. She was an observer outside her body, looking at herself, waiting for the body to become angry, to kick and shout. But the body remained still; fact had separated from reality. For the moment, the mental anguish subsided.

Sally imagined this would be what it was like in the moments after death, watching your own body as your soul hovered nearby before beginning the long trip to wherever spirits went.

Sally wished she *were* dead; then the terrible shame would be gone.

Hours later when she dozed off the violent kicking began again, this time as part of a dream in which she was screaming a frantic but soundless scream. The terrifying vision woke her up, restarting the cycle of passive observation and violent physical movement. She hated herself for getting into a situation where Wade could overpower her. She felt dirty and ashamed, convinced she should have done more to prevent what had happened, but not understanding what that could have been.

Around eight, Sally gave up and decided to go for a walk, to tire herself out so real sleep would come.

"Oh, I'm glad you're up," Lydia called after her. "Feeling better, I hope. Do you need to see a doctor?"

Sally felt her heart give a gigantic thump before launching into a high-speed gallop. *How did she know? Did I say something in my sleep? Did someone call? Maybe she spoke with Mrs. Spencer!* The panic sucked the wind out of her and choked off her ability to speak.

"Did the diarrhea stop?" Lydia asked, unaware of the terror that the word "doctor" had brought on. "Do you need something? Imodium, or whatever?"

Oh, Sally thought, as surprised as she was relieved. *She bought my story after all.* Sally found that she could breathe again. "I'm actually feeling a little better," she replied as evenly as her still-elevated adrenaline level would allow for. "Thought I'd take a walk. Get some fresh air."

"Good plan," Lydia replied. "Let me know if you need anything. Don't get too far from the house."

"I'll be okay," Sally replied, wanting to add, *There's nothing nobody can do to me that already hasn't been done.*

"You might need the potty," Linda called.

ಬಇ

That night Sally slept in fits and starts, sleeping a little, struggling a lot. She got up around noon on Sunday, still experiencing the same cycle of anger, fright and numbness. She felt terribly alone, even though her mother was in the house with her.

Sensing that something was still not right, Lydia suggested they go to the mall and to a movie. At first Sally declined. Then she relented, dreading an empty house.

That night Sally fell into a deep sleep, only to wake up with a start at one in the morning — the exact time of the rape. Sally's brain replayed the attack yet again, and she watched in horrified silence as her body was brutalized by Wade Spencer. She re-experienced his scent. A scent that had been so intoxicating in the car, now made her sick to her stomach. Sally raced to the bathroom, barely making it in time to vomit into the sink.

Fifteen

On Monday morning Sally was called to the office of the school principal. The Principal, Natalie Hill, was seated behind her desk when Sally walked in. Mr. Henderson was in the small office as well. He was sitting in front of the desk across from Miss Hill. Before either Henderson or Hill could speak, Sally demanded to know why she was there.

"Take a seat and we'll talk about it," Miss Hill said in a mildly unpleasant tone. She was a woman in her early fifties with hard eyes and a perpetual frown. Sally sat in a chair next to her teacher also facing the principal.

"I'm told you were seen going up to the third floor with a boy on Friday night," she began. "Would you care to explain?"

"More like a man than a boy," Henderson interjected.

"Right," Miss Hill, echoed. "A man. What about it, Miss Mascar?"

"He was my date," Sally replied. "He had to use the restroom."

Henderson turned toward Sally. "Let's stop with the pretense," he said, looking straight into her eyes. You know where the restrooms are, do you not?"

"Well, yes."

"Then please tell us whether there are restrooms near the auditorium."

"There are some across from the auditorium doors and on each side in the hall," Sally answered meekly.

"So, even if your friend *was* looking for a restroom, which I very much doubt, why not go to one of those?"

Sally didn't have a good answer, although later she thought of some. They were full. The line was too long. He got lost. But under fire, "I don't know" was all she could manage.

"What do you mean, 'I don't know'?" Henderson pressed, shooting a quick glance in the direction of Principal Hill.

"I was following him. I thought he knew his way."

"To where?"

"To the restroom."

"But you know the restrooms are on the ground floor, right near the auditorium. You just told me that. And you're well aware that the upper floors are off limits after hours, right?"

"I guess so."

"So tell us again why you were going up to the third floor."

"I was following him."

"Does he have a name?"

"Yes"

"So what is it? What's his name?"

"Wade."

"Is that his first name or his last name?"

"Wade Spencer."

"I *knew* I recognized him," Henderson exclaimed. He turned back to face Principal Hill. "We had him some years ago. Let's see—" Henderson thought for a moment. "Graduated five years ago to be exact. Son of Jackson Spencer."

Miss Hill picked up the thread of the interrogation from there. "So he must be in college now?" she asked.

"Uh-huh."

"So tell us again," Hill demanded. "Why were you and big-man-on-campus Wade Spencer on the steps to the third floor?"

"I was following him, to show me something; he said it was neat."

"So he wasn't going to the restroom after all." Henderson said, throwing a *I knew it* look toward the principal. "What was it? What did he want to show you?"

"I don't know."

"Did you see what it was?"

"No."

"Did he tell you what it was?"

"No."

"Why not?" Henderson demanded. "I mean, he went to all that trouble to take you to the third floor and then didn't show you what he had in mind? Is that what you're saying?"

"Because you told us to go back downstairs."

Henderson paused, trying to remember if the movement he had seen was on the second floor or the third.

In that pause, the principal jumped back in. "Sally, were you and this college boy doing anything improper?" she asked, drawing out the last word. And then an even more drawn out, "I think you know what I'm getting at."

Sally felt as though a knife had been plunged into her stomach. Some small part of her wanted to blurt it all out, but that small part of her was no match for the shame and fear that were solidly in control of Sally's actions. Fear of her mother. Fear of what people would think of her. Ashamed of what she did. "No, ma'am," she replied. "Nothing like that happened. We came down when Mr. Henderson told us to."

Sally's denial didn't sound convincing, even to her.

Indeed, Sally's demeanor telegraphed to Principal Hill that the state of affairs was just as she and Mr. Henderson had suspected. Their aggressive approach to the interview was, in fact, a deliberate attempt to shake Sally from what they knew would be an attempt to lie her way out of the situation. For all the outward gruff, and her reputation as a dried-up and bitter old maid, Miss Hill was a keen and adept educator, dedicated to her students' academic and emotional well-being. Especially to the girls.

"Sally," Hill began in a much quieter tone, "it is important not to lie about this. That boy is over eighteen, maybe even twenty. You're only fourteen. If he did anything to you, touched you, anything, I need to know. You're under age. You really need to tell me."

Sally was positive that if they knew what she had done she'd be sent to reform school. She remained silent.

"Sally," Principal Hill said, "It's written all over you. I can see the...the...hurt in your eyes. If anything happened I need to know."

Sally forced conviction into her voice. "Really," she heard herself say, "nothing happened. Nothing."

"Sally, please tell me what happened. I can see it in your face. Something is wrong."

Oh, yeah, something is wrong, Sally thought, but there was no way she could speak of it.

"Okay, Sally," Miss Hill said, when Sally did not respond, "it's only fair to tell you I'm going to have to speak with your mother to tell her what I suspect."

Sally's stomach knotted and she felt as if she would faint. But she managed to keep her head up and her mouth set tight. This was her problem and she would somehow deal with it herself.

The principal thanked Mr. Henderson for his help and then turned back to Sally.

"You can go now," she said, "but you need to stay away from boys who are older than you." She paused and, for a brief instant, her attention seemed to have drifted elsewhere. "Stay away from them," she repeated. "Only bad can come of it."

If only you knew. Sally pushed herself up from the chair and, without a word, hurried from the principal's office, making it all the way to the toilet before she vomited.

Sixteen

Maggie and Joe Harris were overwhelmed with the preparations required before they could even hope to bring Caroline home. Joe's mother, Ida, suggested that Cecil come up to Dallas for the month of July. "You two have your hands full down there with Caroline. Oh, that poor girl. I still can't believe what happened. It's the least Henry and I can do. She'll require your full attention and Cecil will just be in the way."

Joe's father, a petroleum engineer who had taken early retirement because of a heart condition, insisted they could manage their grandson, saying, "How hard can it be? I look forward to him being with us. All I have is time on my hands. We'll all be just fine."

So it was settled. Cecil would spend the month of July in Dallas with his grandparents. The boy was told only that Caroline had been in an accident and that she would be in the hospital for a while. The family preferred to know more about Caroline's prognosis and what it would mean to their living conditions before they attempted to deal with Cecil.

Pappa, as the boy called him, welcomed the boy's passion for things mechanical. After a few days, mostly spent observing Cecil tear down and rebuild his old lawn mower engine, Henry decided it would be good to introduce Cecil to his friend Lucas, whose hobby was restoring antique cars. Lucas had recently sold his dry cleaning business, put a lot of money in the bank, and now busied himself with his hobby.

Lucas came to the house and observed Cecil tear down and rebuild the lawnmower engine yet again. He turned to Henry. "I've never seen fingers that agile. The best mechanic I know is a guy named Nellie. He's not near as good as Cecil. That kid's a natural. I've never in my life seen anyone work on engines in a spiral pattern. That way he doesn't have to step over any part when rebuilding the engine. Brilliant I'd say."

"My son told me about that, but I couldn't visualize how he did it. I understand he just has to see something once and he can master it."

"Listen," Lucas said, "if he's in Dallas all summer I'll go ahead and buy the car I've wanted for a while now. It needs to have the engine replaced and I can't do it alone and this is a tough one."

"You sure you want Cecil to work on it?"

"It might be challenging. We're going to rebuild a gas turbine engine and put it in the car. But if he's as good as it appears this should be a piece of cake."

"I thought you were the car-rebuilding expert," Henry said.

"I'm pretty good at bodywork, upholstery, maybe some deep tune-ups, but certainly not a full rebuild of a gas turbine. Especially when the parts are hard or impossible to obtain. What I have in mind is hardly easy. From what you've told me about Cecil, and what I've seen of the boy, I'm confident he can design any part we can't find. I've never seen anybody do what that kid can do."

"You'll need a machine shop for that stuff," Henry observed. "Cecil's never worked with power tools. He may be good with hand tools, but I wouldn't trust him with big stuff. He'll cut his hand off."

"I'll line up Nellie. He's the best there is—at least when he's sober. Between him and Cecil we'll get it done."

Henry rolled his eyes. "When he's sober, huh?" Listen, I don't want Cecil around any drunk. He's too impressionable."

"I don't allow Nellie to drink when he's working for me. He'll stay sober all right 'cause I don't pay him 'til he's done—and remains sober. That's always our deal and it works just fine. 'Ole Nellie can manage to stay off the bottle for a month or so."

"And the car? What are you actually planning to buy?"

"I've heard of some guys putting gas turbines in a Ghia. I've wanted to do that myself for a while. Going to take some real ingenuity. We'll see how good the boy really is. The Ghia I have in mind is a real mess."

"I thought you car buffs never changed the original equipment. You're confusing me."

"It's not an antique. It's just something some of the guys have been fooling with. Mostly it's about the turbine engine. But the body is a mess as well. It'll be fun."

"Are you sure Cecil can do it?"

"All we can do is try. Nothing ventured, as they say. It's just money."

"I'm glad it's your money and not mine. When the kid gets nervous, he locks up."

"Loosen up, Henry. It'll be fine. It'll be good to have somebody young around the house. I'm looking forward to it."

ಬಂಚ

Joe and Maggie were thankful when Henry called to propose keeping Cecil in Dallas for the remainder of the summer. Caroline had been moved to a rehabilitation facility and it was slow going. Her broken arms were healing well enough, but there was now talk of a possible amputation of her left leg. Only time would tell.

"Any movement at all?" Henry inquired. "Can she at least move her arms?"

"No, Dad, not really," Joe Harris replied, his voice filled with profound resignation. "She can move her fingers ever so slightly, but she can't even lift a pencil. Hell, she can't even hold a Kleenex for that matter. Maggie is crying all the time now."

"And how are *you* doing?"

"Not much better, to tell the truth. Most days I don't want to get out of bed, and that's on a good day. It's painful to see Caroline struggle and to know that no matter how hard she works she'll never leave her bed on her own power."

"You must have hope," Henry counseled, not for the first time. "Your mother and I will visit for a while when we bring Cecil home in August."

"Truth is, the longer he's there the better," Joe responded. "After that fiasco with the school play I don't know where we're going with him."

"He's doing just fine with us. We have a nice project lined up for him. Right up his alley." Henry went on to describe the Ghia remake.

"Just be damn sure the boy doesn't hurt himself," Joe said. "One's enough. I can't deal with any more."

꧁꧂

The gas turbine engine arrived a week later. Lucas, with Henry's help, uncrated it. Cecil stood off to the side, seemingly in a trance as he waited for the engine to emerge from its wrapper. When it did, his eyes went wide. Then he smiled. Then he laughed and began to prance around.

The men, using a portable hoist, lifted the engine onto a metal stand and secured it with tie-down bolts. Cecil watched, hopping impatiently from one foot to the other. "This is what's called a gas turbine engine," Lucas explained. "It's a rotary engine that extracts energy from a flow of combustion gas. It has—"

"I know how it works!" Cecil yelped. "Can I take it apart? Can I? Can I?"

"How do you know how it works?" Henry asked. "You've never seen one of these before."

"I can see it. The pressure builds up here," the boy said, patting the outside of the pressure chamber. "And this has a rotor in here. It turns, except you can't see it 'cause it's on the inside."

"Never seen anything like the boy," Lucas exclaimed. "Okay, you can take it apart, but only if you can rebuild it exactly like it is. Do you think you can?"

"If it's built correct now, I can."

"Good point, actually. This baby was used in a small army tank some fifty years ago. It was rebuilt once in the eighties, but they didn't run it but one time, so the boy may be right. It might not be right. That's a good reason to strip it down and rebuild it before we install it."

"Can I start? Can I start? Can I start?" Can I—"

"Cecil!" Pappa commanded. "I told you. None of that while you're here with us! Understand?"

The boy looked down and his shoulders fell, but the mantra stopped.

"Let me be real clear about this," Pappa continued. "If you start that mantra stuff, I mean repeating words over and over, I'll pack you up and take you home. You won't get to work on the engine. Understand?"

Still the boy remained silent.

"Cecil, I'm speaking to you."

Lucas started to say something, but Henry cut him off. "No, the boy will behave himself or go home. It's up to him. What will it be, young man?"

Cecil still refused to speak. Pappa took him firmly by the arm and marched him toward the overhead door leading out of Lucas's garage.

Halfway to the door, Cecil pulled free and ran back to the engine. When Pappa caught up, Cecil said, "I understand."

"Okay. Next time, answer me the first time."

"Ok, Pappa," Cecil responded. "Can I start now? Can I?"

This time instead of repeating the question over and over, Cecil waited for an answer.

Henry looked to Lucas who said, "Go ahead, Cecil, but for goodness sake be careful what you do."

Seventeen

Cecil worked on the turbine for twenty minutes and parts were already in their customary spiral pattern on the garage floor when suddenly he yelled, "Broken!" He was holding a bent tube. "Wrong part," he said. "That's why it broke."

It was not only bent, but appeared to be newer and of a different material than the other parts. "I'll mark this with blue tape, so we remember."

"Don't have to. I know," Cecil replied, already at work removing the next part.

"Okay, humor me. I need to mark it so that *I'll* know." After the tape was put on, Lucas positioned the tube in the open space Cecil had left for it. The boy had already removed two other parts and eight bolts. "At this pace," Lucas commented, "the whole thing will be disassembled before the end of the day."

Even as they were speaking, parts were lining up, and the spiral was closing in on Cecil. Cecil refused to stop for lunch, absorbed in the gas turbine, the first one he had ever seen.

Lucas and Henry returned from lunch forty-five minutes later to find Cecil struggling at the workbench, a large wrench in one hand and a hammer in the other.

"Whoa! What seems to be the problem?" Lucas called from the doorway.

"Can't get it to move." Cecil positioned the wrench on a nut and gave the end of the wrench a solid rap.

Nothing moved.

He gave the hammer four hard raps in quick succession with no results.

Lucas peered at the nut. "It's probably rusted and locked. Let's put some penetrating oil on it and let it sit."

Cecil looked puzzled, but stood back so that Lucas could go to work with the oil and a rag.

"You hungry?" Pappa asked. "I brought you back a ham sandwich and a Coke."

The boy stood while he devoured the sandwich, his eyes never leaving Lucas.

"I see you put blue tape on several of the parts. Does that mean they are broken?" Henry asked Lucas.

"Some wrong. Some broken."

"Okay, tomorrow Nellie will be here and we can put him to work. You'll tell him what we need, and he'll make it for you."

"That will be fun," Cecil responded, more excited than he had ever been in his life. "Tomorrow we can clean the parts. Some have rust."

"I see that. I'll get some wire brushes and we'll make everything good as new." When Cecil had drained the Coke, Lucas said, "Okay, you can try the bolt. The oil should have done its magic by now."

"Magic?" Cecil said. "What magic?"

"Never mind, Cecil," Pappa said, "just try it."

Cecil rushed over to the engine, anxious to see how the oil worked. To his surprise, the nut moved on the second hammer tap. "I can finish now," he exclaimed.

Within an hour, all of the parts were on the floor ready for cleaning and reassembly.

"Can we start now?" he pleaded. "Put it together?"

"Not ready for that, yet, Cecil," Lucas said. "First we have to clean all the good parts and make replacements for the broken ones. It will be a while before this is back together."

"He'll be finished in a few days," Henry observed. "Then what?"

"First of all, it's going to take weeks to get the broken parts made," Lucas explained. "It'll also take some time to clean all of these. Then when it's back together we need to install it into the car. That will take some effort, new brackets, that type of thing."

"By the way," Henry asked, "when is the car arriving?"

"Monday. Then the real fun begins. We need to make up all the brackets, linkages and even the gear train. This is just a warm up."

"You expect Cecil can do all that?" What does he know about linkages?"

"More than I do, I bet. The boy's a natural, I tell you. You see that wrench in his hands? When his fingers move, it's like watching a musician," Lucas exclaimed, echoing the observation that Joe Harris's friend, Bart, had made so many years before. "This will be a fun summer."

"I'm glad you're enjoying yourself," Henry said, ribbing his friend. "From what you're telling me I'm guessing this is going to be one expensive car."

"Just watching your grandson is worth the price of admission," Lucas replied. "I can't wait."

Eighteen

"What's been wrong with you this summer?" Lydia Mascar wanted to know. "It's already past the Fourth of July and you've hardly left your room since the end of school. All year I couldn't tear you and Alice Spencer apart. Now you won't even call her. What happened?" Thinking back to her own early teen years, Lydia softened her voice. "Are you two fighting over a boy or something? Anyway, you're too young for boys. You should just enjoy yourself with your girlfriends."

"I'm okay," Sally snapped. "Leave me be. I want to be by myself."

"They're your friends. You should be with them."

"I flunked math and English! They'll be in high school and I'm still in baby eighth grade. You think they want to be with me?"

Lydia exploded. "Did Alice say that? I'm calling Jennie Spencer right now!" She reached for the phone.

"No. Don't!" Sally screamed, her stomach clamping down on what little she had eaten for breakfast. "Can you just leave me alone? Can you just?"

"I'm worried about you. It's been well over a month since school ended. You can't mope about all summer."

"I just want to be by myself. Give me a break!"

Just when Sally had begun to feel normal, her breasts became sensitive and she lost her appetite. Then nausea set in every time she opened the refrigerator.

She was tired all day even though she barely got out of bed. At first she believed it was because her period was late. Then she began to spot, and was happy that she was getting back to normal. But her life fell apart the next morning when her pad was smeared with a brownish substance.

That's when she recalled the physical education lecture of Miss Ryan. "Missing a period," the teacher had said, "sometimes happens naturally. But if you've engaged in intercourse your periods can change. Often that means you are pregnant, especially if you're experiencing nausea, or perhaps your breasts are sore. If that happens, you need to tell your parents immediately."

"Oh, God!" Sally screamed. "What will I do now? I can't tell Mother, she'll kill me!"

Sally continued screaming until her voice gave out. Thank God her mother was at work. The gnawing fear that she had lived with for the past month—the fear that someone would find out about her and Wade in the woods—was nothing compared to how she felt now. She stamped and jumped until her feet couldn't take it. She flung her dolls and her bears and her pillows from one end of her room to the other hard enough so that one of the pillows spewed feathers everywhere.

Sally found herself on the floor in the middle of her room, feathers still coming down on her head. How long she had been there she didn't know. Nor did she know if she had slept. But what she did know was that somehow she felt calm somewhere deep inside her. She focused on that calm and, with deep breaths, nurtured it to a point where she gained control of her thought process.

Her plan had been to keep the rape to herself, to never tell anyone *ever*. But keeping it all a secret now wasn't going to be possible. Doing nothing was no longer an option.

"Think," she urged herself. "Gotta think. Think of *something*."

❧☙

Sally was waiting in the kitchen when her mother came home from work. "Mom," she began, surprising herself at how calm she sounded. "I've been thinking."

"Oh? About what?" This was a different Sally than Lydia had seen of late. "What have you been thinking about?" Lydia's tone made it clear she was cautious of the sudden change—cautious, but hopeful.

Sally took a deep breath and pressed on. "I think it's about time I got to know Nellie."

"Say what?" Lydia gasped, looking for a chair to fall into. "You want to do what?" The suggestion about Nellie had come out of left field.

"I think it would be good to get to know my dad."

"And what brought this on?"

"I was just thinking. I don't know him at all."

"What makes you think we can even find him?" Lydia stammered, struggling to understand her daughter.

"Is he still in Dallas?"

"I really have no idea where he is. He could be in Dallas. He could be on the moon. For all I know, he could be living under a bridge." Lydia actually thought her former husband was most likely dead by now. He hadn't come by in years.

"Mom!"

"Well, it's true. You know full well he's a confirmed drunk. I don't know how he survived as long as he did. I mean, as long as he has."

"Can you find him?"

"Sally, this is a really bad idea. Really bad." On one of Nellie's infrequent visits Lydia had broached the subject of him getting to know his daughter. The man nearly leapt out of the window.

"Mom, I need to know him. I do."

"Why now? What brought this on?"

"Because I can't know me until I know him." Anyway, she added, "what's wrong with a person wanting to get to know her dad?"

"Nothing. If that's all it is."

"That's all it is. What else could it be?"

"That's what I'm trying to figure. You're not yourself."

"Well, do you have his number or not?"

"I might have a number," Lydia admitted hesitantly. "He left me a piece of paper with a phone number that he said I could call. A friend of his I think. He said to call if there was something happening with you that he should know about. I guess this qualifies."

"Please, Mother. Get that paper for me."

Not without grave misgivings, Lydia went to her room to retrieve Nellie's phone number.

"Here," she said, a few minutes later thrusting the paper in Sally's direction. "This is your father's friend's number."

"Is Lucas his friend?" Sally asked after glancing at the paper.

"Huh?"

"Lucas. It says 'Lucas' right here under the phone number."

"I suppose so. But I'm not sure."

Sally went to her room and rehearsed what she was going to say. Finally, taking a deep breath and, perching nervously on the edge of her bed, she slowly dialed the number.

When a male voice answered the phone on the third ring, Sally said, "Hello, my name is Sally Mascar. My father's name is Nellie. My father gave me—uh, actually he gave my mother—your phone number. He said we could reach him there."

"Your father?" said the man. "Who did you say this was?"

"Sally Mascar."

"Mascar? Really? Are you talking about Nellie Mascar?"

"Yeah. Right. That's him. That's why I'm calling."

"Really?" the man said again. "You're his daughter? I had no idea Nellie had any kids. He's never said anything about having a daughter."

"Can you put him on the phone? I need to talk to him," Sally said, frustrated that this conversation seemed to be going nowhere.

"How did you say you got this number?" the man asked.

"He gave it to us," Sally said, noticing that she had begun to bounce her leg up and down. "Can I talk to him, *please*?"

"Nellie doesn't actually live here," said the man.

"But this is Lucas, right?"

"How did you know that?"

The leg was bouncing even faster now.

"It says 'Lucas' here under this phone number."

"Well, I'm Lucas," said the man. "What did you say your name was?"

"Sally. I'm Sally, his daughter," she said, annoyed at having to tell him her name for the third time. She managed to restrain herself from adding "*you old fart*" to her answer. "If Nellie doesn't live there any more, do you know where I could call him?"

"He'll be here tomorrow or the next day. I have work for him. He'll be here the rest of the summer."

"Oh, great. Thanks," Sally said. Then, without knowing why, she blurted, "I want to visit him."

"Visit him here?"

"I don't know," said Sally, really sorry that she hadn't already hung up. "Visit him where he's living, I guess."

"He doesn't live in any place where you can visit him," Lucas said. "But it so happens he'll be sleeping here for the next month. You can stay here, too. Big house, plenty of room. And just how old are you, Sally Mascar?"

"I'm fourteen."

"Oh. Fourteen, huh?" A pause, and then, "Did your mother say it's okay? I mean you coming to Dallas." And then, "Where did you say you live?"

Sally knew that she hadn't said where she lived, but this was no time to bring that up.

"Cosper," she said. "I live in Cosper."

"That's over five hours away. Would your mother drive you? How would you get here?"

Drive me? thought Sally. *I'll be lucky if she lets me go at all.* Her plans did not include her mother. She figured buses went everywhere and she could find a bus to Dallas.

"Well, um, my mother wouldn't be coming at all. Just me. On a bus or whatever."

"Hmmm. You better put your mother on the phone," Lucas said in what struck Sally as a sort of abrupt, grown-up tone.

Sally ran to the kitchen. "Lucas wants to talk to you," she said excitedly. "He said I could stay at his house."

"What?" Lydia Mascar, shrieked. "First you tell me you want your father to come here. Now some friend of your father—who I don't even know—wants you to stay at his house? Are you berserk?"

"Just talk to him. He's nice. Nellie will be staying at his house. I can visit Nellie. Can you just talk to him, Mom? Can you just?"

Lydia approached the phone as if it was a coiled rattler, hissing and ready to strike. She picked up the receiver with two fingers so gingerly that it almost slipped out of her hand. She adjusted her grip and brought the phone to her ear, her free hand squeezing her temples with her eyes squinted closed.

"This is Lydia Mascar," she began. "Who am I speaking with, please?"

Sally tuned out after that, preferring instead to try to imagine how she would handle getting to know Nellie. At least it would take her mind off of what was going on inside her.

Nineteen

Cecil was in the back of Lucas's garage using a small power tool to ream out a corroded oil inlet. Under Nellie's guidance, he had become very proficient using small power tools. Today Nellie had promised to show him how to use something called a plasma cutter to cut out a bracket. Then they were going to drill it with the big drill press that Cecil had been eyeing. Nellie had also promised to show Cecil how the massive metal bender worked because they had to bend the bracket to make it fit properly.

Cecil had jumped out of bed an hour early anxious to have Pappa drive him to Lucas's house so he could get to work. This would be his first exposure to tools of this magnitude and he couldn't wait to turn them on. The morning was dragging because all of the parts he was responsible for were already cleaned. It was approaching noon, but Nellie, who usually came in around ten, hadn't arrived yet.

Cecil looked toward the garage door as he had done every five minutes for the past two hours hoping to see Nellie arrive.

Nellie was a tall thin man who hadn't spoken much in the few days they had worked together, but he sure knew what he was doing with the tools.

This time when Cecil looked up, a person was indeed in the doorway. But instead of Nellie it was Lucas. And next to him was a girl. A girl he knew. Seeing the familiar face of his classmate at first seemed natural; she was always appearing around Cosper in strange places and at strange times. He would be in the hardware store with his father and she would come over to him and ask what he was doing. When she had first started doing that he thought she was teasing him. He'd get angry and walk away. Over the course of time he realized she was genuinely interested in what he was doing. She just never spoke much, apparently content to simply watch him.

One day he invited her to his house to see his latest engine project. They had walked home together after school, Sally listening while he explained how the engine worked. She sat with him when he took it apart. When he started rebuilding the engine, she actually handed him the parts in order. At one point, she asked if she could put the manifold on. Her fingers were not well coordinated, and she struggled with the small bolts.

He had expected her to make fun of him in school the next day, but she never did. Sally had come to his house several times after that and the visits only stopped when Alice Spencer made fun of her in class one day for spending time with him.

When he looked up again, Lucas was gone, but Sally was still standing at the front of the garage, waiting. He then remembered he was in Dallas and not Cosper. *What is she doing here? Her face is different, more agitated. She's moving slower as well. Maybe it really isn't Sally. The heat must be playing tricks.*

He finished reaming the inlet and made a mental note to rebuild it if they had time. There was a slight pitting inside the opening that offended his sense of perfection.

Lucas came through the door from the house. "Sally, I'm afraid your father's not here. He got up early this morning and left. I thought he was coming back, but apparently he's not. He packed up and left. I'm terribly sorry."

Sally nodded, but kept her eyes focused on the driveway. "Does he know I'm here?"

"I told him last night you'd be here today. I'm sorry."

"Sally," Cecil called from amidst the parts, "what are you doing here?"

"Cecil!" she responded, her face opening wide to him, "what are *you* doing here?" She ran to where he was, hopping over the debris on the floor. "Why are you in Dallas?"

"I came to visit my Pappa," Cecil replied. "I'm working here, rebuilding an old car!" Cecil was excited about showing someone what he was doing. "Why are you here?"

"I've come to see Nellie."

Cecil's face went blank.

"Nellie's my father," Sally said, mostly to the floor.

"Nellie's your father?" Cecil exclaimed. "I didn't know you had a father."

"I don't really. I came to find him."

Again, Cecil's face went blank. "Is he lost? I can help find him."

Lucas came over to where the teens were standing. "I suppose you both know each other. I'm sorry. I hadn't put it together. You're both the same age and both from Cosper. You must be in school together. What a small world! Come, let's go get lunch. Cecil, your grandfather's waiting out by the pool."

On the way back to the garage after lunch, Henry and Lucas walked several feet behind Sally and Cecil. Henry commented, "I've never known Cecil to talk so much. You can't usually get the boy to speak when you want him to. Did you hear him at lunch? He got real animated."

"I never looked closely at him before," Lucas volunteered, "but he's a handsome boy. You can see it when his face comes alive. Doesn't seem to happen all that often though. When he's concentrating on the engine his serenity is a pleasure to behold. It's as if nothing else in the world exists."

"For him, that may be true. He's in his own universe. He has a single focus. I took him to a doctor last week. They ran some tests. The doctor says he's got something called Asperger's

Syndrome. I don't know much about it, but it seems he fixates on one thing at a time. When he does, nothing else matters. He has no social clues, doesn't even know when someone is joking—or angry for that matter. He's a good boy. Means well."

"He and Sally sure get along," Lucas commented. "She's a nice kid, but a little...slow I think. Never knew her daddy. Then suddenly her mother said the most important thing in the world is her coming here to be with him. Nellie got all nervous and cut out. I don't expect him back."

"When she's not talking with Cecil she...she...well she looks worried. Almost like she's hiding something."

"But she sure listens to Cecil," Lucas replied, "when he talks about the project. I heard him explaining about the gas turbine and the turbocharger he put together. He told her how it worked and what he planned to do next."

"I saw them talking," Henry admitted, "but didn't hear what they were saying."

"And Sally's no slouch either when it comes to engines. She was eating it up and asking questions about what Cecil was telling her. I suppose it's in the genes. Like father, like daughter."

"It's too bad Nellie split. He was good for Cecil and would have been great for Sally."

"That man's got problems. He doesn't relate to kids. He's frightened of them somehow. When Sally called, I wanted to say something to her, but thought better of it. Nellie told me a few years back what it was, but I forgot the details. Something happened when he was young. Dropped something, maybe a sister. He was rambling when he told me, started to shake. He wasn't making much sense, and I couldn't push him."

"That sounds like it was babies. These are teens."

"All I know is that when I told him about Sally coming he got jittery. Left the house early this morning. I'd be surprised if he comes back."

"So what are you going to do with the engine spread out all over the floor and the car on its way?"

"Plan B."

"And that is—?"

"Cecil and I — and I suppose Sally — will put it together."

"What about the machine tools?"

"I know enough. Cecil knows exactly what needs to be done. We'll do it."

"It's your car. But Cecil doesn't know beans about big power tools."

"You'd be surprised what he knows. You need to see the turbocharger he built. I happened to have a kit from another project. Before I knew what he was doing, it was together. He drew a picture for a modification to make the turbocharger fit with the engine we built. I tell you the kid's a genius. He sees a machine and instantly knows how it works. He also usually knows how to make it work better than the original design."

"What are you going to do with Sally?"

"She'll stay with me. That's what I promised her mother. There's plenty of room. Since I lost Emma, the place's not been the same. It'll be good to have someone moving about. I sense she didn't come for Nellie. Her mother was shocked that she even wanted to see him. According to her mother, the girl has refused to acknowledge Nellie her whole life. So I have to question why now?"

"If she gets to be too much for you, Ida and I will take her. We have an extra room as well."

By the time Lucas and Henry arrived back at the garage, the teens were deeply engrossed in the engine. Cecil was busy explaining the workings of the engine to an eager Sally.

Lucas gave them time to make it through the engine and then joined them. "I thought I'd turn on the saw and we can cut some brackets. You two can watch and then I'll show you how to set the press up for drilling the parts."

After cutting the first bracket, Cecil announced, "I can do that."

"You sure?" Lucas responded.

"I can do that," Cecil repeated.

"Okay, be careful. Hold the metal like this." Lucas started for the boy, but before he reached him, Cecil had positioned the metal and the blade was halfway through it. Lucas observed the boy for a moment, then commented, "You do that better than I did. I never thought to hold the metal that way. I've never seen anyone do it that way either."

"Saves metal," was Cecil's response. "More parts."

Lucas had to acknowledge that the boy was right. The cut-out pattern was so perfect that with just one extra pass two brackets fell out instead of one.

When the brackets were cut, Cecil walked to the drill press, selected a bit and inserted it in the chuck. Lucas stood back and watched. "And just where did you learn how to work that? Your grandfather says you've never been around power tools."

"Just know, is all."

And so the day went. Sally remained at Cecil's side, positioning herself to catch the scrap, but declining Cecil's offers for her to run the equipment. They talked while they worked and several times Lucas admonished Cecil to pay more attention to what he was doing. But any close observer of the boy would have seen that he was concentrating on the machinery with a keen intensity. Cecil was in a world of his own. A world he was eager to share with his friend, Sally Mascar.

The next several days passed in this way, each day ending with the four of them going to dinner. On Sunday they knocked off early and Grandma Ida joined them for a movie. They saw the opening of *The Lion King* and afterward went back home for ice cream. Pappa watched the Rangers lose a close game while the teens played Atari games.

Ida and Henry were excited that Cecil was so content and yet so alive. They were, however, worried about Sally. Several times when the girl thought no one was looking, her face fell and she seemed lost within herself. The girl appeared to be overcome with sadness so deep it sent shivers down Ida's spine.

ఴ☙

The Ghia arrived on Monday, a mass of rust, broken mirrors, broken lights and bent fenders. Someone had cut X's in the interior upholstery and liners. The few remaining window and door handles were mostly useless.

Cecil surveyed the car. "Piece of junk is what it is!" he pronounced.

"That's the point," Lucas replied. "We get to rebuild it the way we want."

The boy's face came alive. "Use the handles for patterns. We can make new ones that work better."

"Looks like we got our work cut out for us," Lucas announced. "Let's get at it. I suggest Sally and I rip out the interior. Cecil, you can measure for the mounting brackets."

"And the handles," Cecil added.

"And the handles as well," Lucas responded.

The tasks assigned, they all got busy, breaking for lunch and finishing around four in the afternoon. Cecil and Sally changed into bathing suits and jumped into the pool.

The next day Cecil and Sally decided to remain in the garage during lunch. Cecil suggested it would be fun to sit in the back seat and listen to music. Without waiting for a response, Cecil covered the open seats with cardboard and shop rags. He then busied himself connecting three power cords together and ran the long line across the floor to the car. He then plugged in the shop radio, and music filled the garage.

Being so busy getting the car ready for them, Cecil did not realize Sally had turned her back and walked across the garage. The image had triggered a vision of her and Wade and the repressed terror flooded through her. The sound of the radio reminded her of the songs she had sung to Wade before he... before he...

"Come, Sally!" Cecil called. "It's all ready. Come see how it looks."

Sally turned to face Cecil, but could not force herself to walk toward the car.

"Come, Sally," Cecil called again. "It's nice in there. I made it nice for us."

Sally reluctantly walked across the floor to where Cecil was standing, his face beaming as he held the door open for her.

"I can't get...I can't—"

"You won't get dirty. I promise. See I covered everything. We have the radio and all."

Looking into Cecil's innocent eyes Sally relented and, sucking in her breath, climbed in the backseat.

Cecil got in after her and Sally said, "I'll sit over here and you sit over there."

Cecil did exactly as he had been instructed and when Pappa and Lucas retuned with sandwiches and Cokes they found the two of them in the back of the Ghia, their legs outstretched facing each other, listening to a top-40 station with their heads bobbing in unison to the beat.

The remainder of the month slipped by quickly, as did the first two weeks of August. Nellie had not put in an appearance and, indeed, was not missed. The car was stripped completely and, following Cecil's instructions, they had begun the lengthy and time-consuming rebuilding project. Clearly they would not finish by summer's end.

On the last day of work, the teens agreed it had been the best summer ever. They high-fived and promised each other they'd finish the car the next summer.

Ida baked a lemon-coconut cake in celebration of Sally's fifteenth birthday. They held the party poolside at Lucas's house and celebrated with barbeque chicken, roasted corn on the cob and Ida's homemade potato salad.

Cecil spent his time in the pool, mostly watching the pool sweep, and coming out only to eat. Sally sat on the side, dangling her feet, a large shirt hanging over her shorts.

After clearing the table, Ida eased herself down next to the birthday girl. They sat in silence for a while. Then Ida leaned in close next to Sally. "Is something wrong, dear?" she inquired solicitously. "You seem tired. No doubt my husband and Lucas have been working you too hard. Maybe it's good you're going back to school."

"Oh, no," Sally quickly replied, "I love doing the work. I've learned so much. I really like watching Cecil. He's so good. He's amazing."

"Perhaps you need to get more sleep then. You're about dead on your feet. And you didn't eat very much."

"I'll be okay. I was up late last night."

"I dunno," Ida said. "It just seems something is wrong. Want to tell me?"

"Nothing's wrong, Mrs. Harris," the girl replied, leaning away. "I'm just thinking about going back home. I'm sad the summer's over. Cecil and I work so well together. He's different, but we're good friends, you know."

"Yes, I know. It's real nice to have a friend."

"Back home they make fun of him," the girl said, "but I like him."

"And it appears he likes you, dear. Please remember, if you need anything you can call me anytime."

When Sally didn't respond, Ida called to Cecil. "Time to get out of the pool. In fact, it's time to call it a day. Come say goodbye to Sally. We're leaving early in the morning."

"Can I stay a little while and talk with Sally?" Cecil pleaded. "We won't be in the same school when we get home."

"Just a few minutes. We have to get up early."

Cecil ran to the house to change and was back a moment later. Sally hadn't left the side of the pool. Cecil sat down next to her. "School starts in a week," he said. "I'll miss listening to music with you, and talking. I have to leave tomorrow. They're driving me home."

"I'll miss you too," she replied softly. "You're my only real friend."

"I'm coming back at Thanksgiving to finish the Ghia. Can't wait to fire her up! Can you come back with me? That would be fun."

"Sure," Sally answered, half-heartedly. "That'd be nice."

"Hey, I have a good idea. Want to drive home in the car with us? We can make room. Pappa has a big car."

Cecil's smile faded when she said, "No, thanks. I'm taking the bus home."

"Come with us. It'll be a fun ride. We can talk about the project."

"I said I'm taking the bus! Now leave me alone, Cecil. Summer fun is over."

Sally had never once spoken to him that way. He turned away from her. Quietly, the mantra began, "I don't understand. I don't understand. I don't understand."

TWENTY

Caroline Harris turned eighteen on August twenty-second. If things were different, she would be excited about starting her senior year in high school. But the only modicum of excitement she felt was about the removal of the cast from her leg. It wasn't that she would feel anything different because she felt nothing. The excitement, if what she felt could be called excitement, stemmed from knowing that now her physical therapy could move forward in earnest.

Birthday presents were piled high on the stand in her hospital room, but she couldn't open any of them without help. The truth was she didn't really care if they were ever opened. The only thing she wanted was the one thing she was told she would most likely never have—the use of her arms and legs.

Grandma Ida and Pappa were there; they had brought Cecil home from Dallas the day before. Grandma had insisted on baking a huge chocolate cake. Candles weren't allowed in any patient rooms, so the party was held on the first floor in the not-very-inviting environment of a staff conference room.

She was nervous as her bed was wheeled out of her room on the way to the transport elevator. The only time she had been off the fifth floor since her accident was for the interminable CAT scans and therapy. She was depressed at the thought of years of therapy leading nowhere. She said as much to her father.

Joe had responded, "With hard work you'll be able to move around on your own, even go to college. Many, many people do it. You can as well."

That thought held out hope, and it was that hope that Caroline used to get through each day.

Several people called her name and wished her well as the bed moved down the hall. But Caroline didn't recognize any of them, nor did she try to respond. She felt as if she was on display, a prime example of who-knows-what being paraded down the hall.

Grandma Ida held the cake high, its flaming candles threatening to burn down the hospital, when Caroline's bed came through the door of the conference room. "Two for good luck," Ida explained.

"Thank you, Grandma," Caroline managed. "It looks nice." She was learning to speak slowly and to control her breathing. She had been assured by the speech therapist that with time her speech patterns would return to normal. She had also been assured that within a month the halo holding her head rigid would be removed.

Tears gushed down Ida's cheeks when her granddaughter couldn't manage enough breath to even blow out a single candle.

Maggie, forcing back her own tears, stood over the bed, opening the presents, wondering if her daughter would ever be able to enjoy any of them: books and clothing mostly. "Get well soon," was the theme of the cards, and the impact of each one cut deeper than the previous.

Cecil stood in the back of the room while the presents were being opened, afraid to touch his sister for fear of hurting her worse than she already was. When Caroline had first been wheeled in he had caught a glimpse of excited recognition in Caroline's eyes. A brief second later, however, the sparkle was replaced with the deepest sadness he had ever seen. Cecil looked down. It was the first time in his life that he had ever understood what a person was feeling just by looking at that person.

Maggie moved around the room picking up pieces of ribbon and birthday wrapping, her cheeks wet with tears. Cecil looked at her but did not understand why she was crying or why she couldn't stop crying. His attention turned to his sister when he noticed her legs twitching. "Your feet are moving," he called out. "I thought—"

"It's a mechanical device," his dad explained. "It stimulates her nerves and muscles."

"Can I see?" Cecil asked, running to the bed and stripping the covers back.

"Hey," Caroline managed, "stop that."

"Cecil, this is not the time," Joe said, moving to stop his son.

"But I want to see how it works."

"Not now, Cecil!" Joe said. "This is not the time."

"Get him away from me." Caroline demanded, evidencing more emotion than she had at any time since the accident. "He creeps me out." Her head fell back on the pillow, exhaustion overwhelming her anger.

"Come Cecil, let's take a walk." Joe suggested. "Caroline needs to be alone for now."

"I have pictures of the turbine I rebuilt," the boy protested, reaching for his back pocket. "You haven't even seen my pictures!"

"We can look at them on our walk. Let's go."

"Caroline won't see them."

"Who cares about your stupid pictures!" his sister cried. "You don't get it, do you! I'll never get out of this bed, and all you can think about is your stupid pictures!"

"That's enough!" Joe snapped. "Come Cecil." With that he grabbed his son's arm and began to pull him from the room.

"It's not just pictures!" Cecil shot back over his shoulder. "I can fix things. I can help."

Joe hooked his foot around the door to close it behind them. Turning to the boy, he said, "Your sister's in trouble and you're thinking about how some piece of machinery works?"

"I want to make her better."

"You can start by just staying away from her. The two of you...well...just stay away from her. Don't worry about how her equipment works — or why it works. The doctors will take good care of her."

"I want to help. Nobody lets me help. People make fun of me. I like Lucas. He doesn't make fun of me. He lets me help."

"Listen, Cecil," Joe patiently explained. "Your sister's never going to walk or use her arms ever again! She's going to need someone to feed her, dress her, and my God even help her with the bathroom. That's a full time job. We need your cooperation."

"She can't go to the bathroom by herself?"

"She can't do *anything* by herself. We all need to help. Even getting her to the point where she can go home is going to be long and difficult. Please try and understand."

"I understand. I understand everything." His eyes fell to the floor and he started mumbling, "I understand. I understand. I understand."

Joe, hoping to distract him, said, "By the way, I just received a call from Sally's mother. She's very upset. Sally wasn't on the bus. Do you know if she was planning to go anywhere else?"

"Sally is my friend. She worked on the engine. We're friends. She's the only friend I've ever had."

"I know all that. Lucas put her on the bus, I understand. Did Sally say anything to you about...about getting off? Going somewhere else?"

"Nothing."

"Sure?"

"I'm sure." Cecil reached for his back pocket and his eyes came alive. "Look at my pictures now?"

Joe was anxious to get back to Caroline, but he was mindful of his promise to look at Cecil's pictures. Taking the stack of prints from Cecil, he gave them a quick shuffle-through without allowing Cecil the time for any commentary. "I have to get back to your sister," he explained. "We have to take her back to her room. You can explain these to me some other time."

☯☾☽

At home later that night Cecil was listlessly disassembling an old engine that Joe's friend, Bart, had brought by. Pappa, after observing him for a while, said, "Your heart's not in it, Cecil. What's troubling you?"

"Nothing."

"I watched you all summer, and I know when you're not yourself. Is it your sister? Is that what's bothering you?"

"Sally. She's my friend. Sally's lost."

"What do you mean lost? She can't be lost. Lucas put her on the bus to Cosper."

"Daddy said she didn't come home on the bus. She got lost."

"That's not possible," Pappa replied, frowning. He liked the troubled girl.

"She's lost," Cecil insisted.

"Joe," Henry called out to the kitchen, "can you come in here?"

His son dutifully strode into the den, drying his hands on a dishtowel.

"What's up with Sally?" Henry asked. Cecil says she didn't arrive home."

"I don't know anything more than that. Her mother called this morning and wanted to know what Cecil knew. I checked with Cecil and he says he knows nothing."

"What's the mother's number? I liked that girl. Your mother thought something was wrong in Dallas. She asked the girl about it. Sally claimed nothing was wrong. She was tired is all. Your mother was concerned about her."

Joe went into the kitchen and returned with the Mascar's phone number.

A few minutes later Henry had a distraught Lydia Mascar on the line. After explaining who he was, Henry managed to calm the woman enough to elicit from her what little she knew. Sally had boarded the bus in Dallas bound for Cosper. She never arrived.

When the woman began to cry, Henry tried to comfort her by saying, "I know Lucas gave her several hundred dollars as payment for her work on the car. At least she has money on her."

There was nothing more Lydia could add. Both the local and the state police were investigating.

Henry hung up and immediately called Lucas. A few minutes later Henry turned to Joe. "Strange. Lucas saw her board the bus to Cosper. Apparently, the bus changed drivers in Austin, but the second driver claims there was no teenage girl on board when he took over."

"She got on, she had to get off," Joe said, glancing toward Cecil. "Could she have gotten off in Dallas before the bus left?"

"Lucas says she was on the bus when it pulled out of the station."

"The kid's fourteen! She must be in some sort of trouble," Joe said, settling on the sofa across from his father.

"Fifteen," Henry corrected. "We had a birthday party for her in Dallas. Your mother commented at the time she seemed depressed and worried."

"Are you talking about me?" Ida asked, coming down from the bedroom where she had been resting.

Henry looked up. "How come when I want you, you can't hear a thing I say? The minute I say something about you, you're all ears."

"Learned it from you, I suppose," Ida shot back. "What's this all about, anyway?"

Ida looked tired. Seeing her granddaughter in the hospital, unable to do anything but lift her head, had drained her. She slumped down on the sofa next to her son.

Henry repeated the news about Sally. When he finished, Ida said, "That girl is in some sort of trouble. I never did believe that story about her coming to Dallas to meet her father. When he didn't show up she didn't seem to care. Henry, didn't you even say how she actually seemed relieved? All she seemed to care about was that car."

"And talking with Cecil," Henry added. "The two of them were inseparable all summer. They ate almost all their meals together. Cecil padded up the back seat frame and the two of them ate lunch there every day."

Joe's interest peaked. "They didn't—"

"Not so far as I could tell. I'd look in on them from time to time. He was on one side, she on the other. They talked, listened to music, nothing else. Far as I know, they never even held hands."

"They went swimming at Lucas's," Ida said, "Maybe they —"

"Someone was always around," Henry responded, feeling the need to defend his performance as chaperone. Actually, Sally stopped swimming after a few weeks. After that, she didn't even wear the swim suit Lucas bought her."

"Come to think of it...I...I—" Ida began. Then she stopped.

"What?" Joe asked.

"Just a thought. Can't be."

"What?" Joe pressed.

"I don't know. If I didn't know better I'd say...I'd say she was...in the family way."

"Nonsense!" Joe responded instinctively. "Sally? Pregnant? My God, the girl's barely fifteen!"

Ida shrugged. "That's why I didn't say anything. It makes no sense. I was thinking it at her party, but couldn't get her to talk to me. I told myself I was just a confused old lady."

"Now, Ida, don't be starting stories," Henry said. "She's a nice girl."

"I'm just saying what I thought. And besides, nice girls do sometimes get that way. But she's so young." Ida lowered her voice, and said, loud enough so that only Joe and Henry could hear. "I don't know what you thought, but Sally doesn't seem to me to be overly bright. She's a bit slow. I could never get more than one-word answers from her all summer. I asked her about books once and she said she didn't much care for reading."

"Her mother told dad she flunked math and English, and maybe even history," Joe said, acknowledging his mother's comment.

"Some boy took advantage of her, is my guess," Ida said, grimacing.

Joe glanced over at Cecil who was having trouble removing a drive belt from the engine he was working on. "Hmm. She *was* with Cecil all summer," he allowed. He studied the boy for a while, then added, "Never saw him have trouble with a drive belt before. The boy's agitated."

"It's not him," Ida cautioned. "Boy's got only one thing on his mind, and it's not girls. And besides," she added, "I've seen enough pregnant girls in my day to be pretty sure that it happened before she came to Dallas."

The phone rang. Joe answered, then called to his father, "It's Lucas."

Henry took the call in the kitchen and when he returned all color had drained from his face. "The police have now definitely traced Sally to Austin. Seems she bought a ticket only to Austin and not to Cosper. That's why the bus driver left without her. But here's the real kicker: phone company records show a call from Lucas's house two days earlier to a pregnancy hot line."

"So I was right," Ida said.

"The agency won't give out any information," Henry continued, "other than to say they didn't pick up or meet anyone at the bus station on that date."

"What do they think it all means?" Joe asked.

"I don't know. Lucas was just giving us a heads up. He expects the Cosper police will want to talk with Cecil and maybe to you."

"Shit! That's all we need!" Joe fumed. "I've taken so much time off the job since the accident I'm going to get fired! And now this! The company's got my route covered well enough, and they're supportive and all, but there's a limit. Between Caroline and Cecil, I don't know how I'll ever get back to work."

Twenty-One

Lucas's prediction came true. Detective Mackay Scott called the next morning to ask Joe to stop by the Cosper police station as soon as he could. Joe had known Scott from their high school days when Scott was the senior quarterback and Joe was a sophomore defensive end. It had been Joe's job to harass Scott in practice and Joe had done an exceptional job of making Mackay's quarterback life miserable. The two of them had words in the locker room on more than one occasion.

They were now seated opposite each other in a windowless closet of an office. Neither had maintained their high school physiques and the room barely held them both. Detective Scott expressed his regrets about Caroline and Joe nodded absently. Then Scott, trying to lighten the mood, said, "They keep promising us a new building, but it never happens." He shrugged his shoulder, as if to apologize for the cramped and messy space. "Need to pass the bond issue."

"I'll vote for it, but people don't want more taxes."

"This is what you get, then. Well, let's get on with it. Tell me what you know about Sally Mascar. I know your son was in Dallas this summer with her. Was he there because of Caroline?"

Joe explained why they had decided to send the boy to spend the summer with his grandparents. He went on to relate what his father and mother had told him.

"Your mother's right-on about the pregnancy. Sally called a hot line. That much we now know for certain. It's a national hot line actually. When Sally told them she was in Dallas but wanted something out of town, the call was routed to Austin. She told them she was eighteen, so no bells went off."

"So where is she? Do you know what happened?"

"That's why you're here. We *don't* know. She walked out of the Austin bus station. That much we know. Then she vanished. Trail's cold."

"So what can I add? I was in the hospital with Caroline all that day and every day."

"Did Cecil say anything—anything at all—about Sally?"

"I told you all I know."

"He didn't help her in any way?"

"Kid's into engines. That's all he knows. Frankly, he's not very social."

"You certain he didn't say anything that would help us?"

Something in Detective Scott's tone, or in his eyes, sent off alarm bells in Joe's head. He pushed back from the desk and the chair hit a box of files. "We finished?" Joe asked, standing to leave.

"Just about," Scott replied. "I just want to be sure you don't know something I should know."

"I don't know any more than I told you. Cecil doesn't know anything. Please leave him out of this. The boy gets all upset and that's the last thing in the world I need right now. We already have our hands full. Shit, Maggie blames herself somehow for Caroline's accident. She cries day and night. Any time she's away from Caroline, she's crying. We're both at the breaking point."

"I can't very well do that," Scott said, referring to Joe's plea to not involve Cecil in the investigation. "Your boy spent the whole summer with Sally Mascar. I don't know what happened or didn't happen, but the simple truth is he's the person who knows more about Sally than anyone else at this point. He's our only lead."

"What are you saying exactly?"

"Fourteen-year-old boy and girl. Remember back then what that was like for us."

"This is absurd! Cecil's not a typical fourteen-year-old. He has social problems. The last thing in the world he's thinking about is girls."

"Well, the girl didn't get herself pregnant. It didn't happen by itself."

"This is preposterous!" Joe was in the hall, his back to Scott.

The detective called after him. "I agree," he replied. "That's why we're going all out on this. It's not just a case of a girl getting knocked up. She's possibly dead."

"Dead!" Joe responded, turning abruptly. "What makes you think—"

"State police have been investigating a series of missing girls. All of them came by bus to Austin. Sally's disappearance is the first time they've been able to positively link a disappearance with the pregnancy hotline. The hotline appears to be legit, but someone has tapped into it and they know when a frightened, pregnant girl is coming to town. State police believe the girls are picked up at the bus station believing they are going with representatives from the hotline." Scott took a deep breath before continuing. "Two girls have been found dead. There's reason to believe others are being held as slaves for prostitution."

"Oh, my God!" Joe responded, "I had no idea that stuff really existed! Sally, poor child!"

"I'll need to speak to your parents. Please ask them to stop by later today. I'll be here working the phones. And if you think of anything, please call me. I want to get to the bottom of what happened to that young lady."

꧁꧂

"Let me understand," Henry said when Joe repeated his experience with Detective Scott, "they think Cecil got Sally pregnant? They're fools, is all I can say."

"He didn't come right out and say it, but it's on his mind alright. Cecil's got enough problems as it is. They want to talk to Cecil. That's what I'm upset about. The boy will go to pieces."

While Joe was discussing the situation with his parents, Scott was already at the high school talking to Cecil in the principal's office. After acknowledging his name, Cecil refused to speak further, keeping his eyes focused on the floor.

The principal, a man in his mid-sixties and a year from retirement, had no patience with this strange kid. "Listen, son, you're new here and already in big trouble. You need to answer the detective's questions. You ever hear of Juvenile Court? Well, that's where you're going if you don't start behaving yourself."

Scott asked, "Did you touch Sally this summer?"

Cecil, his eyes on the floor, nodded his head. "Sally's my friend."

"Is that a yes?" Scott asked.

Cecil again nodded his head.

"Answer the question in words!" the principal demanded, "or so help me you're going to Juvvy!"

"Yes," Cecil managed. "I didn't do anything. Sally's my friend."

"That will be determined," the principal responded. "Now answer the questions."

"You say you touched Sally Mascar," Scott repeated, his pen making marks in a note pad.

"Yes."

"How many times?"

"Every day."

"Where did you touch her?"

"Legs."

"Anywhere else?"

"No."

"Did you touch her private parts?"

Cecil's face went red, but he remained quiet.

"Answer him!" the principal demanded, the color in his own face deepening.

"No."

"No, what," Scott asked, his voice gentler now, trying to balance the heat coming from the principal.

"I didn't touch her...there." Cecil replied, refusing to look up from the floor.

"Where didn't you touch her?" Scott pressed.

"Private places."

"Boy, this is serious!" the principal said, his face now deep red. "Do you know how girls become pregnant?"

Cecil continued to look at the floor, his fists beginning to pound on his legs. He said nothing.

"I asked you how girls get pregnant," the principal demanded, leaning forward over his desk. "Answer me this instant!"

"Did nothing! Did nothing! Did nothing! Did nothing! Did nothing! Did nothing!" Cecil's eyes remained riveted to the floor, but the mantra continued. "Did nothing! Did nothing! Did nothing! Did nothing! Did nothing!"

"Stop that this instant!" the principal, his composure now gone, screamed. He pounded the table with his fist. "Your behavior is unacceptable! I won't have it in my school! I won't have it!"

"Did nothing! Did nothing! Did nothing! Did nothing! Did nothing! Did nothing!"

"I said stop it!" The principal jumped to his feet, "Do you want to get expelled? His voice was loud enough to be heard in the waiting room through the closed door. "I'll have none of this behavior in my school! None at all!"

"Did nothing! Did nothing! Did nothing! Did nothing! Did nothing! Did nothing!" Cecil was deep into his stuck-in-set perseverative behavior and no amount of yelling by the principal or by the Detective could bring him out of it. The chant continued with Cecil locked in a trance, unaware that the principal had grasped his arm and yanked him to his feet.

Scott stood as well. "This is going nowhere," he said, trying to calm the situation. "Leave the boy be. We'll pick this up later."

"Take him with you!" the principal barked. "He's expelled!" He shoved Cecil toward the door. "I don't want him in this school! He doesn't belong here! Get him out of my sight!"

Detective Scott put his hand on the boy's shoulder. "I'll take you home now, Cecil." His voice was firm, but gentle. "I need to talk to your grandparents anyway."

"Did nothing! Did nothing! Did nothing! Did nothing! Did nothing! Did nothing!" The mantra was deeply set now, even as Cecil was led out of the office and through the waiting room.

Twenty-Two

Two days later, Detective Scott's phone rang.

"This is Richard Henderson. Am I speaking with Detective Mackay Scott?"

"You are? What is it?"

"I'm the eighth grade teacher over at the grade school and I may have some information on Sally Mascar. I read about her disappearance in the paper and I'm concerned."

"Go ahead," Scott said, picking up a pen and positioning his notebook in front of him on the desk.

"This may be nothing, but at the class play back in May I caught Sally creeping around the school. Actually, she and an older boy were on an upper floor, either the second or third, I can't recall. They shouldn't have been up there at that time. When we, the Principal and I, asked Sally about it she maintained they were looking for a bathroom. But there are at least two men's rooms on the first floor where the auditorium is."

"And when exactly was this?"

"May twentieth, Henderson said. "I've already confirmed it on my calendar. That was a Friday. We spoke to Sally on Monday. She was...hiding something."

"The boy wasn't Cecil Harris by any chance, was it?"

"Goodness no!" the teacher replied. "Cecil? He wouldn't know what to do with a girl." Henderson laughed a nervous laugh. "The boy's some kind of mechanical savant. Genius with things that move, but only *mechanical* things that move, if you know what I mean. He's oblivious to everything else. In fact, Cecil was with me at the time I saw Sally. She was with the Spencer boy."

"The Spencer boy? The ones who own the *Sentinel?*"

"Exactly."

"I know the family," Scott said, pausing to think this through. "They only have one son. Isn't he over at Holbrook? He's got to be, let's see, he's at least nineteen, maybe even twenty. What's he doing in the grade school?"

"That's what we asked Sally. But we never got a straight answer. His name is Wade Spencer. I remember him from when he was here. He changed a bit since eighth grade, but it was him."

"You're sure?" Scott asked, his pen racing across the paper.

"Sally confirmed it was Wade. You might want to check with the principal. Her name's Natalie Hill. She has good insight into these things and has a sixth sense about what makes kids tick."

Scott raced over to the school to follow up with Principal Hill. She confirmed what Henderson had said and volunteered that in her opinion, the two of them had done something beyond holding hands.

The next day Scott interviewed Wade Spencer in person. Wade confirmed that he had been with Sally Mascar at the play. He said he was only looking for a bathroom when Henderson caught them on the upper floor. He insisted that he left her at the school when the play was over. He hadn't seen her all summer. No, he didn't know where she was and didn't know she had been in Dallas all summer.

Scott again interviewed Lydia Mascar and through tears and hysteria, the mother again related what she remembered from her confrontation with Sally the morning after the play. "Something was wrong with her. Sally's not the smartest person in the world. She does a lot of dumb things, but she's always been a good girl. I had the strong feeling she was lying to me, covering up something."

"Something is missing here. Wade says he last saw Sally at the school when the play was over. According to what you just told me, Sally claims she had burgers at *The Pit* after the play. How did—"

"Lydia's eyes went wide. "Now I recall. There was a terrible accident at *The Pit* that night just after the play. Sally says she was there and did not see an accident. I thought it strange at the time, but I didn't know the exact timing so I thought it was possible."

"How did Sally get over to *The Pit*? Did she tell you?"

"Let me think. So much has happened, I don't...oh, yes. She said Jennie Spencer took a bunch of them for burgers."

Detective Scott said, "May I use your phone?"

"Certainly."

He then called the Spencer house and asked to speak to Jennie. A few minutes later he said to Lydia, "Seems you were right about the timing of that accident. Jennie Spencer said they went for ice cream instead. Traffic was all backed up."

"Why would Sally lie?"

"That's what I'm trying to find out."

ಬಿಸಿ

Scott conducted a second interview with Wade Spencer and he insisted he had left Sally at the school. Wade would only say that he went to the play with Sally, got lost looking for the men's room and had no idea where the girl was now.

An hour after the second interview, Jackson Spencer arrived at Scott's office. "Son," he began, making no pretext of being friendly, "if you have something on my son I want to know it," he demanded. "If not, leave him the hell alone! You understand me?"

"What I understand, Mr. Spencer," Scott responded, "is that your twenty-year-old son was seen in the company of a fourteen-year-old girl. We believe the girl became pregnant about that same time. Could be coincidence, could be statutory rape. Now she's disappeared. Other than her mother, your son may have been the last person in Cosper to see her."

"Sounds like an awful lot of speculation if you ask me. Sounds like you don't know for sure she was pregnant. And even if she was, there's no proof Wade was involved. Hell, what would he want with a fourteen-year-old? There have always been plenty of girls his own age coming around." Jackson lowered his voice. "And there's always, *Cospers Own*, if the boy gets horny. Hell, his granddaddy started that place and it's still going strong. Catch my drift?"

Scott didn't respond. It was his belief that *Cospers Own* was living on borrowed time, even protected as it was by powerful political forces. Exploitation of women did not sit well with him.

"And even if my son was involved with that Mascar girl there's not an iota of evidence linking him to the girl's disappearance. He told me he left her at the school after the play and hasn't even seen her since. Unless you can prove otherwise, I strongly suggest that it's in your best interest to leave him alone. If you ever find a link between my son and the girl's disappearance you call me and I'll bring him in to see you. But until then, you leave him be. You understand me?"

What Scott didn't say is that if he had a link between Wade Spencer and Sally Mascar's disappearance he would bring Wade in himself — in handcuffs, big-shot publisher's son or not.

But for now, Wade Spencer was a dead end.

Scott added an entry in his notebook. *WS possibly lying. Tone wrong. Follow up.*

༄༅

Four years later, Detective Scott was fatally injured in a drug bust gone bad. His notebooks were dutifully filed away. Among them the notebook for 1993 — the notebook in which he had made the entry *WS possibly lying*. Scott had updated the entry to note that *WS had checked into the hospital at 3:48 AM on May 21, 1993 complaining of a rib injury suffered in a fall and a nasty cut under his right eye. WS was vague concerning the precise location of the fall. Under pressure, he directed me to a rock he claims he tripped over. Rock too small? What was he doing out there at 3 AM? What caused the facial laceration? More here. Where's Sally Mascar?*

Despite the questions noted by the detective, the Mascar case was re-categorized from "pending" to "unsolved" when Scott died. And a short time later his captain, upon ascertaining that Lydia Mascar had moved away, had the file marked "closed." A four-year-old missing person case, especially one in which the leading suspect was a member of a prominent family, was not at the top of anyone's priority list.

BOOK TWO

Twenty-Three

Every year, Cecil Harris celebrated his birthday twice. Once on December 31, and then again the next day on January 1. His birth certificate showed his birth date as December 31, 1978. But his parents, in a stubborn attempt to adhere to the true facts of his birth, had always celebrated his arrival on New Year's Day. After their divorce, this dual birth date actually served a useful purpose, allowing each parent to celebrate a *real* birthday.

Turning twenty-two was no exception. Thus it was that on the last night of the year 2000, Cecil treated his father to dinner at the French Room at the Adolphus Hotel in Dallas. Joe Harris had moved to Dallas two years earlier with his new wife, Patty-Ann. As Joe told the story, after Caroline had her accident, Maggie devoted herself a hundred and fifty percent to taking care of their daughter, even going so far as to sleep in the same room with Caroline for fear the girl would need help in the middle of the night. A year passed and Maggie still hadn't returned to the marital bedroom. Whether out of parental concern, or from an unspoken sense of guilt, Maggie devoted every waking moment to the care of Caroline.

Casual sex is how Joe characterized it when he first slept with Patty-Ann while away at a sales meeting. It had been two years since his wife had moved out of his bedroom and Patty-Ann looked exceptionally good. She was the company's executive secretary and hostess for the meeting. Joe had met her several times in years past, but had only spoken to her in passing.

A year later Joe moved out of the house in Cosper and filed for divorce. Two years later he accepted a position as Vice-President of sales at a competitor's company. The position required him to move to Dallas, which he reluctantly did. Patty-Ann joined him in Dallas and they were married within a month.

The New Year's Eve party at the French Room was Cecil's idea. Lucas had hosted a party for him in this very same room a month earlier and Cecil liked the atmosphere. Sitting across the table, his father raised his glass. "Happy birthday, Cecil," Joe began, "and many happy returns of the day. Who could have imagined that getting tossed out of Cosper High School would have been the best thing that could ever have happened to you? You've done well for yourself. You look handsome in your tux. Happy twenty-first."

Cecil, holding his glass high before plinking it first against Patty-Ann's and then against his father's, replied, "Attending the Dallas Magnet School for Science and Engineering was good, but being expelled from high school in my first week was certainly a bummer. It was especially bad because they thought I got my best and only friend ever pregnant." What he didn't mention was his abiding resentment at having been essentially tossed out of the family and banished to live in Dallas with his grandparents. His doctor had told the family they could fight the expulsion. But his parents were overwhelmed with caring for Caroline and allowed the expulsion to stand unchallenged.

Cecil proceeded to chug the champagne non-stop until the glass was drained.

"Be careful there," Joe admonished, "you're driving to Cosper later."

"I'm a big boy now, Dad. I can take care of myself real well."

"With as much as you've consumed tonight, you'd do well to drive in the morning," Joe pressed.

Cecil turned to face Patty-Ann. "What do you think? Am I too far gone to drive?"

"I don't believe anyone should drive when they've been drinking," Patty-Ann replied, not appreciating being dragged into this discussion. As long as she had known Joe she had observed the tension between him and his son. The boy visited his father only on rare occasions even though they both now had homes in Dallas.

"I can handle it. I'm good with cars, don't you think? You can't deny I'm good with cars."

"Building them, I agree. I'm talking about driving them," Patty-Ann replied, not one to back down.

Joe, trying to head off a confrontation between Cecil, who had not approved of the divorce, and Patty-Ann, who did not have the brainpower to keep up with Cecil, said, "You certainly are good with mechanics. How you managed to design those robots to help Caroline while you were still in college I'll never know. She's a different person now that she can climb out of bed herself. You have no idea how much that means to her."

"I did it for her. I told you I could help her."

"And built a company to help thousands in the process," Joe added.

"Lucas did all that. I only designed the bots. He did everything else."

"In college, no less," Joe commented.

"It was easy. The lab assignments were lame. I just found the parts in the robotics lab and built a prototype. The dean is a robotics expert, built a whole lab just for building things."

"I remember when Caroline first tried them out," Joe said, a slight smile replacing the tenseness he had been feeling. "Nearly broke her neck all over again."

"I fixed them after that."

"You sure did. The next time they worked perfectly."

"Got an A in the course."

"As well you should have."

Patty-Ann asked, "How did you get through high school so fast? Not even three years if I'm counting right."

"Pappa got tutors for me. I took tests and passed them. Then I skipped some grades. UT Dallas took me in early."

"But you never graduated. College I mean."

"Not necessary. I know how to make things work. More courses won't make a difference. I've got all the money I'll ever need."

Joe broke in. "Cecil's right. He learns better off by himself than he ever did in a class. Proof's in the pudding."

"Pudding," Cecil said, finishing his third glass of champagne, "I like pudding. What kind do we have?"

"Just a saying," Patty-Ann said, nodding in the direction of her husband.

Cecil turned to her. "You didn't answer my question. Can I drive or not?"

Joe again interjected, "It just makes more sense to get up early and drive in the morning. This is New Year's Eve. There's a reason they call this amateur night; a lot of people will be out driving who don't belong out there. By five in the morning they'll all be home or in the morgue. Either way, the roads'll be safer."

"Actually, I already told Mom I wouldn't be there until midafternoon. I'm staying here at the hotel for the night."

"Good plan," Joe said, relieved that Cecil, despite his recent wealth, showed good sense. "I'm proud of all you've accomplished and all before the age of twenty-one. It's remarkable. I'm only sorry your grandfather didn't live to see what you've become."

At the mention of Pappa, Cecil, who had learned to control his emotions, looked away for a moment. Then he refilled his glass and raised it. "To Pappa, wherever he is. I know he's looking down. I owe it all to you—and Lucas." Again Cecil drained his glass.

Patty-Ann glanced at her husband as if to gauge his reaction to Cecil's words. Joe sat quietly, simply placing his hand over his wife's, as if to say, *it's not worth getting into it with him.*

When Joe did speak, it was to say, "Thank you for making such a generous gift to the retirement village. Now for sure they'll take good care of your grandmother."

"I saw her today, and she…she didn't know who I was."

"She has her good days and bad."

"She went nuts."

"Alzheimer's. There's a difference. And keep your voice down. People are starting to look over here."

"Who cares? She doesn't know her ass from her elbow. I say she's nutso-rooney. Call it what it is." Cecil drained another glass and reached for yet another refill.

Joe, purposely lowering his voice, hoping his son would do likewise, replied, "Pappa did a good job of covering for her. The doctor said he suspects she's been deteriorating for quite a while."

Cecil consumed the refill, checked his watch, and then said, "Time for beddy-bye." He pushed his chair back from the table, stood and started toward the door. His right foot caught on the napkin that had slipped from his lap and he stumbled. Catching himself on the back of his chair, he exclaimed, "Waiter should have taken the napkin! Too bad I already tipped him. I thought this was a fancy place!"

"Cecil! People are looking. Keep your voice down, please."

"I paid my money. I can talk as loud as I want! It's a free country! They should mind their own business. All my life people are always telling me to stop saying something. People never listen to me." He put his hands over his ears. "Now I'm the one who doesn't have to listen!"

Joe was appalled, but kept his voice calm. "You've had more to drink than you should," he admonished. "I'm glad you only have to make it up to your room. Want us to help you? We can join you for midnight and watch the ball drop."

"Ball dropped already. It's in New York. It's past midnight in New York. I'll say goodbye down here. Nice seeing you both. Happy New Year!"

Joe and Patty-Ann stood aside and watched as Cecil slowly navigated the few steps down from the French Room to the main lobby. They saw him weave his way past the grill and turn the corner toward the elevator. Not once did he look back to give one final wave.

"He might be a millionaire," Patty-Ann commented, "but he's still a troubled child."

"Try sixty-million and counting," Joe answered, refusing to acknowledge that Cecil still had issues. "He'll be fine."

Twenty-Four

Cecil and his mother were sitting in the kitchen waiting for Caroline to join them. Cecil was on his second cup of tea, having consumed five cups of coffee on the five-hour trip from Dallas.

"You look terrible," Maggie commented. "What in the world have you been doing?" She had never seen him with his hair in such disarray and with such deep shadows lining his eyes. "You're not taking proper care of yourself."

"Too much celebrating with Dad is all." He didn't want to say anything about all the champagne he had consumed at dinner with them, let alone the bottle that he polished off afterwards in his room—a present from the hotel. "So how's Caroline doing? Does she like the latest update?"

"I'll let her tell you herself. She'll be down any minute. We expected you about four, not eight, so she went up for a nap. She doesn't have much stamina these days, but her spirits are good. You've done wonders for her, you know. I can't thank you enough, for both of us. You made my life easier as well."

"Don't talk about me behind my back," Caroline announced, slowly making her way into the kitchen.

"Hey, Sis!" he exclaimed, "The fact I didn't hear you coming means you've mastered the bots. That's great."

"You made it easy. Give me a big hello first before talking shop."

Cecil threw his arms around her. He would have picked her up and pulled her close, but from bitter experience he had learned that was not a good idea. So he kissed her gently on the cheek. "Come sit with us. I was just having some tea." He moved off to the side and watched intently as the robots he had designed propelled her across the floor. To a casual observer, not noticing the titanium struts running from her feet up the sides of her legs, and from her hands along the sides of her arms, it looked as if her legs and arms were bending naturally as she moved forward. In fact, Caroline was concentrating hard on balancing herself over the bots as they bent at her knees and elbows in a natural walking motion. She was controlling the motion by slight head and finger movements that she knew from painful experience could easily get out of control.

"You look like you need something stronger than tea," she said to Cecil when she stopped just short of the table. "I wasn't sure that was you when I turned the corner. Something wrong?"

"Like I was just telling Mom, too much celebrating."

"You mean too much alcohol. That stuff will kill you. Better stop while you're ahead. How's Dad?"

"Fine, I suppose. I didn't spend much time with him. Just dinner. Patty-Ann makes me uncomfortable. Does he get down to see you?"

"Sometimes. He says his new position keeps him busy in Dallas."

"You appear to have mastered the bots. I'm working on some improvements. Mostly to make it a bit smoother."

Maggie reached to pull out a chair for her daughter. "No, Mother," Caroline exclaimed, her breath now coming hard. "Let me do it. I have to show the genius how his gadgets work.

He'll hound me if I don't show him." Caroline's right hand shot forward and came to rest on the back of the chair. Slowly her fingers bent of their own accord to grasp the chair.

Suddenly, Caroline's arm shot back and the chair slid away from the table. "Shit!" she exclaimed. "I thought I had that mastered."

"I'll work on the controls," Cecil replied. "We'll get it fixed. You're doing fine. That's my fault."

Caroline's fingers opened, releasing the chair, but her arm did not move, as if frozen in place.

Cecil waited, willing his sister to take command of the arm bot. He knew how much concentration it took and wished he could immediately fix it. But he had tried for months to get the sensitivity just right. For now, this was the best he could manage.

Finally, her arm lifted and pulled back to her side. Caroline then moved into position to begin the slow process of sitting in the chair.

When she was finally seated, Cecil gently slid the chair, with her in it, under the table. "I have to work on the sitting motion," he said. "So far, I haven't been able to capture it perfectly. Sorry."

"Stop already!" Caroline exclaimed. "You can't imagine how good it feels to be able to move around without a wheelchair. Oh, I still need the chair for some things, but I can get in and out of bed with the bots. Best of all, I can do my *activities of everyday living* as the therapists like to say. Well, mostly all of them, anyway. All thanks to you, brother dear."

"Hey, in case you haven't noticed, Sis, this is no longer only about you. Lucas now has over ten thousand people using our devices. He sure knows how to run a company."

"I can't believe you started all this just for me. What you've done is spectacular. I can't thank you enough."

"Simple really. The robotics existed. I just made it so you can slip the fitting over your arm or leg and train your body to activate the elements. They pick up even slight muscle movements, and of course, verbal commands. I had help with the verbal command stuff at the school. I don't know much about electronics. Lucas hired some guy to put it all on circuit boards."

"That's the key though. I can't make my muscles work, but I can learn to pull or bend a little and that's enough to activate them properly."

"Hey, you two," Maggie called. "No more shop talk for the night. Cecil needs a good meal. Do you want to go out or eat in?"

"In," Caroline immediately responded, "I'm really not up to going out."

"You never want to go out," her mother said. "You've become a recluse. Cecil gets to decide. He's the birthday boy."

"Maybe tomorrow. Let's celebrate his birthday tomorrow."

"I'm not really hungry," Cecil said. "We can have the cake now. And Caroline's right," he added. "We can go out tomorrow."

"Okay. Let me get the cake and you can blow out the candles."

When the festivities were over, Maggie said, "I'm going to let you two be by yourselves. Cecil, be sure you stay with her until she's in bed for the night. Every now and again the thing stops and she's stuck."

"You never told me. I should adjust it."

"Not tonight you won't," Maggie answered. "Enjoy your first night home in two years." She kissed him and left for her room.

When she was gone, Caroline said, "You don't know how good it is to have you home. For me, as well as Mother. Taking care of me is an incredible burden on her. Just this one night off for her means so very much. She listens with one ear all night, every night. She used to sleep with me, she was so concerned. Now we have an elaborate speaker system so, if I just grunt she comes running. I try to tell her not to, but she continues."

"I didn't know."

"There's a lot you don't know, dear brother. A lot."

"Then why don't you start by telling me."

"Not in the kitchen. Go make a fire in the den and I'll make my way in there. It'll be nice to sit in a cozy room and talk."

Cecil built the fire and sat on the stone hearth watching the budding flame, lost in thought. A few moments later, from the corner of his eye, he saw his sister come into the den. He watched as she came toward him, one painfully slow movement at a time. Certainly, life would be easier for her if she used the motorized wheelchair he had designed and built for her. But she wanted to walk upright in the worst way.

Despite the fact that he rarely visited, he spoke with his sister almost daily. The reason he didn't make it to Cosper more often had to do with the way the town had treated him. For reasons Joe Harris didn't fully understand, Cecil held his father, as well as the entire town, accountable for him being sent to Dallas. His mother, he always felt, had been a victim, unable to separate herself from Caroline long enough to focus on his, or for that matter, her own, needs. Cecil had become victim to her unwavering focus on Caroline. Apparently, so had his father.

Caroline finally made it to the sofa and slowly settled in. Cecil moved to a facing chair and said, "You're getting along very well with the bots. Tomorrow we can talk about improvements. I never intended them to replace the chair."

"People are meant to walk upright. I want to walk, not ride."

"But I don't know about long term. You should use the chair, at least some of the time."

"I know, I know. That's what the doctor says as well. But I love the fact all I have to do is speak a command, or twist my head or neck, to control it. It makes me feel...well...human."

"Don't overdo it. The bots are designed for light duty."

"Then redesign them for heavy duty."

"Perhaps we will. With the market cap we got on the IPO we can now do just about anything we want. Lucas knows what he's doing. I do the design and I'm what's called a CTO, Chief Technical Officer. I get paid a lot of money to think."

"You've done more than just think, little brother. The trust fund you set up for me made all the difference. You know, when I was lying here in the early days, all I could think about was how was I going to take care of myself. I knew Mom and Dad would do it while they could. But after that, when they couldn't anymore, how would I cope? When Dad ran off with Patty-Ann, I went crazy."

"You never counted on me."

"You were a spaz when you were here. Sorry, but that's how I knew you. Then you got in trouble with the school and you were gone. Why would I have ever thought about you helping me?"

"I'm your brother, that's why."

"Now I love you. You've made a life for me."

"You would do the same for me."

Ignoring Cecil's comment, perhaps because she knew it wasn't true, she said, "I was thinking the other day. Pardon me, that's all I can do is think — and talk. I was thinking about why you got in trouble, trying to remember what I was told. It had something to do with that Mascar girl, the one who went missing."

Cecil's stomach knotted and his fists clenched. He started to look down, but instead focused on her eyes as he had been taught to do by his therapist. "Eyes tell you a lot about what a person is thinking," the therapist had counseled. "Start by looking at eye color. Later you can learn to interpret the clues."

For the first time in his life he noted how pretty his sister actually was, with a tiny nose and mouth and big hazel eyes. The color of her eyes matched his exactly, but his nose was broader and his chin rounder. He imagined they were the same height, but since Caroline could never stand up straight he would never know.

As hard as he worked at it, he still didn't know what clues he was supposed to see. But as he looked at Caroline all he was sure about was that she was not wearing makeup because she'd have no way to put it on. "She ran away," he finally responded. "People thought she was pregnant. School said I did it."

"You! At fourteen! With a girl! That's a laugh."

"Wasn't funny. Don't laugh at me!"

"Before he died, I heard Detective Scott talking to Daddy about Sally. He was positive somebody local had a hand, or some other part of his body, in it."

"Did he say who?"

"Sally had been seen with somebody early in the evening the night of the play. The next morning she was acting strange. He wouldn't say who it was. But I think the detective knew."

"How do you know all this?"

"Police report was made public a few years back. Actually, you can get it on-line. It should have been held private, but someone screwed something up."

"What ever happened? Did they find out who it was?"

"Nothing. Detective Scott couldn't prove anything. He couldn't even prove Sally was pregnant."

"Maybe she wasn't," Cecil responded. "It's all speculation."

"Hey, speaking of the newspaper. A piece of news for you! Old man Spencer dropped over dead a few months back. Joke around town was that it was a slow news day and he was looking for something to publish." She laughed, then struggled to catch her breath.

Cecil remained quiet, trying to understand the joke.

"Wade Spencer now runs the newspaper," Caroline continued when she caught her breath. "He's a jerk. I saw him at his sister's house a few times way back when. He's a few years older than me."

"I don't know Wade."

"He keeps to himself. Isn't married. Mother says he doesn't date."

"How does mother know?"

"Mother and Jennie Spencer are best friends. Mother says he's awkward around women."

They sat by the fire bringing each other up to date on their respective lives. Caroline hadn't felt this content for as far back as she remembered. When they were finally sitting quietly, Caroline asked, "So tell me, brother dear, do you have a love interest?"

"Nothing now," Cecil said, dodging the real answer.

"What does that mean? Nothing now. Have you ever?"

"I take the Fifth," he replied.

"Constitution does not apply to this sofa. Gotta answer," Caroline teased.

"Nothing serious."

"Does that mean, *nothing*?"

"Yes, if you must know."

"Surely you've met women you could date. With all your money they must come flocking."

"Can't get interested. That's all I know."

She looked at him a moment, and then said, "You like boys?"

"No! And no more of this! I don't ask you what you prefer."

"You kidding me! I'm a quad! Maybe a quad with bots, but a quad nonetheless. For me, anything would do. Don't even know if I could manage it."

"Stop it! I don't like that talk." Cecil stood. "It's been a long day. I'm exhausted. Let's get some rest."

"Promise me you'll sit with me tomorrow night. Since Dad left with that...that bimbo, I've not had anyone but mother sit with me. Promise me."

"I promise. Now, want me to help you up?"

"Stand close just in case. I'll try this myself. You need to design a better way to control getting up. It's awkward."

"It was designed to be used with a helper. You've gone beyond the design limits."

"And you're a millionaire because of it."

"So are you, my dear sister. So are you."

Twenty-Five

Cecil spent Tuesday afternoon researching everything he could about the Mascar disappearance. He was puzzled to find that the on-line archives had nothing more than a missing person report in the Police Blotter section. The report had been filed by Lydia Mascar listing her fifteen-year-old daughter Sally as not arriving home from a trip to Dallas. Nothing more was reported.

He could not locate the police report Caroline said had been inadvertently released. After thinking about it for a while, Cecil drove to the *Sentinel* headquarters and searched their computer index for back issues containing the police report. Nothing appeared.

He searched using every combination of words and names he could think of. Still nothing registered. At five, Cecil was politely asked to leave. He was told he could resume his search at eight in the morning.

On Wednesday, instead of continuing to search at the paper, Cecil went to police headquarters. They refused to retrieve the files from storage, but he did obtain one useful piece of information. The desk sergeant, a man who appeared much too old to still be on the force, and from the sound of his voice certainly smoked far too many cigarettes, said, "Young man, why are you harassing us over this file? The darn thing was published in the *Sentinel* a few years back. Go ask them for it."

"You happen to have an old copy around?"

"Are you kidding me? I doubt if we could find it if'n we did."

"*Sentinel* doesn't have it. At least I can't find it in their computer."

"Don't say. Darn thing was there bigger than life. Chief reamed butts for letting it get out."

※

That night while building the fire, Cecil thought about his conversation at the police station. Everything he had found coincided exactly with what Caroline had told him, except he couldn't find the published police report. That made no sense. There was a piece missing here somewhere.

Hitting a dead end, his mind wandered to his conversation with Caroline the night before concerning Wade Spencer. She had known Wade in high school because she had been friends with Wade's other sister Janet. Cecil pressed her for details of why she had called Wade Spencer a creep. Caroline had responded, "He always looked at me funny. Like he was looking through me. He'd bump into me at the weirdest times. Like when I was coming around a corner he'd just happen to be standing there. One time I got the feeling he was out on the lawn behind a tree watching us undress."

"Why were you—"

"I was staying at Janet's house. She's my age."

"Brother spying on sister's girl friend does not seem—"

"I might be wrong, but I had the impression he was more interested in Janet than in me. That's why I think he's creepy."

"It *is* creepy trying to see your own sister," Cecil responded, shuddering at the thought. He couldn't imagine wanting to see Caroline naked.

Now, waiting for her, he realized how comforting it was to be home with people he cared about. He knew it was that way also for Caroline because she hadn't wanted to leave the den the night before.

"Penny for your thoughts," Caroline said, making her way across the room in slow deliberate movements that Cecil could only imagine were extremely taxing. "You seem lost in your own world."

"Just thinking of how nice it is to be here. Spending time with you, that sort of stuff."

"How nice of you to say that, brother dear." Caroline slowly willed the bots to lower her onto the sofa. Halfway down she lost control of the leg bots and her knees buckled.

Cecil, failing to anticipate what was about to happen, arrived at her side a split second too late to prevent her from crumpling to the ground. Caroline lay with her back resting against the sofa, her legs folded awkwardly under her.

He straightened her legs and moved into position to pull her up. "Don't!" she exclaimed. "I have to do it myself." It was several minutes before she mustered the strength to even begin the struggle to stand.

Cecil sat on the floor beside her waiting patiently, observing a reddish-purple bruise form on her arm where it had hit the sofa.

When she began the tedious process of standing, Cecil moved to the edge of the sofa ready to catch her if she couldn't make it fully erect. He apologized, saying, "I was so busy watching your motion, I forgot to position myself to catch you. I should have been there for you."

"It's not your fault. I lost control. I must remember to concentrate on what I'm doing."

"When I leave, I'm ordering in full-time helpers."

"You'll do no such thing!" Caroline commanded. She was now sitting on the floor, her back straight, summoning the strength to move up to the sofa.

"You want me to have helpers, stay here and help. You don't need to ever leave again."

"I can't do that," he protested, but could think of no real reason why not. Lamely, he said, "I have to design the next generation bots."

"You can do it from here."

"You do have a point. But—"

"But you don't want to."

"It's not that, it's—"

"You don't have a love interest, or at least you say you don't. You're all I have. It's perfect—for both of us." She waited for Cecil to respond, and when he remained silent, she added, "If you remain, I'll let you bring in helpers then. So you don't have to be responsible all the time. Just be here with me." Taking a deep breath, she began the process of willing the bots to move. Slowly, her arms rose and her hands eventually rested on the sofa. Then her legs began to fold back, the right one first, followed by the left.

Cecil studied the movement intently. When Caroline's back began to slide upward against the sofa he knew for certain she was undertaking an impossible task. The angles would not allow her leg bots enough upper force. Before her butt would reach pillow height her legs would slide out from under her. This, he knew from his study of anatomy, was dangerous and might result in her ripping her fragile shoulder muscles.

He sat mesmerized with the motion, seeing in his mind the solution he could make to the programming—and to the physical structure of the leg bots. With the addition of a lever mechanism, the problem would be solved.

He watched as her feet began their inevitable slide, the scene playing out exactly as he had predicted. His eyes darted to her shoulders to see their angle. There again, they were positioned just as he had foreseen. Suddenly, and almost too late, his arms shot out and locked under her armpits, removing the pressure from her shoulders. Cecil managed to get just enough leverage to prevent the damage he had feared. With all his strength he tried to stand her up. But he made no progress.

He commanded, "Go limp. I'll get a hold of this easier if you go limp."

Caroline allowed her arm bots to release their hydraulic fluid-controlled pressure. All her weight fell onto his arms.

Slowly, he eased her back down to the floor. He then positioned himself in front of her, pulling her upward to the sofa, propping her in the corner where she had been the night before.

He looked up into her wet eyes. Thinking he had hurt her, he said, "Sorry, Sis. I didn't mean to hurt you. Is it your shoulders? Should I call the doctor?"

"I have no feeling there, so it's not the pain. I'm crying 'cause I failed. I wanted so much to show you I could do it. But I failed."

Cecil moved as close to her as he could and extended his arms until they circled her tiny waist. "No," he softly answered, "I failed you. The design is flawed. I'll fix it. I promise you, I'll get it right."

Her checks were wet, moisture dripped down onto him. She had no ability to wipe her face, so he gently cleared away the tears with the palm of his left hand.

"I'm so helpless," she sobbed. "Everything I do I need help with. I wear diapers and can't change them. When mother's not around, I sit in my mess like a baby waiting for its mother. She tries to be here, but there are times...oh, I thought I got over this years ago!" She took in a long breath of air, then said, almost to herself, "It never goes away. Never gets any better. I'm useless. Useless!"

"I failed you," Cecil said, his head on her shoulder, letting her tears run down across his face. "I'll fix it for you. I promise, I'll fix it for you. Don't cry. Don't cry."

"But you can't fix me! Nothing can fix me! I have no one to hold me, to touch me, to really care for me. Do you know what that's like? Do you really know what it's like?"

I know exactly how you feel, my sister. I have no one either. He started to mouth the words, but sharing personal thoughts was uncomfortable. Instead, he replied, "I can try. I can try. Now let's talk about pleasant things. My therapist always says it's better to—"

"Like your therapist knows how I feel!"

"She knows how I feel. And she's right."

"Okay, brother dear, I'll play your game. Tell me about that car you're driving. What is it?"

"An old Ghia we rebuilt the summer you got...the summer I spent in Dallas. It has a neat gas turbine engine with a turbocharger. My friend Sally and I worked on it all summer. Lucas gave it to me when we formed the company."

Cecil again thought back to the delightful hours he had spent with Sally in the backseat, talking and giggling. She had taught him to giggle. She had also taught him to enjoy listening to music. But he had problems with music because a melody, or a phrase, would become lodged in his mind, repeating itself over and over and over, effectively blocking his thinking.

Sally had taught him other things as well. All summer when she saw his head go down, she'd whack him hard as a reminder to lift his head and face directly what was tormenting him. She scolded him when things didn't go his way and he got all locked up. A life's lesson he still struggled to master.

"I didn't mean to lose you. What are you thinking about?" Caroline's voice broke through his musing. "You have such a pleasant expression. Hey, it's not often I see you smiling. In fact, I don't recall the last time."

"I was thinking of Sally. Wondering what ever happened to her. You don't just fall off the planet."

"Ran away, I suppose. Didn't the detective have reason to believe she was pregnant? Dad even said once he thought she had died."

"Sally's not dead! She's my only friend! I know she is not dead."

"Hey, don't get all angry at me. But they were pretty certain she was pregnant."

"That's what Grandma Harris told them. But Grandma's nuts! She doesn't even know who I am!"

"Grandma, before she lost it, was intuitive. I wouldn't count her out. And she's not nuts!"

"I got tossed out of high school 'cause they thought I got her pregnant. I hate this city for that! I can't stay here, 'cause I hate it here!"

"Dad says you got tossed out 'cause you pitched a tantrum in front of the principal and went into Mobius mode. That's not the city's fault."

"*What* mode?"

"Mobius. An endless loop. Mother calls it your loop mode."

"They didn't have to throw me out! Dad was only too happy to ship me off to Pappa's. That way I was out of the way."

"I'm sorry, Cecil, it's all because of me."

"I don't blame you. You're the victim. I actually managed better than people thought I would. Thanks to the tutors Lucas arranged. They got me though high school in less than three years. AP classes allowed me to get advanced placement at UTD. That's why I could build the bots my first year. I had plenty of lab time. I was way ahead of the class."

"It's all worked out for you, hasn't it?" Caroline fell silent, staring into the fire for several long minutes. "Better than for me, that's for damn sure! Better than it will ever be for me."

"I'm sorry, Caroline. I wish I could make it all better."

"Your bots help. You've done your part. Enough of this. I need you close by me." Caroline again studied the fire, while Cecil studied his sister. He watched with amazement as the anger and resentment in her eyes and mouth slowly transformed into soft and wonderfully pleasing lines. Her body relaxed against him.

Cecil lost himself in the warmth of the moment, curled up against his sister, at peace with himself, even if it was only for this brief moment.

Twenty-Six

The next morning Cecil was at the kitchen table reading the paper, enjoying a cup of coffee and answering a million questions presented by his mother. Most of all, Maggie wanted to know what he and Caroline had been talking about so late into the night.

"We mostly just sat by the fire. She fell asleep and I carried her up to her room."

"You can't just leave her in bed like that," Maggie scolded. "She must be cleaned and checked to see if she needs a catheter."

"Mom, I can't undress her. And I can't be doing any of that other stuff. You know—"

"That's what I'm for. You should have got me up."

"You need your sleep."

"Your sister has needs. Hygiene is critical. Her diaper needs to be changed, her bottom cleaned. If she's using the indwelling catheter, the volume needs to be noted."

"Mother!"

"Well, it's a fact. She has special needs. It's time you're aware of them. Life's not just about moving around. Life's about changing—"

"Mother! I don't need the details! Please!"

"She's your sister, Cecil. Without me, or you, she has no one to take care of her. Your dad ran off with that ...that woman. Left me here to...to...listen to me, you must learn to insert the catheter when she needs it. You never know when—"

"Mother! Stop!" Cecil's face burned and he found himself looking down at the floor. The word *stop* played over and over in his mind and he forced himself to look up and not to say it over and over. "She'll just have to...to do it in a diaper, that's all."

"Cecil, you need to grow up and—"

"I can't be touching her. I can't! Not on her...not down there! I can't be putting a catheter—"

The telephone interrupted. Maggie answered it on the third ring. She held the phone out to him. "It's Alice Spencer."

"Alice?" Cecil began, holding the phone away from his ear as if it would bite him, "this is a surprise."

"I saw you at the paper the other day," Alice began. "Thought it was you, but wasn't sure. You're so...so grown up."

"We all get older, don't we?" He visualized her back at the ice cream parlor, taunting him, ice cream dripping from her nose. He had to take a deep breath to control his remembered anger.

"Some age better than others," she cheerfully volunteered. "How about meeting me for lunch today?" Alice's voice was sweet and sincere. "Be nice to say hello, hear about what you've been up to."

"Sorry, I—"

"Cecil, don't be a pill. Just lunch. I'll buy. How about *Scotts*? Great burgers and fries."

Cecil's curiosity got the better of his common sense. "See you at noon."

"Can you make it one? The crowd will be gone by then."

"One will work," Cecil replied. "See you there."

"What was that about?" Maggie asked the moment the phone was back on the hook.

"Got a lunch invite. She saw me at the paper the other day."

"You watch that girl. She's married to Clyde Higgins. The guy's a jerk."

"Then why did she marry him?"

"You remember Alice. Always the lively one. She was a cheerleader in high school. Into everything. Clyde played on the football team. Big guy on campus sort of thing."

"Mom, how do you know all this stuff?"

"People talk. Since Jackson died, Alice's mother and I are friends. Clyde's been stepping out on Alice."

"Mother!"

"Well, it's true enough. He's running around with a real hussy. She moved here not long ago and works in the grocery store. She's way overweight and keeps to herself, except for Clyde that is. She's slow. Her checkout line's always the longest."

"Mother!" Cecil exclaimed, clasping his hands over his ears, "stop it! You and your friends need a life. Gossiping about people is not good!"

"Alice is after you now," Maggie chided, "'cause you have money."

"Is it common knowledge I have money?"

"It's been in the paper. You're big news in this town. Local boy makes good."

"They threw me out for God sakes! I hate them all. As far as I'm concerned, I'm not from Cosper. If it weren't for you and Sis, I'd never come back here. I wish you'd move up to Dallas."

"My friends are here. I'm staying put."

Cecil wanted no more of this talk, so he said, "I have errands to run." He gave his mother a peck on the cheek. "Tell Caroline we're going for a drive later today and having dinner out. She needs to get out."

"She won't go. Since her accident she's afraid to get in a car. We've tried, but she won't go."

"We'll see about that," Cecil replied, thinking only of the mechanics of it and not the emotional aspect of Caroline getting back in a car.

❧☙

Cecil wondered what Alice would look like after a few years of marriage and maybe a baby or two. He thought about her husband running around with the chubby grocery clerk and wondered if she knew. Would she care? Cecil didn't understand relationships and this one was no exception.

Before meeting Alice, Cecil again used the *Sentinel's* computers to search for the story. After an hour replicating his steps of two days earlier, he was satisfied he had not missed it. The story simply was not in the paper even though he had been assured it had been.

Disappointed, he drove the mile to the restaurant, parked his car, and steeled himself to meet the one person he had hoped never to see again. He walked through the door and looked blankly at the few faces still remaining. It wasn't until Alice waved at him that recognition came. It wasn't that she had gone to fat, because, in truth, she had only gained a modest amount of weight. Her face, however, was that of a woman in her late thirties, not the face of a twenty-one year old who shared his birthday.

"Happy birthday," he announced, approaching the table in the back corner where she was sitting. "Never expected to be having lunch with you. You look older."

"Just as blunt as ever, I see." Extending her hand, Alice continued, "If I recall right, the last time we were together you jammed ice cream up my nose." When Alice smiled, the harshness eased, but her chin was hard and jutted out more than he remembered.

"You deserved it. You called me a jerk."

"Seems we've taken up exactly where we left off."

"You invited me. It's not too late to send me away."

"Please sit," Alice said, smiling pleasantly. "We can smoke the peace pipe; at least pretend we're friends."

"How about just having a hamburger? I don't smoke and I really don't like pipes."

Alice expected him to laugh at his own lame joke, but quickly realized from his somber expression that he was serious. "And as literal as ever I see. You never did have a sense of humor. Let's order, I'm hungry."

While they waited for the food to arrive, Cecil said, "I hear you're married. Any kids?"

A shadow passed across her face before she replied, "Clyde doesn't want kids. I do. It's a sore point."

"That's a problem. Do you work?"

"At the paper. Father died and Wade runs it. My sister and I work there. She writes. I do bookkeeping."

"I thought newspapers were dying. From what I saw over there you guys are going great guns."

"We're lucky. This town is doing well. *Axtel Industries* fuels it. They advertise their products with us. Frankly, I think they throw money our way to insure favorable press. They're sued a lot and the tenor of the paper has a lot to do with jury verdicts."

"Are you saying the paper slants its news to the highest bidder?"

"That's not what I said. I said they advertise. That makes us think twice before cutting off our noses. That's all."

"Same thing."

"Speaking of sisters," Alice said, steering the conversation away from the paper. "How's Caroline doing? I keep meaning to stop by and see her, but never seem to find the time. I feel awful. Mother keeps me filled in. She's friends with your mother, you know."

"Caroline's doing as well as can be expected under the circumstances."

"The story we ran says helping her was the inspiration for your company. Is that accurate?"

"It is."

"But Caroline refused to allow us to run a picture of her using the, what did she call them? Bots or something?"

"They're bots. Short for robot. She values her privacy."

"I can understand that. Privacy is hard to come by in this town, I'll tell you that much."

The waiter set their meals in front of them and they fell silent.

"You married?" Alice inquired, after finishing most of her hamburger. She tried to make the question sound casual, but her inflection carried a measure of tension.

"No."

"Why not? You're rich and well...you've grown up and don't look so...so...I mean when you were here you were a nerd. Now you're so...different."

"I'm not different. I'm still the same—"

"Good different. I see it in your eyes."

"My eyes are hazel, like Caroline's. There's nothing else to see." *She's after you now because you have money.* His mother's words rang in his head. Cecil looked down at his plate.

"You have anyone special?"

"Comes and goes," he answered, trying to be unspecific. Wiping his mouth, he added, "Right now, nothing. Can't speak for tomorrow." He studied her eyes, looking for the *social clues* his therapist had instructed him to look for. All he could see was brown. He could never see anything else and was not convinced anyone else did either.

"You really have changed," Alice commented. "Not what I had expected at all. You're more...more sure of yourself than I had imagined. But then...then you lapse and I can see the way you were."

"I am what I am." Cecil repeated the words of his counselor while trying to remain positive about himself just as he had been taught. "What did you expect?"

"Hate to say this, but a geek of the highest order."

"Then why ask me to lunch?"

"You're news. I work at a newspaper. Connect the dots."

"What dots?" Cecil looked around to see if he had missed something. "What are you talking about? I don't see any dots."

"I work at a newspaper. Newspapers print stories about interesting people. You are an interesting person. Get it?"

"So, I'm a work project?"

"Curiosity mostly. Kid goes through grade school, everyone picking fun at him for one thing or another. Kid gets thrown out of high school within the first week. Kid goes to Dallas and becomes a millionaire by his twenty-first birthday. Whole town's curious. What gives?"

"For one thing, lots of counseling. The technical term is Asperger's Syndrome. I fixate on things mechanical. It's called channeling. My grandfather sent me to a top doctor in Dallas. Medication and behavioral therapy get me through."

"Circumscribed interests I believe is the term. When someone fixates on something as you do. That loop thing you do is perseverative thought."

Cecil studied Alice for a long minute, absorbing and processing what she had just said. She knew entirely too much about his condition for this to be a casual lunch.

Then it came to him.

He pushed back his chair and stood. "You researched me, didn't you? Paper wants a story and knew I wouldn't speak to a reporter. Let me tell you something, Alice Spencer. You think ice cream up your nose is horrible, you print anything about me and you'll find out what horrible really is."

Without waiting for a reply, he marched out of the front door. Alice had called him for the lunch; she could pay the check.

Twenty-Seven

On the drive back to his mother's house, Cecil replayed the disturbing conversation he had just had with Alice Spencer. He hadn't liked her in school and he liked her even less now.

Catching a movement in his rear view mirror, Cecil glanced again but it was gone. He turned his head to obtain a better view of the back seat. He caught a glimpse of a shadow and strained to see what it was.

The piercing sound of an air horn directly in front of him jolted his vision back to the road. His car had wandered over the dividing line and was in the direct path of an oncoming Greyhound bus. Before he could react, the bus veered to its right, missing his car by less than two feet. For an instant, time stood still as the images of wide-eyed passengers burned into his mind's eye.

Cecil swerved back onto his side of the road, the adrenalin rush causing him to over-compensate. The wheels hit the gravel on the shoulder and the car began to spin out of control. A traffic sign loomed ahead. Cecil froze as the wooden pole raced straight for the center of the car.

"Hit the brakes!" The command had come from the back seat, the voice vaguely familiar.

Cecil, not realizing his foot had still been on the gas pedal, quickly did as he had been instructed. The car came to a stop with only inches separating it from the sign post, the sound of the shrill air horn still ringing in his ears.

Cecil sat for a moment, willing his body to stop shaking, willing the vision of Carolyn's lifeless limbs to go away.

"Find a place to get off the road," the voice said. "We'll be killed out here."

Cecil, his arms still shaking, slowly edged back onto the roadway. In a quarter of mile he turned onto a hard-packed dirt farm-to-market road. He found a wide grassy area and pulled over.

When the car was safely parked, Cecil turned to face a woman sitting in the backseat, a hat pulled low blocking a clear view of her face. "Who the hell are you?" he demanded. "And what the hell are you doing in my car?"

Slowly, the woman pulled the hat from her face and opened her mouth as if to smile. The gesture revealed several broken teeth and, given the chubby face, conjured up the image of a Halloween pumpkin.

"Who are you?" Cecil repeated. "Get out of my car!"

The woman pulled her legs up onto the seat and shifted so that her back was against the door.

The position triggered a vivid visual memory. "Sally! Sally! Is that you? Oh, my God, it is you, isn't it? I knew the voice!" Cecil's mind raced. Things were out of place. *Wrong! Wrong! Wrong!* His brain was screaming. He forced himself to say, "Sally Mascar! I thought you were dead!"

"Sally *is* dead! My name's Samantha...Nelson. Friends call me Sam."

Wrong! Wrong! Wrong! Wrong! Wrong! echoed in Cecil's head. He fought for control. "Come up front," he finally stammered. "It's been so long. So much has—"

"Drive further down the road. They all have their noses in my business."

Dutifully, Cecil drove deeper into the country, the movement of the car momentarily soothing him. By the time he found an unpaved road he was more under control. He turned onto the road, his tires throwing up clouds of dust. They traveled five more minutes before he brought the car to a stop alongside a gently sloping small rise. "Now come up front," he called to Sally. "I feel like a stupid chauffeur."

"Come back here," she replied. "Like old times."

There was a certain logic to her request. He walked around to the passenger side and climbed into the back seat, just as he had done every day during the best summer of his life. Soon their legs were entwined as they had been the last time they were together. Only this time it was mid-winter, and even though they were in South Texas they both wore jackets.

"What happened?" Cecil asked, not able to contain himself any longer. "You disappeared. Where did you go?"

"Didn't want to be home is all."

"Why? You should have told me."

"Couldn't. I wanted to, but couldn't. They'd make you tell."

"Where'd you go?"

"Austin."

"They looked for you there. You disappeared."

"I had my reasons."

"Tell me."

"Can't. Is this your car now?"

"It's mine. It came out nice."

Her face fell, and her eyes closed.

"What's wrong? You upset because I have the Ghia?"

"He's dead, isn't he?"

"Who?"

"Lucas. It's his car. He died and you got it."

"He's very much alive and runs my company. He gave it to me as a present."

"What company?"

"We make robots to help people move who can't move on their own."

"Why you do'n that? You should build cars and engines."

"Maybe someday. Now the bots help my sister."

"Your sister needs them?"

"She's paralyzed. You remember, we talked about it sitting right here in this car."

"I forgot. I forget a lot of things," she confessed. "I had a real hard time."

"How long have you been here? In Cosper?"

"Got here a few months back."

"What're you doing here? You work or anything?"

"I worked at the market. Been a checker."

Cecil recalled his mother's comments about Alice's husband running around with a fat checkout girl. "So, then you must be the—". Remembering what he had been taught, he caught himself. "You're at the grocery store then."

"Not any more. I quit just today." Defiance, mixed with anger, filled her face. "I told them what I thought. Then I walked out. I'm tired of those women saying nasty things to me."

"What things?"

"Nasty things. That's all I'm saying."

"So now what will you do for a living?"

"I've got me a good job."

"Where?"

"Promise you won't get mad at me?"

"Why should I get mad at where you work?"

"Promise?"

"I promise."

"*Cospers Own*"

"Cospers!" he exclaimed, stunned that Sally would even think about working at a bordello. His mother had called the place a whorehouse masquerading as an upscale members-only dance hall.

"You promised," she snarled. Her face set hard. The sparkle disappeared from her eyes. "You promised!" She turned away and wiped her cheek. "A person's gotta live! Life's not treated me as good as you! Nobody'll hire somebody like me. No education. Fat and ugly."

"You're not fat and ugly."

"But they all make fun of me!" She studied Cecil's expression. "Hey, I may be heavy, but men still want me! Besides, I'll lose it. That's a good reason to do it."

She tried to untangle her legs and Cecil grabbed her thrashing ankles. "Stop that!" he commanded. "Let's talk like friends."

"You don't approve of what I'm doing, I can tell."

"I have no right to disapprove. I just want to understand."

"You can't understand! You have your *company*, and your Ghia! I have nothing but myself and...and...nothing else. I need the money bad. There's something I'm saving for."

"I'm sorry, Sally. I wish I could roll back time."

"I'm not Sally! You can't begin to know what happened to Sally! Sally died long ago!" She yanked herself free. "Take me back to town. This was a big mistake."

"Sally...Samantha...tell me what happened. I miss you. Can't we be friends again? Like we were."

"This was a mistake. Take me back. Your friend Sally is gone. Nothing can bring her back. Nothing!" Samantha pulled her legs up to her chest and sat that way until Cecil finally gave up and went back behind the wheel.

"Come, sit in the front at least."

Samantha pulled the hat over her eyes and remained silent, not moving. Cecil fired several questions over his shoulder, and when she didn't respond, he stopped trying. They rode back to town in an uncomfortable silence.

Samantha wanted to be dropped off in front of the supermarket. Cecil pulled up to where she pointed and said, "How can I get in touch with you? I want to be your friend."

The passenger door opened and Samantha slipped out with not so much as a glance back as she hurried away.

൧ൠ

Caroline was in the den when he arrived home. She called to him to join her. "Build a fire so I can get warm. I've been waiting for hours for you to get back. How was your lunch? You were gone a long time. Something going on? Tell me all about it. I want to hear all the details. Mother says 'ole Clyde is stepping out on Alice. She paying him back?"

"She was on a mission for the paper. All she wants is to get a story. I refused. That's all."

"You spent a lot of time with her. Give her anything good to write?"

"I told her I'd sue her and the paper if she tried."

"You're testy today. Mother thought Alice wanted you for something else you know."

"She's got a husband. Besides, Alice and I never got along before I left, so why now?"

"Mother says—"

"Mother has an active imagination," Cecil shot back, not comfortable where this was going.

"Mother needs a man, that's what Mother needs."

"Don't talk that way! I don't like it one bit."

"That's what I need also. A man."

"Stop talking that way!"

"You think because I can't move my arms and legs I don't need someone to talk with, to share things with? I've never had a man even kiss me—other than Father I mean. And you know what, dear brother? I need sex! Period!"

"Caroline! Stop talking that way! And keep your voice down," Cecil scolded. "Mother will hear you."

"Let her hear me! She needs sex also, but she won't admit it. No, not her. Miss Martyr. Hear her tell it, she lost her husband because of me. Truth is, she lost her husband 'cause she stopped sleeping with him." She glanced toward the kitchen, "Come sit close to me. I want to feel your warmth to chase away this awful coldness deep within me."

Cecil checked on the whereabouts of his mother. Satisfied that she was preoccupied, he said, "I'll sit next to you, but no more of that talk."

"What's the matter, makes you uncomfortable? Are you telling the truth when you say you've been with women? I think you haven't. You're a virgin just like me!"

"Stop it!" he barked. His face was even hotter than it had been before. "I won't stay with you if you continue." But he made no move to break away.

"I understand Mother scolded you for leaving me in bed last night. Next time, you'll have to change my diapers. Clean my bottom, powder me like a baby."

This time he did pull away, moving to the far end of the sofa. "What's gotten into you today?"

"I suppose it was thinking of you getting it on with Alice Spencer. I suppose I should call her Alice Higgins. After all, she's a married woman. Got to pay proper respect, even if she doesn't."

"You've been drinking. That's what I smell. You cover it well, but you've been into something. How do you do it? The bots aren't designed for—"

"You did a better job with those darn things than you think. They're designed to grasp rectangular objects. Just need to drink what comes in that shape container."

"Who brings it into the house?" He looked toward the kitchen, then exclaimed, "Don't tell me!"

"Not for me, stupid. For her! Says she needs it to sleep. Who am I to complain? Come back over here, I'll be good."

"Promise?"

"Of course, I promise."

When he was again on her end of the sofa, their bodies inches apart, he said, "Sis, mind if I renege on our dinner tonight? We can go out tomorrow. I'm not up to it tonight."

"Too much Alice Higgins! She'll do it to you every time."

Caroline was right, only it wasn't Alice who had dampened his spirits. It was Sally Mascar, or what remained of her.

Twenty-Eight

Later that night, after a dinner consumed in the den by the fire, Maggie, who had waited on the two of them like a maid servant, announced, "I'm turning in early tonight, I'm tired."

"So am I," Cecil responded. "Don't know why, but I'm exhausted."

Caroline chirped, "As I said, that's what Alice Higgins will do to you."

"Stop that," Cecil replied.

"Told you she was after you," Maggie chimed in. "She's bad news. Stay away from her if you know what's good for you."

"I didn't spend any time with her, if you must know. Lunch didn't go so well."

"Good for you. Come Caroline," Maggie said, turning to her daughter, "I'll prep you for bed."

"Not sleepy. I want to sit by the fire a while longer. Stay with me Cecil. You can sleep on the sofa if you wish. I'm enjoying just having you in the room with me."

Cecil relented and retraced his steps across the room to the sofa where Caroline was curled into the corner. Maggie called from the base of the stairs, "I'm going up now. Cecil, wake me when she's ready for bed so I can prep her. Don't repeat last night."

"I'll wake you, Mother," Cecil promised. "Good night."

The two of them sat quietly enjoying the warmth of the fire, and the warmth of each other. Caroline broke the silence. "It's nice having you here, brother dear. Please stay in Cosper."

"That's not a good idea," he replied. "It's really not." But with Sally Mascar in town, the thought was not so disquieting as it had been. "I need to get back to Dallas, but I have an idea. A change of scene will do you good. How about a visit to Dad? It will give you a break and allow Mom some time off."

"Mother will just sit here, brood and worry about me. Worry about you. Worry about something."

"If mother agrees, will you go with me?"

"If you promise to sit with me like this in Dallas."

"That won't work too well. You'll be at Dad's and I'll be at my place."

"It's the only way I'll go. You can stay at Dad's. Or I can stay at your place."

"Promise you won't...make me...uncomfortable like before."

"I can't promise what you'll feel."

"No more sex talk."

"I'll try, but some days that's all I can focus on."

"Promise?"

"I promise."

"The change of scene will do you good. I'll call Dad in the morning."

They dozed on the sofa together. Around two in the morning Cecil woke thinking he heard somebody in the house. He got up, carefully removed his arms from around Caroline's tiny waist and went to investigate. The alarm was set. He heard nothing further.

He returned to the den. The fire was just smoldering ash and the room was chilly. Caroline was struggling to sit up, but was having trouble controlling the bots.

"You're tired, Sis," Cecil called, running over to where she was slumped. "It's hard when you're tired. Let me help." He gently got her sitting upright. And as he had done the night before, he picked her up and carried her up to her bedroom.

"Don't wake Mother," Caroline said, "You can get me ready for the night."

"Me! I don't know the first thing about—"

"Time you learn. If I'm to travel with you, then you have to take care of me."

The logic of it seemed right. The fact of it seemed inappropriate—and frightening in its implications.

"Don't look so stricken. And besides, right now I'm not messy, just wet."

He continued toward the door to fetch his mother.

Carolyn called, "I won't go with you unless you know how to do this."

That stopped him. Coming back to her side, he said, "Sure you want me to...to undress you?"

"There's no other way to clean me and change the diaper." She smiled her crooked smile. "And besides, it's time you learned what the female anatomy looks like."

"Stop talking that way. You promised."

"Think of me as a machine. One of your stupid engines. Just a bunch of parts. That's all I am anyway, a bunch of broken parts. Bet you can do it then."

First, he unfastened the bots from her limbs, placing each of them carefully in their respective charging stations. She might have been experiencing a low battery downstairs. He made a mental note to check on the batteries and to see if a design change could be implemented to improve work time. He had never imagined anyone needing the bots for as many hours a day as Caroline seemed to use them.

He safely stored the machinery for the night, then reluctantly unsnapped her pants. Carefully pulling them down he was stunned to see how thin her legs were. The muscle was mostly gone, and very little fat surrounded the bones. The mechanics of her hip and knee joints appeared visible through the translucent skin. It was as if he was looking at an X-ray. He marveled at the perfection of the structure. Indeed, she did resemble a machine.

"Don't look so shocked. I'm not a marathon runner. I can barely make them move with the bots."

"You've lost mass even since I fitted them. We have to work on that." His mind raced with possibilities for improvements to the leg bots to prevent muscle loss. Perhaps he could restore her leg muscles if it wasn't already too late.

"Now get the diaper," she instructed. "In the top drawer. Looks like undies, but thicker."

He was operating mechanically now; his mind focused on the design changes he was planning to make. When the diaper was almost in place, she said, "Don't forget the cream. Without it I'll be a mess in no time. It's on the dresser, the green jar."

Cecil retrieved the jar, opened it and realized that she intended for him to wipe the cream substance, more like petroleum jelly, over her private parts.

"Oh, no! I'm getting Mother."

"And I won't go with you to Dallas! You have to take care of me. I can't do this alone."

"But—"

"Listen to me Cecil. When that truck hit, I ceased having feelings in my arms and legs. But that's not the only feelings I lost. Along with it went any hope of dignity I could possibly ever have. Until you came along with those wonderful bots, I had no privacy at all. When I make a mess, someone else has to clean me. When I have an itch, someone else has to scratch it. I can't even put a morsel of food in my mouth by myself. You think it's a big deal to wipe the cream on me. Pretend it's a machine part you're putting grease on. Pretend what the hell you want! Just do it and get the hell out of here!" Tears flowed freely down her cheeks. She had no ability to stop them or even to wipe her face dry.

He finished with the diapers and slipped her pajama bottoms on, refusing to deal with the tops. She could sleep in her sweater. At least he could allow her some measure of modesty.

He dried her face and bent to kiss her. When his lips touched her cheek, she whispered ever so softly, "Please, I beg you, stay with me. Sleep next to me. I need you here close to me."

✥

Halfway to Dallas the next day, Caroline, sitting in a prototype swivel seat designed by Cecil, rotated toward him and said, "Did you see the look on Mother's face when she found you in bed with me? I wish I had a camera. She didn't know whether to scream or hide."

"I was dead to the world. The door slamming woke me. I thought the house had exploded."

"What did she say to you when you asked her to dress me?"

"Said we seemed to be getting along just cozy. 'Finish what you started,' she told me. 'Dress her yourself!'" Cecil surprised Caroline by imitating his mother's voice almost perfectly.

"When I came down," Caroline said, "Mother had my breakfast ready and I thought we'd have words. But all she said was, 'Hope you slept well.' She's in shock. Doesn't know what to make of us."

"She's the one who told me not to just plop you in bed at night. So what's she complaining about?"

"Funny, she doesn't think it's...improper...and, frankly, neither do I, for you to insert the catheter. But sleep in the same bed. Now that's a two-tailed cat. I'm a quad for God's sake! And you slept across the bottom of the bed. Couldn't be further from me if you tried."

Changing the subject, Cecil said, "Dad's excited to have you coming, even if he'll only see you for a few days."

"What's that about? I didn't hear that part."

"They're leaving for a trip. He suggested both of us stay at his house and get someone to take care of you. I told them not to postpone their vacation. There'll be more visits."

"You can take care of me. I don't want a stranger. I've had enough strangers poking and prodding."

"I have to work sometime. I have some ideas for improving the bots."

"Is that all you think of? Machines?"

"Sorry to say, but yes. I know what they'll do, how they'll behave. But with people it's different. I never know what they'll say or do. Never have."

"You don't read the clues, that's your problem."

"Are you talking about social clues? I don't hear or see clues. I hear words and many times I'm confused about what they mean."

"Have you always been that way?"

"Always. My therapist says it's one of the traits of Asperger's. She says I need to learn to read people. But I can't. I've been trying to concentrate, but the only person I can read is Sally."

"No wonder the kids picked on you, called you names."

"Let's change the subject."

"When Dad goes on vacation, can I stay at your house?"

"We'll see."

"What's that mean?"

"Depends on if you behave yourself."

"Me?" She shot him a hurt look. "I've no way to misbehave."

"You know what I mean. That sex talk makes me... uncomfortable."

"I can't help it if it's on my mind. I can't make my mind stop 'cause it makes you uncomfortable. Minds don't work that way. Least mine doesn't."

"Then keep it to yourself," Cecil said.

"I'll do my best."

"You promised."

"My fingers were crossed," Caroline said, a twinkle in her eye.

"You can't cross your fingers."

"If I could cross my fingers they would be crossed."

Twenty-Nine

"She's creepy," Caroline complained to her father about the helper Joe had hired for the times when he and Patty-Ann would be away. "I don't want her touching me."

"I'll get someone else. This is the third one you've...rejected. We're running out of time. Listen I'll cancel our trip if you like."

"Don't cancel. Cecil can do it."

"Cecil? You got to be kidding. Maybe if you were an engine he'd have no problems. But not—"

"He took care of me at Mother's. Changed my diaper and everything."

"Cecil? I can't imagine your mother allowing that for one minute."

"She was sleeping. Cecil didn't want to wake her."

"And you were okay with that?"

"I like having Cecil close. We spent hours by the fire talking."

"I've not known him to talk to anyone for any length of time." Joe thought a moment and then corrected himself. "Except for that poor Sally girl way back when...when he spent the summer with your grandparents in Dallas."

"When you sent him away you mean."

"We had to. Anyhow, he had a great summer. My father told me all about him eating lunch every day in the back seat of the Ghia with Sally, the two of them talking and listening to music. You spending time talking with him is nice, but hard to imagine."

"It's true. Ask him."

At dinner, Joe broached the subject of Cecil taking care of Caroline while they were gone. To his surprise, Cecil replied, "I didn't think she'd accept any help so I've arranged to work from home. She and I will be fine."

Patty-Ann, not fully on-board with the arrangement said, "You know that means bathing and dressing her...and...and... well changing her diaper. All the things I've been doing this week."

"He can do it," Caroline answered quicker than she should have.

Patty-Ann's eyebrows puckered, but before she could say anything, Caroline added, "Anyone who can take an engine apart and put it back together with such precision and care can manage to dress me properly." She laughed, "To him, I'm nothing more than a machine."

"I wasn't referring to the mechanics of it. I was thinking more about the...well, the lack of...shall we say, modesty."

Caroline looked toward Cecil who was fidgeting in his chair. It was the way she remembered him as a child. "Cecil and I discussed this already. I'm okay with it. Cecil's okay with it. So what's the problem?" What she wanted to say, but didn't, was that she actually enjoyed his presence.

"I've had my say," Patty-Ann answered through tight lips. "I'm staying out of this. You two work it out."

Joe, taking a clue from his wife's tone, turned to her. "So what's bothering you? Let's get it on the table. I don't want to hear about it on our trip."

"It's really not my business."

"Last chance. Or forever hold your—"

"Okay. If you insist! All I have to say is it seems wrong, that's all. Brother and sister. It's just not natural that's all."

"Early on, I thought that also," Joe began, selecting his words carefully. "It's Caroline's modesty that's at stake here. Caroline said years ago her dignity had been permanently compromised, that she couldn't ever regain it. It's really her choice if she wants Cecil to take care of her, keeping it in the family so to speak."

"I didn't exactly say it that way," Caroline said, "but that's what I feel. He's helping me out of love. The others are doing it because it's a job."

"Cecil," Joe said, turning to his son, "don't disappear on us. Where do you stand on all this?"

"Stand?" Cecil repeated, puzzled by the question, and not looking in their direction. "I'm sitting right here. Can't you see that?"

"I mean, what's your feeling on the subject?" Joe pressed.

"I want the best for Caroline." His answer was directed to the back window, as though he were talking with someone out in the yard. "I wish I could perfect the bots to do it all for her. But I've failed her."

"That's not the question. What I'm trying to determine, and you're not helping, is if you're willing to take care of your sister while we're gone? That means doing everything that's necessary?"

Without looking away from the window, Cecil replied, "If that's what she wants, I'll do it."

"I would hug you, if I could," Caroline said, air-kissing him from across the table.

"Our place or yours?" Joe asked. "You're welcome to stay here."

"My place. It's easier for me to work."

"Okay. We'll transfer everything over in the morning. Patty-Ann can get her settled."

Caroline beamed while Cecil continued to study the window.

"Cecil, please join the conversation," Joe snapped. "I mean, look at us." When his son finally looked their way, Joe said, "There's a rumor floating around that your company is about to be acquired. How do you feel about that?"

"I was told not to discuss that."

"That's fair. Will you be asked to remain?"

"Dad," Caroline scolded, "he can't discuss it. But I can. Cecil will be required to remain as the CTO, or whatever they call him. Without him, the company will die."

"I can't discuss this," Cecil repeated. "I can't discuss this."

"He's agitated. So he's resorting to Mobius mode. Better change the subject."

"Mobius—" Patty-Ann began.

"Never mind." Caroline turned to Cecil. "We've dropped the subject. Now just relax and enjoy the dinner. No more unpleasant talk."

To Joe's astonishment, Cecil's eyes cleared and he announced, "After dinner let's all go to the mall. Caroline, you'll love the stores."

"I don't have the energy to—"

"We'll get the chair," Cecil pressed, anxious to test the newest prototype. I'll control it. I got a new controller."

"If you insist," his sister answered, "If you insist." Clearly, she was not thrilled with the prospect.

ಸಿಆ

Slightly after ten that night they returned from their expedition. Caroline had fallen asleep in the chair so they cut the visit short. The prototype wheelchair was almost to the top of the stairs at the Harris house when one of the hydraulic valves jammed. The sudden jerky movement jarred Caroline awake.

"Sorry, Sis," Cecil quickly said. "I don't know why the valve's been sticking, but it has been doing that all night. I'll keep working it until I get it right."

"What...Where are we?" Caroline questioned, disoriented and surprised to find herself suspended in a wheelchair at the top of a flight of steps.

"You fell asleep at the mall, so we came home. The folks went to their room. I said I'd tuck you in."

"You should have woken me up. It would have been fun you feeding me popcorn. What time is it anyway?"

"Ten. Why? You got something to do?"

"Wish I did. A hot date would be nice. Instead, I get a hot towel on my bottom."

"Sis! You promised!"

"A promise is not forever. I was just dreaming of having a lover. We were on a picnic and he rolled on top-"

"Stop it! One more word like that and I'll leave you right where you are! Suspended between floors."

"I'll yell."

"I'll take the controller with me."

"You wouldn't dare."

"Keep up that *I need a man* talk and see what I'll do."

"I'm simply stating a fact. And, let's face it. You need a woman."

"Stop it!" Cecil jammed the controller in his pocket and started down the steps.

"You win!" Caroline immediately called. "You always win. I have to beg for everything I want."

"Stop that talk, or I *will* leave you hanging here."

"You do that and I can just see the *Sentinel* headline back home. *Local millionaire arrested in Dallas for leaving helpless sister stranded halfway up a flight of stairs. Quad falls to her death trying to free herself.*"

The thought of the headline brought a smile to Cecil's face, realizing that Alice Spencer would really enjoy writing such a story. He relented and maneuvered the chair up the last few steps and then steered it into Caroline's bedroom.

Cecil then watched from the doorway as the chair transferred his sister to her bed flawlessly. There was hope for his design yet.

"Don't bother calling Patty-Ann," Caroline said, "You take care of me tonight. Did you see the relief on her face when she realized after tonight she wouldn't have to change me anymore?"

"I already told her I'd take care of you. And besides, you're imagining it."

"If you hadn't been throwing a tantrum, you would have seen it yourself."

"I wasn't throwing a tantrum."

"You had your head turned away like a petulant child."

"I get uncomfortable when you start that talk."

"Get over it! You're a successful man. Richer than anyone in Cosper by a long shot. And if you ask me, the best thing that can happen to you is to allow your company to be bought."

"How do you know about the sale? I'm not supposed to say—"

"I heard you on the phone. You know, when your cell died and you used the house phone."

"I didn't say much on that call. You've been reading my—"

"Got curious. All those calls when you left the room. I peeked at the papers Lucas left for you."

"That's not right! I shouldn't—"

"We're family. You and me. I'm just looking out for you. Besides, I have good advice. You listen to me. Hold out at first. Two good things will happen. First, they'll up the offer for your company. Make them put up more cash. Their stock is fine, but more upfront cash never hurts. Second, without you, the company is not worth as much. Make them give you an office in Cosper and a few million a year in salary, say for five years. That can be a non-compete payment."

"Where did you learn this stuff? Lucas mentioned something along those lines as well today."

"I've been doing some on-line learning. Ever since you started the company and gave me all that stock, I thought I'd learn business. I took one of those business school programs. Got myself an MBA, at least in my own head."

"Imagine what you could accomplish if you had the use of your arms and legs."

"That's not right! Don't say things like that! I can do anything I put my mind to, except get a lover. Once you taught me how to use the computer by talking, I can do anything you can do. I can't do machines like you. But then, no one in the world does machines like you. But running a company, I can hold my own with anyone. Brains are what it takes. Not arms or legs."

"How about I design a bot to work the keyboard? Would that be good?"

"I'm doing just fine talking, but a bot might be better. Just do your non-compete clause so you can work on computers."

"I can always do bots for my company," Cecil responded. "That's within our scope."

"I was thinking of building a new company that we can run together."

"I don't know about—"

"That would be fun. I can be president since you don't like to deal with people. Think about it, Brother Dear."

"Listen, Caroline, if we sell out now, you'll be worth over twenty-million. You don't need to work."

"And do what with my money? Sit here wilting away? You can design stuff to help people, and I'll run it. That will at least give me reason to get up each day. It might also help people."

"I don't think—"

"Hey! I've got a good idea. Build me a lover bot. We could take walks together and hold hands—or whatever these gripper things are called. It would be nice to have someone to talk with, someone who understood me." Tears welled up in her eyes and ran down her cheeks. She was helpless to wipe them away. "Oh, hell, Cecil. It'll never happen outside my dreams."

"Maybe someday you'll meet someone."

"I never meet anyone."

"Of course not. You never go anywhere."

"This is upsetting. Put me to bed."

Cecil walked over to his sister and touched the back of her hand just above the wrist. It was one of the few areas where her nerve ends worked.

A slight smile spread across her face. "Change me and tuck me in. We have a big day moving tomorrow." She closed her eyes and threw her head back, the smile spread across her otherwise taunt face.

Cecil undid her belt and unzipped her slacks, slowly pulling first one pant leg and then the other down over her knees. When he spread her legs to apply the moisture protection, he noticed a slight movement of her midsection. He was fascinated because he had been certain she couldn't move at all.

It suddenly hit him. He took a quick step back away from her. His heart raced and his face grew hot. He remained silent though as the words, "No! No! No! No!" raced through his brain.

Caroline's eyes were closed and her face was at peace. The movement of her hips settled into a rhythm, even as his discomfort grew. The words he had fought so hard to contain burst from him, soft at first, and then with increasing intensity. "No! No! No! No! No!"

Thirty

"I'm here to see Sam," Clyde Higgins told the bleached-blonde working the reception desk at *Cospers Own*. "The new girl, the one who started a few weeks back."

"Have a drink at the bar. I'll be back to get you when she's ready."

Checking his watch, he asked, "How long you figure it'll be?"

"Depends. Might be five. Might be fifty-five."

"I don't have fifty-five," he replied, again looking at his watch. "My wi...my time's limited. No more than twenty."

"I'll see what I can do. If it'll be too long, do you want someone else?"

"Sam only."

"Want to wait in a private room or is the bar okay?"

Clyde opted for a private room. Even though the long standing code of the place discouraged anyone from talking about what went on here and who was seen in attendance, it was worth an ounce of precaution. After all, he had been meeting

Sam regularly when she worked at the grocery store and half the town already knew it. Hell, his wife Alice knew it as well. Why she hadn't left him he hadn't figured out. Perhaps it was something to do with the paper.

The blonde was back within five minutes. "Good news. Worked some things out. It'll only be a minute or two."

Five minutes later the woman poked her head into the small room as if she were afraid to bring the rest of her body inside. "Sam's available now," she announced.

"How much is she getting?" he asked.

"That's between her and you."

"Give me a range, will ya?"

"None of my business. But if it was to be my business I'd say a hundred would do it for straight stuff."

He followed her swaying hips down the corridor and past several closed doors and then up a flight of steps. At the top she pointed to the second door on the right. "No need to knock."

He opened the door and slowly entered the room. The room held a bed, a small chest of drawers with a lamp perched on top and a single rocking chair. No pictures, no mirror, no color of any sort. The single window had light tan wooden blinds painted to match the walls. A slowly revolving ceiling fan hung over the bed.

Sam was sitting in the chair. "Hi Clyde," she said. "I see you found your way here. Took you awhile."

He closed the door behind him. "I'm not happy you're here, you know."

"You have another solution? Giving it away free in your truck doesn't pay my bills. I'm now what they call an official sex worker. Time's money. You here to talk or get it on? Your choice."

"How much are you charging?"

"Hundred even. Special for you."

"That's a lot of money."

She stood, took the few steps across the small room, and rubbed against him. "It's worth every penny. You, of all people, ought to know that full well."

"I can't afford that much."

She was now snuggled against him, her hand on his thigh. "I can't afford not to charge that amount. Some I charge a hundred and a half. Gave you a real special price. Friend's discount."

"Just this once," he said, his fingers working feverishly at his belt.

Precisely twenty minutes later she escorted him to the door. "See you soon," she cooed. "Hurry back."

The door closed behind him.

Two more to go tonight and she'd clear an even five hundred. One of her best nights so far. What had surprised her the most in this town, unlike the other towns she had worked, was how many of her customers were married. This was an easy life compared to walking the streets of Austin and the other Texas cities where she had worked, always in the shadow of a handler. This beat doing it in back alleys and filthy flats with riff-raff who didn't know the meaning of the word bath.

Being brutalized by the cult in Austin was the price she had paid for keeping her baby. Sure, they had paid for the medical care and the hospital, but after that she had to repay them. And the debt was never satisfied, no matter how many tricks she turned, and no matter how many beatings she took.

When her handler had made the mistake of threatening her child if she didn't turn more tricks, she slipped a knife between his ribs. Mother and daughter then disappeared together into the dark night.

Thirty-One

Caroline sat by the front window of her brother's Dallas Uptown condo, passing the time by surfing the Internet and reading a book, using the mechanical page turner Cecil had constructed for her.

She carefully placed the book on the table, then ever so slowly turned and made her way down the hall to Cecil's office. Once there, she confronted him by asking, "I've been here two weeks now and not once have we sat and talked. I miss your company."

"Sorry, Sis. I've been busy with the sale. It's working out just as you said it would. Price went up and they gave me a sweetheart deal. Our lawyers have been beyond great. They put together a non-compete that only keeps me out of designing robots that handle the traditional activities of everyday living. That allows me to design computer-aided devices and perhaps even a machine for controlling driving. Anything to do with the wheelchair is also open for me."

"Sounds like you have a good team. A bit expensive, as I heard you tell Lucas, but, in the end, worth every penny."

"They're great."

"I can't believe how many patents you have. I checked, and from my count, it's ten."

"With another ten pending. And that's just the United States. Got three times that many around the world."

"All this by the age of twenty-one. You're something."

"Tomorrow is what they call the pre-closing. Don't know for sure what that means, but they tell me by Friday we'll be fully closed. By next Tuesday the money will be in our accounts, free and clear."

"How will I manage all that money? I've never even thought about what that all means."

"Don't worry, it'll be managed by some really good professionals, diversified and all. You'll have thirty-five million in cash. About forty-five in stock. The stock is frozen for six months, and then a percentage can be released every quarter. So why are you so down?"

"Since when do you recognize feelings?"

"Little by little I see things. First it comes in people I care about. I still can't for strangers."

"So you care about me? That's at least good news. I thought after the night at Dad's you—"

"Let's not go there, Sis. I can't do what you want. I can't."

"Can't or won't?"

"Same difference."

"Why not?" she demanded. "You helped me walk." Caroline nodded toward her useless legs. "Don't get me wrong. I'm grateful. But...but... you're so careful not to touch me, except when it's essential. You're more interested in the damn bots than you are in me!"

"Brother and sister, it's not right. You need someone who can—"

"And just where is this someone coming from? You planning on wheeling me into a bar and hoping some guy'll come along and take pity on me?"

"Don't talk that way. I don't like it when you talk that way."

"What's right in all this? I'll tell you. Nothing! Without your bots I'd be on my back, watching TV, maybe using the computer a little, but only with someone's help. You gave me freedom from all that. But when it comes to what I crave most, someone to be with me when I'm alone, someone to talk with and confide in, someone safe, you're all I have. And you're all I'll ever have! And you turn your back on me!"

"You make it sound like I'm out to hurt you. I just want you to live a normal life. You can, you know."

"I'm not normal and never will be! Tell me, Cecil, tell me! Why are you torturing me! It's not fair! It's just not fair!" Tears streamed down her face and Caroline's right-arm bot started to move upward. But then it stopped in mid-motion. Then the arm fell back, slamming against Cecil's desk.

Twice more the bot began to move, only to fall back to her side. Caroline was unable to focus on the nerves and muscles needed to control the mechanical motion required to wipe her wet cheeks.

Cecil made a mental note to allow for a change in sensitivity under verbal command. All the while realizing he could never solve all the mechanical problems inherent in making his sister fully independent. She was right, of course. Her entire being was dependent upon the intentions, good or bad, of other people. All the money in the world could never change that fact. Cecil wiped her face dry and then wrapped his arms around her and pulled her close. When he stopped concentrating so hard and felt her frail body against his, the words he had been trying to say; the words he had carefully practiced with his therapist, finally released. "Caroline, I love you deeply, and I always will."

Exactly as he had been instructed, Cecil moved slightly away from his sister so he could look at her face. "I know you want me to touch you in sensitive places. I understand that. But it doesn't feel proper for a brother to do that for a sister. You may feel differently, others may feel differently, but not for me. I'm not the person."

"Who is then?" she cried, "Who is? Bring me such a person if you won't!"

Remaining calm and focused as he had been coached, Cecil replied, "Doctor Thornton says there's something called a surrogate partner. A person trained in giving you experience, and more importantly, confidence in having a partner."

"Oh, God, Cecil. Has it come to this? I don't even know if I can...can do it. I don't know if my body will cooperate. I don't want a stranger touching me. I don't know if—"

"They're trained," Cecil replied, continuing with the script. "They know what they're doing. A partner will work with you and teach you."

"But I want you! You're family."

Cecil, carefully following the therapist's instructions, again kissed her cheek. Salty tears on her face ran onto his lips. "I can't do it, Caroline dear, it's not possible for me."

"Oh, God, Cecil, You're not—"

"Let's just leave it that I've problems of my own."

"Maybe I can help solve those problems," Caroline began, hope rising in her voice, her eyes frantically searching Cecil for a sign of compliance. The last time she had pushed him he had gone into a mantra that had lasted far into the night. "While you help me, I can help you as well, dear brother. I'm a twenty-four-year-old virgin for God's sake!"

Calmly, Cecil replied, "Doctor Thornton says that's not the way for either of us. I have the number of the agency you should call."

Caroline's body stiffened. "What am I supposed to say? *Hello, I'm Caroline Harris and I need someone to come to my house so I can get laid. Please hurry!*"

"First of all, you can start by not being so coarse. You have normal needs and you're asking for professional help. It's perfectly acceptable. If you want me to call, I will."

"If that's the only way," she relented, her head buried against Cecil's chest, sobbing uncontrollably, "then please, dear brother, do what needs to be done."

Thirty-Two

A week earlier when Wade Spencer caught a glimpse of a young woman walking out of the grocery store something in her movement brought a banished memory alive, sending a knot into his stomach. Almost instantly years of suppressed anguish flooded into his waking brain.

Thinking back to that night eight years ago, he vividly recalled how terrified he had been that Sally Mascar would go to the police and he'd be arrested. He remembered coming home from the hospital and sitting up all night waiting for a knock on the door. As the days passed and the knock didn't materialize, the terror slowly subsided. By summer's end he had convinced himself Sally had not told anyone. He certainly would have known if she had told his sister, Alice. That meant he was in the clear.

Then when Sally disappeared and the police investigation began, the terror returned. He assured his father he did not know what had happened to Sally Mascar after the play. His father had been skeptical, especially since Sally had stopped coming to the house that summer. But in the end Jackson had stood by his son.

The terror eased when it was thought Sally had died. Instead of mourning her death, he welcomed it. But as the years passed the fact that he had rejoiced in Sally's death came to haunt him. He often awoke in the middle of the night when, as often as not, he'd dream of Sally hovering above him pointing wildly in his direction and yelling something he never could quite hear.

At first the dream was a distraction, a mild discomfort, a fear of being caught. But then it deepened into a relentless torment that took hold of his life.

Whenever he struck up a relation with a woman, no matter how casual it was, Sally would be there, floating in the air, her finger directed at him. Consequently, relationships proved impossible. The few times he attempted to have sex outside *Cospers Own* were a disaster with Sally ever-present and accusing. His skin would become clammy and often his heart would race out of control. Gynophobia, a form of agoraphobia, is what the therapist called it. Fear of women. But Wade steadfastly refused to discuss the basis of the torment, preferring instead to sit through the endless psychotherapy sessions talking about his relationship with his father and sisters.

Rapists, Wade repeated often, were the worst of the criminal world. And child rapists were the worst. Over the years he had run countless stories condemning sexual assaults. He had made a mistake — a bad mistake — and he had paid for it dearly ever since. But he didn't think of himself as a bad person — as one of those criminals.

If the woman he had seen turned out to be Sally Mascar, he knew he had to do something. But what? Nothing made sense to him, other than to seek her forgiveness.

She hadn't come looking for him, so why was she here? She hadn't gone to the police — at least not that he knew. But she had taken up with his sister's husband. Was that a warning? Was she going to get to him through his brother-in-law?

He thought about what his therapist had concluded, based on the fact that he was able to work with women, especially reporters and secretaries. He experienced his employees different from the way he experienced a possible date. "It seems to me," the therapist had said, "that when sex is ruled out, you do fine. At least you're able to function in the work environment and run the paper. Be grateful. That's more than many others with your symptoms can do."

"Does that mean I'll never marry? Never have a relationship with a woman?" Wade had asked, visualizing himself growing old alone.

"Do you wish to marry?" came the reply.

"I don't know. I'm probably better off not even looking."

"I suggest you not try until you are comfortable in that setting. You seem terrified of sex. I don't yet know why. In my experience, the roots of sexual concerns often can be traced to bad sexual experiences. You have never told me anything of that nature and I have no reason to believe you are homosexual, so until we can figure out the cause, I'd say it's unlikely you'll have a positive experience."

The countless hours of talk had not prepared Wade for what he would do if Sally came back. But had she? Wade needed to know for certain if the woman now working at *Cospers Own* was, in fact, Sally Mascar.

⁂

"The new girl?" the *Cospers Own* manager asked. "We got two. "Lily or Samantha? Which one you talking about?"

"The one with...with the broken teeth," Wade Spencer replied, impatient to obtain the information he came for.

"Sam's the one with the busted teeth. She's not your type, Mr. Spencer."

Wade noticed the tightness flash across the manager's face and immediately knew something was wrong. He had been here frequently enough so he knew he wasn't on their watch list. And besides, the *Sentinel* was careful to keep the club's name off its pages, so they owed him. "What do you mean by that?"

"Pardon me for saying it, but she...carries more weight than...the other girls you—"

"That's who I want tonight. Just get it set up."

The manager pulled out what appeared to be an accountant's log book and thumbed through it. Finding what she was looking for she looked up. "I'm terribly sorry Mr. Spencer, but Sam's not available."

"Booked all night?"

"Afraid so."

"Set me up for tomorrow then. I want two hours."

"She's not available tomorrow either."

"What the hell's that about?" Wade demanded. "Just when the hell is she available?"

"I'm sorry but I don't see anything open."

"Give it to me straight. Is there a problem?"

"Listen, I'll level with you. You being who you are and all. Samantha has your name on her no-see list. I can't—"

Wade pounded his fist into the counter hard enough to cause the bouncer to take a step toward him. Wade glanced in his direction. "Back down, Johnny. I'm leaving now." Turning back to the manager, he said, "I'll give you twenty-four hours to fix whatever problem exists. You know me well enough to know I'm not a threat to any of your girls. You understand me?"

"I understand you very well, Mr. Spencer. Very well. I'll do what I can. But I can't promise."

"Do it, if you know what's good for the club!" Wade turned and flung the front door open and stomped across the porch and down the steps angrier than he had been in years. He did not even notice his brother-in-law, Clyde Higgins, sitting on the porch swing awaiting his turn to see Samantha.

The fact that Wade had been effectively ushered out of the facility told him what he had surmised. Samantha Nelson and Sally Mascar were one in the same. Otherwise there would be no reason for her to block someone she didn't even know. Why she had changed her name was unclear, but he was certain she had. Samantha had gained weight and had an ugly scar across her face. The manager had been right in one thing. Samantha was not someone he would normally be interested in.

He had gone to *Cospers Own* to apologize to Sally and to do whatever it took to free himself from the torment that consumed his life. All he wanted from her was forgiveness. He wanted to explain how he had tried to set it all right by anonymously establishing a charity that worked with rape victims and women who were in abusive relationships. He knew he couldn't turn back the clock and undo what he had so foolishly — and horribly — done to her. But he needed to talk to Sally, to apologize, perhaps even give her money to get her life in order. He was certain she'd understand. In time maybe he'd be able to heal himself.

Thirty-Three

The heat of the summer was taking a long time to dissipate. Samantha Nelson awoke in late October to find the morning temperature had dipped below eighty for the first time in months. In early spring she had started a small garden along the side of her rental house. The heat had discouraged her from working outside all summer so the remaining vegetables were hidden among the tall grasses and weeds.

To help her cope with the anxiety growing within her, she took advantage of the milder weather to clean up the garden. After thirty-minutes the sweat poured from her forehead and temples. She sought shade against the northern wall of the house. Using the garden hose, she drenched her face, then sat down to allow her body to cool. As she sat slumped against the house, her mind reengaged with reality. Her agitation stemmed from the events of the night before.

Sam's shift at *Cospers Own* had started with Clyde Higgins flashing two one-hundred dollar bills. Where he managed to get the money she had no idea. He had demanded a full hour.

'Mostly to talk,' he had said. He kept his word about that. He used the time to try and convince her to leave the brothel. He wanted her to 'go back and work a regular job,' as he had put it.

"So you can get free tail, is that what you want?" Samantha had snapped back at him. It had come out harsher than she had intended, but she was tired of everyone telling her what was good for her.

"No, I'll pay," he immediately replied. "I don't like you... you know...doing this with every guy waiving green at you."

"I need the money."

"For what?"

"I don't ask you what you do with your money — or even where you get it — so it's not your business what I do with mine!"

"I don't want you doing this."

She had seen the hurt in his face and tried to soften her tone. "You were happy before I worked here. You knew I was seeing other men. You said nothing."

"It's different now. I don't like this."

"There's one way to stop me. Only one."

"What would that be," Clyde had replied, smiling a bit now in anticipation of being able to accommodate her.

"Marry me."

His face fell. Before he could respond, she said, "See what I mean. The last thing, the very last thing, you want is to marry me. And yet you think you can tell me what to do."

"I can't. It's impossible."

"Then get on with the business you came here for. You're almost out of time." She had pulled her jumper over her head revealing her naked body to him.

Undressing with the lights on was a mistake and she realized that immediately. But it was too late. His eyes went wide at the sight of the welts extending across her stomach and chest. Welts inflicted a week earlier by a whip when a drifter had experienced performance problems. Yesterday had been her first day back to work.

The fact that the cowboy had been dumped ten miles out in the country with both legs broken and no transportation did nothing to repair her body, or to compensate her for missed opportunities.

"Who did that to you?" Clyde demanded, fire in his eyes. "I'll kill the sorry bastard!"

"Goes with the territory, I'm afraid. Forget it." She turned the lights low. "Come to Sam, honey. I'll take good care of you."

He gingerly touched her face, pulled her slowly against him. "I'll kill the bastard if I ever find out who it was."

After work, Samantha's manager stopped her. "The man on your 'no-see' list stopped by earlier. "I told him you were booked the entire night. But...he got angry."

"Why are you telling me this?" Samantha asked, anticipating where this was leading.

"It's not good for business, Miss Sam. Not good to refuse a man with his power. He could dish us a world of hurt."

"I won't see him, and that's final!" Sam snapped. "Want me to move on, just say it. But he's not getting near me!"

Not wanting to ruffle the feathers of the woman who, after just a few months, had become one of their top producers, the manager answered, "You're new to these parts. You might be having the son and the father mixed. Son's fine. Never had any problems. Always tips nice. His father, Old Jackson Spencer, well, he's a different story altogether." The manager's eyes closed and her face set hard. "That old man was a problem. He would have been jailed if he hadn't controlled the town. Came in here with whips and sometimes tire chains." She unzipped her skirt and let it fall to the floor. "See this scar?" the manager asked, pointing to a red welt two inches long across her right thigh, "He did that to me one night. And that wasn't the worse he did. That was the night he got so carried away he up and died. Right here in this room. Johnny and the boys drove him down to the paper. Left him in the paper's parking lot."

"Why are you telling me this?"

"I'm thinking you heard a story and got the son and father mixed. You have no reason to blackball the son. If he brings a whip, it's to use on himself. Sometimes he needs...let me just say...a little stimulation. But what I'm saying is Wade's not known to be a problem, not like his old man."

"I don't have them mixed up!" Samantha barked. "I won't see Wade. And that's final."

"Okay," the manager capitulated, "we'll handle it. Don't you worry."

But Samantha did worry. Mr. Wade Spencer might be the big-shot owner of the *Sentinel*, but he also raped her when she was fourteen. Yes, it was true that without him, her daughter, Malinda, who was more precious to her than life itself, would never have come into this world. But the fact remained, she would not, indeed could not, ever forget or forgive what he did to her. She was determined, and every day she renewed that determination, to make Wade pay for the way he had ruined her life.

Hearing the news of Wade appearing at *Cospers Own* was the second thing that had happened last night. Bad things, she knew always came in threes.

But it was the third thing that had kept her up most of the previous night. *Cospers Own* had received a phone call seeking a booking for tonight. The caller had offered to pay five thousand dollars in advance, and a thousand dollar bonus if she gave him what he wanted. He had also stipulated that she would see no one else that night. And while the man had refused to divulge his name, he had promised he would provide sufficient identification when he arrived to satisfy their requirements. The call had come from a pay phone, so they could not immediately verify its authenticity.

Sam was assured that these types of arrangements, while uncommon, had occurred in the past and had never caused any problem. The manager had, however, refused the caller's request to take Sam off premises. The recent beating she had suffered was fresh on her mind.

The manager reminded Sam, "This club's been operating for over sixty years with very few problems. Everyone in the county, including every wife and girl friend, knows we're here. They also know we serve a useful civic purpose. The girls here are clean, violence is rare, and nobody gets their name in the paper. The cops leave us alone 'cause sex crimes in our county are lowest in the state. Everybody wins. We need to keep it that way."

"So why'd you let that creep get to me?"

"Mistakes do occur, Sam. I'm sorry. I thought he worked permanently on the Janeck spread. Turned out to be a drifter that Jesse didn't filter properly when he called, which is why I fired her. I know that doesn't make your attack any less horrible, but at least that low-life won't be bothering anybody else for a long, long time."

"I read in the paper he got himself thrown from his horse."

"Imagine that," the manager giggled, "even his own horse couldn't stand him."

The rates that Sam commanded for her services were the highest of all *Cospers Own*'s girls, but yet her clients were willing to pay. The manager had asked her on more than one occasion what her secret was, even going so far as to comment, "Pardon me for saying this directly to you, but truth is, you're not the greatest looking filly in this stable. And goodness knows your weight is...well...I know you've worked at getting it down...and you're doing a good job so don't get me wrong...but, let's just say it's...it's still higher than some of the others. So what's your secret?"

"I care about each one of them. They all have problems. I talk to them. I don't hate every man who comes through the door like most of the others here do. That's why they come back. It's not all about the sex."

A bird flying close to Sam's head jolted her out of her reverie. She went into the house for a drink and while in the kitchen she once again checked her hiding spot and counted her money. With what she would receive tonight she was halfway to her goal. Pleased, she slipped out a little of the cash and took six-year old Malinda to the new Walmart.

"Go ahead, dear, pick out a movie."

This was the first time Sam had allowed her daughter to buy anything and the girl was excited. She spent over a half-hour looking through the DVD selection and finally settled on Disney's *Toy Story*. Then the child said, "Mommy, another one. Another one, please. I want this one." She pointed to *George of the Jungle*.

"Sure, Honey, you can have that one too." She hoped that the DVD player she had picked up at a garage sale the day before worked. These were the first two DVDs Samantha had ever bought.

Thirty-Four

"I found a house in Cosper that is perfect!" Caroline exclaimed when she hung up the phone after a long conversation with the realtor. "There's an office suite for you and everything's on a single floor. It's perfect."

"What makes it so perfect?" Cecil asked, yielding to Caroline's excitement.

"It was custom built for the wife of the *Axtel Industries* president. She had a stroke and is confined to a wheelchair. It's on the outskirts of town on a large lot with plenty of separation from neighbors, just as you suggested. The realtor says the husband was fired. They won't be moving in."

"I read about that. The company had a gear train recall and the stock price fell. I looked at their gear train and the stupid thing is they can save a ton of money by a simple design change that doesn't even require the worm gear. In fact, there are three gears doing the job of one, adding friction and weight and cost."

"I'm talking about buying the house and you're dreaming about design changes to some worm gear," Caroline said, half chiding. "What about the house?"

"Buy it if you like."

"Will you live there with me?"

"Where else would I live?"

"It's settled then," Caroline said, knowing when to stop negotiating.

"Whatever," Cecil replied, visualizing the inner workings of the *Axtel* transmission using his new design.

"What'll happen to the workers?" Caroline asked. "More importantly, what'll happen to the town?"

"Unless someone buys the company and fixes their problem, I'm afraid they'll all be laid off, most likely within a year."

Caroline frowned. "*Axtel* is the economic driver for Cosper. There's no other company there who can employ all those folks. The town'll die."

Cecil's focus returned to his sister. He had never before heard her express concern for other people. He had no love for Cosper and wondered why all of a sudden his sister did. They had enough money to live anywhere in Texas—in fact, anywhere in the world—so why Cosper?

Maybe it was the result of her psychological counseling and the therapy sessions with the surrogate that had changed her attitude toward others. He knew she had met with the agency back in mid-January and since that time had not said one word about how it was going. There had been other subtle changes in her, but he was unable to figure out exactly what they were, other than there had been no more discussions of sex.

Cecil had been counseled by his own therapist not to discuss his sister's therapy with her unless she brought it up. So far, and to his relief, she had not. It was now completed, six months being the limit allowed by the agency. From what he had read, she was now on her own.

"Something's troubling you," Caroline said after several minutes of silence. "What is it?"

"Nothing much, other than I'm puzzled over your sudden interest in the well-being of the folks in Cosper. I thought you disliked Cosper. What gives?"

"I was just thinking. If the men are out of work and trained in gears and things, wouldn't it be a great business to buy? We can use them to build our next product."

"Barely six months out of my company and you want to start a new one. Let's wait a while, settle in, get our house set up. Then see what life brings."

"That was yours. This will be ours. And the timing is perfect."

"You can't just buy a company and then tell everyone they'll be making something they never saw before. Besides, the factory, the whole setup, production-lines, everything, is tailored to produce drive-trains for cars. That won't work for personal bots."

"That's a shame," Caroline said, seemingly agreeing with Cecil. "The reports certainly aren't hopeful. They're about to close the factory. Actually, they have no other choice. With the recall, they'll run out of capital."

"So you've been studying them. What are you thinking? Out with it."

"Just something Liz said got me thinking."

"Liz," Cecil said, puzzled. "I don't know—"

"Liz Mascarati. You might remember her as Classico. Liz Classico. She was in the accident with me."

"Is she also—"

"She's fine. Married to a cop. Nice guy. She's my best friend. About the only person who came to visit when I first got home. We talk on the phone almost every day. She was saying how the town seems to be dying. They're even cutting back the town budget. Her husband's concerned about promotions."

"So what's that got to do with *Axtel*? He's a cop, not a welder."

"Buy it cheap. If you redesign the drive train like you said you could, it'll be better than what everybody else in the industry is doing. It will also be cheaper."

"I have no experience running factories, or in selling to automotive companies. We'll get killed."

"We can hire the best plant manager in the business. Let him run the place. I'll be behind the scenes. It'll be fun. Most importantly, it'll give me a reason to get up in the morning."

"Banks will never loan us the money. Not without experience."

"That's where you're wrong, brother dear. We can get all the capital we need. You just sold a company you started from scratch. And it sold for over two hundred-fifty million. You have what they call credibility."

"Lucas is the one who did it. I just designed the bots. I don't know a thing about working with people. I can't understand them."

"Don't sell yourself short. We can do it. We can get Lucas to help."

"He retired."

"We can do it."

"You're crazy. You know that?"

༺༻

The conversation over the *Axtel* venture was lost in a flurry of move-in activities until late October. After dinner one evening Caroline said, "Build me a fire tonight. The weather's cooled enough so we can test out the fireplace. Let's see how it works."

"What do you mean the weather's cooled? It's still in the nineties out there."

"Close enough. Build a fire, a test run so to speak."

"How about tomorrow night? I was going out for a few hours tonight."

"And leave me alone in this big house? I can't stay here alone. Not yet."

"The bots are working fine now. No more battery problems. No more unexpected lock ups. You'll be fine. I hardy even have to touch you anymore."

"You never know with mechanical things. Something always goes wrong at the wrong time. Count on that."

"I'll call Mother," Cecil responded, picking up his cell phone. "She'll come over and stay the night."

"Don't bother her. This is Wednesday night."

"I know it's Wednesday. What's that got to do—"

"Mother's night out with the girls. They play some card game or other. Never misses it."

Cecil thought about his mother and the image flitted through his head of her going to a place like *Cospers Own*, only for women. "I didn't know Mother went out."

"How would you know? When you lived here all you cared about was taking engines apart. Then you went away."

"They sent me away. There's a difference. Banned from Cosper is what really happened!"

"Anyway, don't bother Mother. Stay with me. We can talk. I miss that. I miss companionship, someone to be here in the room with me."

"I have something I want to do." He was not about to tell Caroline about his plans to visit Sally at *Cospers Own*. He also knew he could never tell her about his feelings for Sally. Caroline would just get angry and demand more of his time. "We can build the fire tomorrow."

"As soon as I ask you to do something for me, you put it off. All of a sudden you have something more important. You got a girl, it that it?"

Cecil realized this was going to end badly. He relented and built the fire. They settled down together, neither of them taking the lead in initiating conversation. After a while, Cecil drifted off to sleep. When he woke, Caroline said, "See you're exhausted from all this moving. Taking care of me is trying as well. It's a full-time job."

"You're easy. You do so much for yourself."

"Do you care about me?"

"Of course I care. What brought that on?"

"Never once have you asked about my therapy."

"I was told not to."

"Who told you that?"

"Thornton."

"How does she know what's right?"

"She's a therapist, she knows these things."

"Everyone's different. You want to know what happened or don't you?"

"Not if it's going to make me uncomfortable. If you're going to talk about sex and stuff, then—"

"Grow up already! You're always uncomfortable. I think you're uncomfortable around women, period."

"We were talking about your therapy, not mine."

"Yours is more interesting. Mine is because I'm a quad. My body's different. Yours is in your head. Hey, look up and stop pouting. I thought you were over that."

"You know I'm not comfortable talking about these things."

"Get comfortable, will you. Okay, I'll talk about mine. The good news is that I'm no longer a virgin! The better news is I do have some feeling. It's better than nothing. Maybe someday you can design a bot to move my hips properly. But I now know I can do it with a man—if I find a man willing. That's a really big if."

"I suppose that *is* good news," Cecil managed, his face and neck burning. He forced himself to look up from the floor. "Let's change the subject. Let's talk about the bot that—"

"Are *you* willing? I mean to work on a bot to help me? You'll have to learn the proper motion. Go over to *Cospers Own* and take some lessons. You and Clyde Higgins can share the same woman."

Cecil at first didn't realize what his sister meant. But as he continued to focus on what she had just suggested, his head fell and the words of a mantra formed. *Stop this. Stop this. Stop this. Stop this.* He managed to keep it inside. Instead he said, "I won't work on the bot if you do that again."

Caroline exclaimed, "I should have known you didn't love me, even though you say you do. I should have known better. You don't, do you?"

He slowly looked up at her, saw her pleading eyes, her chin quivering, and replied, "Yes, Caroline, I love you. I love you very much. But—"

"There can't be any buts in love! Either you do, or you don't! Actions speak!"

Cecil's face burned and he did not know what to say. He moved even further away from her and again focused on the floor. Softly at first and then gradually louder and louder, the mantra formed. "I can't! I can't! I can't! I can't!"

"Stop that!" Caroline demanded. "You're acting like...like a spoiled child!"

"I am not!" he managed. He wanted to tell her that Higgins's girl was Sally. He wanted to tell her that he was in love with Sally, but all that came out was, "I can't! I can't! I can't! I can't!"

Caroline, attempting to stand and take herself to her room, lost control of the leg bots and fell. She landed face down on the floor at his feet.

Cecil's chant continued. "I can't! I can't! I can't! I can't!"

The leg bots were now useless and the bot on Caroline's right arm had come loose. She willed her left arm to move ever so slowly toward Cecil's legs, thinking that if she could engage his ankle with the pincher motion of her fingers it would break the mantra.

But the angle was wrong. All she could manage was to bring her left hand under his where his eyes seemed to be focused, but she could not force it to move close to his leg.

"I can't! I can't! I can't! I can't!" the chant continued.

The mechanical motion of the bot finally came into focus below him. In his mind he could see the angle was wrong; the pinchers were not lined up properly and were in danger of becoming bent. His attention riveted on the mechanical linkages. His chant abruptly ceased. "They're all wrong!" he exclaimed. "They'll break!" He bent forward. "I'll relieve the pressure here," he said, taking hold of the left arm bot. It'll move this way better."

Cecil's attention focused entirely on the engineering problem laying in front of him and it wasn't until he adjusted the pinchers that he realized Caroline was lying on the floor, crying and in obvious distress. "What are you doing down there?" he asked, clearly puzzled. "Did you slip? I'll help get you up so we can finish adjusting the bots properly."

He gently turned her over and eased her back up onto the sofa. "Are you hurt?" He was concerned that she might have been injured internally. "Should I call the doctor?"

"Nothing a good mechanic can't repair," she snapped, tears continuing to stream down her face.

"What happened?" Cecil asked when she was sitting upright on the sofa, all four bots again operating properly.

"I lost control trying to stand."

"That hasn't happened in months."

"It happens when I lose concentration."

"That's not good."

"Tell me something I don't know."

"You know it. So don't do it."

"Easy for you to say, brother dear. Easy for you to say."

THIRTY-FIVE

"So, he stood you up," Sam's manager said. "It's his money. You had a night off, and got paid exceedingly well for it. What more can a lady want?"

Sam had come in early the next morning to chat with her manager. "It's bothering me who he is. You sure he can't be traced?"

"Honey, when someone with that kind of dough wants to remain unknown, he remains unknown. Period! End of story. Not good for business if we tried."

"There must be something from the check."

"Bahamas. Some partnership or something down there."

"You think it's drug money?" Sam asked, her concern rising.

"Could be anything. Leave it alone. He'll rebook. We'll check it out then."

"Could it be Wade?" She couldn't think of anyone else who had that kind of money. She thought back to the various creeps she had dealt with since Austin. Not one of them would pay that kind of money for anything, even assuming they had it to spend. "I'll not accept Wade for any amount of money."

"It's not Wade. His voice I know. But whoever it is, if he's willing to put up that kinda money, he'll be back. That much I can promise."

"I'll leave it up to you. But no Wade."

"That reminds me, what's up with his brother-in-law, Clyde Higgins? Man's here regular like. What he and Alice do in their bedroom I can't vouch for, but seems they get along, go places together."

"He likes me, that's all I know."

"Does he make you perform special?"

"Talk is what he wants most of. Sex he does 'cause he feels he has to. Manhood thing. He likes to be held close. He talks about his life. I listen real good."

"Where's he get the dough?"

"Drives a truck for the paper. Does the repairs himself and keeps the repair money."

"Does he ever get rough?"

"Not Clyde. When he saw the welts, he like near went crazy. Said he'd kill the man who did it."

"Cowboy's in a wheelchair over at the charity hospital. They sold his horse, won't be need'n the ole mare for a long while. Don't tell Clyde, or he might just finish the asshole off."

"Clyde's a good man. Wish I could find me one like him."

"Don't we all, sweetie, don't we all."

ಸಂಬಂ

Business at *Cospers Own* had been tapering off because of the continuing layoffs at *Axtel* and at Halloween the manager ran a half-off special to anyone wearing a costume.

That night Sam entertained Jack the Ripper, two gorillas and a large penis. She was tempted to ask the penis impersonator why he hadn't dressed up, but the episode with the cowboy was still too fresh in her mind. Her hand went involuntarily to the still tender welts on her stomach.

Clyde came in without a costume. When Sam asked him why, he said he knew she needed the money, so he didn't feel right paying half. When she told him he could have just refused the discount, he replied he hadn't thought of it that way.

"Suppose the layoff's been hurting your business," Clyde said when they were snuggled on the bed. "The paper's hurt'n. And revenue's way down. Things are looking bad. Rumor has it *Axtel* will close by year's end."

"We're all in this together it seems. I've been savin' and savin' and can't get enough for what I want."

"Why won't you tell me what you're savin' for?" Clyde asked, not for the first time.

"It's a surprise. Can't tell you."

"Pretty please."

"Don't start that. I won't tell."

"There may be good news. A rumor's floating that someone's going to buy the plant. It's all mysterious and hush-hush like. I hear the new owner has a new design ready and all."

"When will you know?"

"Better be soon or this town'll be gone."

"Maybe I'll be moving on then. Don't want to wait too long."

"Oh no, Sam," Clyde exclaimed. "Don't leave! What'll I do without you?"

"What you did before."

"I was miserable before. You make life bearable."

"Girl's gotta do what a girl's gotta do. Now let's get on with it."

"Not tonight. You just got me real upset over your moving on. Please don't go."

"I won't if the plant stays open. If not, then — "

"Don't say nothing. I don't want it comin' true."

ಖಡ

Later, when Sam was checking out for the night, the manager said, "Even with the discount, we did better tonight than any night in the last two months. But even so, if'n things don't pick up soon, don't know what'll happen."

"Clyde says someone is buying the *Axtel* plant."

"Who'd want that ole place? From what I hear, machinery is old, and not working well. Their transmissions don't work well. It'll take a lot of money to fix it up."

"Some folks who don't want to be known, Clyde says."

"Speaking of not wantin' to be known, this is your lucky night. That rich guy who stood you up's comin' back."

"When?"

"Tomorrow night. Money will be in the account in the morning. Same terms."

"Another five thousand!"

"Plus the bonus."

"I get it even if he doesn't show, right?"

"Like before, minus our cut."

"Then I'll have all I need."

"For what?"

"Me to know."

"Go home to your gorgeous baby. By the way, I never did ask you. Who takes care of her when you're here?"

"Got an arrangement with a guy. I feed her and get her ready for bed. He watches TV with her and puts her down."

"You paying him?"

"He gets a place to eat and sleep. Gets himself a freebie once a week."

"More than some husbands," the manager smiled, "judging from the traffic we get here."

"Has my no-see been back?"

"Funny you should ask. He came around two nights ago asking for you again. This time he knew your name. Said he knew his brother-in-law was cheating on his sister with you and wanted to confirm it. We politely declined to discuss it. He had several drinks in the bar and then left. Then today an article appeared in the paper, written by, of all people, his sister Janet

Spencer, condemning us. She accused us of home wrecking. Got a call from the sheriff asking if I saw the article. Told him I had, but that I didn't know what Spencer was talking about. Told him we run an honest dancehall here."

"You think there'll be trouble?"

"This place's been here a lot longer than Wade Spencer — or the sheriff for that matter. Fact is, Wade's granddaddy founded this club. It'll blow over sure as we're standing here."

"I'm worried. This ain't good. I can't afford to get arrested again. This time they'll take Malinda."

"Your baby'll be just fine. Go home, get some sleep. Tomorrow night we'll all get to meet your wealthy secret admirer. I'm as curious as you are."

Thirty-Six

"Alice," Wade called to his sister, "stay for a moment, would you?" The staff meeting had gone on longer than expected and the reporters were eager to get back to their deadlines. "Close the door," he said, "this is private."

"What's going on?" Alice asked, curious as to what was on Wade's mind. He had been pretty clear at the staff meeting that the paper was suffering. Everyone had expected him to announce layoffs. When that hadn't happened there had been a collective sigh of relief.

When Alice was seated, Wade began, "As I said, the financials don't look good for the long term, but so long as *Axtel* continues to advertise at the level they have been we can make it. What I didn't say is that I see no reason for them to continue. When they pull the plug, we're not far behind."

"Everyone knows that. Goes without saying. Something else is on your mind?"

"Can't a brother and sister have a chat without some other motive?"

"At the paper I'm an employee. Friendly talks are at home. Isn't that what Dad taught us?"

Wade thought for a moment before he spoke. He had been pacing the floor and now stood with his back to the only window in his office. His head was perfectly framed in the branches of a live oak older than the building. "Even with *Axtel* we'll be lucky to last a year, two at most, unless something big happens."

"So why are you telling—"

"Money. You and Clyde both work here. When the paper's gone—"

"Don't you think I know it? But there's nothing out there for either of us."

"It's not only that, but...but listen to me. Clyde's not being prudent. He's over at *Cospers Own* and you—"

"What the hell you think I can do about that?" she snapped. "Throw him out? Then what?"

"He's spending every penny he makes on that hooker."

"If you must know, and it's really not your business, I've had words with him about it. He says it's nothing. I told him to stop. He promised me he did. I thought he had. But...but...it might be too late for that." Tears formed in the corners of her eyes and she looked away. "If you must know, we're in separate beds now."

"Do you know who the woman is?"

"Her name's Sam. Samantha something. That's all I know." When Wade didn't respond, she asked, "And just why do you care who she is? You know something I should know?"

Wade shrugged and looked away, but not before his sister caught a flicker of what she interpreted as fear in his eyes.

"What is it? You clearly know something I should know."

Wade slowly walked to his desk and slumped in his chair. Without looking up, as if talking to himself, he said, "I think she's someone who lived in this town years ago. But I'm not certain."

"Who?"

"I'm not going to say until I know for sure."

"Do I know her?"

"Don't think so," Wade lied. "This was long ago."

"Have you been...seeing her? Is that what this is about?"

"I was just curious if you knew who she was? That's all. I also want Clyde to stop seeing her."

"Only thing that'll stop Clyde at this point is if he runs out of money." The tears started again.

Wade excused himself to go to the men's room, closing the door behind him to give his sister privacy.

ಬಐ

"Now that you own it, what's the next step?" Cecil asked Caroline. They were discussing *Axtel Industries* while he prepared dinner. Caroline was sitting in her wheelchair looking out into the back yard. She had been using the chair more and more lately because it moved her around faster than maneuvering with the bots.

For the first time since Caroline's accident, the passage of time meant something to her. The number of documents she had to review and discuss and argue over was overwhelming to the point where she had finally allowed Cecil to hire helpers for her. A bit of bribery was involved. The helpers were her concession for him working on the *Axtel* gear train. She knew that once he became immersed in the project he would be hooked. Focus was his strong point. Lock him onto something and he never let go.

True to form, once Cecil analyzed the current gear-train, he realized that the entire design was faulty. He then undertook a complete redesign even before the closing.

"Next step," Caroline said, concentrating on a pair of mockingbirds, "is waiting for you to say that the new design is ready. Once we get to that point, we can build a few prototypes to confirm the design."

"I was thinking along other lines," Cecil replied. "The deal closed today. The workers are agitated. There are rumors in town about the plant closing. Why not make an announcement of the new product and let it be known everyone will be rehired by the first of the year?"

Caroline held her ground. "How do I know how many people we'll need and when they will be required? We'll stage them coming back."

"You talk like an old-line manager," Cecil observed. "What happened to the *let's save all their jobs* slogan you were mouthing a few weeks back?"

"It's my money at risk here," Caroline snapped. "We need time to make this work. Whose side are you on anyway?"

"Just trying to figure out where you're going with this thing. The new design will work. You can build prototypes all you want, but it'll work."

"How do you know?"

"I can see it. They can mock one up in a week. I designed it to use the parts already being made, just fewer of them, and arranged differently. If we make the announcement tomorrow, we can move forward. We can organize the manufacturing process and I can meet with the chief engineer and work through everything."

"Won't we need sign-off from the car manufacturers to use the new design?"

"I can't imagine that will be difficult. If we move fast enough, the new design can be used in place of the older one for the recalls."

"I'll think about when to make the announcement," Caroline said. "But remember, I don't care how hard they press you, you can't reveal I'm involved. I don't want to be dragged into the public spotlight. The paper trail shows an off-shore company as owner. No amount of digging will get to me. The best they'll find is the name of a fictitious businessman by the name of C. H. Armstrong."

"Is Lucas still working with you?" Cecil asked. "You're starting to sound just like him."

"He's very helpful," Caroline admitted. "We talk every few days. He's in the background and just gives me comments."

"Dinner's ready," Cecil announced. "Let's eat."

"We're eating early tonight," Caroline observed. What's up?"

"Going out. Mother will be here. I invited her to eat with us, but she had a book club dinner. They all go out once a year to celebrate. Your helper will stay until Mother gets here."

"Where are you going?"

"Out."

"With a girl?"

"I'm going out. Leave me alone. Every time I try to go out you badger me. I'm entitled to do what I want at night."

"You're meeting someone. Fess up. Who is it?"

Cecil's face flushed, but he struggled to remain in control. "An old school friend."

"Boy or girl?"

"Boy."

"You're lying. It's written all over your face. Besides, you have no school friends."

"Did so."

"Who then?"

"It's private."

"It's a girl! You're meeting a girl!"

"No."

"Don't tell me you're getting mixed up with that hoity-toity Alice—what's her married name—Higgins? She can't even keep her own husband satisfied. He goes to that disgusting *Cospers Own* club at least twice a week."

"How would you know something like that?"

"Mother tells me everything that goes on in this town. Some guy pinches an ass on Main Street and Mother's phone rings."

"Was it like that when Dad lived here?"

"I don't know. But a lion doesn't grow stripes."

"Lions don't have stripes."

"You know what I mean. Tigers do."

"Tigers? What do tigers—"

"Never mind. Drop it."

"You're giving Mother far too much credit. She can't know everything."

"Mother says ole Clyde followed that fat girl to the *dancehall*. You know, the one from the supermarket with the broken teeth."

"You've never seen her. How do you—"

"Like I said, Mother knows everything."

"Mother should mind her own business."

"She says Clyde spends more money on that woman than he makes, unless she's giving it away."

"You're disgusting! Is that all you ever think about?"

"Before I bought the company it was, yes. Now, I have other things to keep my mind active."

"That's a relief. Maybe you can get Mother involved in something also. Make her your assistant."

"Afraid nothing will pry her from her gossip. She gets out of sorts on days when her busybody network isn't humming at full capacity."

Caroline studied her brother across the table and suddenly a mischievous grin appeared. "You sly weasel!" she teased. "You're going to that...that *dancehall* club to get yourself laid." That embarrassed look gave you away. Took me a while, but that's where you're going, isn't it?"

Cecil glared at her, but said nothing.

"I can't say as how I blame you, brother dear. I'd do the same if I was able—and if I was a man—and if there were places like that for women."

"Stop talking that way! You know I don't like it."

"By the way," Caroline continued, ignoring her brother's discomfort, "*Cospers Own* was in the paper yesterday. The story was written by Alice's sister, but I bet Alice put her up to it or maybe even wrote the article herself. Anyway, it called on the sheriff to close the place down. Mother says Alice is upset 'cause her husband's getting it on with that slut over there. But I have a different theory. I think Alice doesn't care about him getting laid. Just cares about the money he's spending."

"You're getting as bad as Mother. Worse even!" Cecil declared. "And stop referring to her as a slut!"

"What's it to you?" Caroline shot back. "That's what Mother calls her 'cause that's what Alice Spencer's mother calls her. They talk to each other several times a day."

"Don't stoop to their level."

"Oh, I get it," Caroline said, as the mischievous grin returned. "You know her real name. Hah! You know who the slut is. Gimme a name, then I can correct Mother."

"None of her business — or yours either."

"Oh I get it," Caroline replied, obviously enjoying getting a rise out of her brother. "Clyde's not the only one she's seeing. Is that it?"

Cecil avoided the question. "It just bothers me to hear people called names. I know what that feels like."

"How about bringing home one of the johns hanging around over there? I'll give it away free. It's been six months and I'm getting pretty needy."

"Stop that!"

"Just keep me in mind if you find any candidates."

Thirty-Seven

Cecil was an hour behind schedule by the time he arrived at *Cospers Own*. Caroline had insisted that he not leave until Maggie called to say that she was on her way.

He parked the Ghia several blocks away, in a public parking lot, not wanting his car seen outside the brothel. His heart nearly leaped out of his chest when he turned the corner and saw a dozen state police cars and arrest vans parked in front of the club. He would have turned away instantly, but the thought of Sally being arrested overcame his reticence of being seen in proximity to the brothel.

He edged closer and watched as several men were led out in handcuffs — the bouncers, Cecil figured. They were followed by about a half-dozen women. Cecil moved closer, trying to see if Sally was among them, but he could not see their faces clearly enough. But all the women he saw appeared to be more or less petite and so Cecil was satisfied that Sally was not among them.

It seemed that the police were removing people based on gender, or maybe job description, and since Cecil had arrived in time to see the bouncers be led away, he concluded that Sally must still be inside. He inched even closer, pushing his way to the front to be sure he didn't miss seeing her.

Bright lights suddenly flashed directly toward him. Cecil was blinded for a moment while several people were marched past him moving toward the waiting vans. His vision cleared as the first of them disappeared into the van. He could not get a good look at any of the latest arrestees. He slammed his fist against his leg in anger.

Cecil remained where he was for another hour, as one by one the vans and cars pulled away, their blue and red lights screaming for attention. A uniformed trooper stopped directly in front of him and turned to face someone across from Cecil.

Suddenly, the bank of TV lights swiveled to illuminate the trooper. Cecil had to shield his eyes to keep from being blinded. Gradually, his eyes adjusted and when his vision returned there was a female reporter standing beside the trooper. She held a microphone in one hand and had an earphone jammed in her right ear.

Facing the camera, she began, "Thank you, Scott. As you said, I'm here in front of *Cospers Own*, a long-established men's club, talking to State Police Captain Vincent Stefiano." She turned sidewise to the camera and addressed the slightly overweight, middle-aged officer. "Captain," she continued, "I understand your home base is Austin." She paused long enough to allow Stefiano to nod in agreement, and then continued, "But you're on special assignment here in Cosper."

"That's right," the trooper confirmed.

"We've seen several women and a few men brought out of the club in handcuffs. This club has operated for many, many years without incident. Can you tell us what has changed? Did something happen?"

"We've had this establishment under surveillance for a while now," Stefiano said smoothly, clearly no stranger to TV cameras. "But until recently we had no reason to interfere with the local sheriff's department who has primary jurisdiction out here."

"Did something happen to change that arrangement?"

"A man was found not far from here with severe injuries. We have reason to believe those injuries were inflicted by one or more employees of *Cospers Own*."

"I understand that incident is being investigated by the sheriff. Does this mean the state is taking over the investigation?"

"All I'm at liberty to say at this point is that the incident is under investigation."

"Can you confirm or deny the rumor that the sheriff himself is being investigated?"

"No comment."

"Is the investigation of the sheriff linked to the injury that you refer to?"

"No comment."

"People are saying that *Cospers Own* will be open for business as usual tomorrow. Any comment?"

"I doubt that will be the case. The ladies you saw being brought out in cuffs are being charged with prostitution. They'll sit in jail until they can be arraigned and then raise bail money. There certainly will be a distinct lack of...professionals available to serve any of the clientele." A slight smile replaced the captain's hard-set chin. "In fact, I also believe there will be a distinct lack of clientele for the foreseeable future. Pictures in the local paper will see to that."

"We're also told that sex crimes are lower around here because of *Cospers Own*. How do you answer those who claim that places such as this actually make Cosper safer for women?"

"I'm not at liberty to address those kinds of speculations," Stefiano replied. "What I can say is that we have evidence that sex crimes in and around Cosper are grossly underreported by the local authorities."

"Is that why the sheriff is being investigated?"

"No comment."

"Okay Captain, I know you have a busy night ahead, so I'll let you get on with your work."

"Thank you, Nancy Jean."

The woman again turned to face the camera. "There you have it directly from State Police Captain Vincent Stefiano. *Cospers Own*, a popular private club here in South Texas, raided tonight for alleged prostitution. When the club will reopen is not clear. This is Nancy Jean Collins, WDHT Eyewitness News, reporting live from Cosper, Texas. Now back to you, Scott." The lights went out and the reporter handed her microphone to a technician. As Cecil stood there, wondering what had become of Sally, he overheard the reporter continuing her conversation with the captain, after apparently listening to instructions piped into her earphone.

"Off the record now, Vince," she began, "what's the real reason for this raid? This is the first in anybody's memory of a problem. What's changed?"

"Off the record, when the local paper turns against these places, the governor hears about it. This being an election year and all — well things just happen."

"Did you arrest all the women?"

"All but three that we know of. Somebody must have tipped off somebody because the manager was nowhere to be found and one of the girls had skedaddled with a bouncer a few minutes before we arrived."

"And the third?" the reporter asked.

"No basis to arrest her," the trooper replied. "She was just sitting in her room, fully dressed, staring vacantly at the door. No john in sight."

Thirty-Eight

Cecil's head pounded. He tried to read the clock but couldn't determine if it was ten in the morning or one in the afternoon. He had not gone straight home from *Cospers Own*, preferring instead to get drunk for the second time in his life.

All he remembered was the bartender forcing him into a cab, saying something like, "Get your car in the morning, Buddy. You'll not make it a block in your condition."

His head hurt and the pounding was getting louder.

Then the pounding stopped.

A few moments later, it started again. This time, sounding like a knock on his bedroom door.

A voice called, "Mr. Harris, a man to see you. Says he needs to speak with you. Mr. Harris, you okay? You never sleep this late."

The voice sounded familiar, but he couldn't place it.

More knocks. The voice again. "Mr. Harris, are you okay?"

He grunted, "Go away." But it came out a deep moan. Then he recognized the voice. It belonged to Caroline's helper, Miguel.

"Mr. Harris, sir, a man is here to see you. What should I say to him?"

"Go away!"

"Him or me?"

"Both!"

Cecil sat up. His head pounded even harder. The room spun. Gradually, the fog cleared. He thought back to last night and immediately his concern for Sally overwhelmed him. *Maybe Sally was in trouble and needed his help?* "No, wait," he called, "I'll be down soon."

Holding onto the bed, and then the dresser, Cecil took tiny steps across his bedroom. By the time he made it to the bathroom he was mostly upright without support. The pain and dizziness came and went.

He splashed water on his face and didn't feel anything. He did it again and the motion brought on nausea and he lost the contents of his stomach in the sink. Nothing solid. Two more heaves. Then nothing at all.

He drank a glass of water. Halfway through the second glass the sick feeling stopped.

He went numb.

Numb was better than sick. At least being numb he could walk straight. He pulled on a pair of sweats and an old shirt. Not exactly office attire, but he wasn't going to an office. This was his house he told himself, and by God he could dress as he liked in his own house.

Slowly, he made his way from the sleeping wing to the living room, gaining confidence in his ability to navigate as he progressed.

Sitting on the sofa holding a cup of coffee was the last person in the world Cecil had expected to see in his house.

The man placed the coffee cup on the side table and stood when Cecil entered the room. "In case you haven't seen it, and from the look of you I'm sure you haven't, I brought you this morning's *Sentinel*. Appears you made the front page." The visitor thrust a newspaper into Cecil's hand. "Open it."

"Oh, sure," Cecil managed. "What are you doing here anyway?"

"I'll explain in a minute. Just open the paper."

Cecil did as he was told. The front page of the paper had a picture of last night's raid on *Cospers Own*. There he was, big as life, smack in the center, standing behind a line of women being led away in handcuffs. The discreet sign of *Cospers Own* was visible directly over his head.

"Quite frankly, Cecil, I was surprised to see you in that picture. Didn't know you and my brother-in-law were friends. Didn't know you frequented the club. Hadn't ever seen you there before."

"Your brother-in-law? What are you talking about? That's—"

"The guy standing next to you. That's Clyde Higgins, my brother-in-law. He works for me."

Cecil was stunned, his mind in overdrive, seeing lots of possibilities, but comprehending none. He forced himself to take a deep breath, as he had been taught to do in moments of high anxiety. "Just passing by," he murmured. "Saw the commotion and stopped to see what was going on."

"I don't believe that for a moment," Wade responded. "But it's no skin off my nose what the hell you were doing."

"Skin off your nose?" Cecil studied Wade, trying to do as he had been taught and read a clue. But he saw no clues. "Oh, a saying. I get it. I need coffee, clear my head. Please just sit. I'll be right back."

Cecil returned to the living room carrying a coffee cup. His hands shook so badly that liquid had splashed over the rim filling the saucer almost to overflowing. He carefully placed the saucer over the cup and tipped it to drain the liquid back where it belonged. Most of the errant coffee made its way back into the cup, but some spilled onto the carpet. "Not a good way to start the day," Cecil observed. "Had a few too many I suppose."

"More than a few too many from the looks of things," Wade laughed. "Hope you had something good-looking to celebrate with."

Cecil eased himself down into a chair opposite Wade. The two men hardly knew each other and Cecil was naturally uncomfortable. "I don't understand why you'd drive out here to talk about stuff like that. Or, frankly, to talk about anything. You must have better things to do."

"Actually, I'm working. I came to talk to you, on the record if you will, about your involvement with *Axtel*."

"No comment," Cecil replied, borrowing the phrase from the interview he witnessed last night. Cecil was not aware of the implications of "no comment" and did not realize he had just confirmed Wade Spencer's suspicions.

"Let me tell you what I know," Wade pressed. "I know you, or someone close to you, bought the company. I know you have designed a new transmission. I don't know the real owner."

"No comment."

"What's the story behind the transmission? Why design a new one?"

"No comment."

"You sound like that state police trooper on TV last night. If you haven't seen it already, you will. It's being rerun every hour."

"Why'd the *Sentinel* turn against them?"

"My mother has always hated that place. She said my dad spent too much time and money there. My brother-in-law practically lives there with...with Sal...with some broken-down tramp. He's been stealing truck repair funds to give to that bitch. I tried to go in to see her, to..." Wade caught himself, "to put a stop to it. They wouldn't allow me to see her. That pissed me off big time. That club's outlived its usefulness."

Cecil remained silent, not knowing what to say. He didn't like people calling Sally names, but felt helpless to say anything.

"*Cospers Own* is a diversion," Wade continued. "Talk to me about the new transmission. You saved this town. We've been on deathwatch for a long while now. If *Axtel* folds, the paper's finished and the town will wither. So, on a personal note, I thank you."

"No comment," Cecil repeated.

"Look, Cecil, I know you're behind this. You've been seen out at the plant talking to the workers. At least tell me about the new design."

In his element with mechanics, Cecil relented and told Wade about how the new drive train worked, and how it was more cost effective. He discussed how he expected the demand to grow because of the fuel efficiency the new transmission would produce. "Fuel efficiency is what it's going to be all about. I expect to double the output of the factory within a year."

Wade took copious notes. Cecil drew him a diagram of the gear interaction that coupled motion with lubricating fluid injection. Belatedly, Cecil remembered the admonition of his patent counsel not to discuss how the gear train worked. "Don't print this sketch. It's still secret."

"Okay, I'll treat that part as background. Now I'm not a mechanic mind you," Wade said, "but I happen to know a fair amount about transmissions. This one is very different. How do you know it'll work?"

"It'll work all right."

"Well, I'll say this," Wade began, "if the gear train works as you say, this town will be stable for years to come. Again I thank you for stepping in."

"Stepping in" was an expression Cecil knew the meaning of. "I'm not the owner," he said. "Just a contractor helping them with the new design."

"Who owns it, then?"

"Some secret buyer."

"Who?"

"Don't know."

"I know you know."

"Don't."

"You wouldn't be doing this if it wasn't someone you knew."

"I grew up here and I want to help. And besides, it's a good design challenge. When they asked me, I couldn't help myself."

"Cosper threw you out! If they had done that to me I'd never set foot here again. If I had your money, I'd buy the place and pull the plug."

"What plug?" Cecil asked.

Wade waited to see if Cecil was serious, or just pulling his leg. When Cecil's puzzled expression didn't fade, Wade said, "Pull the plug, as in, turn it all off. Close it down."

"I don't own it. I can't do that."

"And you won't tell me who does?"

"Can't."

Wade stood. "If you won't tell me who's behind this then we have nothing further to discuss at this time. So, thanks again."

"Cecil," a faint voice called from down the hall, "who's there?"

"That your mother?" Wade asked. "I haven't seen her for years."

"My sister."

"Your sister. But I thought—"

"What did you think?" Caroline asked, moving slowly into the room. She was walking upright using her bots. "Wade Spencer!" Caroline exclaimed. "What a surprise. What brings you out to this neck of the woods?"

"Hello, Caroline," Wade replied, immediately uncomfortable in her presence. "I haven't seen you in a dog's age."

"Now whose fault is that? It can't be mine, as you can plainly see. I don't get out much these days."

"My fault, I know," Wade answered turning toward the door. "I have to go now."

"Don't leave so soon. How have you been? I haven't seen you since...since I don't know when."

Wade, fighting the urge to flee and feeling his neck begin to burn, turned back. "In high school. You were a sophomore, I believe, and I was a senior. You're moving around very well on those things. Very impressive. What are they called?"

"Bots. Short for robots. Cecil made them for me. The first product of the company he just sold. They changed my life."

"They appear to work well," Wade responded, the reporter in him pushing his anxiety into the background. "Now I understand how Cecil made so much money. Impressive." He studied the bots a moment longer and then said, "I would like to know how they work, but I really must be going. Can I interview you sometime? I mean about how they work."

"Cecil is the one to interview about operational aspects. I just use them."

"Both operational and...and practical."

"I would love to, but not for publication. We can do it now if you like," Caroline coaxed. "No one ever comes out to see me. It would be nice to talk. Have some coffee?" Seeing his hesitation, she added, "I'll even demonstrate how they work."

"Thanks," Wade replied, "but I really have to be going." He opened the door and slipped out. A moment later Caroline heard a deep throated-car start, the tires squealing as the car sped out of the driveway.

Caroline spotted the paper Wade had brought. Turning to Cecil, she said, "You two talking about your big night at the brothel? You did well to keep out of jail."

"What the hell are you talking about?" Cecil exclaimed.

"Watched it all on TV with Mother. Wait 'til she gets on your case, brother dear. She waited up for you to come home. But I was right. I told her you'd go hide somewhere."

"Why the hell were you and Mother watching TV at that hour? Mother never—"

"Wade's mother called and told her about the raid. And there you were, front and center. You and Clyde, old buddies having a night on the town. The two of you couldn't have paid for a better seat."

"Not funny! In the wrong place at the wrong time is all."

"I'll bet it's right here on the front page," Caroline said, pulling open the folded paper. "Yup. Here it is. Above the fold, even."

"It's wrong, it's wrong, it's wrong, it's wrong," Cecil began, his eyes now focused on the floor. He retreated to his room, continuing the mantra that wouldn't let up for over an hour.

Thirty-Nine

Samantha woke a little after two-thirty in the morning. She had slept fitfully, her mind alive, flitting from one thought to another. She had arrived home from *Cospers Own* at ten-fifteen, which was hours earlier than normal. The state police had detained her only long enough to take her picture. They actually were planning to arrest her along with the other women, but she had defied them.

"Hey, I'm alone here!" she had exclaimed in the most indignant voice she could summon. "And as you can plainly see, I'm fully clothed! So what have I done wrong?" It wasn't as if she hadn't had plenty of experience with the law. Samantha had been arrested for prostitution any number of times in the six years she worked for the Austin cult before she made her break and had been warned that one more arrest and her child would be taken from her.

"Sorry, miss. You're in the wrong place at the wrong time," one of the officers had muttered, not expecting to have his authority challenged.

"Whatever," Samantha had continued in her indignant tone, "you ever hear of false arrest? Put a hand on me and you'll learn all about it!"

The bluster had worked. The police told her to beat it out the back door. Sam raced home, only to find Dil, the guy who babysat Malinda, acting strangely. He had jumped from the sofa turning to face her, a startled expression on his face. Malinda, who should have been in bed sleeping, fell to the floor and began to cry.

Sam ran to her. "She should have been in bed long ago," she cried. "What's going on here?"

"We were watching one of her new DVD's and she fell asleep. I didn't want to disturb her." But the tone of his voice was wrong. If there was one thing Samantha did well, it was to read men and Dil was clearly hiding something.

She bent over her daughter. "It's okay, honey," she cooed, "Mommy's home now." Not seeing any evidence of injury, Samantha asked, "Did you hit your head?"

"I'm okay," Malinda said, still sniffling, but mostly quiet. Tears dripped down her cheeks and Sam wiped them dry. "My shoulder hurts, but it's mostly okay."

Samantha helped her daughter to the bedroom, gently pulled on her pajamas and in doing so checked her again. She was looking for any evidence of wrongdoing by Dil. Seeing nothing obvious, she put Malinda in bed and offered to read her a story.

Malinda replied, "I'm sleepy, mommy." She closed her eyes and was instantly asleep.

Sam returned to the living room to confront Dil. The expression she had seen on Dil's face had told a story she didn't like.

But Dil had gone to his room, leaving the TV on. Except it wasn't playing a DVD, it was tuned to the news. There stood Clyde Higgins in front of *Cospers Own*. And next to Clyde was Cecil Harris, a bewildered expression on his face.

Now, as she lay tossing in her bed, she couldn't stop fixating on the same questions over and over: *What were those two doing out there? Do they know each other? Do they talk about her? Who is Cecil seeing?*

When she exhausted the possibilities she started on Dil. *And why had her daughter been on the sofa with Dil? And they weren't watching a DVD. If that low-life did anything to Malinda, I'll castrate him!*

Suddenly, she heard a noise. She bolted upright in her bed. She then reached under the bed for the baseball bat she always kept handy. It was a precaution she had adopted her third week in Austin. After a little searching, her fingers closed on the shank.

She moved to the door and silently opened it. She heard footsteps moving in the direction of the kitchen. Baseball bat at her side, Samantha walked slowly down the hall and paused outside Malinda's room. Opening the door a crack she saw that the child was sleeping on her side clutching her stuffed elephant.

Samantha continued down the hall and noticed that Dil's door was slightly open. Peeking inside the small room she could see an empty bed. Then she heard another sound clearly from the kitchen. She froze with the bat ready to swing.

The sound came again, only this time she recognized what it was; the kitchen pantry ladder being opened. Sam pressed herself back against the wall to avoid throwing shadows from the faint light coming in through the living room window. The next sound she heard made her blood run cold. Her heart beat wildly and her focus narrowed. She ran the remaining few steps to the kitchen, the bat now high over her shoulder.

She entered the kitchen just as Dil stepped off the ladder, a metal container in his hand. He would never have seen the bat smash against his head, except that Samantha let out a sharp cry as she took the final step across the kitchen. He managed to raise the can to a position between the bat and his skull as the blow struck.

The impact deformed the can and sent it flying. It also sent Dil reeling against the refrigerator, his head having been grazed by the deflected bat. Paper money from the can filled the air.

"You son of a bitch!" Samantha screamed. "You bastard! I'll kill your sorry ass!"

Dil twisted sideways as the bat again came down, this time cracking against his chest.

"Christ, you broke my ribs!" he managed to cough out, his face contorted in pain. He rolled sideways to dodge another blow. "Christ! You're killing me!" he spat, blood mixed with saliva, as the lethal bat made contact with his ankle.

Dil rolled away, tried to stand, fell, scrambled to his knees, and then pulled himself up using the doorframe for support.

Samantha took a step toward him and he hopped toward the front door, trying to scoop up his duffle bag on the way out. He managed to carry the heavy bag halfway across the living room before his ankle gave out and he fell. He used the sofa to stand and all he could manage was, "Shit!" before he disappeared through the front door, leaving his belongings behind.

The only reason Dil made it across the room was because Sam stopped to retrieve the money that had spilled from the broken tin. She knew there had been roughly eight thousand dollars, mostly in hundreds. That meant she was looking for at least seventy-five Benjamin Franklins. She actually found seventy-eight, plus some twenties. "It's lucky it's all here, you asshole," she screamed in the direction Dil had vanished. "Otherwise I'd come after you and beat your filthy brains out!"

Then she slumped to the kitchen floor.

༄༅

Samantha was still on the floor twenty minutes later, when the doorbell rang. Believing it was Dil coming back for his clothes, she ignored it.

But the bell rang again a moment later, this time accompanied by a loud pounding. She got up, baseball bat in hand and walked to the door. "Who's there?" she yelled.

"Police. We need to speak with you."

It certainly wasn't Dil's voice. She dropped the bat and opened the door. Parked directly in front of her house was a police car with its lights flashing. She could see the outline of someone in the back seat, but could not make out who it was.

Standing at the front door was a police officer, a middle aged man with a slight paunch. A name-tag on his shirt read "Schneider." Standing behind him and slightly off to the side was a policewoman, her hand on her holster. Her tag said "Ann," which struck Samantha as terribly inappropriate. Maybe these weren't cops at all. Maybe they were reporters looking for a story. But the police car looked real.

"Evening ma'am," the man began. "I'm Sergeant Irwin Schneider, Cosper PD. This is my partner, Officer Kathy Ann. Is this your house?"

"I live here, if that's what you mean."

"And your name?"

"Samantha Nelson."

"We had a report of an altercation on these premises, Miss Nelson," the officer continued. "Know anything about that?"

"I tossed out my babysitter."

"What's his name?" The officer paused. "Or is it a her?" he said, correcting himself.

"Dil. Dilson Tylor."

"Just exactly what happened?"

"It's all okay. Everything's fine. I'm fine." Samantha made a move to close the door.

"Hold on, miss" the officer admonished. "It's not as easy as that. We had a report of screaming coming from these premises. On our way here we picked up a Mr. Dilson Tylor. He was injured pretty bad and stumbling down the street. He claims you beat him with a baseball bat. He claims he was in the kitchen looking for some cookies when you barged in like a madwoman and hauled off on him. So, just exactly what happened?"

"He was stealing my money," Samantha blurted out. "The no-good son-of-a-bitch tried to steal my entire life savings! Shoulda killed him!"

"That would not have been a very good idea," Schneider said, studying her eyes, trying to determine how serious she was about killing Dilson. "You're lucky he's not hurt worse than a few broken ribs, maybe an ankle. Anyway, I'm going to run him over to the hospital and get his full statement there. Officer Ann'll be taking your statement here. Then we can sort this all out."

"Am I under arrest?"

"For now, we just need to hear your side of what happened," Schneider replied. "Premature for any arrest."

"As long as it doesn't take too long. I got to get some sleep. My daughter gets up early and I need to get up when she does."

"Half-hour at most," promised Officer Ann, her hand still resting on her gun as she moved forward. "A half-hour and I'll be out of here."

The two of them watched as Schneider started toward his cruiser. Officer Ann then turned back to Samantha. "I wouldn't want to mess with you when you're angry," she said with a slight smile. "From the looks of it he has at least a couple broken ribs and if I'm any judge of it, a busted ankle. Nasty welt on the side of his head, too."

"Tell him if he ever comes around here again, he won't live to tell about it," Samantha shot back.

"It's not wise to go around making bodily threats like that," the officer advised.

She pulled out a pad and started writing.

"It's not a threat, officer. It's a statement of fact. You can tell him that as well!"

Forty

The next day Wade called to speak with Cecil. "Oh. It's you," Cecil exclaimed when he was called to the phone. "I've nothing more to say about *Axtel*."

"That's not at all why I called. I wanted to ask you if you think your sister would mind if I came by tonight? She's certainly an interesting person. I very much enjoyed my time with her."

"Call her if you want to."

"I was really asking you if you'd mind," Wade responded, his enthusiasm wearing thin. It had taken all his courage to even call Cecil. After leaving Caroline he realized that despite his initial anxiety, panic had not set in. Why that was so, he didn't know. But he did know that Caroline seemed safe for him.

"Why ask me? Why would I mind if you came to see Caroline? I don't understand."

"You seemed so...so...agitated when I was out there. I don't want to impose."

"You're coming to talk to her, not me. Not my business."

"Didn't want to disturb your routine."

"It's okay."

"Just thought I'd check. Sorry I agitated you again."

"Call my sister if you want, no business of mine."

After speaking with Wade, Cecil drove out to the *Axtel* factory to work with the production foreman in setting up the new production line. From the prototype test reports he had read, the drive-train had been performing perfectly and everyone was excited.

Cecil made his way to the glass-enclosed foreman's office overlooking the production floor. "Just the person I wanted to see!" the foreman exclaimed. "I've been studying your design and it'll be simple to mass produce. It's so...so...what's the word I'm looking for... elegant. That's it. The drive is elegant. Been in this business all my life and I've never seen one like it! We'll have no problem getting the workers up to speed. They're already pumped."

"I knew the train would work," Cecil responded, "but I've been concerned about assembly. I know nothing about that aspect."

"It's in good hands. No worries. The way it's designed, even a child could assemble it."

꽁꽃

Maggie was in rare form when Cecil walked into the house later that afternoon. A full hour after he arrived, his mother was still going strong, peppering him with questions about his being at the brothel.

"I've told you at least five times, Mother," Cecil said at one point. "I was only on the outside of the place. You can see from the TV I was standing outside. On the outside. Get it? Outside."

"You have no idea how humiliated I am," Maggie continued to press. "People I haven't heard from in years are calling. The men who were caught were at least smart enough to cover their faces so their moms and wives wouldn't be embarrassed. But no, not my son! My son plants himself directly across from the camera so that everyone in South Texas will see him. You shouldn't be anywhere near that place! What you need is a decent girl, someone to be with. Get married, give me grandchildren."

"That's enough, Mother! I won't discuss this further." Cecil stood to leave the kitchen. "Bet Mrs. Spencer hasn't called," he snapped. "Clyde was there."

"She's got her own hands full with her no good son-in-law cheating on his wife as he does. But at least it's not her son. Wade Spencer wouldn't be caught in a place like that. No, siree. Wade's a good boy. Hey, where're you going? I'm not finished."

"I've had enough of this. I'm tired."

"Don't you walk away when I'm talking to you! Come back here this instant!"

"Mother," Caroline piped up, having sat quietly off to the side keeping herself out of the line of fire, "Cecil's a grown man. He can do as he pleases. Leave him be."

"You stay out of this, young lady! This is between me and your brother. If I want your opinion, I'll ask for it."

"Mother, what's gotten into you? You're way overreacting."

"I don't know what to do with the two of you. I'm going home. Why I bother, I don't know."

Cecil returned to the kitchen when the front door slammed closed. "Something's going on that she's not telling us."

"She seemed fine last night," Caroline replied. "Agitated when she saw you on TV, but nothing like just now. Changing the subject, she asked, "So what's going on at the factory? Is it a go?"

"Yup. Everything's in order. The gear train runs smooth. They said they can manufacture it without a problem. No real start-up time. The cost savings will be greater than expected so we can drop the price even further. The margins are that good."

"That's good news. So what's bothering you? I see it in your eyes."

"They have too many workers by half. You're going to have to lay off a whole lot of people if you're gonna turn this around."

"I've got a better idea. Go off and design another new something we can build. You now know what the plant is capable of, so design something that takes advantage of what we can produce."

"Easy for you to say."

"Yes, and easy for you to do. I have the utmost faith in you."

Cecil started off toward his home office. Caroline called after him, "If you can't think of engines or car parts, then focus on robotics."

"Can't. We have a non-compete."

"No, that thing is narrowly worded, remember. It only keeps you from robots that you designed for me. And even then only for the basic activities of everyday living. You can design stair-climber wheelchair robots and even bots that control computer keyboards, that sort of thing."

"I have a great idea for an improvement to your wheelchair, but the plant is geared to heavy duty equipment, not light metal titanium and aluminum. Conversion would be too expensive. I'll stick to car drive-trains for now, maybe a new transmission."

"Suit yourself. Oh, by the way, Wade's coming over tonight. You okay with that?"

"Why shouldn't I be?"

"Okay, just checking. He said he talked to you. He seems... well, different."

"Different?"

"More reserved than when I knew him years ago. Almost..."

"Almost what?"

"I don't know. If I didn't know better, I'd say, shy. No, not shy, frightened."

ಌ☙

It wasn't until Christmas that Maggie finally stopped hassling Cecil over the *Cospers Own* incident. And then only because Cecil had refused to have Christmas dinner with her if she didn't give it up. Caroline supported him. "Not even an eye roll," Caroline had insisted to her mother, "or out you go."

The three of them spent the early part of Christmas Eve in front of the fireplace in the den. Then, as was their custom, they ate dinner by candlelight followed by the exchange of presents.

At precisely eleven, the doorbell rang. Caroline's face flushed. "Oh, that's Wade," she exclaimed. "He said he wanted to bring a present by. I told him this would be a good time."

Cecil shrugged and went to open the door. In came a red-suited Santa with a bag full of presents.

"Ho, ho, ho," the Santa cried, "Merry Christmas to all."

Cecil pushed the cheerful Santa back onto the porch and slammed the door.

Immediately, the doorbell rang again.

"Let him in, Cecil," Caroline called from the den. "It's Wade."

"Oh, sorry. Got confused."

When the door reopened, Wade said, "Thought you were angry with me there for a moment, Buddy." He followed Cecil across the room to where Maggie and Caroline waited and then turned to face Cecil. "You're naughty for slamming the door in the face of Santa."

Wade's red Santa hat had been knocked sideways and, catching a glimpse of it in the mirror, reached up to straighten it. He then turned back toward the women. "Ho, ho, ho. Santa has presents for all. Maybe not for Cecil. He's been naughty."

"Oh, how nice of Santa to bring presents," Caroline chirped, a broad smile illuminating her face. "We have a little something for Santa as well."

Caroline, seeing her brother's head fall, immediately realized what was troubling him. "Of course you haven't been naughty, Cecil. Santa was just fooling around. I'm sure he has a present for you as well. Don't you, Santa?"

Cecil looked up and saw the broad genuine happiness of his sister, something he had never really seen before. His agitation vanished. "I didn't mean to push Santa...I, I mean Wade. I just got confused."

Wade, following Caroline's lead, said, "Of course I wouldn't hold back on Cecil. He's the man single handedly saving this town. I hear the new gear-train is a real winner. Rumor has it Ford is considering using it for their trucks. Workers are excited. But hey, I didn't come out here for business. Let's celebrate. I bet we could all use something to wet our whistles, if you know what I mean."

"I don't have a whistle," Cecil responded, again looking at the floor.

"Caroline's not allowed any alcohol," Maggie scolded.

Caroline rolled her eyes in the direction of Cecil.

"Oh, you mean have a drink," Cecil said, moving toward the kitchen. "I'll bring her cranberry juice. What do you want, Mother?"

"Same," Maggie replied.

They settled by the fire, and after presents were distributed, Wade said, "I have one more for Caroline." He dug to the bottom of the now mostly empty bag and pulled out a box wrapped with silver paper and a big red bow. "You're a hard one to shop for," he said, handing the box to Caroline. "But I finally found something I thought would be nice."

She tried to rip the paper open with the bots, but her excitement caused them to work sporadically. After several failed attempts, Wade reached for the package, ripped the paper off, and handed the box back. "Can you open the box?"

"If I slow down. Excitement causes problems." Her eyes filled with tears. Her inability to perform the simple task of ripping the paper from the box brought her back to reality. She forced a smile. "Oh, I'm sorry. Frustration gets the best of me at times."

Slowly the right hand bot grasped the top of the box and pinched the cardboard. The top lifted off, revealing something silky. Caroline looked up at Wade. "Please take this out for me. I don't trust the bots to handle something so delicate."

Wade dutifully unfolded a silk lounge suit. "I thought this would be comfortable since you spend so much time sitting. Something different from the sweats you usually wear."

"It would be a nice change," Caroline admitted. "I'd have to have help getting them on though. They'll snag on the bots if I try to do it myself."

"Jeez, I hadn't thought of that," Wade said in a rueful tone, clearly embarrassed. "I can exchange them if you'd like."

"Oh no! I'll just have to teach myself how to do it. It will be nice to have something different, something a bit more...more, shall we say, feminine."

Cecil, uncomfortable with the direction of the conversation, said, "I didn't know you'd be here or I'd have a gift for you." He was wearing the driving gloves Wade had brought for him and he pulled them off. "Thank you for the gloves. I love the soft leather. I'm sorry...I should have—"

Wade held up a hand, cutting him off. "With what you've done in the past few months in this town, hey, that's gift enough."

"You give me too much credit," Cecil replied.

"I doubt that," Wade replied. "In any event, I'd sure like to thank the new owner in person, if I could find out who in the tar it is. I'd love to run a story featuring the town savior. Sure you won't help me on this?"

Cecil restrained himself from glancing over at his sister. "Can't do it. Sorry."

At midnight, Maggie served warm apple pie and vanilla ice cream, just as her mother had before her. It was a long-standing family tradition that she had no intention of parting with. After the dishes were cleared away, Maggie announced, "I'm going home now. I have an early day tomorrow and a long one. I'm volunteering at the Veterans Hospital, feeding the patients and giving out Christmas presents."

"I guess you're going with my mother then," Wade said. "She's been doing that since before I was born."

"She got me started."

Wade turned to Cecil after Maggie had gone. "Ever since that raid, my mother's been all over my brother-in-law, Clyde, for getting his picture in the paper. She even came down on me. Said I should have cropped him out. Sometimes you just can't win."

"My mother's been yelling at me as well," Cecil replied. "Caroline came to my rescue."

"Don't know what's got into those ladies," Wade said, "but I'll drink to them getting off our backs." He picked up the Scotch bottle and, after leaning over to refill Cecil's glass, refilled his own.

"Here, here." Caroline said, forcing her bots to move the juice glass up to eye level. "Put a little of that real stuff in here."

Wade looked at her. "I thought—"

"Just pour!"

They clinked glasses and Cecil said, "Now that *Cospers Own* is closed, your mother should be happy Clyde can't spend any more time there."

"It's not working out that way," Wade replied. "The boy's lost over that girl. He's beside himself. She got herself in trouble with the law. Beat the snot outta some guy trying to steal her money, so she claims. Now she's being sued because she broke his ribs. Got his head smashed in as well and his ankle broke. She did a real job on him."

Cecil assumed that Wade's position as publisher of the local paper was what enabled him to know such details. In any event, the news of Sally being sued got his attention. His mind drifted yet again to the question of what had happened after her disappearance to make her such a different person. Her temper flared easily and there was a hardness to her that troubled him. "So what's that all about?" Cecil asked, trying to keep his voice from revealing his true feelings.

"Cecil's got an interest in that girl as well," Caroline piped in. "So be careful what you say about her."

"Do not!" Cecil replied. "Do not!"

"The guy she hit was living with her. She says he was her babysitter. She caught him stealing money she had saved. Hearing comes up right after New Years."

Babysitter? Cecil thought to himself, trying to sort out the implications of what Wade had said.

"Girl's run out of money for her lawyer," Wade continued, "so Clyde's been giving her money. My sister put her foot down, and now the girl's in trouble cause, without money, the lawyer is refusing to move forward. Babysitter will win his suit. Classic case of the law getting it backward."

"Hey guys, remember me?" Caroline called from the sofa. "I can't believe you two would sit around on Christmas and discuss the woeful life of a common whore."

"Not a whore!" Cecil said, his head bending forward.

"Forgive me," Wade apologized. "I was caught up in the moment."

"Come sit next to me, and I'll work on forgiving you."

"I'm going to my room," Cecil announced. "Call me when you need me to get you ready for bed."

"Why would you need him?" Wade asked, after Cecil had left the room. "I'm here."

"Bedtime ritual. I need help getting ready for sleep."

"Nothing I can do?" Wade asked, looking puzzled.

"I wish you could," Caroline said, ruefully. "How I wish you could."

Forty-One

"Mommy, why can't we have a Christmas tree like everyone else?" Malinda Nelson sat cross-legged on the floor in the doorway to the tiny kitchen as Samantha poured the last of the milk into a small bowl of Cocoa Puffs. "Last year we had a tree."

"I was working last year, baby. Things have gone bad now. If you want, I can buy a little tree for the table."

"Uncle Dil did this. I hate Uncle Dil."

Suddenly, Samantha was alert. Had Dil, in fact molested her? "Why do you hate him, honey?" she asked the child, careful to keep her voice soft and not threatening. "Did he do anything to you?"

"He tried to take your money. Now you lost it all. I hate him!"

It crossed Samantha's mind that it would have been better to have let that bastard take her money than to have given it to the lawyer. *Legal thievery. What's the difference? Nothing good ever came from lawyers. I'm broke either way!*

And now Clyde was in trouble at home as well for helping her. Actually, he wasn't exactly giving it to her; she was still earning it, only in her own bedroom.

Samantha put her hand on her daughter's shoulder. "It'll be all right, honey. Mommy promises."

Where she was going to get money for more cereal and milk she didn't know. Earlier in the week she had asked for her old job back at the supermarket. The manager, a regular patron of hers at *Cospers Own*, politely told her he'd get fired if he hired her back. She suspected he was more afraid of his wife finding out about his activities than his boss.

"Come," she said to Malinda, "eat your cereal. Then you can open your present." Samantha had saved enough money to buy her daughter a new pair of pajamas to replace the ones that were tattered and outgrown. She had also put aside just enough money to buy them both tickets to the new Disney movie, *The Emperor's New Groove*. That was her Christmas present to herself.

What she didn't tell her daughter was that they would be moving on New Year's Day. Dil had called this morning and threatened to make her prostitution public. "If you don't pay me," he had shouted into the phone, "for my ribs and cracked head, you're gonna lose your precious kiddo! From what I hear, the courts don't like whores raising kids!"

"I should'a killed you when I had the chance, you no-good slime ball!" Samantha bellowed into the phone. "Next time you won't be so lucky! I catch you, I'll cut your balls off!" She had slammed the phone down so hard the case cracked. What she hadn't heard was the click at the far end as the recorder turned off.

Dilson Tylor may not have been ambitious, or even bright enough to get a job, but he was a master at working the system.

FORTY-TWO

Cecil woke on Christmas morning and knew instantly his life had changed. He had worked late on a modification to the gear-train and fallen asleep in his chair. He had not been disturbed all night.

That could only mean that Wade Spencer had put Caroline to bed. He thought back over the past two months since the two of them had met, and realized this had been the first time they had been alone at bedtime.

Caroline was certainly old enough to take care of herself. If she wanted Wade as a boyfriend, or as a lover, that was her business. Cecil regarded this as welcome news. Now he was free to pursue Sally and get to the bottom of what was troubling her.

Sally! He had tried twice to meet her, and each time something had prevented them from getting together. Now he was determined. First things first, however. He decided to find the lawyer representing her and pay him for the trial. He could not allow her to become indebted to some bum thief.

Cecil went to retrieve the morning paper and discovered Wade's car in the circular drive. Either the man was too drunk to drive home and called a cab, or, in line with what Cecil had earlier thought, the relationship had progressed to the next level.

Knowing Caroline's libido, he bet on the latter.

Cecil spent most of Christmas Day online trying to find mention of a trial involving Sally Mascar or anyone named Samantha. He was also hiding from his sister, not wishing to face up to her new relationship. Wade, he noted, had driven off shortly before noon.

Maggie arrived shortly before six. Not finding Caroline on the first floor, she rushed to her bedroom.

Cecil heard the unusually fast pounding of his mother's shoes on the wooden steps and remembered that he had not seen Caroline all day. Other than the opening and closing of Caroline's bedroom, the house remained quiet. He returned to his sketches.

About an hour later Maggie paged him for dinner.

When Cecil arrived in the kitchen, he found Caroline sitting in her wheelchair, hands folded on her lap. She seemed fine. In fact, had Cecil been capable of reading the signs, he would have seen that his sister was glowing. Her eyes were alive and her lips, for once, were curled upward ever so slightly.

With barely a nod in her direction, he busied himself helping his mother prepare her traditional Christmas Day dinner consisting of roasted chicken, mashed potatoes and green beans with almonds. Dessert was pecan pie, his father's favorite.

They ate at exactly seven-thirty, as they always had.

At eight-thirty, his father called. His first question to Cecil, even before saying, "Merry Christmas", was, "So how's the pecan pie?"

"Great, as always. Merry Christmas, Dad."

They chatted awhile with Joe doing most of the talking. Then Cecil asked, "Do you mind if Caroline and I arrive a little late tomorrow? I have something I need to do in town here before we leave."

"Actually, that will work out," his father responded. "How about delaying a day? Patty-Ann's not feeling herself. Says it's something she ate. She's not venturing far from the bathroom."

"Tell her I'm sorry to hear it. We'll check with you before we start out."

The next morning, Cecil went to the *Sentinel* office and searched the files. It took him a full two hours, but he found what he was looking for. A line item in the police blotter section in an issue from late October caught his eye. One Dilson Tylor had been found dazed and injured, broken ribs, possible ankle injury and a concussion. Samantha Nelson had been named as the assailant. Possible robbery was noted as the reason for the altercation.

Cecil searched the paper's computer index and found a lawsuit filed in County Civil Court, entitled *Tylor v. Nelson*. He copied down the file number, thanked the receptionist for her time, and walked the three blocks to the courthouse.

Twenty minutes later, armed with a lawyer's name, address and phone number, Cecil was back in his car on his way across town to the lawyer's office.

The office turned out to be in a shopping mall next to a pet store. A sign in the lawyer's window read, William Towers, *Lawyer, Criminal Proceedings and Personal Injury. Nothing too small or too large. Free consultation.*

"I'm here to see Mr. Towers," Cecil told the pencil-thin woman sitting at a desk. She was examining nails so long they curled downward on themselves. Cecil wondered how she could function in an office environment with nails like that. Curbing the overwhelming impulse to say to her, "Why don't you cut those nails!" he instead said, "This is about the Samantha Nelson matter."

The woman twisted open the top of a nail polish bottle before she responded. "Mr. Towers is out of the office today."

"Is he in town? If so, please call him. It's important."

"He's at his ranch," she replied, concentrating on applying polish to a nail. Without looking up, she continued, "He asked not to be disturbed, except in an emergency."

"What makes an emergency?"

"A new client—with money," she responded.

"Then call him and tell him it's an emergency. I'll be back in an hour. I'm going for barbeque across the street. Haven't been in there in years. Is the pulled-pork as good as it was?"

"How'd I know? Don't eat meat," she snapped. Looking up, she asked, "You got cash?"

"I said it's an emergency. Call your boss. That is, assuming you can even dial the phone with those stupid nails."

The woman glared at him. "You better have the money, buster. Lawyer Towers don't book it with fools. He'll eat you alive."

Forty minutes later, Cecil stood to carry what remained on his tray to the trash. He bumped into a man wearing a flannel shirt overhanging his jeans. There were streaks of mud splashed across his alligator boots. The man loomed over him and wore no jacket, even though there was a definite nip in the air.

"You the rude guy looking for me?" The voice seemed to come from the sky. "I'm Towers. Sit down so we can get to the bottom of this emergency. Better be good to get me off the ranch on my day off. My secretary says you have the money to pay for my time today. Rate's double on my day off."

The man was even larger than his name. Instead of Towers, Cecil thought his name should be Giant. Slumping back into his chair Cecil faced the lawyer across the table. At least now he could see the man's face. "I'm Cecil Harris," he began tentatively. "I need some information. I have the money."

"Billy Towers," the man said, reaching a massive hand across the table and nearly crushing Cecil's in the process. "What's your problem? Hey, now that I've had a good look at you, I've seen you somewhere. Never ever forget a face. Never. Hey, wait a minute. You're the guy who sold the robot company for big money and also the one saving our poor-ass town. Read about you in all the financial magazines." He again stuck out his hand. Cecil reluctantly reached up to shake it. This time the grip was gentle. "Hey, glad to meet you. Sorry if Cindy Lou was rude to you. She's that way with everyone. Now that I look at you, you're also the same guy who got your picture taken in front of *Cospers Own*. It's sad to see them shut that place. That club did a lot of good for the community."

"This is about Samantha Nelson," Cecil said, not knowing how to begin the conversation.

"I presume you know that I can't discuss a client's confidential matters."

"I understand she's being sued by some slime ball called Dilson Tylor."

"I can't talk about it. Now what's *your* problem?"

"I saw some stuff in the paper," Cecil replied. "Can't you talk about what's in the paper."

"Depends."

"I'm also told Samantha's out of money, in which case she'll lose and that weasel will be into her."

"Assuming it's true, then he'll get a default. It is really as simple as that. I'm not a charity lawyer. I tell all my clients that up front."

Cecil reached for his wallet and started counting out hundred dollar bills, placing one on top of the other. "Tell me when to stop so that she gets the best defense possible."

"Stop," the lawyer called almost immediately. "Those are hundreds! You're out of line here."

"That certainly can't be—"

"Save your money, son. The problem with you rich guys is that you think money can buy anything. Money won't work in this case."

"You won't take my money? Just name the price. Money's not an—"

"Wish I could. You're a bit late."

"What?"

"Look, I can't talk about clients. But I can tell you about a call I got just this morning from Dilson's lawyer. That's not confidential. Hell, I suppose half the county has heard this by now anyway. Your friend was caught on tape, I'm not sure when, threatening to kill Tylor and telling him she'll cut off his gonads. That girl's got some mouth on her. Gets her in trouble, it does. And a temper as well, I might add. Tylor's prepared to play the one card I had hoped to avoid. That's the prostitution card. Jury's not going to like hearing she left her little girl home with a rat while she went to work, so to speak. *Cospers Own* is not very popular with the women folk these days."

"I don't understand how—"

"Let me spell it out for you, son. The worse I paint Tylor for the jury or even for the judge if we end up waiving a jury, the worse Samantha looks for leaving the kiddo with him. It's a classic no-win situation."

"Did she know this would happen when she started all this?"

"She didn't start it, he did. He sued her for breaking his ribs and his ankle. Asshole's lucky he didn't try to steal *my* money. They'd find him on my kitchen floor, his head blown clean off! Wouldn't even go to the Grand Jury. Guy's a real scumbag!"

"So what did you tell her?"

"Can't talk about what she or I said to each other. But let me just say, she knew what she was in for."

"So why not give him what he wanted?"

"She wanted her day in court. Truth is, the jerk's a low life. There may even be child abuse on his part, but if we get into that the Court will come down on Samantha like a ton of bricks. So put your money away. She paid me enough already."

"So what's your advice?"

"I can't tell you what we discussed. But hypothetically speaking, someone with her problem comes to me, I tell them to pay the scum off or move-on." The lawyer thought for a moment, then continued, "She changed her name once and she can do it again."

"How'd you know about her name change? She tell you?"

"I do background checks on my clients as a routine matter. Can't be a criminal lawyer and believe anything anybody says. That young lady you met in my office may be good for little else, but one thing she does well is insulate me from liars."

"Tell her I'm sorry if I upset her. I just told her what anyone with a brain would tell her. Those nails look stupid and are useless."

"Son, we all do things others find no sense in. Take my advice, so long as it ain't hurt'n you, leave it be. You'll live a happier life if you do that."

"How much will it take to make him go away?"

"Don't rightly know for sure. I can't do anything without my client's permission. But if some stranger were to call up his lawyer and offer some settlement, I bet this can be gone by the end of the day." Towers produced a pen and wrote a name on a napkin. "I don't know his number off the top of my head, but he's in the book. Don't say I sent you, that's all. Give him an offer he can't refuse. Guy's got three busted ribs, a busted ankle and a concussion. Blow to the head in his case, unless it killed him, could do no damage. Zero from zero...you get my drift? He'll walk with a limp for a long while. That baseball bat of hers did a real job."

"Hate to give him anything, guy trying to take the money she saved."

"The first blow to the head did it. He was trying to get away after that. Swinging the bat when he was crawling across her kitchen and smashing his ankle is going to cost her. Like I said, she'd be fine if he would have died in her kitchen."

"Then you're saying a gun's better than a bat."

"Sometimes it is. It depends. With a bat you gotta make the first blow count."

"The kid's a low life. Deserved what he got."

"We can't exactly paint Samantha as a model citizen either, you know."

"She's just trying to get by."

"The worst part of this whole thing is she'll end up with no money no matter what she does. My guess is she'll now do what she should have done all along."

"And that is what?"

"Start fresh where she can raise that child of hers. Somewhere where no one knows what she does for money. Imagine what it'll be like for the girl to be in school with everyone talking about her mother being a lady of the night. If she's not careful, CPS will take that child from her."

Cecil's head fell. All he could think was, *Got to help her. Got to help her. Got to help her.*

Forty-Three

The year 2001 started out a bit different for Cecil than previous years. Patty-Ann was still not feeling well, so Cecil celebrated the December 31st part of his twenty-second birthday in Cosper. Cecil was subdued, which Caroline attributed to Wade's constant presence in her life. Maggie believed Cecil's sullenness stemmed from *that loose woman*, as she now called Sally.

They were both wrong. Cecil was waiting for a call-back from Dilson's lawyer to see if the scum-bag, Dilson Tylor, would accept the settlement that Cecil had offered.

Birthday candles were blown out, cake was served and presents were opened. Life was going on around Cecil, but he was not part of it. At the first opportunity, he disappeared into his room.

The New Year's Day part of Cecil's birthday found him by himself for most of the day. Wade had convinced Caroline to go for a ride. Maggie, put off by Cecil's mood, went home.

The deal with Dilson's lawyer wasn't completed until January third. In the end, they agreed on two thousand dollars to Dilson, three thousand for the lawyer, and an agreement to pay all medical bills arising out of the incident.

Samantha's lawyer, Billy Towers, called to thank Cecil. "You did the right thing, son," he said. "It's probably a good thing our Miss Nelson didn't hang around to hear the news. No telling what she might have done to him. Probably be hiring me to defend her on a murder charge."

"What do you mean she didn't hang around?"

"She's gone. Left me a phone message yesterday that she had skipped town on New Year's Eve."

"Any way to find her?" Cecil asked, devastated at the news.

"My experience with people such as this is when they want to be lost, they get good and lost. Me and you, we got too many ties, accounts and things. Drifters drift. That's why they keep their money in tin cans and don't burden themselves with things. One day they're here, the next day, like Houdini, they're gone. That's the reason I get my money upfront and in cash."

"Any suggestions on finding her?"

"You won't like it. You'll have to apologize, but Cindy Lou, the girl with the nails in my office, is the best in the business. She knows everyone in the state. Call the office and work it out with her. If Samantha's findable, Cindy Lou will find her."

൞ଓ

Cecil had no concept of what he had done wrong, so it was difficult for him to say he was sorry. He fumbled around without success trying to say the right words.

Cindy Lou came to his rescue. "Just say you're sorry. That's all. I don't care if you know why you're saying it; just say you're sorry."

"I'm sorry, but I—"

"Just stop at *you're sorry.*"

Cecil looked at her across the counter. All he could focus on was her fingernails curling into what he deemed a primitive form of life.

Standard Deviation

"Look, just say you're sorry! Nothing more. Just you're sorry."

"I didn't say anything that wasn't true."

"Enough! You want my help, you say you're sorry. If not, get your sorry ass out of here!"

"I'm sorry," Cecil mumbled, his eyes on the floor.

"Okay, now tell me what you need."

Cecil explained what he wanted. Cindy Lou listened, took a few notes and told Cecil, "If I find her for you that'll be five hundred. If not, fifty for expenses." Before Cecil could respond, she corrected herself. "On second thought, make that an even thousand. You don't deserve the friend's discount."

ಬಂ

The month of January proved difficult for Cecil. Thankfully, he was busy at the plant overseeing the production of the new gear train. He also spent as much time away from the house as possible because Wade had essentially moved in. When Cecil was in the house he remained holed up in his office, reviewing drawings and specifications for the new production lines.

In early February Cecil made several trips to Detroit to demonstrate the new gear train. First he went to General Motors and then to Ford. Because of limited manufacturing capacity in the Cosper plant he told them both that *Axtel* could only handle one of them. He then went to Ohio to talk with the chief engineer of Honda who immediately requested a factory tour.

"I'll be frank with you, Mr. Harris," the Honda Chief Engineer, Jeff Jaspers, said a few weeks later during a visit of the Cosper facility, "we are looking for improved performance of the hybrid we're introducing in the spring of 2002. Your design is perfect. What you have here gives us what we need. My hat's off to you on the simplicity."

"You're not wearing a hat. Of course it's off."

"You're funny, Mr. Harris," Jaspers replied, smiling politely.

"I'm not funny at all," Cecil replied, continuing with his presentation. "I've visited GM and Ford already. Our capacity is limited. The first to act gets it."

"We're in," Jaspers declared. "I'll have our lawyers draw the formal deal." The man reached in his bag, pulled out a set of papers and handed them to Cecil. "Here's a term sheet we put together. I trust you'll like the quantities and pricing."

"I'll have to discuss this with my sis...the company," Cecil answered. "I'm not in a position to accept or negotiate. I only design and demonstrate."

"One issue, and I assume it won't be a problem, is that we want to assemble the transmission in our facility in Ohio."

"That's not possible. I designed the gear train to keep the *Axtel* facility running at maximum here in Cosper. We can't allow you to manufacture it somewhere else."

"I'm afraid we have the same issue as well. I hope we can come to terms. Your company will make a ton of money."

"It's about employment here in Cosper, not about money."

Jaspers studied Cecil a long while before he replied, "It's never about employment, Mr. Harris. It's always about money."

ಬಒ

The next morning, after Wade left, Cecil found Caroline working at her bedroom desk studying numbers on the computer. "You've been missing in action lately," she commented. "I trust you're working on the demos and not pouting in the corner."

"Why would I be in a corner? I'm happy you found somebody you care about."

"You haven't spoken to me for several days. I don't know what's gotten into you, but I miss our little fireside chats."

In fact, Cecil missed being with her more than he had imagined he would. "I do miss our talks," he confessed. "But I know how important having someone in your life is. You care about Wade, that's what's important."

"He cares for me as well. I'm so happy. You can't imagine. Someone to tuck me in, to be there when I need help. I'm not so terrified of the night any more. In fact," she said, her eyes dancing with delight, "I rather enjoy the nights now."

"I imagine you do," Cecil said, turning away. A moment later, after it become clear that Caroline was done with bedroom stories, Cecil turned back. "I came," he said, all business, "to talk to you about the Honda deal. They want an exclusive on the new drive train."

"The numbers are sensational! What's the issue?"

"They want to manufacture in Ohio. Jasper said something I didn't understand about some sort of tax incentive."

"The price is right. More than right. Our margins are good. The lawyers say it's simply a technology transfer deal. Pure profit."

"Whatever happened to jobs for Cosper folks? Isn't that why you bought the company in the first place?"

"Partially. I also bought it for something to keep me occupied. And, might I add, to make money. This deal will certainly do that."

"You and I will make money, but not the workers. Cosper will die. I'm not in fav—"

"I'll handle the negotiations from here. Just have the specifications ready for a transfer if that's the way the deal goes."

"But what about the workers here?"

"Most are busy with the redesigned original drive train. And besides, I have every confidence you'll design a second drive train to keep the rest of the workers busy. We can sell this one to Honda and manufacture the second one here."

"The one I just designed is the best in the world."

"So the new *Axtel* transmission will be second best. You may not know it, 'cause you don't follow this stuff, but the industry loves the new design."

"So why is GM and Ford taking so long to accept the new one?"

"Probably internal politics. Those guys don't like it when an outsider beats them. You ever hear of *not invented here*? That's what's going on. We'll sell them the next one."

"I don't like taking the work out of Cosper."

"That's my worry, not yours. Besides, I thought you were the guy who hated Cosper."

"Not these guys. I like them." Cecil turned to leave. He was agitated and his head was down.

"Oh, and one other thing before you leave," Caroline called to him. "Wade and I are talking about getting married and building a house designed for my needs. Just wanted to tell you so it wouldn't be a surprise."

Even though Cecil had felt isolated in his own house for the past two months, the thought of his sister leaving him hit hard. "I don't understand," he managed to reply, his eyes continuing to focus on the floor. "You both can live here. I'll stay out of your way. I don't understand."

"What you don't understand is that Wade and I will be formally engaged soon." Caroline, ignoring Cecil's chant, continued, "Wade says it's better if we have our own place. I agree. I want to be with him as much as possible. It'll take us a while to have it designed and built. Maybe a year, maybe even longer."

"Remain here. Remain here. Remain here. Remain here," Cecil repeated, not seemingly hearing what his sister was saying.

"Stop that this instant!" Caroline scolded. "Remember your lessons. Take a deep breath. Calm down. Relax. Everything will work out just fine."

"Remain here. Remain here. Remain here. Remain here."

"If you're locked up, then get out of my room! I love you, Cecil, but I have to live my own life. Do you understand me? Wade's the only person who's ever taken time to get to know me. I can't lose him. I just can't! I have no one else!" Caroline spun her wheelchair around and rolled over to him. When he refused to look up, and with the chant continuing, she wheeled herself into the hall and down the corridor toward the den, putting as much distance between herself and her brother as she could.

Even with the door to the den closed she could hear Cecil crying out for her to remain in the house. Tears welled up as she sat alone, torn between her love for Wade and her conflicted feelings for her brother. She loved Wade deeply. The thought of him not being in her life sent shivers through her mostly unfeeling body. She loved her brother, not so much for what he was, but for what he had given her—the gift of mobility. And with mobility she had recouped a semblance of the independence she had enjoyed as a child. That independence was perhaps the most important gift of all.

Forty-Four

Sally Mascar, now using the name of Salina Olsen, had always known her stay in Cosper would be limited. Her only regret was that she hadn't found a satisfactory way to deal with Wade Spencer. That and the chance to introduce Malinda to her grandmother were the real reasons she had come back to Cosper. She had failed on both counts.

Sally tried to rationalize that if she hadn't been raped, Malinda would not be in her life. But even the blessing of Malinda was not enough to erase the torment Wade had set into motion.

As happened all too often, Sally's thoughts drifted back to Austin. Shortly after she had stepped off the bus in Austin on that fateful day in 1993 Sally was met by a girl by the name of Tamalia who was only a few years older than Sally. Tamalia drove her to a nicely furnished apartment and then took her shopping for clothes and food. "Friends call me Tam," she had told Sally. "I got pregnant at your age so I know what you're going through. I'm here to help."

Every day Tam came to the apartment and some days they just watched TV together and on other days they'd go for walks or just walked the streets window-shopping.

The apartment had a view of the lake and often the river filled with what looked to Sally like long rowboats holding teams of men. She loved to watch as their oars moved in unison propelling the boats up and down the lake.

Then one day it all changed. A man, not much older than Tamalia, came to her door and told her he had been sent to take her to see the doctor. When she asked where Tam was, the man answered, "She's not feeling well today. Come, we're already late."

But they didn't go to see a doctor. Instead, he stopped at the far edge of town, got out of the car, walked around and opened her door. She refused to get out, and he grabbed her by the arm and yanked her to the sidewalk and marched her up the front steps of a seedy-looking four-story apartment building. He then proceeded to push her up all four flights and into a small room on the top floor. The man then closed and locked the door behind her, leaving her alone — and frightened.

The room had a filthy refrigerator, a sink, a table with one chair, a hot plate, and no other furniture. A door led to a small area the size of a closet that held a toilet.

That night she slept on the floor, crying herself to sleep. The next day she found a few cleaning supplies under the sink and cleaned the apartment as best she could. But the grime had been imbedded over many years and resisted her efforts.

Every day for a week the same man returned, unlocked the door, put food inside and left. The only time he spoke was to warn her not to try to escape or scream because if she did nasty things would happen to her.

A week later he moved her to another, even dirtier place. This place had a filthy bed. Here, despite her fears, she slept on the bed because nasty things crawled across the floor at night.

Now, as she looked back on it, she understood she was being moved around to make certain she wasn't being followed. They had wanted to insure that any police investigation would lead to a dead end.

After two more moves into and out of places unfit for human habitation, she was ushered into a three-room apartment that, with a good cleaning, she made habitable. This place had linens and towels. The refrigerator contained unspoiled food.

The man motioned for her to sit at a small round table while he produced cold chicken, bread, and a bottle of wine. Together they finished off the wine. Afterward, he took her into the bedroom and pushed her backward onto the bed.

In an instant he was on her. This ritual was repeated three nights in a row, with never a word being spoken by either of them.

After the third night, he said to her, "None of this comes for free, you know?" This apartment, the medical expenses of the baby, things like that. We pay all that. You'll repay us by working."

"I have no skills," Sally replied. "What work can I get?"

"You have all the skills you need," he replied. "I've sampled your skill level for three nights now. You'll do just fine. You have good attributes." He nodded toward her now full chest. "I don't know what they'll be like after the baby, but my guess is you'll still be in demand."

He then went on to explain what she would be doing, and how it all worked. He would bring men to her and she'd get a certain amount of money each week depending on how many men she serviced. That arrangement lasted a month before he allowed her to go into "early retirement" pending the birth of her baby.

Three months after Malinda was born he brought a customer to her, lactating breasts and all. He charged them extra for a taste, and by the fifth month the *extra* business was so good that there was not enough milk for Malinda.

That's when Sally ran away the first time. They had anticipated her action and caught her at the bus station. She was brought back to the apartment and beat with a whip. Scars on her back still served as testament to the brutality of the beating.

The day before Malinda's third birthday, Sally, then eighteen, worked a double shift. That meant she had begun earlier than normal and was hustling the after-work crowd. She brought a middle-aged man back to her apartment.

In the middle of the session the neighbor who had been baby-sitting Malinda brought the little girl home to put her to bed because the child had a cold. When the john was leaving, he saw Malinda sleeping in her bed. He went into her room and reached under the blanket.

Sally flew into a rage and slammed the guy against the wall. He turned around and struck her in the face, smashing several teeth. She ran for a kitchen knife and lucky for him—and her—the john had made it out of the apartment before she could get to him.

That night she packed a bag for the second time and managed to get on a bus for Dallas. Her plan was to seek out Lucas and hope he would take her and Malinda in for a few days.

The two of them climbed down from the bus in downtown Dallas, and spotting a McDonalds a block away, walked in that direction. Sally stepped off the curb and a car screeched to a stop in front of her. The back door opened and the Austin soldier flew out, grabbed her with one hand and with the other latched onto a wide-eyed Malinda.

He threw them both into the back seat of the car and jumped in next to them. The car sped off. He put a knife against her throat, and snarled. "Don't ever do this again. You belong to me, you understand me?" Without waiting for an answer, he moved the knife lower. "I have half a mind to cut your cute tits right off. See if you can earn a living then! You ain't good for nothing but being a whore! Whores need tits to make money! You understand me?"

Sally, not knowing what else to do, nodded.

Ignoring Malinda's crying, he continued, "Convince me you won't run away again! Or so help me, I'll cut—"

"I promise," Sally pleaded, "I won't ever do it again!"

"That's not convincing! The moment I let you go, you'll run again. You're of no more use to me."

"No!" Sally cried. "I'll never run again! I promise!"

He moved toward her, knife held high.

Sally reached for Malinda to try to comfort her. The man, thinking she was going for the knife, brought in down. The blade sliced across her chest just below her neck.

"On second thought, next time you act up I'll carve my initials right here." He moved the knife against Malinda's arm. "We'll see how you like it then."

That's when Sally grabbed for his wrist with the vague thought of slashing his throat.

The result was a nasty cut down the side of her neck. The men refused to take her to the hospital and she bled over herself and over Malinda for the entire trip back to Austin. She passed out and when they arrived back home, the men carried her and the child up to the apartment and threw them both in bed.

She was too weak from blood loss to get out of bed for several days. Someone, unknown to this day to Sally, came in every day and cared for Malinda. During that time, infection set in and her temperature spiked. She went in and out of consciousness.

They finally relented and brought a doctor, a worn-out man, who had seen it all. The doctor cleaned and bandaged the wound. "This is nasty," he pronounced. "Knife, I suspect. I don't want to know how this came about. You're going to have a nasty scar. There's nothing I can do about that now. Turn over and pull your bottoms down." When she did so, he stuck her with a needle.

The doctor then examined Malinda. He looked in her mouth, checked her ears and shined a small light in her eyes. "Everything looks okay. Has this girl been to a doctor in the past few years?"

Sally was too weak to respond.

"Answer my question Miss, or I'll report you both to Health Services. She needs her shots."

"No," came the faint response. That was all the strength Sally could muster.

The old man fumbled in his black cracked-leather bag, but couldn't find what he was looking for. "I don't normally carry the serum for kids, but I thought I had something." He wrote a note on a prescription pad and laid it on the table near her bed. "I expect you and the girl in my office one week from today. It's not far from here. I wrote down the address for you. One week, no longer." He shuffled across the floor and out the door without saying another word.

Sally made several visits to the doctor's office, always with Malinda in tow. The girl got her shots and Sally slowly regained her health.

Ever mindful that one false move and Malinda would be maimed, Sally took care to do exactly as she was told. The number of tricks she turned continued to increase, but the money the soldier gave her never changed. She was terrified of complaining, so she remained quiet, plotting and waiting for the right opportunity to present itself.

On her daughter's fifth birthday they both got a present.

The soldier was arrested in a sting operation. Sally, along with a groggy Malinda, took the opportunity to disappear in the middle of the night. This time she went south toward Cosper, hoping to take refuge with her mother.

The plan had a major flaw.

Lydia Mascar had herself moved on. Sally was homeless, but at least this time she had cash. She had broken into the soldier's room and found his money. She took a thousand dollars, together with several phony IDs he used for running his girls.

One of the IDs had the name of Samantha Nelson printed on it. Another ID contained her present name of Salina Olsen. Apparently the soldier liked the sound of S names.

Forty-Five

Sally had planned her escape from Cosper so Dil wouldn't be able to find her even if he hired a detective. Her intended destination was the barrier island city of South Padre Island, located southeast of Cosper. University students—and teachers—who had used her services in Austin and Cosper, had spoken of the island as a spring break destination. There are plenty of bars and restaurants and, best of all, credentials weren't checked very closely.

However, instead of heading directly for the island, Sally and Malinda climbed off the bus in Allende, Texas and immediately caught the bus to Laredo. Mother and daughter remained in Laredo for two weeks before continuing their journey east, this time crossing into Mexico at Hidalgo and taking a room in a small hotel in Del Prado. A few days later they traveled to Matamoras and then crossed back into the U.S. across the Rio Grande at Brownsville, less than thirty miles from their destination.

Passing through the small town of Port Isabel on the mainland just before the causeway to South Padre Island, Salina spotted a sign advertising a trailer for rent. **FIRST MONTH RENT FREE**, the sign proclaimed. Sally signaled for the bus driver to let them off at the next stop.

The two of them trudged the half-mile back to the lot where the trailer was located. Malinda wore a small backpack containing two DVDs, a notebook filled with sketches she had made on the trip and a few pieces of clothing consisting of several dirty pairs of underwear, two T's and a pair of sweat pants for sleeping. Sally lugged two suitcases containing the remainder of their meager possessions.

An hour later the two of them were in their new home. Looking around, Malinda cried, "Mommy, bugs!"

Sally opened the refrigerator and was greeted by a vile smell and greenish blue mold. Tears welled up in her eyes as she fought the overwhelming urge to vomit. Even after all she had seen in Austin she was barely able to contain herself.

Pulling herself together, and forcing a light tone to her voice, she said to Malinda, "We'll go get cleaning stuff and you and I will fix this place up. It will be real nice when we're finished, you wait and see."

"Is this our new home?" the girl asked.

"For now it is, Honey. For now. Come let's go find the store."

"I liked the old home better. Why did we have to leave?"

"A problem came up. This will be fun. Come, we'll fix it up."

"It's creepy. And it smells."

"It'll get better. I promise."

"Make the bugs go away! I'm scared."

"I'll make the bugs go away. It will be real nice. You'll see."

When she had escaped from Austin, she had a thousand dollars. This time she left with much less. Clyde had given Sally money for the escape, money he had taken from his wife's purse. There was less than twenty-five dollars remaining and it had to last until she got a paying job.

Cleaning supplies, a big bottle of Clorox, milk, bread, cereal and a box of Velveeta cheese left her with very little money to spare. When they got back to the trailer, the two of them started from the back and worked their way forward cleaning every surface they could find.

After several hours, Sally pronounced it fit to live in. "Do you agree?" she asked Malinda. "Or do we need to clean more? The bugs are gone."

"I'm too tired, Mommy. It's still creepy, but not so bad now. Make my bed."

"Want cereal?"

"Can I eat it in my bed?"

"Just this once."

"We have no TV."

"Sorry. Have to save up."

"How long will it take?"

"Soon, Honey. Soon."

൪ഗ

Sally hadn't realized that the economies of Port Isabel and South Padre Island have only two seasons when the bars are busy. Spring break and summer vacation. Everything else is sporadic.

Early February was neither.

With Malinda at her side, Sally canvassed every restaurant and bar in Port Isabel, looking for work, all without success. Then she took the free bus to South Padre Island and did the same, starting at the south end of the island and working her way north.

After three full days of relentless effort, she resigned herself to the fact that nobody was hiring. The most anyone would say was, "We may be hiring in March. Depends on the spring break traffic. Check back then."

The two of them were constantly hungry. They were already rationing the cereal, with Sally eating less than her daughter. The milk had run out, so they were using water.

The occupant of the next trailer, a man in his eighties with a sun-dried face and an arthritic left hand, suggested that she go to the local Catholic Church, Our Lady Star of the Sea, and ask for help. "They take pity on mothers with young children. Take the child with you. They won't allow you to starve."

Following his advice, the two of them walked the mile across town to the church. An elderly priest was the only person they could find.

"I'm new in town and out of work," she began. "My husband left us for another woman. I came down here to get work, but nobody's hiring."

Sally detested lying to the priest about her "husband", but she was desperate and was afraid he wouldn't be inclined to help them if he thought her a sinner.

"What work are you looking to do?"

"Anything. Waitress, I suppose."

"I can't do much for you now. No one's here. Give me your address and I'll see how we can help."

Later that day a woman, the widow of a shrimper, came by the trailer with several bags of groceries. The woman wrote her name and phone number on the side of one of the bags. "We can't have a nice girl like you and this sweet child go hungry, now can we? Your husband do that to you?" She was looking straight at Sally's broken teeth.

Sally nodded, again feeling a twinge of remorse.

"Then, it's good riddance, I say. My husband was a good man, but so many aren't anymore. See it all the time." She looked around at the sparsely furnished trailer. "If you need something, you just call this number. We women need to stick together."

Sally and Malinda continued looking for work, Port Isabel one day, South Padre Island the next. Nothing. They were again running low on food, so Sally called the number the churchwoman had left. More groceries were delivered, this time by a different woman who suggested that Malinda could attend the church school for free.

With her daughter taken care of during the day, Sally re-visited every place she had already canvassed. Still nothing turned up, even though the island was bustling with spring breakers.

Since leaving Cosper, Sally has been paranoid about leaving Malinda with anyone. But she was desperate to make money so she could feed her child properly without relying on the church deliveries which, she worried, might stop at any time.

It gradually dawned on Sally that her only option was to return to her former trade. She arranged with the old man in the next trailer to allow Malinda to come over and watch TV in the evenings. "Need to find work," she had told him. "Give you my first ten dollars if you let her stay with you. She's a good kid and she'll watch whatever you watch." The old man agreed, but warned her not to be getting home very late. "Late nights done passed me by."

"If I get hung up and not back in time," Sally told him, "just put her to bed in our trailer. She'll be fine. I'll still pay you."

Sally selected *Laguna Bobs* for no particular reason other than it was situated directly on the bay and seemed to draw a lively crowd. She dressed as provocatively as she could with what little clothing she had. She had lost over thirty pounds since leaving Cosper, causing her to pronounce herself, "Sensational!" upon glancing in the mirror.

The evening wasn't going as she had planned. Yes, it was easy to get the boys interested in her. Yes, they wanted to bed her. That had never been her problem. They even followed her outside. The problem came when she made it clear they would be paying for the privilege. The responses ranged from the mild, "You outta your mind?" To the nasty, "Loads of free stuff floating around! You ain't got anything they don't have. And they're giving it away!" To the borderline violent, "Cock-teasing bitch. I should bust out the rest of your teeth and teach you a lesson."

After several false starts at *Laguna Bobs*, she moved up-island to a funky-looking place called *Parrot Eyes*. She walked into the *Parrot Eyes* around eleven-thirty and was thrilled to see a sizable crowd, all seemingly talking at once. She ordered a beer. The vibes were right. She immediately felt lucky. The seats on either side of her were vacant, providing a vantage point to scan the crowd for likely customers.

A scruffy looking guy came through the door wearing cut-off jeans and a wild Hawaiian shirt, splashes of color splayed in every direction. He took a seat at the bar several stools down from her and ordered a *Miller Lite*. Beer in hand, he turned to face the dance floor, his eyes following one woman after another as they moved past him.

Sally pegged him as a leg man. His eyes never seemed to make it above the waist. She allowed a few minutes to pass and then walked over to him. "You a local?"

"From the Valley," he answered, a slight Latino accent flavoring his voice. "What about you?"

"New to the area," she responded, all the while watching his eyes survey the expanse of skin extending up from her knees and disappearing provocatively under her short skirt. "Don't yet know my way around."

"Staying on the Island?"

"Across the bridge. Came over for a little fun. What about you?"

Now his focus was on her face. "I'm always up for fun. What do you have in mind?"

"You gotta place here?" she asked.

"I have a small place. I like it here, think I'll stay awhile. Settle in."

"That's my plan as well."

He ordered refills for both of them. While they drank, he told her about the Island and the great fishing. "You ever do any fishing?" he asked at one point.

"Not with a rod," she answered with a wink. "But you can teach me. I like to try new things."

"We'll go out sometime. I'll show you how to catch the big ones."

"I'll bet you could. That would be fun."

When their glasses were again empty, he signaled for the bartender. But before he arrived, Sally leaned against her new friend's shoulder. "You interested in spending time with me tonight?"

"Always interested," came the reply. His face was calm, but his eyes signaled delight at the prospect. "What do you have in mind?"

Sally leaned even closer. In a barely audible voice, she replied, "Anything you want. I know how to please a man."

"Does that come with a price or are we just friends having a great time?"

"Everything's got a price. Wives and girlfriends cost, and so do I. Only difference is with me the cost is up front. Well worth it, though."

"It certainly appears that way, I must say." He winked, a knowing smile curling his lips. "About that cost, I've paid dearly in alimony over the years." He put his arm around her and kissed her forehead. "Let's be sure what we're talking about here. Buy you breakfast sort of price. Or are you thinking something else?"

"Something else. Maybe a real fancy dinner price."

"And what would that be?"

"Two hundred for an hour. Do what you want."

"Sounds reasonable. Anything at all?"

"Anything. Let's go to your place. You're on the Island. We'll get to know each other real well."

"I'm ready." He signaled for the bartender, paid the tab and the two of them walked outside, her arm around his waist.

In the parking lot he turned to her and said, "That's two hundred for an hour, right?"

"You got it. I like you. Let's make that two hours, no extra charge. You look like you're up for it."

"Time starts when?"

"When I get in your car."

"Do I pay you now or later?"

"I said I get paid up front."

"How do I know you'll perform? Not just take my money and run back inside?"

"Don't worry your sweet self about that. Your money's green, you'll be happy."

"I don't even know your name."

"You can call me Salina. And you?"

"You can call me Detective Sergeant," the man said with a sly grin. "South Padre Island Police! You're under arrest for solicitation for prostitution."

Sally turned to run. But she managed only one step before his hand locked on her arm. At the same time, two marked police cars appeared out of nowhere, their red and blue lights flashing in the night.

"You have the right to remain silent," the officer began. "Anything you say can and will be used against you. You have the right. . . "

"Shut the fuck up!" Sally shouted. "I know my rights! You should be ashamed of yourself, trapping a girl the way you did!"

Forty-Six

"For the love of God, Caroline," Cecil pleaded. "Tell him who really owns the company! He's been hounding me every chance he gets about the work going to Honda and the layoffs." This was one of the rare nights Cecil was alone with his sister, and he was taking the opportunity to get some things off his chest. "I'm surprised he hasn't already figured it out, having access to your computer and all that."

"Are you saying he'd go into my computer? You don't think much of him then."

"He's a newspaper man. Snooping is what they do. They get paid to bust people."

"Wade's better than that. That's why I like him. He's so... so...considerate of me. He wouldn't ever do anything like that to hurt me."

"I hope not. For your sake, I hope not."

"You're never around here anymore anyway, so what do you care what he thinks or does?"

"Frankly, I don't care what he thinks. I'm just tired of being badgered in my own house. He says he cares about the workers, but actually it's not the workers he's concerned about. He's scared to death his paper will go under. He's a phony, protecting his own family."

"Don't talk about him that way! He's a good person."

"Everybody knows the factory is downsizing, but the amount of money *Axtel* donates to local charities continues to increase. You even bought new uniforms for the football team as well as the band. He's a newspaper man. He must smell a rat."

"I'm not telling him I own it and that's final!" She glared at her brother until he looked away. In a lowered voice, she asked, "How's the new project coming?"

"Ready for release, but—"

"It's not like you to be weeks behind on your timelines. What's the hang-up?"

"My heart's not in it, to be honest. You're living your life with Wade. Your house plans are coming along. Soon, you'll be married. It's time for me to move on."

"You're worse than Mother. What's gotten into you?"

"You bought the factory to keep people employed. But instead, you've turned my ideas into profit centers outside Cosper."

"That's what business people do. Maximize profits. That's what I'm doing."

"You don't need me anymore to do that. I've given you great designs. Just keep printing money, if that's what you want."

Caroline studied her brother a long moment. She had never known him to express his feelings of agitation openly. Usually, he just locked up. The thought crossed her mind that maybe he was finally growing out of his Asperger's. "You have full design freedom. You can design whatever you want to design. That's what you love to do, build engines. So build to your heart's content! There's nothing wrong with making money doing what you like."

"I go out there every day and work with these guys. Then you up and fire them. That's not what I wanted. I can keep them all busy, but you'll send the work other places. They're nice people. You should come out and meet them."

"I know them all."

"You know them as numbers. How much they make, how much they cost you. They're statistics to you. Pawns to be moved about. You don't know them as individuals, with families and hopes and dreams."

"Since when do you pay attention to people's hopes and dreams?"

"I'm learning."

"You've been listening to the union guys. You're starting to talk like those goons."

"They're not goons. They're good people trying to do good for the workers. If I'm talking like them, so what? My new design requires a new production line and a small foundry. We can avoid setting up the foundry by contracting out for the special parts, but there's no getting around the new line."

"So, what's your point?"

"My point is it'll cost you at least five million, maybe as much as eight, to convert over."

"So you think I won't go along?"

"I know what you'll do. You'll look to see if you can find a factory that already has that capacity. Then you'll either buy them or contract the manufacturing out."

"How do you know what I'll do?"

"Because it's more profitable in the short run. Maybe even in the long run, depending on acceptance a few years from now."

"Can these people build your design?"

"No doubt about it. If we're willing to train them."

"And I suppose that's another cost to me?"

"You see? That's what I said. As soon as I release the design, you'll shop the numbers."

"Is that why you haven't released the design?"

"Pretty much."

"And if I promise to keep it all in Cosper?"

"Then you can have it tomorrow."
"Give it to me then."
"You promise?"
"Not 'til I think about it."
"No."
"I'm the boss. Give it to me."
"Not until you promise."
"I won't be blackmailed! You have until noon tomorrow to give me the design."
"Or what?"
"It belongs to the company. You're being paid to design. Whatever you've done belongs to the company."
"I'll release the design when I'm good and ready."
"You'll release it when I say you'll release it."
Cecil got up. "Good night," he intoned. We have nothing further to discuss."
She called after him, "Before you leave, I need you to put me to bed. Wade's out of town."
"Call Mother. Putting you to bed is not in my contract."

༄༅

Cecil left for Dallas early in the morning to visit his father and Patty-Ann, who, as it turns out, was recovering from an appendix removal. He brought flowers, even though the operation had been more than a month earlier and she was back in her normal routine.

"That's so thoughtful of you Cecil," she said, "but you shouldn't have bothered. I'm just fine now. I have to watch what I do. No heavy lifting, that sort of thing."

"So how's your sister?" Joe asked, suspicious that something was up based on the snippy tone of the conversations he had been having with Caroline.

"What's there to tell? She and Wade are building a house. Until they move out, three's a crowd."

"What's with this Wade guy? I keep asking to meet him and she puts me off."

"He owns the town newspaper. His grandfather started it and I'm afraid it won't survive much longer."

"He's that bad at it?"

"Not him so much. Just the Internet is beginning to take its toll. I give him five years max."

"Is he after your sister's money, do you suppose?"

"Who knows? They get along well."

"They sleep together?" Patty-Ann asked, her eyebrows raised.

"He mostly lives at the house."

"But I didn't think quads—"

"She had a teacher, a surrogate, here in Dallas before we moved."

"Can she—"

Joe held up his hand. "Some things we just don't need to know, dear. The important thing, is she happy?"

"Seems to be," Cecil replied, not knowing if her happiness was the result of her relationship with Wade or the spectacular turnaround of *Axtel*.

"Well, that's all that counts really. And your mother, how's she taking the relationship?"

"Hot and cold. Some days she's all in favor, and some days she's biting Caroline's head off. Other days she's after me."

"What's got her so agitated about you?"

Cecil knew that most of it was the raid on *Cospers Own* and its gossipy aftermath. But he wasn't going there. "I don't think she likes Wade," was his reply, deflecting the conversation away from himself and back to his sister. "Wade's good to mother, but I think she's afraid of something. I don't really know."

"Any reason?"

"I don't understand people, so I'm not the one to say."

"Your mother is a good judge of people. If she's uncomfortable, then something's wrong. Sure you don't know what it is?"

"I heard them talking and she asked Caroline what made her switch from thinking he was a creep to wanting to marry him. Mother said he acted funny around women. She said even Wade's mother said as much a few years back."

"What did Caroline say?"

"She told mother to mind her own business."

"Caroline is outspoken these days it seems. I suppose that's what money does to you."

"Money doesn't do that. Caroline is...I won't say."

"What?" Patty-Ann asked.

"Won't say."

Joe, not wanting his son to go into a mantra changed the subject. "You got someone you're interested in?"

Sally Mascar! But how was he going to explain the situation? Just the mention of her name would begin a longer discussion than he was prepared to engage in. "No one at the moment."

"You should find someone," Patty-Ann volunteered. "Being single is not good."

"You're sounding like Mom," Cecil responded, proud of himself for not telling her to mind her own business. Cecil made a mental note to tell his therapist about his restraint.

"Take it from someone who was single all too long. Being single is just not good," Patty-Ann replied.

"I'm thinking of taking a round-the-world cruise," Cecil blurted, trying to stop this line of questioning.

"That's a great idea!" Joe responded. "Have you booked it, or just thinking?"

"Just thinking. But I think I'll do it."

"Do you want company on your trip?" his father asked.

Cecil, who had been working at studying people's expressions, saw Patty-Ann's eyes come alive.

"Just joking," Joe added quickly. "Do you good to be away on your own. Maybe you'll meet someone."

Patty-Ann's eyes stopped dancing.

ಓಡಂ

The next day, Cecil called a travel agent and arranged for a ten-month cruise leaving San Francisco on June first. There would be stops in over forty-five ports, most of which he'd never heard of. The cost was slightly over three-hundred thousand dollars, including the single-person surcharge.

"And how will you be paying for this, sir?" the agent asked, offering a payout plan that allowed for monthly payments spaced out over the ten months of the cruise.

Cecil wondered what they did to you if you got halfway around the world and stopped paying. Probably throw you overboard, he concluded. "By wire transfer," he said to the agent. "Just give me the details and the money will be there in the morning."

"We don't get many people who book the whole route, sir. Most people just do segments. Sure you want the whole route?"

"If I'm going to see the world, then that's what I want to do. Can't do it by segments. Book me a flight to San Francisco, say a week early. I've never been to California. I might as well start by seeing our country first. Hey, change that. Book me a cross-country train, say from Dallas to San Francisco. Make it a scenic tour."

❧☙

When Caroline heard the news through her father, she was furious. She called Cecil to tell him so.

"That's a rotten trick you just pulled! Going round the world. Just like you to run away."

"How so, dear sister? How so?"

"Those plans you drew up for the new product, that's what!"

"You demanded that I give them to you, and that's what I did. I could have wiped them off the computer, but I followed your instructions. Do with them as you want."

"But without you the factory says they can't possibly implement the product."

"I don't understand?"

"They say they don't understand how the mechanism works. They see the gears and the relationships, but they say without you to fine-tune the line, they won't be able to get it working right."

"They can do it. But if not, then I suggest you concentrate on the products you already have going."

"They say the mechanism you designed would be magnificent, if it works."

"Oh, it'll work. It will revolutionize four-wheel drives in the process. In fact, it's possible for every car to have a four-wheel option at no loss in fuel efficiency — and, this may come as a surprise to you — at a lower cost than today's transmissions."

"It'll put our competition out of business. I need you to stay and get it working."

"It'll work. Just tell them to follow the specs carefully and watch the tolerances."

"That's where they need you. They also say assembly is going to be a bear."

"Not so. It's designed to go together easily. I could do it one-handed."

"They say they can't."

"That's your problem. You want to run the company, then run the company."

"I hate you!"

"I'm sorry to hear that. I'll send cards from the ports I visit."

"Don't bother!"

"Okay, so I won't send you cards."

The line went dead before he told her he planned to be back in Cosper for a few days at the end of the month. He would go over the plans with the *Axtel* engineers then.

Forty-Seven

Life went from bad to worse for Salina Olsen, nee Sally Mascar. The police learned she had left a child alone in her trailer. They promptly informed Child Protective Services. At exactly nine-fifteen the morning after her arrest a CPS investigator went to her trailer and knocked on the door.

No answer.

They tried the door and found it unlocked. It took only a few seconds for the woman to determine the trailer was empty.

Ten minutes later the SPI police confronted Sally who confessed that she had left Malinda with the neighbor in trailer 5. The SPI police informed their counterparts in Port Isabel and a few minutes later the CPS investigator, accompanied by two uniformed Port Isabel police officers, banged on the neighbor's trailer door. They were armed with the fact that the man who lived in trailer 5 was a registered sex offender.

There was no answer.

Several more poundings produced no better results.

"He's an old guy," one of the officers commented. "I've seen him around. Seemed harmless enough."

His partner, a tall, former tight-end for UT Austin, pulled over a crate and climbed on top to get a better look in the window. "It could have happened some years back," he said. "Registration is a life-time thing."

"See anything?" the officer on the ground asked, his hand on his weapon.

"Not sure." Climbing down off his perch he proceeded to the front door. "I'm going in."

"We don't have a warrant," the officer with his hand on his gun warned his partner. He glanced around the trailer lot to see if anyone was watching. "They'll bust you."

"Hot pursuit," came the reply. "We're hot after the kid. We have reason to believe she's in there with a registered sex offender. Hell, we'd be busted for *not* going in!" He lowered his shoulder as he had done on the football field and charged forward. The flimsy door flew off its hinges and it was all he could do to maintain his balance.

There was nothing of interest inside the trailer. The sex offender had fled, taking whatever he owned with him.

"Call it in. Missing girl. Shit, we don't even have a description of the man's car! From my recollection, he's slightly under six feet, slender, full head of hair. At his age, could be a wig. Wore dark sunglasses whenever I saw him."

"Canvas the other trailers," the social worker suggested. "See if anyone saw anything."

The tall cop turned to his partner, "Put your gun away, he's long gone. She's right. Someone had to see something, they always do in these places. Let's see what we can find out."

"I'm betting on a lot of *seen nothings, had my back to the window* responses," the partner said, holstering his weapon.

"Talk about getting busted. If we don't canvas, we'll end up guarding tomato cans at HEB."

Their knocks at the first several trailers went unanswered. Near the back of the lot a sleepy couple in their mid-twenties answered the door. They were obviously stoned or suffering from massive hangovers. All they could manage were negative nods before they slammed the door closed.

The next two units were clearly empty or abandoned. The next one after that was answered by a man wearing only graying underwear bottoms. He immediately threw up his arms and cried, "Ain't done nothin'!" he cried. What're you busting me for now? Haven't sold nothin' in months."

"Put your hands down, Juan, we're not here for you this time." The officer then asked about the missing girl and Juan responded, "Seen nothin'. Keep to myself."

"You positive about that? Never known you to not know what's going on."

"If'n I had seen anything, and mind I'm not saying as I have, number 22, back in the corner, would be a good place to start." Juan pointed toward the far corner of the lot in the direction of a trailer sitting separated from the others. It was the only unit with a semblance of a garden planted next to the door. "Old guy lives there. Seen him talking to a little girl from time to time."

Juan's tip proved accurate. Looking in the window, the officers saw a girl matching the description of Malinda sitting across from a grey-haired man. She was eating a plate of scrambled eggs and bacon.

Both officers drew their weapons. The social worker, who had turned pale, was instructed to return to her car and remain there.

"Cover me, I'm going in," the tall cop said to his partner.

"Knocking first?"

"Hell no! I'll take the door down, you get him. I don't want a hostage situation here. And for God's sake, don't shoot if there's any chance of hitting the girl. On my three count."

"One. Two. Three. Go!"

The door flew in and within five seconds the man inside was bent over the table. The tall cop picked up Malinda, chair and all, and set her down outside, trampling the garden as he went.

Back inside, the tall cop's partner yelled, "Guy's name is McDermot. Howson McDermot. Claims he's a retired school teacher. Says he's doing a favor for the man in unit 5. Five was babysitting the girl and this morning when the mother didn't come home he brought the girl over here."

"Your name's McDermot?" the tall cop said to the man whose head was still being pressed against the table. "Spell that."

When the man did, the cop stepped outside to call it in. A few minutes later he came back into the trailer. "You know the man in 5?" he asked. "His name, anything?"

"Nothing. Kept to himself. Don't know her mother either. They moved in a few weeks, oh, maybe a few months back. People in this park keep to themselves pretty much. I like it that way."

"What line of work are you in?"

"I'm a retired school teacher. I taught high school in McAllen for twenty years."

"Let him up. It matches."

While the officers interrogated McDermot, the social worker was busy processing Malinda into the system. No identification was found in Salina's trailer, so the child was named Malinda Nelson Mascar because those were the names the girl gave them.

By dinnertime, Malinda was in foster care. Fingerprinting revealed Sally's true identity and put her age at twenty-two with several arrests for prostitution in Austin. No convictions turned up.

A search of her trailer did not find evidence of drugs or stolen property. The police, however, did find three IDs tucked away under the mattress. "So who is Sherrill Phillips?" Lt. Hinojosa asked Sally.

"Who?"

"Sherrill Phillips?" Hinojosa patiently repeated.

"Don't know anybody by that name. You pinning something on me?"

"How about Sissy Ricos?"

"Should I know her?"

"You tell me."

"I need to get out of here. I want my baby!"

"You should have thought about your child before you began *working* the Island."

"I needed money to feed her."

"What about working a day job?" Hinojosa asked, putting emphasis on the word "day."

"I told you, I tried. Nobody would hire me."

"Why'd you leave Cosper?"

"Nothing there for me."

"What about Dilson Tylor?"

"What about him?"

"He claims you took a baseball bat to his head."

"I wasn't charged."

"Let's start again. Who is Sherrill Phillips?"

"Look, I borrowed some IDs a few years back, okay."

"What about Sissy Ricos?"

"Same."

"We also found an expired license in the name of Sally Mascar. Won't do you much good, but thought you might want it."

"Sally's dead! Gone and buried."

Seeing the anguish in her eyes and the tight fists Sally made, Hinojosa changed the subject. "Tell me about Dilson. He sued you, right?"

"Asshole tried to steal my money! I was saving it for...cost me everything to defend myself. I ran out of money and had to get out of town."

Hinojosa consulted his notes, flipped some pages, went back and reread something, then said, "I'm not exactly clear what happened. How about telling me your version?"

"What happened is I ran out of money, so the bastard won. You get a lawyer, lawyer takes it all. You don't get a lawyer, asshole takes it all. That's how your stink'n system works. He's looking for me now to collect."

"That's not the way I read this." He shoved a computer printout of an official looking document across the table.

Sally studied it, struggling to read the words. She pushed it away.

"My take," Hinojosa said, "is that a settlement was reached and the case was dropped."

"I have no money for any settlement! Just like the system to be screwed up."

"If you have resources you better start using them, else you could find yourself behind bars for a long time."

"I know my rights. I can have an attorney appointed."

"Sometimes there's more to it than that. An attorney might do a good job, but you've got a list of priors the Judge won't like one bit. If he hears about all this, you won't see your daughter for years. You need to do something about your life. The way you're going, it's not going to turn out all that well for you — or your daughter."

Suddenly alert, Sally demanded, "Why are you telling me all this stuff? You want something from me?"

"I want to help, if I can."

"Why the hell would a cop help me? Nobody helps a low life prostitute like me!"

"Maybe 'cause we didn't find drugs in your possession. Maybe 'cause I got a feeling something bad happened to you along the line. You were only fifteen when the kid was born. You're from Cosper. Baby is born in Austin. I was raised in Austin and joined the police force up there, so I know how bad the street was up there. Maybe 'cause if my daughter ever gets herself in trouble I'd want someone to give her good advice."

Sally sat passive, willing her eyes to stay dry. Revealing true feelings to the police was not smart.

"Am I close?"

Sally didn't know how to answer. The man seemed genuinely concerned for her. But she hated men, especially policemen. Nothing good ever came from any interactions she had ever had with the police.

Sensing her reluctance to talk, Hinojosa continued. "You can talk to me," he said, pulling his chair around the table and sitting next to her. "I'm trying to help you as a friend. Also, just to make things easier, I'm going to call you Sally. Drop all those other names you picked up along the way. Sally Mascar from here on."

"They said anything I say will be held against me. I'm in enough trouble as it is. Cops ain't nobody's friends."

"Just tell me what happened to you. I'll go off the record. If it makes you more comfortable just leave out anything you did wrong. Fact is I already know what you did. I want to know what other people did to you."

Sally sat quietly; her eyes watching her toes tap the floor.

"Let me guess," Hinojosa said, "Something happened to you in Cosper. Bet if I called the Cosper police they'd be able to tell me. Judging from the baby's birth date, you got pregnant at the end of a semester. Maybe you were in high school, but possibly still in middle school. You were thrown out — or ran away. I haven't located your mother, but my guess is she didn't know. Life has not treated you well, has it?"

"Middle school," Sally mumbled. Just saying it lifted a weight from her. "It wasn't my fault."

"Yes, you must have been fourteen when you were—"

"Raped!"

"I'm sorry. Life really has been bad for you. Let's see what we can do to turn that all around. But I can't help if you won't talk to me. Your daughter's been taken from you. Unless something changes, you won't get her back for a long, long time."

Tears formed. She was looking at the cop through a mist. Desperate to get Malinda back, she asked. "Will I get in trouble if I tell you?"

"I promise you no. It might even help."

For the first time since she had been brutally raped, Sally Mascar told another human what had happened to her in Cosper that horrible night. She then went on to talk about Austin and how she escaped. She carefully avoided divulging who had raped her, and did not talk about her work at *Cospers Own*. She poured her heart out for the first time since she left home as a fourteen-year old.

Why she had chosen to tell her story to this cop she didn't know. Cecil had been nice to her and yet she had pushed him away. She could have told Lucas, or even Pappa, but she had been frightened about getting into trouble. She had been terrified to tell her mother; she had known the screaming would never stop. Since being raped she felt dirty, unworthy of anyone's love, including her mother's.

Hinojosa, the police officer, remained passive as she spoke, while Hinojosa, the father, felt his own heart break. When she finished, he said, "Thank you for trusting me. I wish there was something I could do to reverse what has happened. But I do want to say one thing to you. Well, maybe a couple. First, not all people are bad. I understand how it appears from your vantage point, but the fact is that there are a lot of good people around. And second, you need to start making better choices about your life. There are good choices and bad choices and each choice has a consequence. Please promise me you'll try to make the choices that lead to good consequences."

"Why should I promise?" Sally demanded. "Nothing good has happened since I was fourteen. Why should it begin now?"

"Because if you promise me that you will make good choices I'm going to make something good happen for you. You have a child to raise and I want you to raise her right."

"I don't even know where she is!" Tears again appeared in Sally's eyes.

"She's in safe hands."

"I want her back!"

"That's not possible right now. It might be in the future, if you make good choices."

Sally, having learned the hard way to conceal her true feelings from the police, refused to let Hinojosa know that what he had just said about Malinda hurt her. Instead, she changed the subject. "What are you going to do for me if I promise?"

"We'll see. Do I have your promise?"

"I promise," Sally replied, knowing from past experiences that promises were meaningless. They were easily broken and, in fact, always were.

Forty-Eight

"Who's this?" Cecil said into his cell phone. The name he had heard was a Lieutenant something, sounded like Horse. *Another solicitation from the Fraternal Order of Police.*

"Lieutenant Hinojosa, South Padre Island Police Department. Is this Mr. Cecil Harris?"

Cecil knew South Padre was in south Texas by the Gulf of Mexico, about a four-hour drive, maybe more, he wasn't sure. The fact that the town was a major spring break destination held no meaning for him because he had never taken, or even thought about, a break. "If you're calling for a donation, call my financial manager. I don't do the books."

"I'm calling about a Miss Sally Mascar. I understand you know her."

Cecil sucked in a deep breath as several thoughts raced through his mind in quick succession. Sally Mascar had disappeared. A cop is calling from an island city. Sally drowned!

"You there?" asked the voice on the phone. "I'm calling about Miss Sally Mascar. I understand she's a friend of yours."

Cecil gathered himself. Remembering his training, he continued to breathe deeply. "Yes," he managed to reply, "I know Sally. Did she drown or something?"

"What makes you think she drowned?"

"Because you're a cop from some island calling about her."

"She didn't drown."

"That's good," Cecil responded, relieved that his friend had not drowned, but unable to express the emotion he felt. "Is she...alive?"

"Very much so. I understand you know her from grade school. Is that correct?"

"What's this about? What happened to her?"

"She was arrested a few days ago."

"Arrested! What for?"

"Prostitution."

"I'm not surprised," Cecil answered, realizing too late he had just made a terrible mistake.

"Why are you not surprised?"

"Did I say that I'm *not* surprised?" Cecil asked, recovering quickly. "What I meant is that I *am* surprised."

"Listen, Mr. Harris, I'll level with you. I'm trying to help your friend. She's in trouble and needs help. If somebody doesn't help her soon, I'm afraid her daughter will be permanently taken from her."

"Daughter? I didn't know about—" Cecil caught himself.

"The girl's in foster care. She's doing okay for now."

"I care about Sally," Cecil said. "But she told me to stay out of her life. Did she ask you to call me?"

"Not exactly. She told me about the summer you two spent together. She said it was the best summer she ever had. She says you were her only friend ever."

"She's my only friend. But she doesn't want me around her. I don't understand. I just want to be her friend."

"She needs your help, Mr. Harris."

"How did you find me?"

"You are not exactly an unknown, sir, as my Google search quickly made clear. There you were, big as life. Impressive.

Worth more money than God himself. I called your home in Cosper and was given this cell number."

"What kind of help does she need?" Cecil asked. "Is it money?"

"I want you to hire an attorney for her. It's more than just the criminal matter that needs to be fixed, I'm afraid."

"I don't know any lawyers down there. There's a guy here in town who might work okay, but he's not—"

"I have the perfect lawyer in mind. He's good at what he does, but he's not cheap."

"How much are you asking for?"

"Not me, Mr. Harris. The lawyer. If you tell me you'll help your friend, I'll have the lawyer call you to work out payment. Is that okay with you?"

"I don't want her to know where the money came from."

"I can arrange that as well."

"Then have the lawyer call me."

"You're doing a good thing, Mr. Harris. A very good thing. For both of them. Mother and daughter. I met the little girl. She's a good child. Do you know her?"

"No."

"She's a precious child. She misses her mother and wants Sally back with her."

"Can we get her out of foster care?"

"Ask the lawyer. Thanks for going along with this. By the way, I assume you're the one who settled that case in Cosper with that Dilson creep. Don't answer if you don't want to, but I can't imagine who else would have done that. Sally's lucky to have you as a friend."

Cecil remained silent.

Hinojosa continued, "When life's handed you what Sally was handed, it's tough to get back up. I was there myself once. A friend, someone I didn't even know I had as a friend, picked me up. That's why I became a cop. Now it's my turn to help. The lawyer will call you."

Abruptly, the line went dead.

Cecil stared at his phone a while before shoving it back in his pocket. He wanted to go to Sally Mascar, visit her in person, and bring her back into his life. The last time they had met it had been a disaster. He was terrified of repeating that situation.

He thought once again of that wonderful summer when they had rebuilt the Ghia. His mind lingered on their talks in the back seat over lunch. And the pleasant evenings they had spent at the end of each day, swimming and talking. Cecil wished they could rekindle the companionship he had felt then. He was certain she had also enjoyed the summer—and his company. The best part was that not once when he was with Sally had he gone into loop mode in frustration.

He had been forced to live away from home in Dallas with no hope of seeing her. High school for him consisted of building things in shop class. He lost himself in his designs, trying to shake off the lonely feelings of not having Sally to talk with. But she was never far from his mind.

Instead of talking to Sally, Cecil began calling his sister. At first it was once a week, then twice a week. Soon the conversation shifted from her struggles to cope with not being able to do anything for herself to what he could do to help. "Make my arms move, Cecil. That's what you can do for me," Caroline cried one afternoon. "Make my arms move."

Cecil then began to focus his energy on the design of machines that could move his sister's arms—and her legs. Months went by and every time she tried them something would fail, or her arms moved wildly in random directions.

With each failure, he went back to the drawing board and worked to improve the bot operation. Slowly, inch by inch, Caroline was able to gain control of her arms. It wasn't much, but it was enough to convince him that with enough concentration she could make the bots work. One foot at a time, Caroline was able to move further from her bed. Then one day, after several more design changes, she walked across the bedroom and out into the hall. By the summer of his second year in high school Caroline was able to take one or two steps before she would collapse to the floor, exhausted and often in tears.

On New Year's Day of his nineteenth birthday, Caroline's present to him was to rise from her bed and walk into the hall, all on her own. She even managed to sit in a chair without help.

It had been a milestone for each of them. For Cecil, it was the enormous satisfaction of giving his sister the ability to move about on her own. For Caroline, it was freedom from depending on someone to tend to her every need.

Thinking back to that time, Cecil now came to realize that no amount of car transmission design, however clever and innovative, could have possibly satisfied him in the way he had been at seeing his sister move on her own.

Recently he had begun thinking of a new project similar to the bots, but different enough, he thought, as to not violate his non-compete clause. His attorneys agreed, but also warned him that despite their opinions, litigation might be brought. "Give it one more year, Cecil," the lead lawyer had said, "and you'll be home free."

Recalling that conversation, Cecil now decided that he would spend time on his world cruise designing the project. His idea was to replace the wheelchair with a walking chair. Instead of having two big wheels on the side, it would have legs like a dog, or more accurately, a small donkey, and its motion would be controlled by head movements as well as voice commands.

Cecil knew the device wouldn't move as fast as a conventional wheelchair, but it would be able to navigate up and down hills without loss of control. Most importantly, it would be able to walk up and down steps as an animal might. The more Cecil thought of the walking chair, the more involved he became. Soon he shut out the world around him and all he could do was focus on his concept. He barely had time to think about his upcoming world trip.

Cecil wrote a resignation letter and handed it to Caroline on his last morning home, after having packed what little else beside his laptop computer that he wanted to take with him.

"Dear Sis," he wrote, "please accept this note as my resignation from your employ. You may keep as yours any design that I have made *up to this date, but please be advised that from here forward everything I design belongs only to me."*

After reading his letter, Caroline rolled into his office. "I'm sorry you're leaving the company," she said. "More importantly, I'm sad you feel you have to run away."

"I'm not running away. I'm just giving you and Wade the space you need."

"I think, brother dear, you are having a tantrum — grown up style. Look, stay here until it's time to leave for the boat. That gives you about two months."

"What's the point? I'll stay in Dallas, out of the way."

"No, stay here."

"Why?"

"Because I asked you nicely." She paused a moment before continuing, "And because Wade and I are planning an engagement announcement and I want you here for it."

"And just when is this big event?"

"Three weeks from Saturday."

"Is Dad invited?"

"Of course. It'll be difficult with Mother and Patty-Ann in the same room, but Mother promises to be on her best behavior. She'll honor that promise because Jennie Spencer will be here. She won't dare do anything in front of Jennie."

"This should be interesting," Cecil replied, smiling for the first time in weeks. "I suppose Alice is coming also."

"Of course. So is her husband, your buddy Clyde."

"*My* buddy? Cecil asked, puzzled.

"From the Big Raid, as it's now called. You know, the picture in the *Sentinel*. You guys are best buds."

"Leave it alone already! I've had enough of that!"

"I wish you wouldn't be so sensitive," Caroline sighed.

"So, let me understand this," Cecil continued, ignoring her comment. "Are you two engaged yet?"

"Actually, we're unofficially engaged. I told Wade I'd wait to wear the ring until it's officially announced. He's giving me the ring at the party. You know Wade, always the newsman. He wants to make a deal out of it. Pictures, that sort of thing. We'll be on the front page of the *Sentinel*."

"When's the big day? I mean when will you actually be married?"

"While you're gone, I'm afraid. June twenty-first—longest day of the year."

Again Cecil was puzzled. "Aren't all days the same length? Twenty-four—"

"No, silly. The longest day means the most sunlight. I want my wedding anniversary to always be a day full of sun."

"I'd postpone my trip if I could, but I don't think that's—"

"Being here for my engagement party is all that I ask of you. The ceremony will be at the house. It's not practical to take a honeymoon."

Cecil thought of his walking chair and how it would change all that. But there was not enough time to design and build even a prototype.

"And besides, the paper's in deep trouble. Revenue's been slipping, costs are up. Wade's barely holding on."

Cecil wondered if the wedding date and the failing newspaper were connected. Certainly, Caroline could financially support the paper for years. But, from things his mother had said, Wade adored his sister. He was unsure as to why Wade wanted Caroline in his life, but as his therapist had said, "Love has many faces and none of us can read what other people see. From what I know about Wade, he has never dated much. Often, and this is only an informed guess, men who don't date have...well...difficulty relating to women. Like you have difficulty relating to women."

"So Wade is like me?" Cecil had asked his therapist.

"I can't say that. What I can say is that Wade's father—and grandfather—were dominating men. Wade is not from the same mold and I'm thinking he somehow feels...inadequate, especially with respect to women."

"But he's...with my sister."

"Maybe it's easier to dominate her."

"No one dominates Carolyn."

"Not mentally or emotionally, but certainly physically. Anyway, he's not my patient so everything I'm saying is pure speculation. But that could be why he and Caroline get along so well. They each fill a need of the other."

༺༻

"My wedding present to you," Cecil announced out of the blue a few days after his resignation, "will be to get the new *Axtel* production-line up and running before I leave. It'll give me something to do until mid-May."

"I love your presents, brother dear," Caroline replied. "I wish you were not running away though."

Forty-Nine

Sally's life took a positive turn. It was not a very sharp turn, but, as Lt. Hinojosa told her, it was a turn in the right direction. Some charity was willing to pay a top lawyer, he had told her, not only for the South Padre matter, but also to work with Child Protection Services to get Malinda back.

Bail was paid within hours. Hinojosa walked Sally to the bus stop in front of the jail. "Now, it's up to you. Go home and freshen up." He checked his watch. "It's eleven-fifteen. You must be in Brownsville, in the lawyer's office by three-thirty. Leave yourself an hour. Do you have any money?"

"Not much."

"The shuttle from here to your trailer is free." He reached for his wallet, counted out five ones, added a five dollar bill to the stack, and handed the money to her. "Here. This will get you to Brownsville. Don't be late."

Sally accepted the money reluctantly. She was afraid to put it in her pocket fearing it would harm her in some way. Cops had always been her enemy and her natural instinct was to reject anything they sent her way. This man seemed different, but still...

"Go ahead, take it. It won't bite. It's a gift."

"Are you sure it's okay? I mean—"

"Of course it's okay. Just don't go home and fall asleep and miss your appointment."

"I'll try," Sally murmured, stepping onto the *Wave*. The small bus pulled away, leaving Hinojosa standing on the sidewalk, as anxious as a father who had just put his daughter on the school bus for the first time.

༄༅

Sally sat across from her lawyer in the fanciest office she had ever seen. He called her Miss Mascar. She judged him to be in his early sixties, soft spoken, not like the hard-ass types she had encountered in the past.

This man is too soft to stand up to the judge and the police. That thought played in her head over and over and she found it hard to concentrate on what he was saying.

The sound of her daughter's name registered, focusing Sally's attention. The lawyer was saying something about plans to get Malinda back.

She interrupted. "I have prostitution charges on my record," she reminded him. "I'll never get her back."

"As I just told you, Miss Mascar, I have every expectation those charges will go away."

"But they got me taking the money. I even saw the pictures those sneaks took. Got me cold."

"Trust me on this. The worse you're going to get is a disorderly conduct charge. Maybe not even that."

"I'll believe it when I see it."

"Healthy distrust is a good thing—sometimes. Let's move on. First you need a job."

"I've applied everywhere on the island."

"You live in Port Isabel. Get a job there."

"Everybody tells me to get a job. But what can I do? I'll tell you. Nothing! I didn't even go to high school. No one hires a grade-school dropout."

The lawyer thumbed through papers from a file on his desk looking for something in particular. "Here it is. These are the notes Lieutenant Hinojosa jotted down." He skimmed down the page. "I thought I remembered this. It says here you worked in Dallas restoring a car. Tell me about that."

Wearily, Sally again repeated her activities during that summer with Cecil. She was uncomfortable sharing such private information with anyone, especially people in power. It was as if speaking about it would somehow diminish the special intimacy of it. She was now sorry she had told the cop.

The lawyer jotted down some notes while she spoke. When she finished, he said, "I think I have just the place for you. There's a small car repair shop in Port Isabel. The only one around that works on interiors." He pulled an address book from a desk drawer and wrote down a name and address. "I'm going to call this guy Lucas in Dallas. If what you told me checks out, I'm sure you will be hired. Give me a day and then go see them. It'll probably be minimum wage or close to it. But it will be a start." He pushed the paper across the desk. "So you'll go and see them, right?"

"I suppose. I don't really have any other choice."

He pulled his desk drawer open and extracted an envelope and passed it over to Sally.

"What's this?"

"Open it."

Sally did as she was told. To her amazement she found a stack of twenties neatly bound with a paper ring.

"Count it, please."

She slid the ring off and carefully counted. "Eight hundred dollars!" she exclaimed. "What's this for?"

"Your benefactor has given you this to tide you over until you receive a pay check. You must call me without fail two weeks from today to report on your employment situation. I expect you to have a job by then."

"That's wishful thinking."

Ignoring her remark, he continued, "And you must fax me a copy of your pay stub every payday. You know how to fax something?"

"Not really."

"Go to any copy store. No wait." He flipped open the address book and added a name and number to her paper. "That's a law office in Port Isabel. I'll tell them you're coming in. Just go there and ask them to fax the pay stub to me. It's that easy."

"What's the point of that?"

"Three reasons. To be perfectly blunt, we need to prove to your benefactor that your money is not coming from prostitution. Second, I'll be working on a budget for you. So much for rent, food, clothes, day care..."

"I know my rent," Sally interrupted. "It's—"

"You'll be moving out of that trailer as soon as you receive your first pay check. You can't raise Malinda there."

"Hey, that's my—"

Ignoring her, he continued, "And third, I'll have a record to show CPS. If all goes well, we'll have Malinda living with you by July. I've already been in touch with the case worker. Your daughter's doing well and wants to come home. There's no sign of abuse or neglect on your part. That's good news. So do as I say and we'll get her back with you."

"I'm a good mommy," Sally stated forcefully. "I want her with me."

"Then do exactly as I say. Exactly! And it will work out."

"I'll try," was all Sally could manage before the tears started to flow.

As the secretary escorted Sally from the office, the lawyer called after her. "Remember, you are due in court on the island Friday morning. Nine AM sharp. Your trial starts at ten. Whatever you do, don't be late."

Standard Deviation

☯☯

The bus back to Port Isabel ran along the Brownsville shipping channel. Had Sally looked out of the window on the right side she would have seen two massive oilrigs being refurbished at *Amfels* shipyard. But her mind was elsewhere. She was concentrating on what she had just been told.

It was actually all too good to be true. If there was one thing she had learned in her life, it was that the system never worked in your favor. Never.

So why should she trust some smooth-talking fancy-dressed lawyer in an expensive office? What did he know of life on the street? He had never in his life been where she had been. The man was so sure of himself. Certain she could waltz right in and get a job in some car shop. Nobody was going to hire a grade school dropout—certainly not one with broken teeth.

The image of Malinda flashed in front of her eyes. She could see her daughter's mischievous smile, her alert eyes and the dimple in her check. When the girl smiled up at Sally it was as if the weight of the world had lifted. Tears welled up and the image faded.

Maybe Malinda was better off in foster care, Sally thought. She recalled the pleading in her daughter's eyes when they were last together, the little girl silently begging for food. With a foster family, Sally wouldn't have to ration dry cereal and Malinda wouldn't go days with little to eat. The girl wouldn't be forced to sleep with strangers while Mommy worked the streets. South Padre Island was out, but there were plenty of other towns where men could take advantage of what she did best. If Texas didn't work out, there was always Louisiana, or even Mexico.

What about Brownsville? Bet there's money to be made in a club down here, Sally thought. Her thoughts moved on to the money aspects of all this, realizing that she'd have to work a week or more at some miserable job just to earn what she made from one or two tricks. And tax-free besides.

Her mind focused on the man at *Cospers Own* who had paid five thousand to be with her for one night? What about him? Once a month, hell, once every three months was all she needed at that rate. Why bother with eight dollars an hour in some stinking hole? A trick a week would give her more than she needed.

The bus turned onto Route 100 in Port Isabel. Sally got off and walked along the road toward her trailer. Her fingers found the lawyer's paper stuffed in her pocket. She pulled it out, studied it a moment and then, on impulse, crumpled it up and threw it in a trashcan.

She walked a block and suddenly the cop's voice was in her head. *That was not a good choice. The lawyer told you to get a job. You need a job. Throwing the paper away was not good.*

If she wanted to get Malinda back, she had to try. Maybe her luck was really changing. And the more she thought of living without Malinda the bleaker life seemed. Sally turned back and ran as fast as she could to the trashcan. Digging through it, she found a mass of damp and filthy rubbish. Her crumpled paper was nowhere to be seen.

Maybe I have the wrong can?

Frantically, she looked up and down the highway, but there wasn't another can in sight. She thought of overturning the can, but the mess would be more than she could handle. If she got caught, it wouldn't go well for her.

I'll just say they weren't hiring.

༄༅

On Friday morning Sally caught the *Wave* to the Island. Arriving at Town Hall she found standing room only in the small courtroom. Sally heard someone comment, "Spring break must have been lively this year, judging from the crowd here today. Not usually this busy."

A small window in the vestibule door gave Sally a pigeon-hole view into the courtroom. At exactly nine o'clock, the judge, a woman dressed in a traditional black gown, took the bench. Soon, people inside the courtroom began moving forward. From past experience, Sally knew their names were being called. She didn't worry about missing her time because she knew her fancy lawyer would find her when it was her turn.

The crowd thinned, but Sally's lawyer was nowhere in sight. A wave of panic flooded over her. *He knows I didn't apply for the job, so he's not coming.*

Her stomach tightened as it always did when she knew she was in trouble. *But he's getting paid, so he should be here!* And then more panic. *Maybe the money for the lawyer got cut off when I disappeared with the $800 without applying for that job. Shit! I'm going back to jail. I'll never get my baby back now.*

By ten-fifteen only a few people remained in the courtroom. Sally pushed open the door and went inside just in time to hear the bailiff call another list of names. A young man stepped to the front. The Judge scolded him for underaged drinking, fined him fifty dollars and banged her gavel. He moved to the side, only to be replaced by another man of roughly the same age.

Same speech from the Judge. The gavel banged and a slightly built woman followed the parade. The gavel banged and she moved over to the corner where the court clerk was collecting fines.

The Judge's gavel sounded a few more times and then Sally was the only non-official person in the courtroom. Her lawyer was still not there and her heart sunk even lower.

Could this possibly be the wrong day? Can't be. He said Friday. Friday morning, in fact. Nine o'clock sharp. So where is he?

The bailiff, a small man with a protruding stomach and an unfriendly face, turned to her. "And who are you?" he demanded.

Sally glanced around, hoping he was talking to someone else. But she was alone.

"I'm Sally Mascar," she managed, her throat suddenly dry.

"Can't hear you! Come up here and speak up!"

Sally reluctantly moved forward and repeated her name.

The bailiff stared up and down at his clipboard and then flipped to a second sheet. "Oh, here you are. You've been adjourned to after the lunch break. Your lawyer should have told you." He glanced up at the judge. "That'll be at one today, Your Honor."

Before Sally could say anything further, the Judge banged her gavel. "Court adjourned until one PM."

"All rise!" the bailiff declared, self-importance ringing from the walls.

There was no one to stand other than Sally, and she was already standing.

The Judge stood, laid her glasses on the bench, and walked out a side door.

Sally fled to the hall in search of her lawyer.

Still not seeing him, she pushed open the big front door and walked into the bright sunlight. The warm day and salt air filled her nostrils. Sunshine or not, all she felt was an oppressive sense of gloom.

Suddenly hungry, Sally turned south, walked a few blocks, and found a place called *The Big Donkey*. It was a Mexican restaurant and she ordered a chicken taco. She wanted more, but didn't want to spend the money.

At twelve forty-five she arrived back at Town Hall. The clerk who had been collecting the fines earlier in the day was now sitting at a desk in the hall. Looking up when Sally entered the building, the woman pointed to a side door and said, "Miss Mascar, please go through here and turn right. First door on the left. It says 'City Prosecutor.' They're waiting for you."

Sally eyed the wall clock. "I thought it was at—"

"This is a pre-hearing conference. Your lawyer's inside."

Sally knocked on the door and a muffled voice called for her to come in. Her lawyer was sitting across a table from a man she had seen in the courtroom earlier. They were both wearing suits. Off to one side sat Lt. Hinojosa.

Her lawyer stood. "Oh, there you are. Miss Mascar this is the City Prosecutor, Dominick Osaga. And I believe you know Lt. Hinojosa."

Sally nodded, uncomfortable in this small room with people who held her future in their hands. Missing from the room was the rat-cop who had tricked her into taking money.

"We've been discussing your case," her lawyer began, "and I think we're all in agreement. The City is agreeable to reducing the charge to disorderly conduct and the sentence will be suspended."

Sally was highly skeptical. "What's the catch?" she asked, an edge to her voice.

"No catch. All you need to do is to plead guilty to being disorderly and we'll be out of here."

"I don't get it," Sally insisted, certain she was being set up.

"Let me just say this," Hinojosa injected, "the officer who arrested you has agreed he might have, just might have, enticed you. Led you on. We're willing to drop the charge of Solicitation of Prostitution."

"Why don't you just drop it all then if you did wrong?" Sally demanded. "I wasn't disorderly, or drunk or anything."

Her lawyer looked at prosecutor Osaga and raised his eyebrows. "You know, Dom," he said, "she does have a point there."

"I'm caught between the police and the judge," replied Osaga, a tall, slender man, with a receding hairline and jumpy eyes. "Judge gets all over me when we drop cases at the last minute." He turned to Hinojosa. "What's your position on this?"

"I agree, drop it," the lieutenant said. "We don't have a case. She's right, she wasn't making a scene."

"Tell you what," Osaga said cautiously, "I'll go see what the Judge's take is. Wait here."

Hinojosa turned to Sally after the prosecutor had left. "Have you found a job yet? I'm told you were going to apply at *Migel's Auto Repair* over in Port Isabel."

He knows more than he's letting on. Sally heard his voice in her head. *Choices are what life is made of.* She was about to lie about *Migel's* not hiring her but chose the truth instead. "I lost the name," she said quietly. "I'm sorry."

"So just when were you going to tell me?" her lawyer asked with more than a tinge of annoyance in his voice. "Time's a-wasting. You want your child back, you better get on it." He bent down and pulled a file folder from his brief case and placed it on the table. A white label stretched across the top read: *Sally Mascar*, followed by a series of numbers.

The lawyer opened the file and flipped through the pages. He pulled a pen from inside his coat and wrote the name *Migel's Auto Repair* on a note card followed by an address. He added the name of the Port Isabel law firm, then handed the card to Sally. "You go see these folks today when we leave here, got it? If *Migel's* isn't hiring then go over to Walmart. They're hiring for certain."

"I understand."

"Your enthusiasm hardly inspires confidence," the lawyer said sarcastically. "Don't screw up again. Either you want a job or you don't. If not, then tell me now so I won't waste any more time or money on this. What's it going to be?"

"I want a job."

Lt. Hinojosa motioned to the lawyer to follow him into the hall. The door closed behind them. Through the small window she could see Hinojosa asking questions of the lawyer. Her lawyer was nodding in response. They were most certainly discussing her.

The file with her name on it lay a few inches away. She checked to make sure no one was looking and then opened the file. Turning the pages, the papers made no sense. Mostly legal letters of one sort or another. She was about to close the file when the familiar blue logo of the *Cosper State Bank* caught her eye. The amount of eight thousand dollars appeared below the date and next to the amount was the lawyer's name. The words WIRE TRANSFER were printed along the bottom.

The door started to open and she hurriedly flipped the file closed and shoved it back to its original place just as the prosecutor came back into the room followed closely by the cop and her lawyer.

Standard Deviation

"The judge is not happy," the prosecutor began, "but she's going to agree to the dropped charges as long as we do it in open court. So come on, let's get this over with so you can go job hunting."

Once in the courtroom they sat at the front table just below the Judge's bench. The bailiff once again cried, "All rise," at which point the judge came through the side door and waved everyone to sit. A few minutes later the bailiff called Sally's name.

All the men at the table stood, so Sally stood as well. The prosecutor announced his name and his title as City Prosecutor. Sally's lawyer announced his name, his firm's name and his representation of Sally Mascar. He then bent toward her and instructed her to state her name and address.

Sally did as she was told.

The Prosecutor then said, "Your Honor. May it please the Court, after discussions with the arresting officer, it now appears that the arrest may not have been proper. We are requesting the charges be dropped."

"Mr. Osaga, you leave me no choice but to dismiss this matter for lack of proper process. But I am not happy. Please instruct the police to follow proper procedure in making arrests." She then turned to Sally. "All I can say to you, young lady, is that you are getting off easy here. I know these officers well and when they make an arrest, it's for a good reason. I don't know what really happened here, and perhaps I shouldn't know. But I can tell you this: Whatever it was you were doing, you better stop doing it. You could find yourself in a world of hurt the next time. Am I clear?"

"Yes ma'am."

"Then I have nothing further to say to you, other than to stay out of trouble." The judge's gavel hit the bench. "Court adjourned until nine AM tomorrow, when we'll do it all over again. See you in the morning, Mr. Osaga."

The words, *All Rise*, echoed in Sally's head as she boarded the shuttle home.

Crossing the bridge back to Port Isabel, Sally studied the water of Laguna Madre for several minutes. Just off the shore, a parasail hung suspended over the deep green waves. The bright colors of the sail formed a backdrop for her real focus; the wire transfer record she had seen in the lawyer's file.

The amount had shocked her, but not as much as had the name on the account from which the funds were drawn. There in bold letters, as if written by a sky-writer in the deep blue sky over Laguna Madre, she clearly saw the notation: CECIL HARRIS, SPECIAL ACCOUNT.

Fifty

Cecil answered the door Sunday morning and blinked twice before he could fully take in who was standing there holding his newspaper. Even though it was after eleven, Caroline and Wade were still in bed. Cecil himself had slept late because he had been working on his *walk chair* and didn't have a good place to stop until way into the wee hours.

Cecil had heard Wade and Caroline down by the fire from his office, the two of them, entertaining each other with stories and games. They had begun playing some form of double solitaire and Caroline had called him on the intercom to ask him to adjust her bots to allow for better control of the cards. This led to a design change that he planned to send to his former company under his agreement with them.

Seeing her by the fire, relaxed, having fun, laughing, made him feel good for her. A deep loneliness resurfaced, a feeling that he thought he had suppressed. He longed for a time just to sit with his sister and talk as they used to do. He missed those times with her and wished for someone to spend time with.

Now, looking out at his visitor, Cecil managed to stammer, "What...what...are you doing here? I thought you were...gone." A very slimmed-down Sally Mascar stood in his doorway. She had the look in her eyes that he remembered so fondly from their summer together. "I suppose I should invite you in. Come on in. I was making coffee. You want anything? Maybe some eggs? Or cereal or something?" He was babbling, but unable to settle himself. Even deep breaths weren't helping. "Anything you want to eat, I can fix for you. The kitchen is over here, follow me."

Sally trailed behind Cecil on the way to the kitchen, still holding the newspaper. She hadn't said a word.

"Do you want coffee? How about milk? Do you want a glass of milk?"

Sally stood mesmerized by the wonderfully furnished kitchen, overwhelmed by its spaciousness.

"What can I get for you?" Cecil again asked. "Are you hungry?"

"This is so...so nice," Sally finally said. "I didn't know—"

"It was specially designed for the former owner. But he never lived here. We bought it before he moved in."

Sally's face fell. "We? Are you married?"

"My sister Caroline and I own this house. She's sleeping."

"Oh, your sister," Sally repeated, her closed-mouthed smile returning. "You live with your sister?" She studied the kitchen for a moment, contemplating how to say what she had come here to say. She formed the words in her head and, with a sudden burst of courage, pushed them out. "I came to thank you for helping me."

Her statement confused Cecil even further. "I...I don't—"

"I know I'm not supposed to know you gave me the money. But I snuck a peak and found out. I had to thank you in person. I'm not much for using the telephone. I never call people." She walked over to where he was standing by the refrigerator and planted a kiss, first on his cheek, and when he didn't pull away, on his mouth.

Cecil didn't know what to do—or say. Here, in his own kitchen, stood the girl he had been thinking about, indeed dreaming about, for years. His very best friend, Sally Mascar, was back. And she had just kissed him. Kissed him as if she meant it.

Sally pulled back. "Do you ever think about our summer? I do all the time."

"All the time," he replied. "All the time. I thought you died when you disappeared from Dallas. Then, when you got into my, I mean *our*, car I was stunned. But you were so...so, not the same. I mean—"

"Forget that time. That was a bad time for me. I was heavy and ugly and broke, and—"

"I know about your work at *Cospers Own*," Cecil blurted. "I mean you told me you were going there, but I never understood why. What were you doing working...I mean working that way?"

"That's past now," Sally replied. "I'm starting over." She looked around, her eyes wide. "Cecil," she said after a moment, "this place makes me uncomfortable. I don't belong here. Can we go for a ride? I want to sit in the car again. I miss that very much."

"Let me get something for us to eat. We can have a picnic." Cecil poured coffee into a thermos and found cheese in the refrigerator. He nervously busied himself around the kitchen gathering things. Finally, he said, "Come, the car's in the garage."

She followed him to the garage and stood back to look at the beautiful restoration. "Forgive me. I was upset when I climbed into the car the last time. Mad at you, mad at the world." Sally opened the front door and before she climbed in, ran her hand over the upholstery the two of them had so carefully and painstakingly installed. It had only been partially completed when the summer ended. She could only imagine how many more hours Cecil had put into it.

Thinking of that summer brought to mind something she had often thought about: what her life would have been like had she told Lucas. As always, she rejected that idea, convinced that had the grown-ups known about the baby it would have been taken from her. Malinda meant everything to her. She forced the thoughts away. Curious about Lucas, Sally called out, "Hey, I was just thinking of Lucas. Ever talk to him?"

"All the time, yeah. My sister also talks to him about the... things. He still rebuilds cars. Sometimes when I'm in Dallas I go over and work with him."

"Why not rebuild your own right here? Maybe I could... help you?"

"That would be good. We could do it when I move in by myself. Maybe Lucas will come down and help."

"Hey, this is gorgeous!" she exclaimed after circling the car. "It's been over seven years and it looks fantastic. There's not one scratch on it."

"There've been a few here and there, but I've managed to rub them out." He waved his arm around the garage. "You can see I've a pretty complete set-up here. Three bays, one car. That gives me plenty of room to work. I use it for my prototypes."

"I heard you were a famous inventor. Bots, whatever they are, or something."

"Robots for allowing people who can't use their limbs to move around."

"Now I remember. You were in Dallas because your sister... was in an accident."

"She can't walk or move her arms. The bots help her. How did you know about me?"

"A teacher where I live. He took care of...he looked you up for me. Says you made a lot of money."

"I did. Lucky, I suppose."

"Is that one of your projects?" Sally pointed to a partially dismantled wheelchair. "Looks like it's got sticks coming out of it."

"I'm trying to make it walk?"

"Did you just say, make it walk?"

"I want to make it walk instead of roll. It's an idea I had. I have too much on my mind to work on it. I can only do one thing at a time. When I get back from the trip I'll get it working. C'mon, ready to go?"

"You're crazy. You know that. Thinking of things no one else thinks about. Back in grade school everyone made fun of you with your engines and things."

"I suppose they did. They don't any more. Are you ready to go?"

Sally climbed in and ran her hand over the dashboard. "I remember when you sanded this down and got all the scratches out. That was a lot of work."

"You did your share. Ripping all the seats out and unbolting everything was hard work."

Cecil headed the Ghia out of town and soon they were passing fields being made ready for late spring planting. Cattle roamed over the slightly rolling land, grazing where they pleased.

They drove mostly in silence, each becoming re-accustomed to being in the other's presence. A lot had happened in the intervening years — both to Sally as well as to Cecil — and neither of them knew how to comfortably bridge the gap.

"What do you with yourself," Sally asked, breaking the silence, "other than design machines and robots, I mean."

"Nothing much really," Cecil confessed. "I like to design machines."

"You should find other things to do. Do you read much?"

"Not *so* much." He hesitated, then added, "I find it hard to read. The words get confused."

"How do you learn then?"

"I remember what I hear. What about you?"

"I don't read much either. Maybe a magazine, when I can afford one," she giggled, her face flushing.

"You have trouble, too? I mean reading."

"I read very slow. I never told anyone. Please don't make fun of me."

"I would never make fun of you, Sally. Never. You are my only friend."

"And you're my friend, too."

"I was told you had to find a job. Did you have any luck?"

Her face brightened. "Tomorrow morning I start in a car repair shop fixing the upholstery. Cars and trucks both."

"That's great! I can't believe it. You'll be working, doing what you like to do."

"I think I'll like it well enough. But I don't know anything about it, really. When we were working on this car, I just did what you told me to do."

"They'll show you."

"Lucas gave a good reference, so they hired me. But I'm nervous I won't be able to do it."

"Sure you can. Just listen to what they want, and do exactly what they tell you." Cecil absently ran his hand across the upholstery. "You did a fabulous job on this one, after all."

"Well, just in case, I applied for a job at Walmart, too. Got that one also, but I won't be able to keep it for very long."

"Why not?"

"Because, it's at night."

"Working at night should be no problem."

"I have a...a problem with nights."

"But you worked nights before. I don't understand."

"It's a personal thing."

Cecil pulled the car over near a meadow full of spring flowers. "Let's get out, we can spread the blanket and have some cheese. We won't have many more days like this before it gets really hot."

She held the food while Cecil spread the blanket. "I can't even remember when I was able to just sit around and do something fun like this," Sally said, leaning back on the blanket, her face turned upward toward the sun. "This is my first picnic ever."

"I don't reckon you would have time, what with raising a baby and working and all."

Sally jerked straight in her seat, her jaw clenched. "How do you know about her?"

"The cop from the island told me. I want to help."

"Malinda is private! I don't need people poking around. Oh, God, I want her back so much."

"I am your friend. I know about your baby. There's nothing to be ashamed of. I mean, having a baby is a natural thing."

"I ain't married or nothing!" Sally shot back. She glared at him defiantly, as if to say, I can take care of her myself.

"I want to be your friend. I want to help you—and Malinda. Friends talk to each other. Please tell me what happened. Why did you disappear?"

"None of your business!"

"It is my business because I'm your friend. You're my only friend. Please tell me what happened to you."

"It's not your business!"

"I'll tell you exactly why it's my business. When you disappeared, I was blamed for doing something to you. I was thrown out of high school and forced to live with my grandparents in Dallas. I saw you at the play with some boy. But I never told them. So it *is* my business. Come, sit like we used to sit and talk with me."

"Did you see who I was with?"

"I've been trying to recall, but his face was in the shadows. I made the teacher go away."

Sally studied him for a long while, and then finally said, "Can we sit in the back of the car with our legs crossed like we did that summer?"

"Of course we can," Cecil replied. He reached down to help her up.

They walked to the car and climbed into the back seat, each sitting where they always had. Sally arranged her legs over his just as they had been the summer of her fifteenth birthday.

After a long period of silence, Sally began to speak. Hesitantly at first, she unfolded the story of her life since Dallas. Cecil remained absolutely quiet while Sally spoke. Questions were piling up in his head, but he held his tongue. Indeed, some of the questions were answered as her narrative continued. But as one sordid detail after another was revealed it became apparent that she was not going to answer the most nagging question of all. *Who had raped her?*

Cecil yet again strained his visual memory for a hint of the person he had seen in the school that night. But, as always, the only image he could see was that of a frightened Sally Mascar being held against the wall by someone taller than she was.

Sally finished her narrative, but Cecil remained silent, having given up trying to think of the proper words of comfort.

Sally broke the silence. "I know I don't deserve your friendship," she started, "but—"

Cecil tried to interrupt, to tell her he was still her friend, but Sally held up her hand.

"I don't deserve you," she began again, "but Malinda, that's my little girl, is a nice kid. I want you to know her, maybe be friends. She needs someone like you. I really trust you."

"Of course I'll be Malinda's friend. I can't wait to meet her."

"I have to prove I'm a good mother first. They have her and I want her back."

"What do you mean?" Cecil exclaimed. "I'm sure you're a wonderful mother."

"I think I am, too," Sally replied. "I try hard. But I have to prove it to CPS before I can have her back."

"And how long will that take?" Cecil asked.

"If I do everything the lawyer tells me to do he says it'll be the middle of June, maybe."

"What do you have to do?"

"Work at my job. Send my pay stubs to him. Spend my money exactly as he says. Get a new place to stay."

"That's a long list."

"He wrote it all out for me. I just have to follow it."

"I thought you couldn't read."

"Books and things are hard. But I can read words if I do it slow."

"Can you do all those things?"

"I miss my baby," Sally suddenly cried. "I want my baby!" Tears poured down her face as though a spigot had been turned on.

Sitting across from her, Cecil could do nothing while Sally cried without pause for a solid minute. When the tears diminished into sniffles, he said, "No matter what, I am your friend. Together we will get her back."

The tears again started. "Cecil," she sniffed a moment later, "I don't deserve your friendship. And you know what else? I hate how I look." She sucked in her breath and plunged forward. "Look at me, Cecil, look at me! My teeth, this scar! I keep the scar mostly covered, but I know it's there. My God, look what happened to me?"

"There's nothing to be ashamed of," Cecil replied.

"That's what I was saving my money for," she shrieked through the tears. "Until that creep Dil Tylor made me piss it away on lawyers! I was so close to having enough money to make myself look good again. Now look at me. I'm so ugly I can't stand to even think about it, let alone look in the mirror."

Cecil didn't know what to say, but it didn't matter. Sally wasn't finished.

"It's not me I wanted to do it for," she sobbed. "It's for Malinda. I don't want her growing up looking at me like I'm a freak. I don't want her having to answer questions from her school friends about what happened. She'll have it hard enough without making excuses for her Momma."

"Thanks for telling me," was all Cecil could think to say.

They fell quiet again, Cecil trying to digest everything that he heard. Neither of them making any move to leave.

Cecil's thoughts turned to his sister and the upcoming engagement party. He was thinking to invite Sally, until he remembered his mother's gossipy accounts of Clyde Higgins being involved with Sally. Clyde would be at the party with his wife Alice.

The silence was finally broken when Cecil followed up on that particular train of thought. "Are you still seeing Clyde," he asked, "or is that over?"

Alice tensed, pulling her legs up against her chest. "How do you know about Clyde?"

"My mother is good friends with Jennie Spencer. Nothing moves in this town without Jennie knowing about it and then telling my mother."

"I like him. He's tied to that wife of his. Thinks he can't find work, except at the paper, so he stays with her for the job. He wants to marry me."

Sally's *'I like him'* assertion was painful for Cecil to hear. "Money seems to be the sticking point for a lot of things," Cecil said, trying his best to conceal his hurt feelings.

"Not for you," Sally replied.

"I'm lucky."

"But you don't have a wife, or even a girlfriend. Actually, I don't know that. About the girlfriend, I mean."

Cecil looked down and fell silent.

"Cecil," Sally continued, "I told you things about me. Very personal things too. You can tell me something like that."

Without looking up, he responded, "I don't have a girlfriend. Other than you."

She reached down and put her hand on his leg. "I am your girl friend. Why are you so...so unhappy all of a sudden?"

Cecil continued to stare at the floor.

Sally pressed him. "Talk to me, Cecil. Tell me what's making you sad."

Cecil locked on the words, *Can't do it. Can't do it. Can't do it.* His lips began to form the mantra. But before any sound came, the voice of his therapist broke through. *When you feel locked you must confront the problem directly.* Forcing himself to heed the advice, Cecil looked at Sally sitting across from him and said, "I've never had sex. I don't—"

Sally reached over and pulled Cecil toward her. "If you come over here we can remedy that this very instant."

He started to untangle his legs and move across the seat toward her.

Then he stopped. "I don't want to be just another man taking advantage. I want you like...like a...lover. Not like...like just anybody. I want you to love me."

"What you mean is, like a whore! I'm not that way anymore! I want you as a lover." She began to cry again, and this time Cecil moved close and wiped her face as the tears continued.

After a while, he said, "I do want to have sex with you. But I want it to be out of love. Do you love me?"

"I think I do, but I don't know what love really means. I've never loved a man. I never allowed myself to think about being in love. Men use me, and I use them back for what I want. Money and security. I haven't had a reason to think about love."

"And me? Why did you want to have sex with me?"

"You've given me so much. Like my life back. I'm repaying you."

"You don't owe me anything. Maybe you'll fall in love with me. Real love. Then we can have...sex. I don't want it as...as a favor."

"Real love. I don't know what real love means. I don't even know if I can be in love."

"Well, we'll be friends then, and just see if it happens."

Again they fell silent. After a while, Cecil said, "I'm starved. I didn't have breakfast and that cheese wasn't enough. Want to go get something?"

"That will be a real treat."

Fifty-One

It was almost four in the afternoon and Sally wanted waffles. Cecil drove to the *Waffle House* out by the main highway. The usual Sunday crowd was gone and only two tables held customers.

They selected a table near the back. While they waited for their waffles, Sally said, "Thank you for such a nice day. I forgot how wonderful it is to be with you. I hate to eat and bolt, but the drive to Port Isabel is more than three hours and I have to be at the car shop in the morning at seven."

"Oh, I'm sorry. I was hoping to take you home to meet my sister."

"Some other time."

They ate their waffles in silence and sat for a few minutes sipping coffee. Cecil had suggested that they both have hot chocolate like they had done that summer, but Sally insisted that she needed something to keep her awake for the drive to Port Isabel. She then went on to tell Cecil about Malinda and what a good girl she is. "Considering all that poor child's gone through, I can't believe she's as good as she is. And she's smart too. Real smart." Sally's eyes watered. "I really miss her. I'm going to make good choices. I promise I will. I want her back." She wiped her eyes. "All I've done today is cry."

"For good reason," Cecil responded. Suddenly he was struck by a thought. "Hey," he began, "this is going to sound crazy. But it'll work. I know it will. I've booked a round-the-world cruise beginning in June. You can go with me! That'll give us plenty of time to talk and be together doing things."

"Round the world! That's crazy! Wow! I can't believe you asked me. Round the world!"

"Remember, we talked about it back in Dallas? You told me your dream."

"I forgot I told you. I've always wanted..." Her face fell. "Wait a minute. I can't go. I just can't."

"There's no need for..." Leaning close and dropping his voice, "sex, unless it works between us. We're just friends for now. It'll be wonderful, and we'll see the world together." Cecil was animated. He was more excited than he had ever been before in his life. "It's not just a cruise. Lucas told me about special projects around the world the government is working on. Missions they call them. I signed up for two, one in Africa, one in the South Pacific."

"Projects?"

"Like helping to design moving steps up a side of a hill on some Pacific island, that sort of thing."

"You mean an outdoor escalator?"

"Something like that. It's for getting tourists up to a scenic outlook or something. They have some special problems they want my help on. It's some sort of U.S. aid. Another is fixing a problem with a ferry boat in Africa."

"You really want to do that on your vacation?"

"It'll be fun. It'll give me something to think about, a reason for going. The problem in Africa is difficult. The ferryboats are always over-loaded. They can't make bigger boats because the rivers are too shallow. They want me to see the issues first hand and then recommend a solution."

"But that's boats. You work on cars and car engines."

"Maybe that's what I've been working on up 'til now, but I can do boats, for sure. It's all mechanics. Anyway, the project is in Dakar in a country called Senegal in northern Africa. The cruise doesn't actually go there, but the government will be picking me up somewhere in the Mediterranean where the boat does go and they'll fly me to Senegal. You can come with me on the missions."

"I just can't go and leave—"

"We can ride the ferry to a place called Dakar so I can see the problems first hand. Then they'll fly us back to meet our boat. It'll be an adventure. You like adventures. You always wanted to see the world."

"That's long gone. Died with Sally."

"But Sally's back."

"In name only. That part of Sally is dead. Anyway, what about Malinda? Cecil, this just can't work out."

"We'll take her with us!" he exclaimed, excited at the thought. "The ship will have sitters and things. She can be with us."

Sally frowned. "But I don't get custody of her until after that. And I certainly can't go without her."

"I'll see what I can do about getting her early. I'll bet something can be arranged. Especially, if we're taking her around the world. What an education that will be." He thought for a moment and then added, "Actually, you and Malinda can meet the boat at any stop if you don't get custody soon enough."

"I don't know. It sounds fantastic! Around the whole world. Wow! But what if—"

"What if we don't get along? Is that what you're thinking?"

"It could happen. One summer being together when we were fourteen is a whole lot different from living together on some boat in the ocean. I can't believe I'm even thinking about this."

"Jump ship. Seriously, at the next port I'll send you and Malinda home. Well, it might work out that I'll keep Malinda and just send you home. Ha, I'm only kidding."

It was not often that Cecil made any kind of joke and Sally just looked at him, her head cocked to the side. "I thought for a minute that you were serious about keeping her." She smiled a troubled smile. "You caught me by surprise. I have to think about it. I'm not much on calling, you know, but I'll definitely call you."

He wrote down his cell number and passed it across the table. "Don't take too long. We need to get passports for both of you."

"This is all way too much for me to think about. Wow! Around the world! I need time. I'll let you know. I can't believe it!

"Listen, Sally," said Cecil, still upbeat, "I made a lot of money, more than I can ever use. I want to share my life with someone. I want that to be you. You *and* Malinda. We enjoy being together. The trip can make us...better friends."

"This is exciting to think about," Sally said, "but I have to get back to my real life for now. It seems so dull after imagining that I might be going around the world. What will you do after that?"

"That's a question for another day."

"Take me back to your house so I can get my car. My neighbor'll be worried. I told him I'd be home by six. It's his car."

"You're not going to make it. But at least we can call him to tell him you'll be delayed."

On the ride back to Cecil's house Sally asked a million questions about where the boat would stop and what they would eat. Cecil did his best to answer her questions, many of which he had never even thought about.

Cecil guided the Ghia up the long driveway. The two of them got out of the car and walked with their arms around each other to the car that Sally had borrowed. Sally slid the key into the car door lock but then turned toward Cecil and cupped his face in her hands. She stared into Cecil's eyes for just a moment before shutting her own eyes and guiding his mouth toward her parted lips. She held him close for a long while and then, without saying another word, got into her car and drove off.

Cecil stared after her until the car could no longer be seen. Then he turned back toward the house, only to discover that Caroline was standing at the window, frowning.

Fifty-Two

"So, brother dear, you found somebody. Who is she?"

"Sally Mascar," Cecil reluctantly replied, preparing himself for the verbal onslaught he knew was coming. His therapists had more than once explained his sister's behavior as being driven by a love-hate relationship she was powerless to control.

"Where do I know that name from? Sally...Sally? Oh, wasn't that the girl who disappeared the summer I was hurt?"

"The same."

"Well, I suppose it's better than you hanging around the brothel. I thought she was...dead. When did she...I mean, when did you two get together?"

"This morning," Cecil answered, continuing across the den in the direction of his room.

"My, you're a fast worker."

"Just friends. We spent the summer together in Dallas when you were in the hospital."

"That was more than a *friend's* kiss."

"Friends, that's all."

"Now I remember Mother and Dad talking about it. That's why you got tossed out of school."

Not wanting to open that discussion, Cecil continued across the room, heading to his office.

"Hey, what's your hurry? Come sit with me."

"Where's Wade?"

"At the office. Emergency board meeting, or some such thing. I think the paper's in deep trouble. Come sit with me. You can be second fiddle tonight."

"What's a second fiddle? I don't even play a fiddle. I don't even play a piano."

"A saying. You're filling in for him. Stop pouting and sit with me. Wade and I are getting married. That should make you happy. You haven't had to change my diapers for a while now. Be thankful."

"Are you sure about Wade? I mean, are you ready to spend your life with him?"

"We get along wonderfully. He's a good person."

"Did you have him sign the pre-nup agreement that the lawyers talked about?"

"Never asked him. I trust him. He loves me. If I ask him it sounds...sounds like I don't trust him."

"I was told everyone with money does it."

"Wade's a good person. And besides...I don't want to risk losing him. He's all I have."

"I can't tell you how to live your life, but you're the one always telling me to follow the lawyer's advice."

"Lucas says the same. Thinks I'm crazy. But I trust Wade. He's good to me."

"If you're positive, then I'll drop it. I feel like an extra gear, that's all."

"By the time you come back from your world tour, we'll be in our own house. That'll give you space."

"I'm not trying to put a damper on your enjoyment. I'm trying to leave you two alone."

"Having time with Wade was a life-saver. It's not like I can go out dancing, or even to bars and hang out. If he hadn't come along, then I don't know what would have become of me."

"You certainly can go out. Maybe not dancing, but out to dinner, even to bars if you want. Just don't overdo it. You're the one who refuses."

"It's far more complex than you can know."

"I don't understand."

"I don't expect you to understand. I can't... I can't drive. Everywhere I go someone must take me. Even when I'm out with you I have flashbacks about the...about the accident. I see that truck coming at us and I..." She pressed her eyes closed. "After we're safely home, I wake up with nightmares about that truck hitting us. You wouldn't understand such things."

"I'm a good driver. You can come out with me and you'll be—"

"It doesn't matter! Liz and I talk about this all the time. She..."

"Liz?"

"Liz Mascarati. Remember, I told you about her. She was Liz Classico then. She was the other girl who...who survived. We talk all the time. She still has nightmares like I do."

"I can take you out for a ride. Show you how safe it is."

"Cecil, you just don't understand. You can never understand these things!"

"I can't help it. I want to make it better for you. That's all I want."

"I'm okay in the house. I just like being here with Wade. He takes such good care of me, I don't need anything else."

"You sound like you're trying to convince yourself."

"Love may come easier when the choices are limited, but love it is. He's good to me. He's never once lost his temper or been impatient when I can't do something. Some things are awkward as you well know, but he's never once even rolled his eyes as you often do. He pays attention to me. What more can a woman want?"

"I don't roll my eyes. I know how hard it still is for you."

"Maybe you don't think you roll your eyes, but you do. Anyway, Wade does it all without complaint."

"I'm truly happy for you both. I hope to find someone someday."

"You will, dear brother, you will. Now come sit with me, like we used to do. Just having you near me brings comfort."

※

Time passed quickly for Cecil as he helped Caroline with many of the arrangements for the upcoming engagement party. Between errands, he found time to talk with Sally's lawyer, satisfying himself that if all went well, it would be possible to reunite Malinda and Sally no later than late May, and possibly even sooner. Cecil was assured that a letter from him vouching for Sally would go a long way to restoring the family unit, which, he was told, was the overriding goal of CPS. He wrote the letter. He asked Lucas to send a letter. Lucas had said, "I can go one better than that. I have a friend who knows the judge. I'll have him send a letter also."

Sally called twice. The first time to ask a million more questions about the trip. The second time she said, "I want to go; that is, if you'll have both of us."

"I asked didn't I? Of course I want both of you."

"Maybe you were being kind. You can change your mind you know."

"I want you both to come with me. That's all I've been thinking about since we had lunch."

"Okay. But only if I get custody of Malinda before the boat leaves."

"I can't wait. Tell you what, go to the Post Office and fill out passport papers for both of you. You'll need a picture of yourself. I'll call your lawyer and have him arrange for a picture of Malinda. You do have birth certificates, don't you?"

"That's a problem. I have hers, but I never had mine."

"Tell your lawyer to get one from Austin. It's going to be tight, but we'll get it done. Don't go to the Post Office until you have the certificate."

Cecil's mind was singularly focused on the logistics. Every night he gave Sally another list of instructions. Finally she exclaimed, "This is all too much for me, Cecil. Maybe I should stay home."

"Don't be silly. I'll help you get it done."

By Friday afternoon, Cecil was convinced he had put all the necessary steps into motion. If all went according to plan, they would have everything in order several days before they had to leave.

Saturday, the day of the party, was taken up with a seemingly unending stream of last-minute errands. By the time the first guests arrived, just after seven, Cecil was exhausted.

Caroline, however, looked positively radiant. She had decided not use the bots because she was afraid she'd lose control with all the excitement. She was sitting in her chair, being careful to keep her dress out of the wheels.

Wade, by plan, had not stayed at the house. He was expected to make his appearance after the guests had assembled.

Clyde and Alice Higgins were the first to arrive, followed by some of the executives from the newspaper and the *Axtel* chief engineer. Maggie paced relentlessly, and settled down only when her friend and mother of the groom-to-be, Jennie Spencer, arrived. When Joe and Patty-Ann came through the door, Maggie fled to the kitchen, busying herself at the counter. She was scolded by the caterer when she rearranged a plate of hors d'oeuvres that were ready to be served.

Jennie retrieved Maggie from the kitchen, saying, "You can't hide out here. You'll ruin the night for Caroline. Wade will be here any minute."

"I can't be in the same room as that...that b-i-t-c-h!"

"Let's not go over that again. You have a nice life. Now get back in there and for heaven's sake put a smile on your face."

Next to arrive was Liz Mascarati. Cecil shot his sister a puzzled look, and Caroline explained, "This is Liz Classico. Remember, I've spoken about her several times. Liz is my matron of honor."

Liz gave Caroline a big hug and then hugged Maggie as well. "So where's the man of the hour?" Liz inquired. "I hope I didn't miss the big event."

"He's not here yet," Maggie replied, a worried expression beginning to appear around her eyes.

"He'll be along any moment," Janet Spencer said coming through the door. "Wade had to stop by the paper to pick something up." She looked toward the front of the house. "I think I hear his car now."

"That may be my husband," Liz commented. "Ever since he made sergeant his time's not his own. Always something going down it seems."

"I thought this was a crime-free town," Caroline quipped. "Can't imagine what he's got going on a Saturday night."

"Since they closed *Cospers Own*, the problems..." Noticing the daggers coming from Jennie Spencer, Liz rethought what she was about to say. "...well, he's busy, anyway."

"It might be Lucas," Caroline exclaimed, obviously excited about Lucas coming to the party. "He was driving down from Dallas and should have been here by now."

Joe came in from the kitchen where he had gone to answer the phone. "Lucas has been delayed," he said to Caroline. "There's an accident on thirty-five which won't clear for a while. He sends his best wishes and says he'll stop by in the morning. He's anxious to meet Wade in person. He says to give you a big kiss from him." Joe did just that, kissing her on both cheeks.

A moment later, Wade Spencer, wearing a black tuxedo with a bright purple cummerbund and bow tie to match, walked through the front door. He held a jewelry box in one hand and had a newspaper folded under the other arm.

"Sorry I'm a bit late everyone. I had a little errand to run." Looking at his future wife, he exclaimed, "My, don't you look ravishing!" He went straight to Caroline, bent down and kissed her. "I wish this was our wedding and not an engagement party," he announced beaming.

Caroline flashed him a wry smile. "Haven't you overlooked something?" she asked. She giggled and then added, "We're all hungry. And besides, I can't wait to get to the presents. It's been a long time since I had anything worth celebrating."

Wade laid the paper to the side and knelt in front of Caroline. He flipped open the box to reveal a magnificent diamond ring. He held it out to her. "Caroline, my precious," he asked, "will you marry me?"

The room was now silent, all eyes on Caroline, sitting with her back to the small fire. "Before I answer you, Wade, my darling, I must ask you a question."

"Anything at all, just ask," Wade replied, a slight puzzled look crossing his face.

"I just want to know if my father has given permission."

"I have now!" Joe exclaimed, not waiting for Wade to ask.

"Well, that settles it," Caroline responded, "I accept your proposal. You may kiss me now, even with all these people watching."

"We'll all close our eyes," Jennie said. Everyone laughed.

When the long kiss was finally over, Wade straightened up and reached for the folded paper. "You can't always predict the Sunday morning headline," he said with an impish smile, "but today you can." Wade then unfolded the paper paste-up he had brought with him.

SENTINEL

PUBLISHER ENGAGED TO LOCAL WOMAN
May 4, 2002

Wade Spencer To Marry Caroline Harris In June Wedding

"All this requires," Wade then said, "is a picture of us." He walked to the front door and ushered in a reporter and a photographer who had been waiting on the porch. The photographer took posed shots of the happy couple and then proceeded to snap candids of the family and friends. The reporter, meanwhile, solicited comments from everyone.

Champagne was passed around, and Joe, his eyes damp, offered a toast. "I can't recall when my daughter looked so...so beautiful and content. May this beautiful couple live together in happiness all their lives. May they continue to bring joy to each other, as they so obviously have tonight."

"I'll drink to that!" Cecil said, and drained his glass. He asked for a refill and then held it high. "To my sister and my brother-in-law to be, I echo my father. I only want to say, Godspeed to both of you." He turned to Wade and said, "You have a good woman here. I trust you will care for her all your life."

"I certainly will, Cecil. And I can only say thank you from both of us for the gift of mobility you have given Caroline. Your creative genius is unmatched. For that we both owe you everything."

"Here, here!" Joe responded.

Fifty-Three

Sally was excited about the upcoming world cruise, but even more excited about her new teeth. At noon on Saturday, when she left work at the repair shop, she raced to the dentist office in Harlingen to have her new crowns glued in place.

Earlier in the week when Sally had called Cecil to accept his offer of the cruise, he had told her about the dental appointment he had made for her the next evening. The dentist had drilled and grinded seemingly for hours. When she finally walked out at ten that night she was wearing temporary crowns over her broken teeth. The smoothness was a strange sensation as her tongue moved around her mouth. These were temporary, but even they looked great. The dentist had instructed her to return Saturday afternoon for the permanent ones. Cecil had paid the dental lab extra to put Sally's dental work at the front of the line.

Sally was now on her way to Cosper to thank Cecil in person. She wanted to show off her new smile. The permanent teeth required some modifications that had taken several hours, but they now fit perfectly. She had also seen a doctor earlier in the week about the scar on her neck. There wasn't time to have it surgically corrected. The doctor's assistant had given her cosmetics and taught her how to apply them. The top layer, being a concealer, went on with a small brush. This was the first makeup Sally had ever used and she felt as though she were a clown getting ready for a performance. After practicing a few times, the scar all but disappeared.

This had been a good week. Her first days on the job had gone well, and she hadn't felt this good about herself since long before the attack. To top it off, her lawyer called to say he had spoken with CPS and they thought a round-the-world trip would be marvelous for Malinda. They would do everything they could to expedite the girl's return to her. The fact that the charges against Sally had been thrown out and that she was changing her residence all weighed in her favor. It also didn't hurt that Cecil had made a large donation of toys for the foster children.

"The last week in May at the latest and most probably even sooner," her lawyer had said, repeating what he had told Cecil.

The modifications to the dental work had delayed Sally's departure for Cosper. The earliest she could arrive would be nine-thirty, and maybe as late as ten.

An hour into the drive, she stopped for gas. While waiting for the tank to fill, possibilities poured through her brain one after the other, planting seeds of doubt. *What if he isn't home? What if he has a date, even though he said he has no one in his life?* She convinced herself this was a bad idea and decided to turn back.

But driving out of the gas station she turned west toward Cosper thinking she would take a motel for the night and see Cecil in the morning.

Shortly after ten, she pulled into the Cosper Motel 6 parking lot. The desire to tell Cecil how much she appreciated all that he had done for her overwhelmed her. Instead of checking-in, she restarted the car and drove toward Cecil's house telling herself the worst that could happen was he would be out.

Sure, he was a rich man. Sure, he would never miss the money. But it was also true he had no obligation to spend his money on her to fix her teeth, to get her baby back, or even to pay her legal bills. All that went way beyond what anyone could expect, even from a friend. This was not something she could say to him on the phone. She had to tell him in person, hold his hand, kiss him. It was important to her to be in his presence to show him what he meant to her. Except for Malinda, Cecil was the best thing in her entire life.

The last time they were together she had tried to repay him with her body. But he had rejected that. Sally had initially felt it was she herself, and not her offer of sex, that Cecil was rejecting. But as the week progressed, she had begun to feel relieved by his refusal.

Then a strange feeling set in. Cecil was the only man she knew who had not tried to take advantage of her. He respected her for who she is, not what she could give him. She had never thought of men in that light. Now, as she neared his house she worried that she would not know when to offer sex again. She would have to want it to satisfy her own need for intimacy before it would be right. The problem with that reasoning, she realized, was that her desire for physical intimacy had been killed by Wade Spencer in the spring of her fourteenth year. Only time would tell if any spark of desire could be rekindled.

༄༅

The lights were on in Cecil's house when Sally turned into the driveway. But there were too many cars out front. *Oh shit! A party is going on inside.*

Sally resisted the urge to wait until morning. She had come this far for this purpose. She decided to go to the door and ask Cecil to come outside. She would show him her new look, express her appreciation, and then leave. It would be that simple and she wouldn't interfere with the party.

Sally pushed the bell button and as she did so she realized the sundress she had bought at Walmart was certainly not appropriate for a party at a house such as this with its fancy kitchen and fancy furniture. Panic took hold and she stepped back from the door. She didn't want to be seen by the guests when the door opened.

But the door remained closed.

She couldn't decide what to do next. Sally pondered her dilemma, finally deciding to leave and to come back in the morning. She was walking back toward her car when the front door swung open and a woman wearing an apron around her waist, called after her. "Can I help you?"

Sally turned, hesitated, then gathering her courage, said, "I'm looking for Cecil. Cecil Harris."

"Just a minute," the woman said and closed the door.

Watching the door close, Sally realized her foolishness for being there in the middle of a party. She didn't belong here now and never would. Cecil lived in a world full of servants and luxury. He was a college graduate and a very rich man. He had everything he could want. She, on the other hand, hadn't even finished grade school. She could hardly read, had a child and a hooker's rap sheet. They lived in worlds that could never come together.

The fragile remains of Sally's courage evaporated into the night. She turned and took several quick steps toward her car. Halfway down the walkway she heard Cecil call her name. *Was this wishful thinking — or real?*

She had to turn back. She had to know. She owed herself — and Cecil — that much.

Turning, she saw Cecil, striding toward her. *Is that anger on his face? Too many shadows to tell for sure. He's moving as if he's upset.* She steeled herself for the worse.

Cecil stopped directly in front of her, a broad smile on his face; his eyes dancing with delight.

Impulsively, partly from relief, partly from sheer exuberant affection, Sally threw her arms around him and pulled him against her. They stood at the side of the curb, swaying back and forth, for several minutes without speaking.

Cecil finally pulled back enough to study Sally's face. "Your teeth are beautiful!" he exclaimed. "You look absolutely stunning!" Then Cecil said, "What are you doing here? I mean I'm so happy to see you, you can't imagine, but I didn't expect you tonight. I thought—"

"I just wanted to thank you in person for all—"

Before she finished her sentence, Cecil pulled her close and kissed her on the lips. A real kiss. A lover's kiss.

"Oh, Cecil!" she exclaimed when they finally broke apart, "I couldn't wait to get here. I need you in my life." The words tumbled out in a new, amazing and totally unexpected way: from the heart. Without rehearsal. Without calculation.

"Well, guess what?" Cecil replied, holding Sally's wrists and swinging her arms in and then out. "You're in my life already, and you're here to stay. Come, let's go inside. We can't be hugging and kissing in the yard all night."

"It's a party. I'm not dressed right."

"Oh, nonsense. Just some family."

"You sure?"

"Of course I'm sure. It's my house. You're my best friend. You and I are going to travel..."

Cecil stopped in mid-sentence and Sally could see, indeed she knew, that something had passed through Cecil's mind that made him not so sure after all.

"You look like you just said something you regret. Something's wrong and I'm not moving another inch until you tell me what just happened."

"It's just that...that I had forgotten in all the excitement of seeing you that your friend Clyde is inside."

"That was my old life!" Sally said, defiantly. "All of that is gone now." Sally then added, "It makes me feel so special that you're concerned about my feelings, but I'm fine with Clyde. Just stay close to me and let's go in and get this over with. I'm terrified."

"Nothing to be afraid about. It's just my family. My sister just got engaged. I think you might know..." Cecil was looking over Sally's shoulder. "Who's there?" he called. "Who's out there?"

The shadow that Cecil was addressing proved to be a uniformed Cosper police officer approaching the porch.

Sensing Sally's alarm, Cecil edged closer to her as the officer came up the steps and joined them on the porch. "Is this the Harris residence?" he asked.

"It is," Cecil replied. "Is something wrong?"

"Wrong?" the officer repeated. "Oh! Hell, no," he said. "Sorry if the uniform alarmed you. I'm Nick Mascarati. Liz's husband. You must be Cecil." He held out his hand. "Congratulations on your sister's engagement. Sorry I'm late. Had a bit of business to tend to."

"Glad you could join us," Cecil told the officer. "This is my friend, Sally Mascar. Your wife is inside."

"Sally, I'm pleased to meet you," Mascarati said, offering his hand. "Mascar. Did your family shorten that from Mascarati? Maybe we're related?"

"I don't know much about my father or his family," Sally replied, her voice tense.

"I'd love to talk more. I've heard so much about you, Mr. Harris. But please excuse me. My wife's already furious with me for working tonight and I'd better be moving on into the house."

When the door closed behind Mascarati, Cecil leaned close to Sally. In a voice barely above a whisper, he said, "I don't usually know what people are feeling, except for you. You're scared. I don't know if it's because he's a cop or because you're scared of meeting my family. So, why don't you take a room at *Dusty Trail Inn*. It's right on the road you came in on about two miles from here. Big covered wagon sign. You won't miss it. I'll call them right now with my credit card. I'll be there around midnight, maybe a little later."

"Oh my God, yes," Sally replied in a conspiratorial whisper. "I'll see you there." After one more lingering kiss and a "goodbye for now" she turned and strode deliberately toward the driveway.

Cecil watched her go, trying to decide which of the evening's turn of events was the more surprising—Sally's unexpected arrival, or the playful tug of his private parts that had preceded her departure.

FIFTY-FOUR

"Who's Cecil talking to out there?" Caroline asked her mother. "He's not been himself all week."

"In what way, dear?" Maggie inquired. "I haven't noticed anything different."

"He's been more off-center than usual this past week," Caroline replied. "He had a visitor a week or so ago, and that's when it started. Told me it was his grade school friend, a girl by the name of Sally Mascar. Who really knows with him? All week he's been on the phone, hiding away in his room. He went on a number of errands for me, and they took him much longer than they should have."

"Sally Mascar?" her father said. "You mean the girl who went missing? Bet he used her name to throw you off. Police believe she was killed."

"Whoever it was, he has a girlfriend he doesn't want us to know about."

"He's not a boy anymore," Joe commented. "In case you two haven't noticed. Let him be."

Maggie pretended not to have heard what Joe said. "So let's get to the bottom of the mystery person. Go out and bring her in?"

Jennie Spencer walked over to the window and peeked out. "That's the hussy!" she exclaimed, her voice transposed into a high register. "The one from the brothel. The one who got away!"

Alice Spencer shot a look in the direction of her husband, Clyde. "You mean the one—"

"Yea, *that* one," her mother snapped. "You know exactly who I mean!" She was looking straight at Clyde. He turned away. "But I must say there's something different about her. She lost weight or something."

"I told him to stay away from that kind of woman," Maggie snapped. "I'll get on him."

"You should," Jennie replied. "We can't have her kind around here. Wade, go on out there and bring Cecil in here. And get rid of that girl!" Realizing her son was not in the room, she asked, "Where's Wade gone off to now?"

"He's in my room with the reporter," Caroline responded. "They're working on the story for the paper. They have a midnight deadline. I can page him if you want. He always responds when I hit this." She pointed to a lever on her wheelchair that Cecil had installed. Using it, Caroline was able to send a signal to Wade's pager. It had proven particularly useful the few times Caroline didn't have enough air in her lungs to call for help.

Joe walked to the window to see for himself who Cecil was talking with. "Can't see any woman out here," he declared. "There's a cop blocking the view."

"That's probably my husband!" Liz exclaimed. "It's about time he got here. The party's almost over."

A moment later, the door opened and Nick Mascarati came inside.

"Hey," Joe called, excitement in his voice, "that definitely is Sally Mascar. Or someone who looks exactly like her. Does she have a sister?"

"An only child, as I recall, Maggie said, pulling the curtain back even further to get a good look. "As I live and breathe!" she exclaimed. "If that's not little Sally Mascar, I'll eat my hat. And land sakes, she and Cecil are going at it! They're certainly more than casual friends. Joe, go and fetch those two in here. Let's get to the bottom of what's going on here."

Clyde Higgins, who had been slinking toward the bathroom at the mention of the *hussy*, thought better of it. He realized that it would not go well for him if he was found hiding, so he returned to the living room and took up a position behind his wife who was seated on the sofa across from Caroline's wheelchair.

Joe swung the big door open and called to the retreating woman. "Sally. Sally Mascar! Come say hello. Cecil, tell Sally it's okay. We want to meet your...girlfriend."

Cecil swung around. "She's leaving now."

"What's that supposed to mean?" Joe pressed. "Hey, Sally, come up here and join the party. It's nice to know you're alive. You can't leave without saying hello."

Sally began to run toward her car, as if she hadn't heard a word Joe said.

Joe confronted his son. "What's going on here, Cecil? Please ask her to come inside."

Cecil looked down, saying nothing.

"It's not right," Joe continued. "I mean her appearing from the dead and then running off without even saying hello. Son, ask her to at least come say hello."

Cecil, realizing they would pressure him all night about Sally if she ran away, turned and called in her direction. "Sally, let's get this over with! Come, we'll do it together."

Sally, her hand on the car door, paused, but didn't turn back.

"Come on Sally, you can't run forever. We can do this — as friends."

Sally took her hand away from the car and slowly turned to face Cecil who had run down the driveway and was now standing beside her. "If you think this is a good choice then that's what I'll do. As friends." She took his offered hand and started back toward the house.

Once on the porch, she leaned close to him. "Look up," she instructed. "Together we won't let them beat us. If Alice or Clyde don't like it, then too bad. But whatever you do, no more looking down."

Cecil lifted his head, and with Sally walking next to him, followed his father into the house, much like a couple being led down the church aisle, or a prisoner being escorted by a bailiff to see the judge.

Together they walked across the room to where Caroline was sitting. "Caroline," Cecil began. "I'd like you to meet—"

"Wait!" Caroline exclaimed. "Let's do this the right way. I want my fiancé here." She touched the lever. "He'll be here in a moment."

It wasn't fifteen seconds before Wade Spencer raced into the room. "What's the problem dear? Are you—"

"Oh, my God!" shouted Sally, going pale. "Oh, my God! It's you!"

Wade lost all color and stood frozen in place.

Sally ran to where Wade stood and started beating him on the chest, shouting, "You're not fit to be on this planet, you monster! You ruined my life!" She tore at his face with her nails opening several deep gouges.

By the time Nick Mascarati realized an assault was taking place across the room, blood was pouring from the wounds. Mascarati pulled Sally away from Wade who then slid to the floor. "I don't know what's going on here," the officer said sternly to Sally, "but you'll have to calm down."

"Get your hands away from her," Cecil demanded. "She's my friend. Leave her alone!"

"Please, Cecil," the officer responded. "Best to let me handle this."

"This is my house and you're a guest in my house," Cecil shouted. "Leave her alone or get out of my house."

"Only if she calms down," Mascarati replied, releasing his grip on Sally's wrists. "I can't allow any further assault. Enough's been done already. Now, both of you stay away from each other. Mr. Spencer, are you okay?"

Getting no response, Mascarati moved closer. "Those cuts need attention. Caroline, do you have a first aid kit in the house?"

Sally, seeing Wade getting up from the floor, and with Mascarati momentarily distracted, leaped for Wade. She punched wildly at his face, landing several vicious blows. She then clawed at his eyes, her fingernails sliding down the side of his face leaving ragged gashes in their wake.

Her hands found his throat and she twisted with the force of unleashed fury. The pent-up emotion of eight years poured strength into her fingers as they closed in a death grip around her rapist's neck.

Wade, his eyes bulging, reached up in a feeble attempt to pull her hands free. He gasped for air, trying to work his fingers under hers.

Mascarati managed to again grab Sally's hands and straining hard, pulled her away. Wade, his throat free of Sally Mascar's iron grasp, remained on the floor gasping for air with his head now twisted at a strange angle.

Mascarati, struggling with an out of control Sally, said, "You're under arrest! Stop fighting this instant!" He wrapped his left arm around her and with his right reached behind him and retrieved his cuffs. He twisted her arms behind her and a moment later Sally's arms were immobilized. He then walked her across the room away from Wade.

Mascarati turned to Clyde. "Bring me one of those," he commanded, pointing to the dining room chairs.

Clyde did so. Mascarati forced Sally into the chair and used a large black snap-tie to fasten the handcuffs to the back of the chair. He turned to Clyde. "I need you to keep your eye on her, but be careful she doesn't turn on you. She's prone to biting," he said, pointing to where her teeth had dug into his upper arm, "and she's a kicker. So don't get too close."

Sally's face was contorted with a rage so primal that everyone had already backed away and was keeping their distance from her.

Cecil, meanwhile, had begun to wail: "Leave her alone. Leave her alone. Leave her alone. Leave her alone."

Joe Harris eased his son onto the now empty sofa and sat with his arm around him while the boy continued, "Leave her alone. Leave her alone. Leave her alone. Leave her alone."

Mascarati spoke something unintelligible into his portable radio. Then he added, "Possible broken neck, hurry." He then turned to Wade. "Can you speak?"

"It hurts," Wade managed, his voice barely a whisper. "My lungs feel...like they're exploding." He gasped, his eyes closed for a long moment, then he said, "I'm dizzy. My head hurts." Only Mascarati and Alice were close enough to hear him.

"Don't move," the officer instructed. "Don't lie down or move in any way at all. I'll hold your neck. If you're about to pass out, please tell me so I can protect your neck."

"I'm dizzy," Wade responded.

"Do you know what provoked her?" Mascarati asked.

Wade didn't reply, but tried to lift his head to see Caroline. His eyes closed and his body shuddered with pain.

"Please don't move! Hold still."

"I want to see Caroline."

Caroline moved the wheelchair closer but couldn't lean forward.

Mascarati repeated his question. "Do you have any idea why this happened?" He then looked around the den. "Did anyone see anything before the attack? What provoked her?"

Cecil, still leaning into his father's shoulder, stopped his mantra long enough to shout, "He raped her when she was fourteen! That's what happened!"

The room went stone silent.

"Tell them, Sally, tell them," Cecil continued in a pleading voice. "Please tell them. Please tell them. Please tell them. Please tell them."

Joe Harris pulled his son even closer. "It's all right, Cecil," he whispered. "It's all right. Everything will be okay."

The photographer chose that moment to snap a picture. The reporter raced to the phone.

Mascarati said to Wade, "Is Mr. Harris correct about the rape?"

"Wade Spencer," Sally shouted, "if you have an ounce of decency in you, tell them what you did to me! Tell them how you ruined my life! Tell them!"

Wade saw the pleading eyes of Caroline and tried to shake his head yes, but the pain was too severe. Instead, he whispered, "I'm sorry. Sally, please forgive me. Caroline, my love, please forgive me. I did a terrible thing. I...I...forced myself on Sally. I'm so sorry."

Mascarati, struggling to maintain a professional demeanor, turned back to Wade. "Mr. Spencer, please understand that anything you say can be used against you."

"The law can't do any more to me than I've done to myself. I've lived with this for so long, it's eating me alive. I'm sorry, Caroline. I'm truly, truly sorry." Wade again tried to look up into her face, but before their eyes met, he passed out.

The ambulance left before Wade regained consciousness. Sally was then led away by officers who had responded to Mascarati's call.

Mascarati walked to where Cecil lay, curled in the arms of his father. "What Mr. Spencer just confessed to is despicable. I don't blame Sally for what she did, but I can't release her once she's been arrested. Considering the circumstances, I would guess the judge will go easy on her."

Cecil was beyond listening. He was intoning yet another mantra: "She's my only friend. She's my only friend. She's my only friend. She's my only friend."

Fifty-Five

The *Sentinel* lay open on the kitchen counter, the picture Wade had planned for the front page showing him sitting beside his bride-to-be had been replaced, just before the midnight deadline, with a photo of him sitting on the floor leaning against a chair, his head cocked at an unnatural angle.

Joe Harris came through the unlocked front door and found his ex-wife in the kitchen, tears streaming down her cheeks.

"You're too late," Maggie said. "If you're looking for Cecil, he's down at the police station. God only knows what he sees in that Mascar girl. She's not only slow, but did you know she has a child?"

"Wade's child, I suspect. Age is right. It now all makes sense. I just came from the station and it doesn't look good for Sally. Wade took a turn for the worse last night. He's in critical condition, but I understand the doctors are optimistic. They won't charge Sally until they know whether Wade will live or die."

"That hussy is not my concern," Maggie shot back, "and it shouldn't be yours either, Joe. It's your children you should be worried about. Poor Caroline never catches a break. The first real smile on her face in eight years and this is what comes of it! And, Cecil, I don't know what'll become of him."

Joe rolled his eyes. "That boy managed to make more money than he can ever spend," he said, "and you're worried about him. Maggie, really."

"Money's not everything. Running around with a slut who turns tricks over at that stink hole is not what I want for my son. I understand he bought her new teeth, bailed her out of some law suits and God only knows what else."

"That's only part of it," Joe said, pouring himself a cup of coffee. "He told me he's taking her on his world cruise. She and the child."

"That's preposterous! The boy's out of his mind. You have to talk to him, make him see what he's doing."

"It's his money, his life. He can do what he wants."

"It's not right. I was hoping he'd meet some nice woman on his trip, maybe come back married."

"That's his plan," Joe replied, "but married to Sally."

"That's *all* he needs! He'll be saddled with a child from the get-go. No way to start a life with an eight-year-old."

"Not to make a pun, Maggie dear, but that ship has sailed."

"What are you talking about?"

"The child's name is Malinda, by the way. She's in foster care down in Port Isabel. Sally got into some scrape or another down there. They took the child away."

"Probably picked up for hustling is my guess. Best thing for the kid in any event. At least she might grow up with good role models, not with that slut."

"Except that Cecil has volunteered to be a foster parent to Malinda. CPS has agreed. Money under the table for all I know. Lucas helped him. It's all but assured, Cecil's getting custody. They're waiting for the court to approve the round-the-world trip. That has caused the judge some problems, but Cecil and Lucas are working it all out."

"Well isn't that the happy thought for the day," Maggie replied.

"Be wound up by the end of the week supposedly," Joe said, ignoring her sarcasm. "And after that, now that he has official custody the kid is his responsibility, Sally or not."

"And speaking of Madam Fisticuffs," Maggie asked, "what do the authorities plan to do with *her*?"

"That all depends on what happens to Wade. If he lives, the lawyer says it's unlikely the grand jury will indict her. If Wade dies then all bets are off."

"Meanwhile," Joe continued, "how's Caroline?"

"How would you expect her to be?"

"Is she awake?"

"I don't think she slept two winks. She won't let me in her room. Go see for yourself."

Joe knocked on Caroline's door but heard no response. He knocked again.

"I said, come in," his daughter responded. Her voice so weak that Joe had a hard time hearing her.

Joe found Caroline sitting in her wheelchair, still in her party dress, her eyes red, the dress stained. The feces smell told him all he needed to know.

"Come," he said, "I'll clean you."

"Why bother! I'll just mess myself again! Let me be. I've nothing to live for!"

"Come," Joe coaxed, not wanting to validate her self-pity. "Lucas wants to come over and see you."

"I don't want to see anybody, just Wade! Just leave me alone."

Ignoring her commands, Joe pushed the wheelchair toward the bed, spread out a waterproof cloth and slipped his arms under his daughter's shoulders. Caroline did not protest as he carefully lifted her frail body onto the bed, taking care not to injure her lifeless legs and feet. Without saying a word, he began undressing her.

Undressing and taking care of Caroline had been awkward when she had first come home from the rehabilitation center years ago. Joe had tried to avert his eyes from her private areas, but she had said, "Dad, any modesty I had is long gone. You won't be able to care for me if you don't look. You have to touch me. You can't insert the catheter with your eyes closed. It's alright."

Those were the same instructions the nurses had used at the center when they taught him and Maggie how to care for their injured daughter. But the permission had to come directly from her.

"Dad," Caroline began, when he had cleaned her and spread the protective cream, "what's going to happen to Wade?"

"He's in critical condition, but they say he's going to pull through."

"No, I mean if he lives."

"He'll most likely be indicted for sexual assault on a minor."

"But it's that slut's word against his," she replied, tears again streaming down her face. "He's the publisher of the town paper, and what is she? As mother says, a common whore is all."

"Not the way it will come out, I'm afraid," Joe responded, trying to be as honest as he could without crushing her. "I'm no expert but I gotta believe that the DNA, or whatever it is they use, will prove if he's the father of that child."

"But what if she gave permission? I mean, young girls get pregnant all the time."

"Not at fourteen they don't," Joe replied. "And besides, Cecil's lawyer tells me that even if she gave permission, Wade has a big problem because a fourteen-year old is not legally capable of giving permission. It's called statutory rape. It doesn't matter if there was consent or not."

"Isn't there a time limit on these things?"

"The lawyer didn't say so. I don't know. But you're talking like...like you want him back. He raped that girl!"

"He's all I have! He's all I'll ever have! What he did happened long ago. People change. I love him. I know him, and he's not a rapist. I need him. He's my whole life!"

"I don't know what to say," Joe commented. "Rape of any sort is horrible. But rape of a child, I can't imagine anything worse."

"Don't judge him!" Caroline pleaded. "It's not fair! We don't know what happened for sure. I'm your daughter, you have to support me!"

"All I'm saying is that it doesn't look promising. We have to give this time. Sometimes you have to take these things one day at a time."

"Can you and Patty-Ann stay in town for a little while? I need someone to talk with."

"Patty-Ann has to get back to Dallas. Lucas says he'll drive her home. But I'll stay. Cecil needs me as well."

"Don't talk to me about that jerk! Without him—"

"Without him, you would have married a rapist and never known it."

"I said I don't care! I need Wade! You think I want to depend on Mother or, God forbid, Cecil, to put me to bed at night. To clean me when I soil? You think that's better than living with Wade, even if he did something wrong years ago? Well, it's not better, Dad. It's really not!"

"Cecil didn't do anything wrong. Don't blame him."

"Cecil was really stupid to have brought her in here."

"What do you mean? What's stupid about Cecil bringing his girlfriend into his house?"

"I just don't want him around me," Caroline said, ignoring her father's point. "He never liked Wade to begin with."

"What makes you say that?" Joe asked, surprised. "Every time I've seen Cecil and Wade together they seem to get along well enough."

"Are you kidding?" Caroline shot back. "Why do you think he's taking that stupid trip of his? Pitching a rich-man's tantrum. He doesn't like Wade living in his house, but he conveniently forgets that it's not *his* house. It's *our* house."

"Tantrum or not," Joe responded, "the trip will be good for him. Maybe he'll mature a bit more."

"Actually, I'd be surprised if he even goes, what with his precious Sally being in jail. Even if he bails her out, how could she leave the country?"

"He's working on it. He expects the charges will be dropped once it's clear Wade will live. I'm sorry to say, Caroline, but the scuttlebutt around town this morning is that most folks are saying 'Good for Sally.' So if Wade pulls though there's not going to be much interest in prosecuting her."

"Anyway," Joe continued, "something else you should know is that Child Protective Services will be giving Cecil custody of Sally's daughter by the end of the week. He's planning to take her on the cruise, too. He's her new foster father."

Caroline's jaw dropped as she absorbed this latest news. "Typical government bullshit!" she exclaimed. "How in the hell can a boy who can't even get himself unlocked take care of a little kid? It makes no sense."

"As you know," Joe answered, "when Cecil puts his mind to something there's just no stopping him. Made himself — and you — rich, so don't be too harsh on him. Lucas and he worked it all out with the judge."

"Knowing Lucas is the best thing that ever happened to Cecil. Without Lucas's support, Cecil could never have made those bots a reality. He's nothing without Lucas."

"Those bots gave you mobility, don't ever forget that."

"How in the hell can I ever forget? I should thank Cecil every day for the gift of movement. But you know what? It gets old."

Tears flowed and Joe Harris gently wiped his daughter's face dry. When she regained control, she said, "Take me to the hospital. I want to be with Wade. I'm doing nobody any good hanging out around here feeling sorry for myself."

Fifty-Six

Cecil had called Sally's Cosper lawyer at home early that morning. Billy Towers had nearly torn Cecil's head off at having been wakened so early. But when Cecil offered to pay him triple his usual fee, Towers saw things differently. Within the hour, he was at the jail to meet with Sally. Cecil had wanted to meet with Towers immediately after the lawyer met with Sally, but the lawyer told him to wait until after lunch.

Cecil was now in Towers' office, going over Sally's situation. This was the third time the lawyer had outlined the possibilities. Cecil wanted to be absolutely certain he fully understood all the possible parameters.

"Look, Cecil," Towers replied, his patience growing thin, even considering the large retainer he had received, "I must assume Wade Spencer survives. As soon as the doctors take him off the critical list, I'm thinking that the police or the prosecutor will find some excuse to drop the charges. The prosecutor knows that as long as Spencer survives, there's no way a grand jury would indict Sally for attacking her rapist, even if it was eight years ago. That just won't happen here."

"But he's the publisher of the town newspaper! The news'll be slanted against her," Cecil repeated, at least for the fourth time. "Opinion will—"

"We've been over this. Listen to me. Wade Spencer isn't well-liked around here. His father, yes. But not him. Child molestation, especially with what happened to Sally because of it, just isn't tolerated in these parts. He'll be lucky if he ever gets out of jail."

"You're sure?"

"Just my opinion mind you," Towers continued, "but I know the people of this county. They are good folks who have low tolerance for child abuse. It's sickening really."

Finally satisfied with what he'd heard, Cecil left Towers' office and started back toward his car. He hadn't taken more than a few steps when Towers called to him from his office doorway. "Cecil! Just got a call from a friend over at the hospital."

Cecil hurried back to the office. "It's your lucky day," the lawyer announced, slapping Cecil soundly on the back. "Spencer's come out of the coma. He has a fractured vertebra. Nothing that a neck brace can't help. He'll be fine I'm told. I've handled whiplash injuries that were far worse."

"And Sally?"

"If all goes according to plan, I'll have her on the street by noon tomorrow. Bond may have to be posted of course, but that's no problem for you."

"Excuse me now, son," the lawyer said. "There's a certain prosecutor I've got to call. This might be over even sooner than I thought."

෴

Joe wheeled Caroline up to the door of Wade's hospital room, but an officer posted there—a young man new to the force—prevented them from going in. "Only close family allowed," he explained. Hearing talk out in the hall, Jennie Spencer came out and explained that Wade and Caroline were engaged. The officer called his sergeant and after some words back and forth, Jennie was allowed to wheel Caroline into the room.

Caroline's chair was brought to the side of Wade's bed. Using the bots to control her arm movements, Caroline touched her fiancé's hand. A few minutes later, her hand still resting on his, Wade's eyes opened.

Caroline sat with Wade for the entire afternoon speaking soft messages of support. He tried several times to speak, but each time the words were cut short by spasms of pain. Around five, the nurse gave him a shot and told Caroline he'd be out until morning.

On Wednesday—four days after the party—the nurse gave Caroline the okay to engage in conversation. The danger period was over. Wade was on his way to a full recovery.

The first thing Caroline said was, "I love you."

Wade responded with, "I don't deserve your love."

"That was in the past. We can go forward."

He pulled her limp hand toward him and placed it on his chest. "Listen to me Caroline. I did something awful to Sally. And I did something even worse to you by not telling you the truth. I will plead guilty and..."

"No! Don't say that! You're entitled to a trial. They have to prove you did it. That girl might have consented. She might have—"

"No, Caroline, she didn't consent. I just...I just took advantage. I don't deserve you. You're too good for me."

"The drugs are speaking. Wait until you're out of here before you decide anything."

"I'm not getting out of here, Caroline. When I'm well enough, they're taking me to jail."

"Don't say that," Caroline pleaded. "Don't say that."

"There are some things you don't know," Wade said. "I have been dreading this day. When Sally first disappeared, I was relieved. Then a few months later I began to realize I had done something terrible. As the months went on and Sally couldn't be found, it ate at me constantly until I couldn't stand it. Then I—"

"Wade," Caroline pleaded, "her hand resting on his, "don't do this. Don't torment yourself. I love you. I'll always love you. What happened is past. I know who you really are."

"—I hired a detective to find her. I wanted to...to apologize to her. I wanted to make it up to her in some way. When she couldn't be found I thought she had died. Then I felt even worse. That's why...why I've never had a girl friend...until you came along."

"Why me, then?"

"I can't explain it. I felt comfortable with you. But even then...even then I was afraid you'd find out. Oh, Caroline I love you, but it can't ever be. I don't deserve you."

"Don't say that! We can make it work."

"I may get out on bail. I may not. I don't even know that for sure. But I'll do time. Possibly twenty years, maybe more. We just can't have a life together. We just can't." He wiped the tears from her cheek. "This is not something either of us can pay money for and make go away."

"But surely someone with your stature, someone—"

He squeezed her hand. "Listen to me. As you well know, the paper's in deep trouble. Mother tells me people are calling to drop their subscriptions. Advertisers are pulling away saying they can't support a child rapist. This is a small community with long memories. My life, as I know it, is over."

Caroline studied his face for a long moment and then, looking deeply into his eyes asked, "Do you love me? Really love me?"

"Of course I do. Do you really have to ask?"

"Then this won't stop me from marrying you! I love you. I need you!"

"Your love is misplaced. You love the Wade Spencer of last week. The Wade Spencer from the masquerade ball. You're now looking at the real Wade Spencer. The rapist Wade Spencer. The ugly Wade Spencer. I'm not worthy of you."

"You are! You are! Please love me."

"I don't know if the real Wade Spencer is allowed to love. I lost that right when I...raped Sally Mascar."

"This is not you speaking. It's the pain medication. I'll wait until you're finished with the drugs before I listen to you."

Every day for the next two weeks Caroline sat with her fiancé, holding his hands. But not once did he kiss her. Every night when Caroline left the hospital she went home and cried herself to sleep.

Fifty-Seven

Sally was not released the next afternoon as her lawyer had promised. The judge wanted to see her entire record. He wanted to talk to the judge on South Padre Island and to the prosecutor. A prominent citizen had been attacked by Sally, and even though there were rape allegations, and even though there had been a confession of sorts, nothing yet had been cast in stone. He simply didn't want to jump the gun.

In the end, attorney Towers prevailed, and on Thursday Sally walked out of the jail and into Cecil's arms. They embraced and then climbed into his car. "Let's drive out in the country so we can park and talk," she suggested. "That's all I've thought about all week. Oh, Cecil, I missed you. I really did."

They parked and climbed into the back seat of the Ghia. "I suppose I lost my new job already," Sally said. "One week and it's gone! I'll never get Malinda now!"

"I had Lucas call the shop. They'll hold your job. They said you had promise."

"But Malinda! Jail just killed my chance of ever getting her."

"That's arranged," Cecil responded, a slight smile forming. "I'll have her. I'll be her foster parent. We can take our trip, just as we planned. Everything's arranged."

"Oh, Cecil, I can't ever repay you! I can't."

"Being my friend is all I want."

"I am your friend, Cecil. Your special friend. I made up my mind on the way up to show you my new teeth. Oh, that seems so very long ago. I was looking forward to us...you know... spending time together."

He touched her leg.

Sally continued. "You know, Cecil, while I was sitting in jail, I was trying to decide if I wanted Wade to live or die. He ruined my life!"

"He's going to pay big time for what he did. His life is going nowhere but down. You did enough."

"Nothing's bad enough for him!"

"You're right about that," he agreed, and then he paused before continuing. "The only thing is that I feel awful for my sister. She was happy for the first time since the accident."

Sally pulled her knees up to her chest and began to cry.

Cecil studied her, wondering what she was thinking, why she was crying. At one time he did understand her. He could anticipate what she was going to say or do. But now she was a mystery. Her crying confused him, so he remained silent, not knowing what to say next.

It was Sally who finally spoke. "You're angry with me, aren't you," she said, "for spoiling your sister's life."

"Not angry with you, but with...with the circumstances. Wade is a bad person and should be punished. He messed up your life and now he's messing up Caroline's life as well."

"Would you mind if I stayed at a motel until all this is over like Mr. Towers promised it would be? That way we can spend time together. I mean, like we did in Dallas."

"That would be nice, but please stay at my house."

"I can't. Not with your sister being there and all. A motel is best."

Cecil leaned forward to pull Sally toward him. When his hand touched her arm, she said, "Later, Cecil. I'm starved. Can we go somewhere to eat?"

"Okay. Then we can find a place for you to stay."

Fifty-Eight

The next two weeks passed in a blur for Caroline. Her time being spent waiting for the brief periods when she was allowed to visit Wade at the hospital. Because of the seriousness of the charges and Wade's inability to appear in court, the judge refused to hear arguments for bail.

When they were together, most of their time was spent talking about the failing paper. Caroline floated the idea of her buying the *Sentinel*, but Wade said, "I wish it were that simple. The fact is that the paper's been on shaky ground for a long time. This just put the final nail in the coffin. The only thing that can save us is for a conglomerate to buy it. I have spoken to one company specializing in buying local papers. They maintain the paper's original name, but they add the logo, A HOMETOWN PAPER under the banner."

"What are the prospects of them buying you out?"

"Price is the only issue now. It's only a matter of time."

"What's holding it up?"

"Me, really. I've been insisting they keep my sisters employed. I think they've finally agreed."

"Let me buy it. I'll agree to keeping them on."

"Wish I could. But people associate you with me and once they find out you're the owner, they'll bail out of their subscriptions. That's just the way this town works."

"Something's puzzling me," Caroline began, hesitant to bring up the subject.

"What is it?"

"A question. Not my business, really, but a question."

"Go ahead."

"The *Sentinel* is your paper. Why did they publish your picture that Sunday after that terrible night? I've been thinking about that and Mother even asked me that very question this morning."

"Goes back many years. The paper once covered up a family indiscretion. My grandfather, actually. He almost lost the *Sentinel* over that. People need to trust the paper. He hired a full-time editor then and gave him full authority. He told the editor to make no distinction in news coverage, even if a family member is involved. My father and I continued the tradition. It's just part of what the *Sentinel* is."

"Still, had the picture not been in the paper, then this—"

"The fact is the fact. I did it and I suffer the consequences. I'm sorry, but there is no other way." Wade took a deep breath, then continued, "In a funny way, I'm relieved. I was living a lie. I lied to myself and, worst of all, I lied to you. It was tearing me up."

Seeing the anguish in his face, she squeezed his hand with what little pressure she could muster. "I love you, no matter what you did. You're a good person, that was...a mistake."

"It was more than a mistake, Caroline. Much more. I ruined a person's life. Sally is lucky to be alive today and I'm to blame."

"Sally made bad decisions as well."

"She was a baby. Fourteen, for God's sake. Fourteen years old! I can't imagine the panic—and terror—she must have felt."

Caroline continued pressing his hand. "We'll make it right. Somehow, together, we'll make it right for her. You don't have to sell the paper to do that. That affects both of your sisters and your brother-in-law, as well."

"Clyde quit. Seems he has a romantic fantasy about Sally. He got himself a job at the filling station. He's actually a good mechanic."

"What's his plan?"

"Don't know and frankly don't care. If he wants Sally that's his business. Hey, no more family stuff."

Caroline moved her hand from Wade's, then asked, "Any news about the Grand Jury? Isn't it set for tomorrow?"

"The lawyer was here earlier and it doesn't look good. Based on what the prosecutor's been saying, and what the lawyer is saying about the kind of people who sit on juries in this county, he strongly recommends that I plea bargain. If I do that he says I'll be out by the time I'm forty."

Caroline again willed the bots to wipe away the tears that seemed to be constantly running down her cheeks. Sounding braver than she felt, she replied, "I'll wait for you. I want you to know that. I love you."

Wade's eyes misted as well. He reached out to touch her hand. "I can't believe I got so lucky to have someone like you in my life. Please find someone else. I'll be away a very long time."

"I promise you that will never happen."

"Sally and your brother are...good friends. They might be married someday. That will make Sally your sister-in-law. Sally's daughter is my daughter, for goodness sake. How can I be part of the same family? It just won't work."

"We'll work out something. Where there's a will, there's—"

"I just don't see how it can happen. You're better off without me."

"We can work through it," Caroline insisted. "I know we can." Caroline fell quiet, her mind replaying a conversation she had had last evening with her father. He had asked her why, if Wade professed to be unable to form relationships, he had formed one with her. Her father sounded skeptical of Wade's true feelings, at one point going so far as to suggest that Wade might be in it for her money.

That thought had played in her mind all night. As she sat holding Wade's hand, she worked up the courage to ask, "Why me of all people? Why did you allow yourself to get close to me? Is it because you took pity on me? Since we met, you've spent most of your time caring for me. Is that your self-punishment?"

Wade closed his eyes, thought for a while, and then said, "I've asked myself that very question over and over. Perhaps I did take pity on you at first. Perhaps, I saw you as...not threatening. Perhaps I saw you as a way to pay back what I owed. I really don't know. Does anyone ever know why they fall in love? But what I really do know today is that I do love you. It doesn't matter how it came to be. I am in love with you today." Tears filled his eyes. "I love you with all my soul."

"Then why push me away?"

"For the rest of my life people will look at me—and at you if we are together—with disgust. Child-molestation is the lowest of the low. Add in rape and there's no escaping the stigma. Even my own mother is cool to me, to say the least. She sits here for hours on end crying her eyes out. I can't ever change that. For as long as I live I'll have to register as a sex offender. There's a bull's-eye painted on my forehead. And it will never go away!"

"You can win people back. I know it."

"How?"

"By doing good things. People will give you a second chance. I know they will."

"I doubt that. Already I hear talk, even here, like what your father said, I'm only out for your money. Nobody will even give me a chance."

"I'm here for you. I need you! You have to fight the charges. I need you more than you can know."

"Frankly, I hate the thought of being dragged through a public trial. My mother, sisters, you, deserve better than that. Sally deserves better than having to relive, in court, all that she went through. My mother can't show her face without someone saying something horrible. I don't want any more public humiliation. Going to jail will make it easier for people to let go."

"All I know is I need you."

"I need you also, Caroline. Until you came along I was lost. Now I find out I have a child I'll never be able to raise. Since I found out it's been eating at me. I want to make it right for her—and for Sally, but there's no way I can ever do that."

"I can. I can set up a trust for them. I can make sure Malinda is taken care of, gets schooling, that sort of thing."

"You're a better person than I deserve. But that's what *you* can do. That's not from me. I have nothing to give. Oh, I don't mean money. I mean from myself. A child-rapist has nothing to give—nothing anybody wants."

FIFTY-NINE

When they were not consulting with Lawyer Towers on Sally's case, Sally and Cecil spent a good part of their days together, driving around, going to movies and shopping for the upcoming trip. For both of them, their most enjoyable times came when they sat together in the back of the Ghia, something they tried to do every day.

"What music do you like?" Cecil asked Sally soon after they settled into their routine.

"I only listen to the radio. I never had money for CDs or anything to play them on."

The next day he handed her a wrapped present. When she asked what it was for, he simply said, "A friend gift. Open it. I think you'll like it."

She ripped off the fancy paper and sat staring at the box. "What's an MP3 player?"

"Music. A new form of music called digital music. You download it from the Internet, or you take it from CDs."

"I don't have CDs and I don't really know anything about the Internet."

"Don't worry about that. Caroline has tons of CDs. I can get music from them." Cecil pulled out the headphones. "Here, try it."

Gingerly, she put them on and pushed the start button as he instructed. Her eyes went wide when she heard Mariah Carey singing, *I'll Be There*. When that was over, the U2 hit, *Mysterious Ways*, began to play.

"I didn't know you liked music," Sally said, "We listened to music that summer, but I thought you didn't like it."

Cecil, his eyes now focused on his feet, confessed, "I didn't. Actually, I still don't, but I thought you might. Those are some songs Caroline has. I didn't know what you liked, so I just looked up the popular ones from when we were in school."

"Thank you, Cecil. You are so loving. I wish I could repay you."

"Just be my friend."

One afternoon as they sat in the Ghia, Sally said, "I'm looking forward to spending time with Malinda. This will be the first time in my life I'm not running somewhere and leaving her with somebody. The trip will be fun, and good for us both."

Cecil said, "I'm going to Port Isabel tomorrow for the final interview with CPS. My interview is at nine, so I'm leaving really early, about four-thirty or five. I should be back before three. Maybe by two. Assuming that goes well, I'll have Malinda in a day or two."

"I wish I could go with you, but the Grand Jury is meeting tomorrow to decide whether I am to be charged with assault on Wade. Lawyer Towers told me to be in his office in the morning."

"It's a formality. They won't do anything. It's Wade they should charge."

"I don't want to think about Wade. I hope it all goes okay and you get custody of my baby. If not, what will we do?"

"Think positive. It'll be fine. I'll get Malinda and you'll be free. Towers says they won't indict you."

"I hope you're right."

"I'll ask my mother if she'll help with Malinda once I bring her home. If not, I'll hire someone."

"Why won't your mother do it? It's only a few days until we leave."

"Sometimes my mother gets crazy. I can never figure what she'll do or say. Fact is I can never figure what anybody will say or do."

༄༅

"Are you crazy?" Maggie barked when Cecil told her that Malinda was going to live in his house until they left for the cruise.

Cecil managed to keep control despite his agitation with her unexpected outrage. "Mother," he replied, "this is my home as well as Caroline's. I have a right to bring anyone I want."

"That wh...girl wrecked your sister's life! Caroline now has no one to be with! Wade's pleaded guilty and he'll be sentenced in a few weeks. Since she isn't married to him, there can be no visitation until he's built up a pattern of 'good behavior.' That could take two years according to his lawyer."

"She told me she'll marry him before he goes to prison."

"That's what she wants. But I disagree with her and, thankfully, your father does too. Even Wade thinks it's a bad idea. He says he'll marry her, but not until he's served some time so she knows what it'll be like to be married to a convict."

"That still doesn't answer the question about Malinda. CPS won't allow her to stay in the motel with Sally, so it has to be here."

"Your mind is obviously made up, but don't expect me to go along with this crazy plan. I can't imagine your sister will be happy about this."

"It's Wade's baby as well," Cecil replied, not at all understanding his mother's agitation. "Mother, after all this time I don't understand why you are still so against Sally. *Cospers*

Own is way in her past and she was turned into a prostitute against her will when she was fifteen. It's not her fault."

"I thought Caroline would never have anyone in her life. Wade was perfect for her. And now...now she has nothing."

"Wade's a rapist, yet you care more about him than you do about Sally — or her child."

"Jennie and I go back a long way. It's her son. He's a good boy. He did one horrible thing and now he'll pay for it the rest of his life."

"But Sally—"

"Sally worked at that disgusting place, doing God knows what!"

"Sally's a good person. It wasn't her fault. Then she made some bad decisions. But she's my friend. I need your help."

"I can't do it and I won't. And that's final."

"Sorry Mother, but Malinda's coming here, with or without your help."

"I won't be here. You can take care of the child by yourself! I won't be used in this way."

"Have it your way, then," Cecil shot back. "Maybe it's even better this way because then Malinda can stay in your room where she can be close to me across the hall."

"My room! Are you throwing me out?"

"You just said you won't be here. So you can live in your own house until we leave."

"What about your sister? Are you going to take care of her every night?"

"We'll manage."

"Manage?" Maggie exclaimed. "Caroline's not even speaking to you."

"She'll have to get over it and let me take care of her. Or you can do it before you go home. Just get her ready for bed earlier."

"You have it all worked out, don't you? Just make up your mind, and everything works! That's what all that money did to you. You're too big for your britches now. Think you can tell everybody what to do!"

"We expect all the charges against Sally to be dismissed. She can live here with Malinda before we leave."

"How convenient! You and your tramp friend all cozy in this house! What's the matter, it's not enough to visit her in that motel. You're the talk of the town as it is."

"I saved this town! They can talk all they want. What I do in my personal life is none of their business."

"That's not the way people see it. Jennie says—"

"Who's Jennie to say anything?" Cecil interrupted. "Her son raped a fourteen-year-old! She's the one who should hide her head in shame. I've done nothing wrong!"

Maggie abruptly stood and stormed out of the kitchen. Five minutes later the front door slammed behind her.

"Was that Mother leaving?" Caroline called on the intercom, "If so, Cecil will you come to my room. Hurry, I need assistance."

Cecil knocked as a courtesy, as he always did, before entering Caroline's room. She was half-sitting, half-lying on the floor beside her bed. Her left arm was twisted behind her and pinned between her and the side table.

"Don't just stand there, brother dear, lift me onto the chair."

Cecil did as he was instructed, and then examined her arm. A welt had already begun to appear. That was dangerous with her poor circulation. "Should I call the doctor? That looks nasty."

"What the hell for? If I called every time I bumped myself we'd need a live-in doctor! I've had worse."

"But—"

"I said forget it."

"What happened?"

"Damn bot refused to move and I leaned too far forward."

"Let me look," Cecil offered. "I need to see what's wrong."

"I know what's wrong! Mother forgot to charge the battery last night. I thought I'd make it to the bathroom myself without bothering everybody."

"I've told you so many times. When—"

"I know, I know," Caroline interjected. *"When the red light is on, don't use it.* I don't need a lecture right now. I need, oh God, I need Wade!" Tears streamed down her face.

Cecil stood, undecided if he should wipe her face or leave her alone.

Caroline settled that issue. "You're not yourself today. Get with it, brother dear. I can't dry my eyes myself and they won't dry themselves."

Dutifully, Cecil retrieved a hand towel from the bathroom and gently wiped her face dry.

"You know," she said, "It's been a long while since you last touched me. I forgot how important you are to me. Just being here, doing things for me."

"I'm sorry about Wade."

"Nothing you can say can make it change, so please just don't say anything. It's my problem, anyway, not yours."

Cecil rolled the wheelchair to the bed and sat in it facing her. Before he could say anything, Caroline said, "What got into Mother? You two get into it again?"

Cecil looked down, his eyes focused on the floor. Caroline continued, "What is it this time? She bad-mouthing Patty-Ann again?"

"No."

"Sally then. She has a thing about Sally. Truth is I don't see what you see in that girl either."

"She's my friend. She's the only person I understand!"

"I know. You tell me that every chance you get. So what is it this time?"

"You mean with Mother?" When Caroline nodded, he said, "I've got custody of Malinda, starting maybe tomorrow I'll be her foster parent."

Caroline made a face so disapproving that even Cecil had no trouble reading it.

"She's Wade's kid as well," he continued. Don't forget that. She'll be living here until we leave for the trip."

"No way! Here? You can't be serious! No wonder Mother pitched a fit!" Caroline glared at her brother. "You *are* crazy, you know that?"

"I asked Mother to help me with Malinda for the few days until we leave. She refused and when I told her Malinda was coming here anyway, she moved back home."

"Any wonder! I'd refuse too, assuming I could help in the first place. This is nuts! You're nuts! What are you going to do with a child, give her one of your filthy engines to work on? There's an old lawn mower engine in the garage. Maybe you and the kid can take it apart and put it back together. You'll at least have something to do with her when she gets here. A little foster father-daughter bonding thing."

"Hey, that's a good idea," Cecil replied.

"You're serious, aren't you?" she asked.

"I want to do things with her. Mother's not going to help, so it's up to me. I'll do it."

Sixty

While Cecil was in Port Isabel obtaining the Judge's approval to take Malinda around the world with him, the Grand Jury back in Cosper, as expected, refused to indict Sally. Late that afternoon, when Cecil arrived back home, he and Sally celebrated her freedom by driving out to their favorite parking space. They sat in the back of the Ghia discussing their future.

The next day they drove back to Port Isabel to pick up Malinda. The little girl was excited to see her mother and the two of them sat in the back seat, Malinda's head resting on Sally's lap, as they talked non-stop all the way back to Cosper. Cecil was content to watch them in the rear view mirror, a smile on his face at seeing them both so happy.

It wasn't until they reached Cosper that Sally told Malinda that she would be living with Cecil because he was her new foster father.

"Where will you be, Mommy?" Malinda asked, her eyes wide with fear. "I don't ever want you to go away again. I don't like it when you go away."

"I'll be at the motel. You'll come over in the mornings and we can play and do things together."

"Can we go to the mall? I want to go to a movie like we did that one time."

"Yes, my love. We can go to the movie and we can buy you nice clothes."

"And a new movie. I lost my movies."

"We can buy you lots of movies."

"Mommy, please stay with me. Don't leave me again."

"Sally," Cecil pleaded, "for Malinda's sake, please stay at the house with us. You can sleep in Malinda's room."

"It's best this way," Sally replied. "Please drop me off at the motel and take her home. She's a good kid and can take care of herself. She's had lots of practice."

Despite Cecil's protests, Sally got out of the car at the motel and refused to change her mind.

Malinda kissed her mother goodbye, and with tears in her eyes, dutifully climbed back in the car. She was hungry when they arrived home and Cecil made her eggs and toast. She cleaned her plate.

"Where do I sleep? Is this a hotel? I've never been in a house this big?"

"No, this is my house. My sister lives here also."

"I want to see my room."

When Malinda walked into her room, she yelped, "It even has its own TV. Does it have a DVD?"

"It sure does. I even have a movie for you."

"I love movies!" she squealed with delight. "Which one?"

"How about Toy Story?"

"I love Toy Story! To infinity and beyond!" she exclaimed. "And Buzz Lightyear! The toys get into trouble. Almost like robots."

"Robots?" Cecil asked, having never seen the movie.

"Like the toys are alive and do things. They move around like robots do. Will you watch it with me?"

"Sounds like fun. Tell you what. I'll go get your things from the car and then you can get ready for bed. Then we can watch the movie."

Malinda jumped on the bed and then bounced to the floor and ran to the bathroom. "It has its own bathroom! This is a hotel!"

"Be right back," Cecil called, and hurried to the car.

☽☾

By the next morning, Maggie, having calmed down, came by to see how things were going. She passed Cecil who was on his way to take Malinda to her mother. They planned to spend the day shopping.

When Cecil returned with Malinda late in the day he found his mother in the kitchen preparing chicken potpies. The aroma brought to mind his childhood when Maggie had made potpies to calm Cecil when he was agitated.

"Thought if we had a guest we should treat her well," Maggie answered when Cecil asked her why she had cooked dinner.

Malinda ate everything put in front of her. After dinner she sat with Maggie in the den, the two of them talking like old friends. After a while, Caroline wheeled herself into the room to join them.

"What happened to you?" Malinda asked, her eyes going wide when she first saw Caroline.

"I was in a car accident."

"How come your legs and arms are so thin?"

"I can't use them. I'm paralyzed."

"When will you get better?"

"I'm afraid never."

"Never. That's a long time."

"It sure is. It sure is."

"Then I'll just have to push you. If you can't use your arms, how do you eat?"

"I have a bot, a robot, that makes my arms move. But it doesn't always work."

"A robot? Like in *Toy Story*?"

"Something like that," Caroline answered.

"I'll feed you. I'm good. I had a dog once. He ran away. But I fed him some of my food. We didn't have much. Mommy told me that's why he ran away."

"It will be nice if you feed me," Caroline replied, her voice upbeat, picking up on Malinda's enthusiasm. "Sometimes I do need help." Caroline smiled for the first time since Wade was arrested.

"Do you want to watch *Toy Story* with me? I'll show you the robots. I fell asleep last night and didn't see it all."

"I'd love to."

"It's in my room. Can I push you?"

"Sure."

Cecil hung back with his mother while the two of them moved slowly down the hall.

"I must say," Maggie began, "I certainly didn't expect anything like that."

"Like what?" Cecil asked.

"Her mother's so...so slow. You can see it in her eyes, not so bright. But this one. This one's a pistol! Smart as a whip. And quick. Keeps you on your toes."

"I'm not on my toes."

"It's a saying. Oh, never mind. You'd better be sharp around her. Come, let's all go watch the movie."

☙❧

Maggie was in the kitchen by eight the next morning and had breakfast ready for Malinda when she woke up. Later that day dinner was again ready when they came home.

Caroline showed up to eat with them and allowed Malinda to feed her. After dinner they played card games and then watched *Toy Story* again.

"It's a shame you're leaving so soon," Maggie commented two days later. "Having Malinda here has been wonderful. I'll miss her."

"I'll miss her also," Caroline chimed in. "She's a good kid. It's hard to believe she's only eight. Who will feed me when she's gone?"

"I'm looking forward to being on the ship with Sally and her," Cecil replied. "Sally's so happy when Malinda's around."

"Have you asked Sally to come stay here?" Maggie inquired. "It's okay with us. Isn't it Caroline?"

"I'm okay with it. Malinda's filled the terrible void. I see Wade in her. Oh, I'm sorry, I shouldn't have said...I don't know what I'll do when you're gone."

"Want me to cancel?"

"Heavens, no!" Maggie exclaimed. "All you've been talking about for the past six months is this trip. I think I know every port, every excursion, every country, you're going to."

"Mind if I go out tonight? Will you put Malinda to bed? Sally and I have to get a few last minute things for her. Some presents for along the way. I don't want her seeing them now."

"Go and have fun," his mother said. "Malinda will be fine with us."

೫೦೦೮

Cecil and Sally finished up at the mall. Cecil turned to her, "Malinda's a delight. You've done a great job of raising her. Mother says you must be a good mother."

"Thought your mother didn't like me."

"Now she does."

"She doesn't even know me."

"Sometimes things work out that way. Do you want something to eat?"

"Let's just go out into the country for a ride. Just the two of us."

Cecil thought he saw something in her face, something he had not seen before. But when he looked again, it was gone. "Sure, let's go. That'll be nice."

"Cecil," Sally began when they had parked, "I have something to tell you. Something important."

They were sitting, as they always were, legs entwined in the back seat of the Ghia. Sally continued, "I've been thinking about this trip—"

"So have I! I can't wait to get to California and—"

"I'm not going."

"What?" Cecil's stomach clenched as though he had been kicked. "What are you saying?"

"I'm not going. Now hear me out. And look at me, not at the floor. This is important. Don't go loopy on me." When he didn't respond, she said, "You and I are best friends. I like being your friend. I'd be in jail without you. My daughter would be gone without you. You've done so much for me. I want to love you. I owe it to you to love you. But I can't." Cecil's head bent even further forward. "Cecil, now look at me! Hear what I'm saying. It's not fair to you if I go with you around the world. If I went, we'd share a bed, but I'd just be paying you back. I can't do that to you. I want to go see the world more than anything. If I work hard and make good choices, someday I might be able to go. But I can't go now."

Cecil was devastated. Despite his attempts, his head fell. Sally snapped, "Stop that this instant! You look at me! I'm making a good choice. I know I am, and I need your support to make that good choice. Now look at me and be my friend."

Slowly, Cecil's head came up. He looked into her tear-filled eyes. In a soft voice, devoid of emotion, he said, "I want you as my best friend more than anything else in the world."

"Then you must go without me. Take Malinda and show her the world. Teach her things she'll never forget. Things I'll never ever know. I'm nothing but a drag on you—and on her. I must stay and get an education."

"I could arrange—"

"Cecil. You've done enough for me already. I need to arrange for things myself. Don't you see that?" I need to learn how to take care of myself. You've given me a start. Now I have to rebuild my life. I can't do it with you doing everything for me."

"What about Malinda?" Cecil pleaded. "She'll be so disappointed. You can't do that to her. You can't."

"I've thought about that a long time. You're her foster father. Give her the opportunity to learn what the world is like out there. It'll be good for her and while she's gone I'll get my act together. Then she and I can have a life together. I have to do it this way."

"And what will you do without her?"

"Truth is, if you hadn't taken her, I'd not have her for a year or more anyway. This mess with Wade would have killed my chances for a long, long time. When Malinda gets back home, I'll be building a new life. I'm going to finish my education and get a high school certificate so I can get a decent job and be a good mother to her."

"You *are* a good mother. I see you two together, you are good with her."

"There's more to being a good mother than going to the mall."

"Please go with us. Even if you can't be in love with me, I want you to come."

Sally sat in silence a long while before she responded. "I've made up my mind, Cecil. This has been very hard. One day I can't wait to go. The next day, I know I can't. But my mind's made up. And I won't change it. No matter what."

"Please come with us. I'm begging you to come with us."

"Cecil, listen to me. A man forced himself on me once. I can't let that happen to me again. That's what this feels like. You're forcing yourself on me. Please, please, understand."

Sixty-One

"You look like you were in an accident!" Caroline exclaimed when Cecil entered her room to help put her to bed. "You didn't wreck the Ghia, did you? I know what that car means to you."

"No, I didn't wreck the Ghia. I gave it to Sally."

"No way! Now I know you've lost your mind."

"She's not going with me. She says we can never be more than just friends. She wants me to go without her."

"That's not a half-bad idea you know. You might meet someone."

"I'm taking Malinda."

"Cecil! What the hell's wrong with you? You're taking a child around the world, a child you've only known a few days! That's preposterous!"

"Why is that so terrible? She's bright. You said so yourself. She can learn what the world is like at an early age. It will be fun."

"It's just that it makes no sense, that's all. No sense whatsoever! It'll be fun for exactly one day! What the hell do you know about kids?"

"Not much, I must admit. But I don't know much about grown-ups either."

"So, brother dear, how in the hell do you expect to pull this off? Surely you must have a plan. You always have a plan. I can't wait to hear what cockamamie scheme you've worked up this time."

"I've been working on a plan ever since I found out Sally and Clyde are seeing each other at night in the motel."

"What?"

"Every afternoon we talk in the car. But something's been wrong for the last several days. And then she said she thought it would be best if I didn't visit with her at the motel in the evenings because she was afraid that it might lead to something before we were both ready. I didn't understand what she was saying."

"Sounds fishy to me," Caroline interjected.

"I know," Cecil continued. "I brooded about it for a couple of days without saying anything to Sally. Then one night about nine I decided to drive over to her motel to make her tell me what the problem was. But she wasn't there. I sat in my car for a long time trying to figure out what was going on. Then a car pulled up to Sally's unit and she got out of the passenger side. Then the driver got out. It was Clyde."

Caroline sighed. "I'm sorry, Cecil."

"Then they went into her room after Clyde unlocked the door with a key he had in his pocket. I waited two hours and he didn't come out."

"You've known about Sally and Clyde, and you still wanted to take her on the trip with you! And become a foster father! You *are* nuts."

"Sally's my best friend. Up to the last minute I tried to convince her to come along with us. I think the trip would be better for Malinda if her mother was there."

"You're serious, aren't you? 'Course you are. I've never known you to joke about anything. She never even told you about Clyde?"

"I think she wanted to spare me from being upset. That's what friends do."

"And you still gave her the Ghia! You are the fool, you know."

"Anyway," Cecil continued, ignoring Caroline's hateful remark, "you asked me about my plan. It's as simple as can be. I want you to come with us. Mother can come along as well if she likes. We'll learn to be a family."

"Not on your life!"

"Why not. You like Malinda. I'll take care of you on the boat. We can hire a helper, if that makes you feel better. It will be fun."

"I can't leave Wade."

"But they won't allow you to see him."

"But I'm here, close by. That's important to me. I love him. I'll have to make do with that."

"Come with me. You can write to him every day. If you don't like the trip you can come home."

"No!"

"I'll take Mother."

"She won't go. She has to care for me."

"I'll get you a helper. Several helpers. They can be here with you all the time. Mother can use a break."

"I said, no! You and Malinda can go and have fun. You leave Mother out of this."

"That's just it. The Court is requiring me to have an approved adult...chaperone...and you or Mother have been approved."

"You heard me. I said we're not going!"

"If you are saying that just so I won't go it won't work. The court has approved a social worker. A woman mother's age. She'll be the chaperone. Lucas said he'll go along as well. We can all go. I checked. There's room for all of us. You and Lucas can talk business all you like."

"I'm not leaving here and I won't let Mother go. And that's final!"

"That's rotten."

"Haven't you noticed, dear Cecil, life is rotten."

Sixty-Two

Aboard the MV Blue Dream
Dear Sally,
August 2, 2002

    I have attempted to call you several times, but your phone seems to have been disconnected. When you receive this letter please call my sister and give her your new phone number. Malinda wants to hear your voice. Malinda has been sending you cards from each port. I hope you received them.

    So far, her favorite part of the trip was when we went through the Panama Canal. I think her second favorite was our time in London. She wants to tell you all about it. As I write this, we are heading to Amsterdam, then to Stockholm. Then we will go into the Baltic on our way to St Petersburg.

    We both wish you were here with us. If you change your mind, I can arrange for you to join us. I hope you decide to come. In a few weeks we will be heading south toward Morocco and Tangiers. After that we will head into the Mediterranean and spend time visiting Valencia, then Barcelona and then on to Nice and Italy.

Malinda saw a movie about Greece last night and can't wait until we get to Athens. There's an island, called Hydra, that uses only donkeys for transportation. No cars at all. I told her we would take a side trip over there. Then onto Egypt. I promised Malinda we would explore the pyramids together.

Sally, I really hope you decide to join us. Your daughter asks about you every day. Seeing the world through the eyes of a child is wonderful.

Your Best Friend,
Cecil Harris

Standard Deviation

Aboard the MV Blue Dream
Dear Sally,
September 15, 2002

    It was wonderful hearing your voice yesterday. Malinda was so excited she couldn't sleep last night so we walked the deck. We are off the coast of Portugal now and it's been stormy all morning so it's hard to see anything but black clouds. The seas have increased and the boat is not as steady as it has been. Malinda is sleeping and when she wakes up we'll go to a movie. She loves Santa Claus 2 so we'll go see it again. It's not out in the States until next month but the boat has it somehow.

    The best news of all is that you are coming to join us. That is why I couldn't sleep last night either. I really miss you and talking to you. It will be nice having you here with us. It will be like old times.

    I wish the boat was going straight to Valencia so you would be with us sooner. But September 27th is only twelve days from now, and since I will be doing that government thing I told you about with Senegal, it is just as well. I am debating whether or not to take Malinda with me or leave her here on the boat with the nanny. It would be fun for her to take the ferryboat up the African coast.

    Can't wait until you join us.

Your Best Friend,
Cecil

SENTINEL

A HOMETOWN PAPER
September 28, 2002

Ferry sinks: 1500 feared dead

BY: NEWS WIRE REPORTS

Authorities have reported the sinking of the ferryboat MV Le Joola in the Atlantic Ocean during a sudden storm. The vessel was Senegalese owned and began its voyage in Ziguinchor. There are unconfirmed reports that as many as 1500 people were aboard the boat, which was believed to be heading toward Dakar, when the accident occurred. Fishing boats in the vicinity are believed to have rescued several passengers. The names of those aboard the ferry have not been released.

SENTINEL

A HOMETOWN PAPER
September 30, 2002

Ferry sinking: Local benefactor missing

BY: NEWS WIRE WITH LOCAL REPORTING BY ALICE SPENCER

Cecil Harris, the man behind the resurgence of Axtel Industries, is reported to be among the missing in the sinking of the ferry, MV Le Joola, off the coast of The Gambia, West Africa. The official count of the missing and presumed dead now stands at 1850. The U. S. State Department has confirmed that Mr. Harris, age 23, was aboard the ferry on a humanitarian mission when the boat sank. Mr. Harris was born in Cosper and maintained homes in Cosper and Dallas. He was on a world cruise after founding and selling a business, all before his twenty-third birthday.

The MV Le Joola was Senegalese owned and operated and was on a voyage from Ziguinchor, which is in the Casamanic region of Senegal, to the Capital City of Dakar. The vessel sank in the Atlantic Ocean during a sudden storm after picking up several passengers on the island of Carabane.

The maximum load capacity of the ferry is 580 passengers and it is believed that over 2000 men, women and children were aboard when it suddenly capsized, presumably due to heavy sea conditions at the time.

The Senegalese Government has announced that it will launch an official investigation into the disaster. It is believed that the French Government is also planning its own investigation.

This disaster ranks third in all-time shipping losses, exceeded only by the 4000 people lost on the MV Doña Paz in 1987, and by the RMS Titanic where 1503 lives were lost in 1912.

Mr. Harris's mother, Maggie Harris, was contacted by telephone. "Cecil was always a good boy," she told The Sentinel. "When he was growing up he had some issues that caused other children to shy away from him. But he always tried to help whomever he could. His sister, Caroline, can get around today because of his brilliance in designing robots that allow her to walk. We thank God every day for that miracle. Cecil was traveling with Malinda Mascar, the seven-year old daughter of his best friend, Sally Mascar. We thank God that Malinda was not with him on his mission to Senegal. She is safe with her mother in Valencia, Spain. Cecil will be dearly missed."

Mr. Harris's sister, Caroline Harris, has refused to comment.

Mr. Harris, who attended high school in Dallas, but whose heart has always been in Cosper, will be remembered for his brilliantly simple and elegant mechanical designs. The continued viability of the Axtel factory here in Cospers is tribute to his brilliance.

A memorial service to pay tribute to Cecil Harris is being planned.

Thank You

I wish to thank my longtime friend Ron Slusky for his extensive and insightful edits and comments. Without his tireless efforts, this book would have suffered. I also owe Judi Tovell and LaRee Bryant for their valuable comments and editing. And a special thanks and appreciation go to Jim Welton and Marvilyn Miller for their tireless editing efforts and suggestions.

In the early stages of the book, a colleague of mine, Tennessee Nielsen, agreed to have The Book Study Group critique the manuscript. The women, who have met in Dallas monthly since 1983, provided meaningful insight into the characters. Many thanks to Tennessee for hosting the group at her lovely home and I am indebted to Group members Dana Harvey, Gwen Longino, Barbara Hunt, Lynn Lemon, Adré Bower, Jill Fleming, Denise Austin, Reggie Campbell, Julie Stark, and Nancy Bierman for their valuable input.

ಶಿಂಚ

Acknowledgement

The robotics aspects of the story was inspired by comments made by Mark Spong, PhD, Dean of the Erik Jonsson School of Engineering & Computer Science and Lars Magnus Ericsson Chair in Electrical Engineering at the University of Texas, Dallas (UTD).

More information on the UTD program can be found at http://ecs.utdallas.edu/markspong.html

ೞఌ

DEDICATION

This book is dedicated to my grandchildren, Kat, Megan and Lauren.

Contact Information

David Harry can be reached at **david@davidharry author.com**

For information on upcoming books and other items of interest, please go to: **http://davidharryauthor.com**

You can follow David Harry on Facebook: **Davidharry**; on Twitter **david1harry** and on his blog: **davidharryauthor.com**

Additional Information

Asperger's Syndrome information:

    www.aspergers.com
    www.osbayrak.blogspot.com
    www.welkowitz.typepad.com
    www.aspergerssyndrome.org
    OASIS@MAPP

Rape and Abuse information:

    www.essortment.com/articles/hotline_100016.htm
    www.thehotline.org/

Domestic violence and rape 24/7 hot lines:

    1-800-799-7233
    1-800-789-3224 (TTY)